CW00541707

The Rose Ring

The Rose Ring

Margaret Mullally

ROBERT HALE · LONDON

© Margaret Mullally 2004
First published in Great Britain 2004

ISBN 0 7090 7562 6

Robert Hale Limited
Clerkenwell House
Clerkenwell Green
London EC1R 0HT

The right of Margaret Mullally to be identified as
author of this work has been asserted by her
in accordance with the Copyright, Designs and
Patents Act 1988.

2 4 6 8 10 9 7 5 3 1

MORAY COUNCIL LIBRARIES & INFO.SERVICES	
2O 11 78 98	
Askews	
F	

Typeset in 10/12½pt Baskerville by
Derek Doyle & Associates, Liverpool.
Printed in Great Britain by
St Edmundsbury Press Ltd, Bury St Edmunds, Suffolk.
Bound by Woolnough Bookbinding Ltd.

For my wonderful mother

CHAPTER ONE

1525

'No!' Alicia's voice was sharp with agitation as she faced her father across the winter parlour of Greenthorpe Manor on that rainy, dark-grey afternoon.

She had promised herself that she would remain calm – that her voice would be gentle and reasonable, her face sweetly serene, like one of the carved stone angels that guarded the gatehouse arch. However, Sir Richard had no sooner started to speak in that hectoring tone than she had felt her whole body stiffen with resentment.

It was an effect that he frequently had on people. Alicia could feel the resentment swirling into icy panic. She was only fifteen but she'd learnt that he could hurt her as nobody else could. Yet the child in her – the rather insecure little girl who had always longed for his approval – stubbornly continued to love him without any hope of reward. For Sir Richard loved nobody but himself.

'I don't think I heard you correctly, girl.' His tone was pleasant enough, but she caught the black thread of menace that lay curled behind it. The feeling of panic fizzed inside her. She was aware of his power, could feel it closing in around her, the way a rabbit feels the cold metal teeth of the snare. She sat up very straight, watching him with wary grey-flecked violet eyes. Involuntarily, one hand reached up to touch the little enamelled locket at her throat, as if she thought it might have some magical power to protect her.

'I said no,' she repeated, more quietly this time. 'I don't want to marry him.'

'I presume you have some good reason?' Richard folded his arms over his chest, surveying his daughter with a blend of amusement and contempt.

How smug and confident he was as he stood there, his back turned towards the fire; a handsome rosy-faced man in his mid-forties, impeccable in dove-coloured doublet and satin hose. His dark-blond hair was unfashionably long, falling in deep heavy waves to his shoulders. It had always been a source of amusement to him that even his enemies were forced to admire his striking looks and the proud cascade of gold untouched by grey was a defiant gesture that had never once struck him as childish. He had an assured chilly elegance, carefully nurtured over the years, which might have seemed effeminate in a man less belligerently male. Alicia thought now how very big he was – almost as big and broad as King Henry himself and, to the frightened fifteen-year-old girl, far more intimidating. It was almost as if he were playing a game with her – one which he knew he would win. She stared up at him imploringly but there was neither pity nor understanding in those hard, bright-grey eyes. She twisted round on the stool, her gaze frantically sweeping the dark-panelled room as if searching for a solution. Almost as an afterthought, it came to rest upon the slim figure of her mother sitting several feet away, her embroidery in her lap, like a servant who is tactfully pretending to be invisible.

So far Lady Dorothy hadn't spoken a word. Sometimes it was hard to believe that she had once been a fashionable court beauty, flirtatious and sought after. Frequent wearying pregnancies had sapped her vitality even as her overbearing husband had sapped her spirit. And yet she'd managed to retain her charm.

Watching those long white hands moving across the embroidery frame as sensitively as if it were a harp, Alicia realized that she could expect precious little help from that quarter. There was nothing for it but to brazen it out alone. She turned back to her father.

'I can't marry Gervase. He's a nasty, sly dog.'

'You talk like an imbecile!' Now there was no mistaking the threat in his voice.

'But I'm not imbecile enough to marry him. I'd rather be sliced into collops and fed to the pigs.'

There, she hadn't meant to raise her voice again but in her own ears she heard it shrill up the scale, desperate and scared. She could feel her heart banging against her bodice as she waited for him to knock her to the floor.

Yet Sir Richard merely fixed her with that unnerving grey stare.

'You're being very childish. Anyway, the marriage with John Houghton's lad will go ahead whatever your whims and fancies, so you'd best resign yourself to it. And if you had a grain of sense you'd see that this is an excellent match!'

'Excellent for you!'

'That's enough.' Frowning, he put up one hand to silence her. Privately he was more than a little disconcerted by his daughter's defiance. His elder girl, Kathryn, had been such a well-behaved child. There were no unseemly outbursts, no displays of stubborn temper, when it came to *her* marriage, he recalled now. She had gone, meek as milk, to her loutish Lancashire knight, and if she'd felt the slightest flicker of rebellion it had remained locked inside her heart where it could neither be seen by, nor offend, Sir Richard. Clearly Alicia lacked her sister's docile temperament. He found himself wondering if the five years she'd spent in Sir Walter Ashby's household had been a mistake. Walter's wife, Bess, was a fat amiable sow who had probably spoilt the girl. And yet, most men of his class sent their children away to be educated in a noble household and they didn't turn into hellcats. Well, whatever the cause of Alicia's wilfulness, he didn't doubt his ability to subdue her as, years before, he had subdued her mother.

He scowled at the small oval face before him. Apart from the colour of the eyes, it was Dorothy's face – pale and piquant with slanting cheekbones and a softly curving little mouth. White as frozen milk beneath a cloud of dark-red curls, the Dorothy-Alicia face scowled back at him. She even held her body with that same air of vulnerability and pride. In that moment he remembered how it used to infuriate him.

The blood was pulsing in his ears as, in an instant, he was swept back to those early weeks of marriage. He could see his young bride, so cool and imperious, looking down her dainty nose at him as if he had horseshit clinging to his boots. (At seventeen she'd had a high opinion of her own worth.) She had even had the temerity to refuse him her bed. Sitting propped among the pillows, the sheet clutched to her bare breasts, she'd fixed him with mocking cat-green eyes and told him he wasn't good enough to lie with her. Eventually he had lost his temper and struck her across the face. And gloated when he saw it crumple in horrified weeping.

He came out of his reverie with a jolt and remembered the girl sitting, nervous and defiant, before him.

'You will do as I say, girl,' he snarled between his teeth.

By now Alicia was shivering with terror, yet she lifted one eyebrow and regarded him insolently. She was pretending that he was a large, savage dog that would pounce if it smelled her fear.

'Sir.' Dorothy stood up and came towards them with an anxious scurrying of skirts. Husband and daughter both looked startled, as if one of her tapestry figures had suddenly come to life. She addressed herself to her husband, as was proper.

'I don't think there's any purpose in discussing this further today. Alicia looks unwell.'

Richard's testy glance swivelled back to his daughter. Her face looked white and strained, and the thought that she might slide on to the rushes in a swoon filled him with acute distaste. When he spoke again his voice was kinder.

'Come now, why all this pother? After all, it can come as no great surprise. Your mother wrote to you last summer after the contract was signed. Why do you suppose we didn't send you back to Ashby Place after Christmas?'

'I didn't expect it so soon.'

'Nevertheless, it *was* expected. You've had time to get over any silly greengirl ideas.'

'Yes, but I thought there was a chance I might be spared.'

'Spared?' Her father's stunned expression nearly made her laugh aloud.

'From having to go to bed with a turd-faced cub,' she explained sweetly.

'That's enough of your impertinence. Gervase is the son of my oldest friend at court and you will speak of him with courtesy.'

He might have said 'my only friend at court', Alicia mused with an inward snigger. The Westbrookes had served the House of Tudor well. Alicia's grandfather, born into the merchant class, had raised money and ships for Henry VII, fought valiantly for him at Bosworth and been rewarded with a knighthood. Richard himself had risen steadily in the first Tudor's household to become Esquire of the Body, but he was unpopular at the court of Henry's flamboyant son and consequently spent little time there.

'Sir, I really think . . .'

'Be quiet, madam! I won't be overruled in my own house. As for you, Mistress Pert, you'll marry young Houghton even if I have to beat you into obedience. You won't be the first silly chit to go to the altar with a bloody back.'

'I will not!' Alicia yelled, leaping to her feet. 'I'll run away to France, and a pox on you and the Houghtons!'

Through a sickening haze she saw his hand swing out, then it slammed hard against her temple. She stood as if frozen to the floor, staring stupidly through a flash of black and red while he shouted at her, his arms flailing through the air like a windmill. She made no sense of the words, for her head was singing.

A hand landed on her shoulder. She whirled round to find her mother standing behind her, her face sick and drained. Nonetheless, she was the only person in the room who appeared to have her emotions under control.

'Go to your room, Alicia – now,' she said, quietly but insistently.

Alicia needed no second bidding. One hand pressed to her pulsing face, the other scooping up her skirts, she turned and fled.

For a long moment Richard and Dorothy surveyed each other. Richard's face was glistening with sweat but he could already feel his rage dampening into a kind of sour satisfaction as he read the anguish in Dorothy's eyes.

At last he spoke, his voice lancing her with contempt.

'Your daughter is an obstinate bitch, madam.'

They were always *her* daughters when he was displeased with them.

Before she could protest he was gone, leaving her to stare miserably at the great oak door as it thudded behind him.

Alicia didn't stop running until she reached the gallery on the first floor, when a sharp little pain in her side made her stop and lean against the wall, waiting for her breathing to quieten. Then she continued swiftly to her bedchamber at the end.

Once inside the little room that had seen so many of her childish tears and rages, she tore off her cap and flung it to the floor before hurling herself full length across the bed in a sudden storm of weeping.

'Sweet Jesus, how I hate him!' A cushion went flying in the direction of a side table, narrowly missing the pewter candlestick. 'If I die of grief it will be his fault.'

She lifted her chin, the tears still running down her cheeks. She dwelt for a moment on the picture of her father pompously explaining to the Houghtons that the wedding could not proceed as his selfish, inconsiderate daughter had died of a broken heart. In spite of everything, she nearly burst into giggling.

Outside it was still raining, the pale drops slipping down the mullioned panes like blobs of candlewax. The fire had long since whimpered to death in the grate and the wood-basket was empty. She couldn't call the servants because they would notice her red-splotched face. And she didn't want anyone to know she had been crying, not even old Joanna who had jounced her on her broad lap when she was very small and sung those romantic ballads that she and Kathryn had loved. Wrapping the moss-green counterpane about her, she went to kneel at the window seat.

It was eerily quiet apart from the dull slapping of rain against the glass. Mouse-coloured clouds scampered across the January sky. Soon it would be nightfall but no one had thought to light the candles, and the windows over-looking the courtyard resembled glittering panels of black diamonds. An air of sullen dejection seemed to hang over the place. It was as if the entire household knew that the master was in one of his ugly moods – which by this time it prob-ably did!

A puddle the size of a fishpond sprawled across the centre of the courtyard where the stone fountain was spilling over on to the cobbles. Alicia trailed a finger down the icy pane, watching idly as her breath turned to mist upon the glass. For some reason her thoughts flew to Kathryn, the sister whom she loved more than anyone in the world but had never really understood.

As a little girl she had envied and adored Kathryn, while knowing she could never be like her. Gilded by blondeness and serenity, Kathryn had seemed with-out any flaw or imperfection, and not only to Alicia. Of the two sisters, it was Kathryn who was invited to court.

'Because she is the elder,' Dorothy had explained to her second daughter.

To Alicia, elder meant better. It meant that even their Majesties had been told how loveable Kathryn was, and wanted her near them.

How she had cried, alone in the apple loft, when Kathryn rode away – cried with loneliness and thick corrosive jealousy which, even at nine, she was shrewd enough to hide.

She rubbed the glass with her sleeve. There was little reason to envy Kathryn nowadays – trapped in a miserable marriage, grieving because after two years she remained childless. Sir Giles Standish cursed her and called her a barren bitch, although he hadn't succeeded in getting his mistress – the beefy sewing-maid – pregnant either. Eighteen-year-old Kathryn bore it all with a dignity that made Alicia want to cry. Her sister was so beautiful and so good yet she remained lonely and unappreciated, except by Queen Catherine, whose waiting woman she was. Rejected by her husband, constantly called upon by the unhappy, middle-aged Queen, Kathryn deferred to the one and loved the other while seeming to have no needs of her own. Yet Alicia thought the Queen selfish, for while Kathryn spent so much time away from home, there was little chance of her conceiving a child.

A yell of laughter outside diverted her. One of the stable-grooms was gallop-ing across the courtyard with a young maidservant on his back. Suddenly he plunged into the puddle with an almighty splash that soaked the pair of them. He spun round, made as if to tip the girl into the water. Her hair was streaming down her back like wet seaweed, yet she was shrieking with mirth and pummelling his shoulder with one of her fists. Still laughing, they disappeared through a narrow archway to the kitchen-garden beyond.

'Trapped, trapped,' beat the dull rhythm of Alicia's heart. 'Trapped,' echoed the rain as it slopped down the window.

An image of Gervase Houghton's face swam before her, white and sullen with the narrow eyes of a lizard and a slice of pale-brown hair flopping over his brow. They had met just once, when Gervase was fifteen and Alicia twelve, but it was enough for her to conceive a violent loathing. He had barely spoken to her, except when prompted by his overbearing mother, but as they'd sat side by side in the winter parlour after supper, he'd looked his fill. Time and again the lizard-eyes slanted towards her, darting over her faintly budding breasts in a sly fidgety way which had infuriated her.

She pulled a face, clutching the counterpane closer. Why the devil did people get married? For women, at least, there was little reward. Alicia had seen how marriage could destroy a woman by slowly abrading her spirit; had seen her mother and her sister crushed in numbing defeat. Yet how different it might be if a man and woman truly loved each other. Joanna's mooing, note-clinging voice had sung of simpering virgins and gentle troubadours; of knights who were probably terrifying in combat but always dissolved into puddles of warm blanc-mange the instant they fell in love.

To marry for love – the idea seemed ludicrous, if not faintly vulgar, to most people. Even her gentle mother had looked startled when she mentioned it to her once.

'Sweetheart, I don't think you understand. One doesn't marry for sentimen-tal reasons, but for the mutual advantage of both families concerned.'

It was all very confusing for an emotional young girl who had read of love in the enchanted volumes of Chaucer but heard adults talk only of money and estates. Yet Alicia knew that marriage could be as warm and rich as a sunlit herb-garden – knew it because of Lady Bess.

All at once her expression grew wistfully yearning. If only she could be back in that noisy, muddled, overflowing household with darling Lady Bess!

Ashby Place was a crumbling mass of rosy-grey stone set in the green heart of Wiltshire. Built early in the reign of Edward III, with straggling wings and numerous outbuildings apparently added at random, it resembled nothing so much as the beloved creation of an architect who couldn't quite bring himself to abandon it. The whole was girdled by a wide moat teeming with golden carp. There was a legend that one of Sir Walter's ancestors had swum in it naked one icy December night, to prove his love to a beautiful but disdainful lady. Unfortunately the young man had consumed too much brandy-wine before-hand, was gripped with cramp and had to be assisted out by two silent, disapproving manservants. The disdainful beauty had married his rival soon afterwards.

Despite its history of romantic pathos, the manor had an air of careless exuberance, rather like a spry old grandfather. Vivid banners fluttered at the turrets, peacocks pranced unconcernedly across the lawns. Visitors would arrive, view the disorder with dismay, then discover that they didn't want to leave.

Alicia, barely past her tenth birthday, stared round the stuffy, crowded great hall in utter bewilderment on that first evening. Liveried servants sped past her, bearing great platters of steaming food. A handful of guests – she learnt later that there was an unceasing flow of them – were clustered round a young man who was singing a French love song while accompanying himself on a lute. Dogs wandered casually through the throng, a pregnant greyhound bitch came to sniff at Alicia's skirts. She was about to bend down to tickle its ears when she noticed a group of young girls – perhaps five or six – being shepherded into the hall by a middle-aged woman. She guessed they must be the companions whom Lady Ashby had mentioned in her letters.

Lady Ashby, a plump little partridge of a woman, stood in front of the red roaring fire, a glass of wine clasped in both hands. Glimpsing the child hovering shyly by the door, she laid the glass down on a nearby table and beckoned, smiling.

Alicia, her bottom still aching from the long hours in the saddle, approached her, then dipped a stiff little curtsy.

'Dorothy's child – at last.' A stubby thumb tilted her chin up, so that she found herself looking into a pair of sparkling chestnut eyes, so warm and alive in a

great mottled moon of a face. 'Welcome to Ashby Place, sweetheart. I'm
delighted to see you.'

She had a rich voice that reminded the little girl of warm gingerbread and she
smelled of carnations. But for her pearl necklace and her elaborately embroidered pink gown, she might easily be mistaken for some child's beloved nurse.
Alicia had a sudden grateful urge to fling her arms round her neck, but remembered her manners in time.

'You're very kind, madam.' Demurely she curtsied again, then a smile flashed
across her face. She couldn't help it – Lady Bess was just like a big, motherly
tabby cat.

Bess noticed the smile and beamed back at her in relief. Cowed children
disturbed her, for several had passed through Ashby Place. Solemn little things
with shuttered faces and prim voices, all the joy and spontaneity flogged out
of them by the parents who loathed them and set more value upon their dogs.
Alicia seemed neither timid nor unduly precocious, so perhaps Richard
Westbrooke had been more successful as a father than he was as a husband.

Lady Bess, somewhat tipsy as she was most evenings, felt a vague tingling of
tears behind her eyeballs. It was as if the years had fallen away and she and
Dorothy were young women again, in the household of Elizabeth of York. How
carefree they had been then – Dorothy so bright and eager as if each day might
bring her some magical gift, Bess already the mother of three small sons but not
in the least subdued by her responsibilities. For all that some eight years lay
between them, the two soon became friends. Bess had sensed the sharp loneliness behind Dorothy's pretty sparkling, while Dorothy came to regard Bess as an
older sister, one who would always look after her. They were seldom apart, that
pale winter at Westminster. Then Richard had married Dorothy and somehow
turned the lovely tender creature into a frightened doll-woman who rarely left
her Hertfordshire home.

Bess, remembering the child standing before her, shook herself out of her
maudlin mood. It hadn't been entirely Richard's fault, for all that he was a surly
brute. Dorothy had been haughty and obstructive, which had only served to fan
the antipathy that had smouldered between them from the first meeting. And yet,
he could have been kinder. He could have been kinder!

'Why child, what eyes!' she boomed suddenly, with a glance at the watchful
little face. 'I vow they're the exact shade of March violets. What do you think,
Walt?' She turned to the neat little grey-haired man who had come to stand
beside her. 'Isn't she just as lovely as Dorothy?'

Sir Walter stroked his beard, gazing thoughtfully at the little girl.

'Indeed she is, Bessy. Indeed she is. And no doubt you'll have found her a
husband before her next birthday.'

'Clattermouth!' His wife flicked her fingers across his nose, which brought roars of laughter from their guests. 'No sensible woman would ever get married if the choice were hers.'

'She has you there, Father.' The young man who had been singing strolled towards them, grinning all over his face.

'This is Roger.' Bess gave a mock grimace. 'Our eldest cub, and more trouble than the whole pack.'

'Hardly a cub, Mother,' Roger protested. He winked at Alicia. 'I was twenty-two last birthday and shall soon have a cub of my own – my second, in fact.'

Alicia looked from one to the other and wanted to laugh with delight. What a jolly family they seemed!

Supper was a sumptuous spread, for the Ashbys didn't believe in denying themselves any of life's pleasures. There was almond cream soup, chicken pie and baked kid in a lake of raisin sauce. Pancakes and cinnamon-flavoured jelly followed, with Gascony wine poured from seemingly bottomless jugs. However, Alicia suddenly felt so weary, she could only nibble at her food. Her eyelids began to droop, while all around her the voices soared and merged into a singing hive.

She woke once in the night to feel a pair of icy feet pressed against the small of her back, and nearly squealed with fright before remembering where she was. A little girl was fast asleep beside her, her body sprawled diagonally across the mattress, one chubby arm still wrapped round a wooden doll. Alicia gave her a shove but she didn't move.

Suddenly she wanted Joanna so badly, her chest hurt. Joanna was short-tempered and could be erratic, but she had always been there.

A fat tear splashed down the side of her nose. Soft snores and whistling sounds were coming from every corner of the dark little dormitory yet she had never felt so alone. It was a frightening, empty feeling, as if she had been carried off and heartlessly abandoned in a forest – a recurring nightmare of hers since she was six years old.

As the next few days trundled past, the feeling of strangeness began to subside. She was kept so busy that there was little time to fret for her old nurse. Although the Ashby household was rompingly informal in many ways, the children were kept to a strict daily schedule. There was Mass first thing in the little stone-floored chapel on the first floor, followed by breakfast at seven. After that they studied French, scripture and needlework under the flinty eye of Madame Jehanne. Madame also taught them dancing and three afternoons a week there were music lessons from a timid, elderly Welshman. None of them had any inkling of how he dreaded those afternoons, nor would they have much cared – their chief delight lay in plaguing him till his face turned dark as a plum. They would fidget and whisper, interrupt him with silly questions, then giggle at his earnest replies. Sometimes the poor man came close to tears as he shouted half-hearted threats at them, but it made no difference. They continued to tease him remorselessly, as they never dared to tease Madame Jehanne.

They all hated and feared Madame for she was a sharp-tongued, humourless tyrant given to terrifying rages which left their victim white-faced and shaken. She disliked children, especially girls, but knew of no other way to make a living. There was no giggling in *her* schoolroom; she wielded the whip for the smallest infraction and seemed to take extravagant pleasure in doing so.

Yet despite Madame, Alicia was happy. She was on good terms with all the other girls, except Jane Seymour. The eldest daughter of Sir John and Lady Margery Seymour from nearby Wolf Hall, twelve-year-old Jane was a prim, self-contained child, and Alicia disliked and distrusted her for that reason. Although her mother had been a great beauty in her youth – her clear-skinned blondeness had inspired the poet, Skelton – Jane herself was a pallid creature with a nasal voice that seemed to scrape along Alicia's nerves whenever she heard it. She was so colourless that she even managed to escape Madame's wrath most of the time. Lady Bess said she was shy. Alicia thought her smug but didn't say so in case she offended her new guardian.

Alicia had been quick to sense the mood of warm gusty optimism that lit Ashby Place like a great torch. It seemed to her that it came directly from Lady Bess.

She loved Bess more than anyone in the world, except Kathryn – loved her gingerbread voice, the carnation perfume that always clung about her, even the way she swore and chewed the end of her quill every time she sat down to tackle the household accounts, which were always in a state of chaos.

There was no malice in Bess and she was incapable of petty spite or sarcasm. She never bullied the servants, though she would deal briskly with any sign of idleness. She was fond of the young girls in her charge without being sentimental about them – that way her big heart stayed intact. Alicia, recalling the tense atmosphere at Greenthorpe, found herself watching Lady Bess speculatively as she entered adolescence.

She had never been beautiful even in her youth, which she had long since passed. Her florid moon face could be most kindly described as 'homely', while two decades of childbearing had taken its toll of her figure. Like Alicia's mother she had known the shock and sorrow of seeing several of her babies die, yet her brightness of spirit had somehow survived, along with her sense of humour. She scurried about the house like a minxish fifteen-year-old, her rather bawdy laugh frequently battering the walls. Some nights she went to bed reeling drunk, singing the coarse songs her father had learnt in the Lancastrian army.

Sir Walter treated his wife as an ally, a pampered mistress and an irresponsible but lovable friend who could dazzle him into all manner of mischief. Alicia liked to watch them, sitting together in the gallery or strolling through the rose-garden, arms linked, as they discussed plans for their home. They always seemed to be touching each other – there were kisses and quick warm hugs, often followed by hearty bottom-slapping. Sometimes their guests would complain to each other in shocked whispers that they'd been kept awake all night by the sounds of love-making coming from the Ashby's bedchamber.

Alicia sensed that for all the teasing and mock insults, the pair were deeply in love. Perhaps, she reasoned with thirteen-year-old logic, it was because they had sons.

Lady Dorothy's failure to produce a healthy boy-child was, Alicia believed, the main cause of her father's sneering animosity. Dorothy was a loving, obedient wife who worked harder than any of the servants at Greenthorpe, yet she received no reward, only sarcastic taunts and, occasionally, blows. Alicia's heart used to flip over in her chest whenever her mother appeared at Mass with bruised lips or a puffy cheek, but nothing was ever said. The brutality that Dorothy suffered at her husband's hands was shrouded in silence, as if by not protesting she could somehow salvage her dignity.

The years shimmered past and Alicia was fifteen, high-spirited and charming, if rather self-willed. She had a delicate yet vital beauty that drew men's eyes and already she knew it, for she had inherited her father's vanity along with his obstinate temper. She spent many diverting hours in front of the mirror, studying her reflection as enthusiastically as an astronomy student might study the sky. It wasn't difficult to take pleasure in what she saw.

Her thick orange curls had deepened to the shade of beech-leaves, tumbling in a glossy mass to her thighs. To her relief, her skin no longer erupted into spiteful little pimples once a month and her body was slender as a wand, though she wished that her breasts were fuller and that she had her mother's and her sister's elegant height. She also envied them their lovely hands, for her own were small and stubby, but at least she'd stopped biting her nails since Madame had threatened to coat them with vinegar. Nowadays visitors to Ashby Place were quick to pay her compliments, especially the men. Alicia found that the almond-sweet words fed her burgeoning conceit. Lying in bed at night she would mull over them greedily, like a newly rich woman with her jewel box. She knew that no one at Greenthorpe would have said such delightful things to her. Imagine Joanna comparing her complexion to a wild white orchid! Only Madame refused to pay her tribute; after five years Alicia's knowledge of French was sparse but she played the lute prettily, danced with a spirited grace and had a natural cleverness with her needle. It seemed ample, for she had been told that there were ladies at the Tudor court who could barely write their name.

In December she went home to Greenthorpe as usual for the Twelve Days holiday, but this time her heart was heavy for she knew that she wouldn't be returning to Ashby Place. Weeping unashamedly, she clung to Lady Bess until the last moment, feeling as if she were being wrenched away from everything in the world that mattered. The pain in her heart threatened to slice her in two.

'Don't cry so, child.' Close to tears herself, Bess hugged the sobbing girl. 'All will be well, you'll see, and once you're married we shall visit each other often.'

Even in her own ears, her cheery tone sounded forced. Of all her young charges, this one had stolen her heart.

Never love another woman's child, she had told herself long ago, when she and Walter first began taking the daughters of friends and neighbours into their home. It hadn't been difficult to keep to that rule – for all her sentimental ways, she was rooted in common sense. Over the years she had been quick to note fear or unhappiness in a child. Many of them had come to her already maimed in spirit, their little faces starved and dull, like abandoned fox-cubs. She had striven to make them feel safe – to instil in them hope and confidence, but they weren't hers to love and so she knew no anguish when they went away. Yet she couldn't help loving Alicia, because she had loved Dorothy.

Out in the courtyard, Sir Walter lifted Alicia on to a silver-grey gelding – their birthday gift to her last October. It now occurred to Bess that Richard Westbrooke might not allow his daughter to keep the animal but she said nothing.

'God bless you, little one,' Walter breathed softly.

Alicia stared at him through a shining mist of tears. It was the first time he had ever spoken to her so tenderly although she had always sensed his steady affection.

Meanwhile one of the grooms was scrambling on to the back of a rather ancient mare. His creased crab-apple face wore an impatient expression; it did the horses no good to be kept standing.

The wagon piled with Alicia's luggage went creaking across the drawbridge. Still she hesitated, wanting to savour the last moment even though it hurt.

The Ashbys stood side by side on the steps, framed by the pale-lemon light of a December morning. Lady Bess's dear rosy face was wreathed in smiles though her eyes were rather moist. Sir Walter had his arm round her plump shoulders, hugging her close to his side. It took all of Alicia's courage to smile back, so that their last sight of her would be a pleasant one. In her heart she was wondering if she would ever see them again.

It had stopped raining at last, though the drops still clung to the panes like tiny ashes. Alicia bent forward in the window seat, chin propped on her knees. Her arms were wrapped close about her body as if to protect it from a blow and she was shivering with cold. The counterpane had fallen on to the rushes but she didn't bother to pick it up. It was as if the dank January chill had soaked into her bones so that she could only sit there, staring blindly into the lengthening grey-

black shadows. One side of her head ached with grinding insistence and there
was an ugly bruise on her cheekbone, staining the delicate skin like a blob of
blackberry juice. Very gingerly, she reached up to touch the spot. Almost at once
it started to throb and she winced.

Damn her father to hell! Why did he care so little for her, for any of them?
And why, even after he had bullied and bruised her, did she feel like crying
because he would never love her? Well, she would be the last to let him know!

Her eyes strained towards the little gilt clock on the mantelshelf. It was nearly
five o'clock; downstairs in the winter parlour her parents would be sitting down
to supper. She pictured them, seated at either end of the table, not even looking at each other while Alban, the elderly steward, shambled back and forth
between them, piling their plates and pretending not to notice the frigid atmosphere.

Alicia grew conscious that her belly was making resentful whining noises.
Even so she hoped Sir Richard didn't order her to the table. She couldn't endure
another of his angry tirades – or his blows.

The empty minutes trudged past, agonizingly slow, while she listened for
some sign of movement in the gallery. After a while the silence grew unnerving. What if her father intended to starve her into obedience? He was certainly
callous enough. But someone – perhaps Joanna? – would surely take pity on
her. Joanna was as sour as a dish of quinces, but she detested cruelty in any
form. She might smuggle in some meat pasties when she came to undress her
for bed. And yet, how dared they leave her alone in the cold and dark without
any food!

Indignantly, she sprang to her feet and went stumbling across the floor, banging her hip painfully on the wooden bedpost as she went. As she flung open the
door, she saw Joanna turning into the gallery at the head of the stairs. The old
woman was carrying a tray and her face looked glum in the orange torchlight,
as if she had a blister on her heel.

She shuffled down the gallery at her usual leisurely pace – Joanna hurried for
nobody. As she drew closer, her mouth suddenly twisted down at one corner.

'Aye, you're to have your supper.' She greeted Alicia acidly in a stout Yorkshire
accent, though it was nearly forty years since she had come south. 'And if it were
left to me you'd get a sound whipping instead, after the trouble you've brewed
today.'

Gloomy old bitch! thought Alicia, yet she couldn't help grinning. Nothing that
went on at Greenthorpe escaped Joanna.

'Do as you like. I'm sick of the girl and the sooner she is off my hands the
happier I shall be.'

It was late that same night. Sir Richard lay back in the big canopied bed, arms folded behind his head as he watched his wife undressing beyond the half-open bed curtains.

He had dismissed her maid last year when the unfortunate girl became pregnant and had stubbornly refused to replace her despite – or because of – Dorothy's pleadings. He'd insisted that Joanna could earn her keep instead of swilling ale in the hall all day – an aspersion which both Dorothy and Joanna sensibly ignored. Now Dorothy had the grudging assistance of the old woman she had come to loathe and her twice-daily *toilette* was a tense, silent ordeal dreaded by both women and consequently relished by Richard.

His eyes flicked irritably round the room, blind to its beauty. The bed curtains were of sapphire velvet lined with silver satin, the velvet counterpane so dark a blue as to be almost black. A sturdy oak chest stood in the corner, covered with a beautiful old Turkey rug. The cushions on the little rosewood stools had been embroidered by Kathryn as a New Year's gift to her parents two years ago. The walls were covered with fashionable linenfold panelling and a couple of Dorothy's best tapestries. It was in this same room that Dorothy's proud and bitter grandmother, Cicely, had spent her wedding night, conceived and borne her children. And *that* was little less than a miracle, Richard snorted to himself. Sir Henry Marsh had been a hopeless drunkard with a taste for young men. In his last years he had been confined to his bed in the gatehouse wing, a rotting mound of humanity, separated for ever from his wife while she ruled Greenthorpe alone, secure in her triumph, her terrible strength, now that she was done with love and could never be hurt again.

'I think Alicia will be happy at court,' Dorothy was saying as she stepped out of her leather stays. 'Kathryn can keep an eye on her and perhaps help her to see sense. It would be for the best.'

Richard didn't answer her straight away; she suspected he was only half-listening. Pulling a violet velvet chamber robe over her nightgown, she went to sit at the *toilette* table, Joanna stumping disagreeably behind her.

She hesitated, surveying the array of bottles and perfume phials, silver-backed hairbrushes and bright lacquered boxes. Then she reached for a bottle of rose-water and began smoothing its contents over her face. Her green eyes were thoughtful as they searched the little curved crystal handmirror which had once belonged to her mother.

Next August she would be forty – an age which was usually dreaded by women yet she faced it impassively. Every woman decayed at her own pace. She had known a woman at court, still charming, animated and bright-eyed in her sixties, and thought her truly lovely. Dorothy's body was still slim and supple and, but for a delicate tracery of lines around the eyes, her face was timeless in its beauty.

'All this talk of happiness!' Richard suddenly thundered from the bed. 'Married life was never intended to be happy – fruitful, I'll own. We shall have to pray that she succeeds rather better there than you and Kathryn have done.'

Dorothy winced at the brutal words but said nothing. Sometimes it seemed as if her only weapon against Richard was silence.

Joanna, her knotty old fingers loosening her mistress's hair, felt her recoil. She let out her breath in a stabbing hiss, then began combing the heavy tresses which were barely threaded with silver. Dorothy's hair was not darkly red like her younger daughter's but a sleek coppery gold that Joanna privately thought more beautiful. Bright as an October forest, the rich swirl glinted and crackled beneath her hand and presently she felt her own stiff, resentful body start to unbend. The least glamorous of females, she had a desperate love of beauty which only another plain woman could understand. Moreover, this was the one task she performed willingly – it always reminded her of the old days and the young Dorothy, who had sat looking into this same mirror, smiling at the smooth face that shimmered back at her and eagerly recounting every detail of her day. Those were the jewel-bright days when Dorothy still trusted her. 'Let her be your penance, madam.' She had once heard Sir Richard say those words to his wife. That had hurt; Joanna, who loved nobody, had once loved Dorothy with a furious, exclusive tenderness that had lit both their worlds.

'Come to bed, madam.' Richard punched the pillow as if it were an old enemy. 'Alicia can go to court if you're so heartset on it – that's if the Queen is fool enough to take her. Let her go where she likes, so long as I needn't fret my bowels over her. But I warn you, she'll breed trouble as a dog breeds fleas.'

With that, he gave the pillow another thump. It was a wonder it didn't burst into a cloud of feathers, Joanna mused sourly, stooping to pick up a pair of scarlet stockings from the floor. Dorothy went on staring into the mirror, her face apprehensive and wary.

'Christ's blood, am I to be allowed no sleep! Stop preening and come to bed.'

Minutes later she was lying beside him in the candle-smoky darkness. His back was turned towards her and, as usual, neither of them spoke. Dorothy's fists were clenched to her sides, so tightly she could feel the nails digging into the palms. Every muscle was taut as a lute string as she fought down the crazy impulse to press her body along the length of his and sob out all her pain and longing. This was how it was every night – lying here miserably conscious of the stiff expanse of sheet between them but not daring to cross it. She had often asked herself which was worse – to have a man in your bed who didn't want to be there, or to have no man at all.

It wasn't the high rapture of lovemaking that she missed, for that was something she had never known. Richard's rough handling of her body had never stirred her senses, yet she'd found comfort of a sort in the physical closeness. However, he hadn't touched her for many months – not since before her last confinement.

She turned on to her back, one fist pressed to her mouth as if to smother a sob. The mound beside her shifted, then was still. There was no pain, no regret, to disturb Richard's rest and he always slept soundly, his dreams untroubled, while she lay awake wondering who his latest mistress was.

There had been a wool-merchant's widow in London who had written him shockingly candid letters which he'd made little effort to conceal. Dorothy had found them stuffed inside an old leatherbound book one evening last summer. The sense of defilement was as potent as if they'd taken their pleasure in her bed, the slicing pain left her feeling weak as after childbirth, but she made no mention of her find. Richard would have cared little for her anguish and anyway, she guessed that he'd have beaten her for daring to probe his secrets. Nonetheless she had found the courage to burn those vile letters over a candle flame, shaking all the while with rage and fear and revulsion. A fine thing if one of their daughters had happened upon them!

Richard had grace enough not to mention their disappearance, but the gulf remained between them. He only came to their bed in order to sleep and he seldom spoke to her unless it was to give an order or to point out some fault. Dorothy believed that the affair with the lusty widow was now over, since he hadn't been to London for several months. Yet he wasn't a man to deny his appetites and there must be a score of women on the estate who'd willingly go to bed with him.

Dorothy sighed, tucking the covers under her chin. If only she had given him a healthy son! Like Queen Catherine, she had not been blessed in childbed. Two little boys, dead before they learned to walk. A series of miscarriages which had left her feeling weak and depressed. And then, last year, a stillborn daughter. That last had carried her to the very edge of despair as she looked upon the tiny still face of her perfectly formed child and wondered at the futility, the sharp unreasoning pain. Now it seemed she was finally done with bearing and burying Richard's children, she felt only relief. It had been such a lonely business, never being able to talk of her grief, the prodding sense of failure, because she knew that he wouldn't understand, only condemn her.

In the darkness she felt tears start from the corners of her eyes and slant across her temples, into her hair. She bit the insides of her cheeks to stop her mouth from wobbling like a child's. As usual, the tears brought no relief. If anything, they only served to remind her of the bleak grey sterility which filled her whole world.

She thought now of her girls – sweet, pliant Kathryn, headstrong Alicia. They were pretty, loveable creatures and yet she scarcely knew them. In any case they had drawn together in silent protective unity against Richard when they were very young and each was the other's greatest love.

Richard not only withheld love, he had destroyed her pride, her confidence, all her belief in herself, while Greenthorpe laughed and mocked, as it had been mocking her since the day of her birth.

CHAPTER TWO

1485

Dorothy Marsh was born in the castle of Sheriff Hutton, twelve miles outside York, on a sultry afternoon when the air was as thick as syllabub and the only sound to be heard was her mother's weeping.

Seventeen-year-old Alice had wanted a son. She turned her face into the frayed silk pillow, refusing to look at the child.

Mistress Peake, the midwife who had just delivered the baby, bit back the retort that danced to her lips and rubbed her aching back instead. She instantly recognized this as something more than a fit of pique. Alice's face looked pinched and grey and there were great tired smudges under her eyes. Of course, she was still in shock, as was the entire household since news of King Richard's defeat on Redmore Plain, near the market town of Bosworth, had reached them that morning.

Richard Plantagenet, last of the White Rose kings. He had been Lord of the North for many years, Sovereign of England for just two. The Council in London had begged him to take the crown after his brother, Edward IV, died and the shaming secret of an earlier, youthful marriage broke out, hurling the succession into chaos. Edward's brood of children by Elizabeth Woodville, his haughty silver-blonde queen, were pronounced illegitimate. Ned, his twelve-year-old heir, would not be 'His Majesty' but 'the Lord Bastard'. Some pitied the lad and felt that he had been cheated out of his rights, but most were relieved for they hadn't wanted another boy king. Like as not it would only stir the old rancour between the houses of York and Lancaster and the blood of good Englishmen would run once again like scarlet rivers into the dust.

So Richard took the crown, after which grief and loss stalked him. Resentment curdled in the hearts of many of his courtiers as they watched favours being heaped upon others. In the end they turned to Henry Tudor, the fugitive heir of Lancaster, though born of a bastard line. Letters larded with pleas and promises were smuggled overseas to Brittany where Welsh-born Henry had been waiting most of his life. He relished the pleas, smiled coolly at the promises – England and the loyalty of all Englishmen, with the added fillip of a golden-haired Yorkist bride. And yet he wanted the crown, which he'd always considered to be his birthright. With an army of French mercenaries and disgruntled Yorkists at his back, he'd made his landing at Milford Haven. As he marched towards the Severn, a mere handful of men straggled into the ranks – nothing like the mighty force that Henry had hoped for from his fellow country-men. Mostly they stood outside their cottage doors or in the fields beside their wooden ploughs and gaped bemusedly.

Had it not been for the calculated, unforgivably delayed support of his step-father, Lord Stanley, the day would have been lost. Stanley's army bobbed on the very seam of battle, cynically awaiting the outcome. Then, as King Richard unexpectedly came thundering across the plain in a direct line towards the horri-fied Tudor, his battleaxe blindly slashing to left and right, felling any who crossed his path, Stanley shouted the order. His men surged forward, encircling the small furious figure on the panting white stallion. The king's scream of 'Treason! Treason!' seemed to linger on the air even after they'd hacked him down upon the earth.

The news, brought to them by a dazed and exhausted lad whose face was still caked with grime and dried blood, had stunned the women at Sheriff Hutton. It had also sent Alice Marsh swooning on to the cushions, her labour already begun.

The women helped her to bed in the hastily prepared room. None of them dared to say what each was thinking yet Joanna, the freckled serving girl who was supposed to be assisting them but kept getting under their feet, could almost smell their fear. The baby wasn't due till mid-October and would almost certainly be stillborn.

'Will she be all right?' A tall blonde girl in her late teens jumped up from her stool as Mistress Peake emerged, Joanna trailing at her heels. 'She *will* live?'

She was dressed in starkest black, wore no ornament apart from a little ruby and gold crucifix at her throat, and her face was puffy with crying. Yet she had the type of lucent beauty which is fragile and at the same time indestructible.

'Who can say at these times, my lady?' Mistress Peake folded her arms across the broad shelf of her bosom. For a moment she appeared almost pleased not to be able to offer reassurance, rather like a disgraced child who feels slightly less aggrieved when she learns that her sister must share her punishment. Then, seeing the rather childish blue eyes turn cloudy with dread, like a puppy that expects to be kicked, she suddenly felt ashamed, and went on: 'You mustn't fret, madam. She's a hardy little thing, in spite of her sparrow bones. Most likely she'll live. As for the baby . . .' she gave a hefty sigh, rolling her eyes piously towards the ceiling, 'well, we shall have to trust in God's mercy.'

Elizabeth of York, the eldest and most popular of the late King Edward's daughters, gave a soft, low moan as if *she* were in childbirth. All at once she began to cry, tears of fright and remorse skimming down her face.

'I should have sent her back to her parents and not kept her here in this dismal place. But she – she said she wouldn't be delivered before St Luke's Day. Oh poor, poor Alice!'

She flung herself weeping against the rigid figure of Mistress Peake, much to that lady's disapproval. Joanna's mouth sagged open, then closed again as she caught Mistress Peake frowning at her over Elizabeth's shoulder. She felt as if she were witnessing some shockingly intimate scene – one from which she couldn't bring herself to glance tactfully away.

At last Elizabeth lifted a wet face and sniffed.

'At least she knows that a man loved her,' she said bleakly.

Mistress Peake smirked at *that*, then remembered she was dealing with a king's daughter.

'*You* will be loved also, madam. The Tudor – I mean His Grace King Henry – will send for you once he reaches London. You'll be Queen of England before the year is out.'

For the life of her she couldn't stem the tartness in her voice. A true Yorkshirewoman, her tough uncompromising heart lay with Richard, who had been a son of York. The women had been told how he'd worn his crown into battle, in splendid contempt of the bastard Tudors. They'd heard, too, how his enemies had flung his naked and broken body into a makeshift grave when it was all over. Hatred had swelled their hearts, threatening to choke them. Apart from all else, it was a foul way to treat an anointed King.

She had seen him once when he visited Sheriff Hutton with his frail wife, Anne. He hadn't spoken to her but a tender, almost shy smile had warmed his rather harsh bronze features when he chanced to look in her direction. And Mistress Peake, knowing his loyal heart, his courage, his fierce abiding love for Yorkshire, found herself smiling back.

She had grieved for him when first his young son and then his queen died, picturing him in his lonely, mournful pride. Now he too was dead, and England had fallen under the heel of a long-lipped Welshman. A hard-bitten woman, Mistress Peake was not much given to tears, but today she wanted to weep.

'How can you say that?' The princess wheeled round, her heavy taffeta skirts swishing distracted circles across the floor. 'I hate his very name. Uncle Richard promised that I could choose my own husband and now . . .'

'And now I must tend to Mistress Alice, madam. Come, Joanna.'

They found Alice tossing upon the bed like a fretful seal, her swollen body twisting from side to side as if to escape the pain. Tears and sweat streaked her face in shiny rivulets, wisps of dark-red hair clung to her temples.

'Come now, mistress.' The midwife's stern face softened as she reached for Alice's hand. 'Try to rest between the pains. You'll need all your strength later.'

'It must be a boy,' Alice panted. Her nails scraped the hot rumpled sheet with a rasping sound that set Joanna's teeth on edge. She thought that Alice looked like a battered doll, lying there on the bed, her eyes staring fearfully out of a dirty face – Alice, who had been so beautiful, it made your heart stop to look at her.

One of the women brought her a cup of wine, tried to prise it between her lips, but she struck it aside with unexpected force so that most of it spilled on to the sheet. 'It must be a boy or it's all been for nothing.' Suddenly she fell back against the pillows and began to sob quietly, like a woman drained of all hope, while the spilt wine seeped across the sheet like a dark, sticky globule of blood.

Later there was blood such as Joanna had never envisaged as the baby was thrust from Alice's loins. She paused, then grabbed the bedpost, struggling against a cold wave of nausea while her breath came in sharp, jagged little sighs that seemed to catch in her throat. Men as strong as bears had died bleeding beneath the pitiless sun on Redmore Plain. What chance was there for this tiny, fragile creature?

Mistress Peake, her hands still working deftly beneath the blankets, looked up in exasperation.

'Brace yourself, girl!' she snapped, relieved at the chance to vent her own tension. 'This is always a bloody business.'

There was a somewhat dazed expression on Joanna's face, greenish-white now beneath the shower of freckles. The midwife suspected she hadn't heard the rebuke and was annoyed. Well, if she swooned she would simply have to lie where she fell!

'I shall never marry,' Joanna murmured, partly to herself. She wiped her face on her sleeve and all at once seemed to revert to her usual stolid self.

Mistress Peake's irritation gave way to a sense of amused pity. Never marry, indeed! If ever a girl was unlikely to find herself besieged by suitors, it was Joanna. Mistress Peake had never known such an ungainly clump of a girl – sullen and clumsy, with a face like a suet pudding. No wonder the other servants teased her.

She was about to chuckle at Joanna's pretensions when she noticed that her patient was trying to speak, and bent over the bed to hear her.

'I'd like to name her Dorothy.' Alice's voice was scarcely above a whisper yet she seemed calmer, almost resigned. Somehow it no longer mattered that the child was a girl. To Alice's parents she would still be a bastard – a bitter canker on their family pride.

'A pretty name.' The midwife smiled encouragingly, but she was puzzled. She had expected Alice to name the child after herself, or perhaps the princess who

had been so kind to her. Still, it was more important that the little one was chris-
tened soon, whatever the name.

Alice turned her head wearily towards the window, where the late afternoon
sun was slanting in over the bed.

Dorothy! Through a tear-spangled mist she saw the baby sister, lost to her
these eight years – arms outstretched, red-blonde curls tumbling about the small,
vivid, laughing face as she ran across the nursery floor, nearly tripping over her
long gown. Alice shut her eyes, holding the image close.

A selfish headstrong child herself, yet she had loved Dorothy with a fierce
affection that had surprised everyone at Greenthorpe. The nurse had always
complained that Alice was selfish, yet to little Dorothy she had readily given her
gingerbread babies, her precious Bartholomew dolls, the whole of her wilful,
tempestuous heart.

When Dorothy was four years old they had laid her away in the blackness of
the family vault and the sun went out of Alice's young life. She had known death
strike before – one brother slain on Barnet Field, the other kicked to death by a
mad horse. However she'd scarcely known the tall redheaded boys who were
already full-grown when she was still in swaddling, and was untouched by their
loss. Now Dorothy was gone for ever, struck down by a childhood ailment that
had at first seemed so innocuous, and her mother said they must never mention
her again. 'Remember Alice, people don't want to hear about your troubles.'

How cold and unfeeling those words had sounded to the grieving child, too
young to understand her mother's white-faced agony. For Cicely Marsh had
borne Dorothy in her thirty-seventh year and had looked upon her as a miracle
child, sent to console her for the loss of her sons, for the sour travesty of her
marriage.

Alice never *did* talk about Dorothy, but the silence became a living shroud, a
sad and frightening burden that she carried inside her, making her flippant and
defensive; fearful of being hurt yet always aching to be loved.

She wanted to ask to see the baby but she felt too tired to speak. Weariness
was spreading across her body like a soggy sheet, pressing her down into a
muddy lake of torpor. She was conscious of the women moving about the room,
restless and uneasy, could hear the child's feeble but insistent crying, yet she was
strangely unmoved.

*When I'm strong again, I'll take her home to Greenthorpe. Maybe they'll forgive me when
they see her. After all, she's their first grandchild.*

Then she remembered her mother's face, pale and stiff as a wax effigy, heard
her drunken father calling her bitch and harlot, and she knew that they would
neither understand nor forgive.

'We should never have allowed you to go to court nor, it seems, to any place
where there are men.' Lady Cicely's eyes had glittered like splinters of green ice

as they ran up and down her daughter's figure that dreadful day in the solar at Greenthorpe. 'Who is responsible – or haven't you decided yet?'

Alice had fled Greenthorpe that very night, with a few angel coins stitched inside her hood and a selection of toilet articles wrapped in a spare gown. She travelled alone for she knew that Sir Henry and Lady Cicely could less easily spare a servant than a daughter who had brought them such shame.

It was a fearful journey for the roads were dark and deserted and badly pot-holed. More than once Alice nearly turned back, but then she had a picture of their hard condemning faces and it seemed to stiffen her nerve. Better to be set upon by a band of robbers and cut-throats than to go crawling back like a dog that has injured its paw!

It was early evening three days later when she stumbled into Westminster Palace. She was very dirty, and limping from a throbbing blister on her heel. Her horse had shed a shoe at Highgate and rather than spend any of her precious coins at the forge she'd sold him to a visiting farmer who'd eyed her matted hair and filthy gown suspiciously but said nothing. No doubt he thought her a whore, like the little party of soldiers who'd jeered and flung her a shilling as they clattered past her down the street.

'Stay with me.' Elizabeth of York, lonely and unhappy, bewildered by her own upturned fortunes, was close to tears as she surveyed the pale girl crumpled at her feet. In spite of everything there still remained that delicate pride in Alice's bearing which had first attracted the princess. Moreover, she was keenly aware that *she* might easily have been in Alice's place, for she was wholly and recklessly in love. Alice bent her small auburn head.

'The baby, madam . . .' she began, then broke off, hands fluttering towards her belly like two sad little birds.

Tenderly Elizabeth raised her to her feet and kissed her cheek.

'Don't worry Alice, I will take care of you and your little one. And now you must have food and a warm bath before you catch a chill.'

The kind words pierced Alice's defiance as her parents' cold implacable anger had failed to do, and she began to cry in the princess's arms.

An hour later she was tucked snugly in bed, clasping a cup of brandy-wine in both hands and staring into the fire. The grinding pains in her abdomen that had troubled her on and off throughout the day had subsided so she saw no point in mentioning them. For the first time in several weeks, she felt safe.

And so Alice joined the princess's household. A few weeks later she accompanied Elizabeth to the splendid but rather gloomy palace of Sheriff Hutton at the King's command. Richard, having just buried his pale frail wife, was like a man whose heart has been scraped raw. The persistent rumours that he planned to marry his niece troubled him as uglier rumours had failed to do and it seemed expedient to send her away. In his brusque way he'd meant it kindly – the gossip and snickering could only hurt the girl – but she was heartbroken, convinced that she had somehow offended him. Now it was Alice's turn to be kind.

In rugged Yorkshire, separated from their families, the two girls soon became good friends. Elizabeth, lonely for her sisters, heartsore for the uncle for whom she bore a secret, guilty love, was cheered by Alice's vivacity. Alice, who had never admired anyone but herself, discovered a deep affection and respect for her mistress. Once the pampered daughter of Edward IV, within a few short months Elizabeth had lost her father, been declared a bastard and robbed of all the pride of her heritage. Her two young brothers had been spirited away although she still believed – hoped – that they were being held in another northern strong-hold. Yet through it all she had shown a quiet courage. Sensitive and warm-hearted with a wild vein of romance in her, she had not yet learnt to control strong emotion. Laughter and tears came as readily as spring showers – not very dignified in a King's daughter – but like her father she knew how to win people's hearts. She had all of Edward's bright charm and none of his violent temperament. Those who loved her mercifully didn't scold her for the laughter or the tears – unwittingly they did her a service. In the bitter years to come she would have little cause to laugh and she would be forbidden to weep.

'I envy you Alice,' she announced rather surprisingly as they sat together in the solar one drowsy summer afternoon. A silver fruit bowl lay between them on the cushions and the atmosphere was mellow, unguarded. Idly, Elizabeth swept the little mound of cherry-stones to the side of her plate, then went on shyly. 'If I'd lain with the king, I might be with child now. It would be like having a part of him still with me.'

Alice selected a fat strawberry and dipped it in her wineglass. She glanced up quickly at her companion but said nothing. Meanwhile she could feel the baby kicking furiously beneath her heart.

'You think I'm wicked, don't you?' Elizabeth's blue eyes were suddenly blurred with tears.

'No, madam,' Alice replied gently. She had learnt by now of Elizabeth's inces-tuous love, was neither repelled nor greatly surprised, yet she always felt vaguely uneasy when the princess talked about it. And she talked about it so often!

Lying in bed that night, she recalled Elizabeth's words. *If I'd lain with the king, I might be with child now.*

The tears came in a hot rush, splashing down her face as she lay there in the dark, arms curved round the pillow, mentally summoning his image. It was a nightly ritual that made her feel sweepingly alive, yet at the same time achingly miserable as she pictured the dark-contoured face with its wary midnight-blue eyes.

'You can trust me, sire.' She had striven to keep her voice low and soothing, that night at Westminster. Moist red lips parted, great purple eyes slanted almost defiantly, she appeared older than her seventeen years – older and recklessly carnal. And yet there was about her an innocence which might have once touched him.

Richard smiled faintly. 'I trusted others and they played me false. Now I know there's no loyalty in men.'

He was looking beyond her to the window blotted with January snow. She guessed that he was thinking of those who'd betrayed him – Lord Hastings, the Duke of Buckingham. . . .

Alice wanted him to think of her.

'But I'm a woman, your Grace,' she protested softly. 'A frail woman who could never harm you.'

She took a step closer, hating herself for acting like a whore but quite powerless against the violent force of her feelings. Nor was she driven by desire alone. Like the Lady Elizabeth she was in love with him – helplessly, intensely in love – and she was offering herself to him in the rawness of a desperation which she had never before experienced. . . .

Now in hot dry August she was delivered of a daughter and there was no one to wish her well except Elizabeth Plantagenet, soon to be Queen of England. Was Elizabeth thinking of her uncle now, lying in his rough, lonely grave? Or was she already planning her wedding gown? She was sufficiently Elizabeth Woodville's daughter to lust for a crown.

Alice opened her eyes and saw the dust motes dancing in a bar of yellow sunshine. Someone was leaning over the bed, fussily straightening the covers.

'Can I get you anything, mistress?' The voice was gruff, like a boy's. Then a freckled face swam through the green-gold mist and Alice suddenly recognized the serving girl who had waited on her all that summer.

'No, thank you, Joanna.' She forced herself to smile but she was thinking, *why can't you just let me be?*

Joanna continued to hover by the bed. With a start Alice realized that the pewter-coloured eyes were watching her intently, almost slyly, as if to remind her of some secret. Her head began to swim in a dizzy haze as she tried to remember just how much she had told Joanna.

Her mother had often warned her against confiding in servants, but that was before she had banished Alice from her life, closed her heart against her, ignored the letter Alice had sent her. (She had also written to her father, but expected no response – he lived in an eternal wine-fuddled twilight of his own and his reactions were neither clear-headed nor predictable.) Sometimes as the old castle slept she had felt terror and uncertainty jabbing at her until she feared for her sanity. It was as if all the anguish that she hid behind a piquant mask during the daytime came flooding into her mind as soon as the candles were lit and her hair unbound; it would swirl around inside her, sickening and cold, like malmsey-wine in an empty belly. And Joanna was always there – not especially sympathetic, but quiet and attentive as servants are paid to be. What in Jesus's name had she said to Joanna? Suddenly it was vitally important that she remember, but she felt too tired.

It was a cruel blow, sniffed Mistress Peake, wiping her bulbous red nose. But then, life was cruel to women, especially unchaste women. Joanna would do well to remember it. (Joanna would never forget!)

Sir Robert Willoughby had arrived at Sheriff Hutton to escort the princess back to London. The castle was aswarm with scarlet-tunicked soldiers, the very walls seemed to shake with the sound of their laughter. Yet no sooner had they gone, bearing Elizabeth away with them like a bewildered blonde trophy, than the house descended into a mood of glum apathy.

Now that she was dead it was as if the women wanted to forget Alice. There was no trace left of her personality and – apart from the frail baby girl bundled away in the nursery – no sign that she'd ever lived among them. Her body had been dispatched to her parents' home in Hertfordshire – a foolish piece of mawkishness, as Mistress Peake pointed out, but they hadn't known what to do. Elizabeth had some notion that the Marshes might want to reclaim their daughter in death even though they had discarded her when living. Now she was to be forgotten, like the bluebell fragrance that had always clung about her person.

In the days that followed, it seemed that Alice's little daughter had also been forgotten. A wet-nurse had been found and, at Elizabeth's insistence, Joanna was charged with her care. The princess was the only one to show concern for Dorothy, weeping so bitterly as she kissed her goodbye, it might have been her own child whom she was leaving behind.

'You will have a dozen babies as pretty, my lady,' Mistress Peake tried to cheer her. Privately she didn't hold with all the fretting and weeping – a royal lady should have more iron in her spine. Still, one couldn't help but pity the girl – it would be a cold bed that she shared with Tudor!

Elizabeth's features seemed to freeze into a glassy mask. She had known even before she lost her milk-teeth that her first duty was to marry and bear sons but now the thought filled her with a creeping dread. To suffer that long, wrenching agony and perhaps to die, as Alice had suffered and died – she could think of few deaths more cruel.

Joanna couldn't remember a summer so relentlessly hot. The bright soggy heat continued throughout most of September, sapping her energy; her clothes stuck to her skin as soon as she put them on in the morning. Worse, there was no one to talk to. Lisbet came only to feed the child and she made no secret of her disdain for a gauche virgin who was so obviously destined to remain so. The sight of Lisbet sitting on the stool with her thighs parted, her bodice open and her greasy yellow head bent over the suckling infant repelled Joanna, yet at the same time filled her with a sense of awe. Lisbet, for all her coarseness, was almost frighteningly sure of herself and she had a sharp tongue that made Joanna wary of her.

And so those late summer days crawled by with Joanna feeling increasingly cross and resentful. Worse than the heat was Dorothy's crying, for it never seemed to cease. That sound drove Joanna to distraction. Sometimes she thought she heard it in her sleep – thin, querulous, persistent.

One day she was standing at the window, staring gloomily out across the parched yellow moors and praying that God would strike her deaf. It wasn't fair, she was no nursemaid. They should have asked that old bitch, Mother Peake; *she* could quieten any baby with an ease that was almost sorcery. But no, if ever there was an unpleasant task to be tackled, it was always 'send for Joanna'.

Outside the leaves hung from the trees in shrivelled brown ribbons. You could almost smell the earth baking under the coppery sun. Joanna felt depressed by the heavy stillness hanging over the castle, for it reminded her of the day Alice died. Streaks of perspiration ran down her cheeks. Irritably she wiped them away with one hand. Why, she could die for lack of air and none of those bitches downstairs would care a fig! She pictured them clustered round the table in the hall, guzzling ale and cakes, gossiping and laughing. Although they had always excluded her from their rather raucous circle, she knew a moment's wistful long-ing to be with them.

In London a virulent plague had erupted into the filthy streets, bringing with it terror and desolation. People called it the 'Great Sweat' for you sweated like an ox while red-hot pincers of pain plucked at your head and chest and limbs and high fever rode in your blood, often leading swiftly to delirium and death. Here in Yorkshire's harsh, rolling countryside there was no plague, yet Joanna felt as much a prisoner as the panic-ridden Londoners trapped in their hovels and great houses. For wasn't she also trapped here in this stinking, sweltering room? Sometimes it seemed as if she would never escape until either she or the child was dead.

Dorothy was still crying. With very poor grace, Joanna stumped across the floor and bent to lift the baby from the long oaken cradle in which Yorkist princes had once been rocked. She was close to crying with frustration herself. Where the devil was Lisbet? Most likely the brat was hungry – Mistress Peake had said she must feed often.

To her surprise, Dorothy stopped crying almost at once, and regarded her steadily with milky-blue eyes. In that moment something happened to Joanna that she was never afterwards able to explain. It was as if she had been struck in the belly by some overpowering force. It left her feeling weak, as if all the air had been punched out of her body.

Hastily she sat down on a stool, clutching the little swaddled bundle to her own body's sticky heat. At last, scarcely daring to breathe, she looked down at the tiny creased face.

'Why, hinny.' She felt slightly foolish, talking aloud to the baby like this, but there was no one to hear her. 'Pretty hinny.' Raising a stubby finger, she traced the fine delicate curve from temple to chin while Dorothy went on gazing at her with cool interest.

Name of God, how small she was! Joanna cuddled her closer. For the first time in a life of dull, unceasing toil, she felt searingly alive with a clamour of emotions. It struck her that this must be how it felt to fall in love – an experience which Lisbet had described with a blend of eagerness and smug sympathy, the way a countess might describe a royal banquet to her laundry-maid.

Mistress Peake had said bluntly that the baby was unlikely to live. Until this moment, Joanna hadn't much cared. Most of the women she knew were brought to bed every year and their babies lived or they died. She had seen her own mother bury a little one, her body heavy and slow with another, and had never paused to wonder what emotions lay behind her numb grey face. Now as she held Dorothy protectively in the crook of her arm, as she bent to kiss the little face beneath the starched linen cap, she was gripped by a swift, choking tenderness. Somehow this child – *her* child – must live.

They arrived at Greenthorpe on a pale blustery April day when the trees were a riot of pink-and-white froth. Fat puffs of cloud dawdled across the sky. Primroses gilded the meadows and dense woodland nearby. As the carriage went swaying up the broad avenue overhung with lime trees, a hare suddenly darted for cover.

Joanna grew conscious of a thrill of nervous pleasure tingling up and down her spine. The leather curtain flapped; she felt the violet-scented wind in her face and wanted to laugh aloud, as foolishly as a drunkard or perhaps a bride. Then she remembered Lisbet, glowering on the cushions beside her, and the moment passed. She didn't want Lisbet telling people that she was too silly and frivolous to be trusted with a baby.

This was the first time she had travelled beyond York and now, with the bone-jolting journey almost over, her new life was about to begin. Her old self – that surly, shambling girl whom everyone thought too stupid to have any feelings – had been left behind in Yorkshire, like a grubby shift that she'd outgrown. At Greenthorpe she would be Nurse Joanna, mantled in all the dignity of her new status. There'd be no more orders from other servants, no one to tell her that she'd get through her work more quickly if she weren't such a hulking great slut. From today, others would run to carry out *her* orders.

She looked down at the child asleep in her arms and, not for the first time, wanted to breathe a thankful prayer. Dorothy had been very poorly all that winter with a succession of colds and a feverish chest infection which had threatened to consume her. Watching helplessly as the tiny body struggled and fought for breath, Joanna had felt her organs turn to ice. She felt herself choking with terror, even as the little creature in the wooden cradle was choking; found herself babbling the names of half-forgotten saints as the days and nights merged into a brown tunnel of despair. Yet Dorothy had survived, gasping and whimpering through those raw winter weeks and now, at eight months, she was a sturdy orange-haired moppet with plump little legs and a saucy, gurgling laugh. For once, Joanna's prayers had been answered by somebody.

Lisbet stretched yawning on the cushions, managing at the same time to give Joanna a spiteful jab in the ribs. She hated travelling and had whined ceaselessly from the outset. She was whining now as the litter bore them along the pale green tunnel. Her back was aching, her neck was stiff as a plank from all the draughts. And if she didn't have some food in her belly soon she'd be dead of hunger, and then who would suckle the little bastard?

Joanna smiled to herself, barely listening to that dreary, petulant voice. She wasn't frightened of Lisbet any more. In fact she had come to regard her as a peevish, rather stupid woman – slovenly, too, with those greasy tresses and the circles of dried milk crusting the armpits of her gown. In a few months time, when Dorothy was weaned, Lisbet would return to her own family and neither she nor Joanna would express any sorrow at the parting.

As they emerged into the cool spring sunlight, Greenthorpe Manor suddenly rose up before them – a pretty honeycomb of a house, set in sprawling parkland, with tall rose-red chimneys curling towards the sky. The walls were of pale amber stone flecked with garnet and cream and chestnut, like a rich pudding glazed with caramel. Two angels knelt above the gatehouse entrance, their lashless stone eyes lowered in weary compassion for a crude world. Their cupped hands seemed to form a mock bridal arch.

Although Greenthorpe was less than sixty years old, it had already acquired an inviting mellowness which managed to conceal any turbulence that might have raged within its walls. Unlike other houses built in that era, it lacked fortification of any kind, yet was miraculously unscathed by the fighting that had been fierce in Hertfordshire during the recent wars. Dorothy's great-grandfather had been a dreamy, sensitive gentleman who'd longed for a miniature paradise in which to write poetry and raise his family, and this fairytale dwelling was the result.

It wasn't until she was standing in the solar on the first floor that Joanna felt her confidence threaten to slither away, like grains of sand in a cracked hourglass.

A tall woman gowned in heavy, stiff black satin stood beside an open window, watching the luggage being unloaded in the courtyard below. After a moment she turned slowly round and Joanna, coming up from a wobbly curtsy, suddenly remembered that her clothes were creased and stained with sweat and baby dribble. As those faintly amused green eyes trailed over her figure, she felt dull and clumsy, like the old Joanna whom she wanted to forget.

They were the same height, but the mistress of Greenthorpe had a spear-slim elegance to which poor Joanna could never aspire. A rope of pearls nestled at her throat like a fat, glossy snake and, as she clasped her hands over her girdle, a ruby as big as a strawberry winked at Joanna. She was not, and never had been, beautiful, but there was an imperious strength in her pale face which was more impressive than beauty.

As they faced each other for the first time, Cicely Marsh seemed to grow more glitteringly aloof while Joanna's hands and feet turned into slabs of lead. She felt a stab of baleful envy for Lisbet, waiting downstairs in the hall with nothing more alarming to face than the impudent smirks of the other servants. Trust Lisbet! she thought viciously, and stared at the floor.

A plump brown-and-white spaniel lay sprawled in a patch of sunlight, looking sulky and bored. Lady Cicely now bent to lift it into her arms with a low caressing murmur that startled Joanna. She watched, her face arranged in respectful lines, as the ruby-starred hand fondled the animal's ears. Lord, but her throat was parched! If she didn't have a glass of ale soon. . . .

'So you have brought the child.' Cicely's voice was like the touch of hoar-frost.

'Aye, my lady.' Joanna started to gabble, not pausing for breath. 'She's below with Lisbet, the wet-nurse. Such a sweet, pretty little moppet . . .'

'You will find everything you need in the nursery. I don't wish to be troubled unless it's a matter of urgency. My husband is ill and . . .'

She broke off abruptly, aware that she was explaining herself to this unkempt serving-girl as if they were equals. Feeling those steady grey eyes upon her, she buried her face for a moment in the spaniel's silken fur, for once disconcerted. How she had dreaded this moment, ever since Elizabeth of York had sent her the news of Alice's death. Yet to Cicely Marsh, her daughter had long been dead. She only wished that they had buried her in that northern wilderness – and the brat with her.

Cicely knew she could never forgive her daughter. Alice had been beautiful and clever – clever enough to make a dazzling match. But no, she had to behave like some low-born tavern slut. She had betrayed her family – betrayed Greenthorpe.

Cicely Marsh had had such glorious plans for her children and now all four were dead. Edmund, her firstborn, had fought and died in the fog-wreathed chaos of Barnet Field. For a while she'd had the comfort of boasting about him, her laughing ruddy-haired boy who'd combined Henry's recklessness with her own obstinate pride. Now a Lancastrian king sat on the throne and it was no longer safe to boast, nor did she feel impelled to do so. Her ambitions were pollarded oaks, her heart a dried-out well.

She had come to Greenthorpe as a fourteen-year-old bride, already in love with the handsome, easy-going young man who had been chosen for her. It had seemed that their life together would be perfect. On their wedding night, light-hearted with happy confidence and what she thought was passion, she promised him sons.

'And daughters, my love.' Beneath the bedclothes, Henry Marsh slid his hand over her flat belly. 'Lots of daughters, all of them as sweet and pretty as you.'

He had fallen back on the pillows then, neighing with drunken laughter while she stared at him in dismay. This was not how she had imagined it.

In the weeks that followed he was almost perpetually drunk – the Marshes had kept that a secret from her father, curse them! – and Cicely's innocent love slowly turned to contempt. She grew to loathe the sight of his face across the table, the feel of his hands on her body, the taste of sour wine on his tongue when he kissed her, yet she steeled herself to endure it. For now in the face of hideous disappointment, it was essential that she have children – lusty, vigorous heirs for the house that she had come to love obsessively and was determined not to fail. (Sadly, Henry had other weaknesses that were to make pregnancy a more anxious and uncertain business for Cicely than for other women.)

Slowly, haltingly, two sons and then two daughters were born of their bitter lovemaking. To Cicely, each baby held the promise of the future in its tiny, wriggling body. Now they were dead and Henry lay in his room above the gatehouse, a pitiful broken creature whom she could not bring herself to look upon. There would be no more Marshes to live and mate at Greenthorpe when Cicely herself was dust. The manor would revert to the Crown and all that she had ever hoped and striven for ground into ashes. Her only legacy was a bastard girl.

As she stood in the solar on that April afternoon, outlined against the cold primrose sunlight, she felt resentment twisting round her organs. Resentment against Alice. Against the new Queen who had so embarrassingly prevailed upon her to raise Alice's bastard. And finally against this unwieldy young woman who'd brought her here and probably expected gratitude. Gratitude! She could scarcely trust herself to speak in case she let loose a torrent of bile.

The spaniel was wriggling protestingly in her arms. Reluctantly she lowered him to the floor and watched as he waddled over to his favourite cushion. Then she turned back to Joanna and waved her fingers in a weary gesture of dismissal.

Joanna curtsied stiffly and turned away, her heart sagging with dull anger. Then as she reached the door, some wild irrational instinct made her turn back and look her new mistress directly in the face.

'Her name is Dorothy,' she said quietly and waited – but for what? What was driving her to goad this inhuman woman?

For an instant she thought the cold proud face would crumble like a piece of marchpane clutched in a child's greedy fist. A muscle began to twitch beside the thin, scarlet-painted mouth. The beautiful tapered hands – those hands that both her daughter and her granddaughter had inherited – writhed together like a pair of storm-tossed leaves. Joanna caught her breath, panic freezing the pit of her stomach. In another moment she would be angrily ordered to leave Greenthorpe – to leave Dorothy.

Then she saw the raw agony in the other woman's eyes and knew that it wouldn't happen. Knew also that she had unwittingly lanced an old wound.

Joanna knew nothing of the little girl buried in the village church, for Alice had never mentioned her. Yet in that moment she was hit by a sharp, overwhelming wave of pity.

'You'd better return to your charge, girl,' Cicely said with a faint sneer, and promptly turned back to the window, her straight back registering arrogance and disapproval.

A cold breeze danced in through the window, fluttering around her veil and stirring the enormous tapestry of Juno's wedding that stretched along the northern wall. Still she stood there like a sculpture of ebony and ashes and ice. Joanna knew then that no appeal could reach her. That some twist of fortune, some sorrow in the past, had bled her of compassion. Perhaps she had always been that way – some people were. Whatever the reason, Joanna neither knew nor cared, since it was clear that she would never take Baby Dorothy to her heart.

CHAPTER THREE

1525

Alicia sat in a curve of the window-seat, looking at her reflection in a silver hand-mirror.

Her white taffeta gown, thickly embroidered with silver thread, was a present from Kathryn. At her throat she wore Lady Dorothy's seed pearls and a little gauze cap was perched on top of her auburn curls. In fact, she looked every inch the court lady, and there seemed no reason why any casual observer might point her out as a newcomer. Nonetheless her stomach was rocking with nervousness and her hands so shaky and slippery with sweat, she was afraid she might drop the mirror.

All around her the Queen's maids of honour were dressing for the banquet. They reminded her of over-excited puppies, jostling for the mirror and scrabbling among the great overflowing chests standing open on the floor. One girl stood in the middle of the floor, fastening a silver-buckled garter over a plump calf. Another was yelling to one of the tiring women to bring her a clean handkerchief.

She noticed a slim dark girl sitting at the *toilette* table, somehow aloof from all the pother. There was a complacent little smile on her carmine-painted mouth, and although there was less than an hour before the banquet began, she was still in her kirtle, her hair streaming down her back.

Alicia frowned slightly. She didn't like Anne Boleyn − few of the women did. Nor had Anne made any effort to remedy this, for they didn't interest her. The younger sister of King Henry's recently discarded mistress, she was already more notorious. Alicia was familiar with her story for, much as the others disliked and disapproved of Anne, it was somehow impossible to ignore her.

She had gone to France as a little girl, in the bridal train of the King's sister, Mary. Two months after the wedding, the elderly, half-senile Louis XII had died from the sheer exertion of trying to keep pace with his sprightly bride, and Mary daringly married her heart's love, the Duke of Suffolk, when he came to escort her home to England.

Anne Boleyn had stayed on at the Parisian court for nine years until symptoms of war hovered once again between the two countries. No sooner had she arrived at Greenwich than she'd fixed those audacious dark eyes upon Lord Harry Percy, Earl Northumberland's heir, who was attached to the household of the mighty Cardinal Wolsey. Although both were plighted elsewhere – she to her Irish cousin, Percy to the Earl of Shrewsbury's youngest daughter – Anne set her hard mind and stubborn heart upon the tall, copper-haired lad. Wary and calculating by nature, in love she was wholly reckless, as was Percy. They were unable to hide the wild tenderness they felt for each other. Thus it reached Wolsey's ears that the two intended to marry.

After his initial bewilderment at their brazen disregard for the proprieties, the Cardinal gave way to one of his famous rages. Percy was summoned to the great hall for a venomous tongue-lashing, to the enthralment of the servants. At first truculent, the sensitive young man soon dissolved into a puddle of tears. Before the week was out, he found himself riding back to Yorkshire in the disgruntled custody of his father. Anne, brusquely dismissed from the Queen's household, flounced off to Hever Castle in Kent, to sulk and plot her revenge.

That had been three years ago and now she was back, defiantly proud and with a new flippancy in her manner that annoyed people, as did her air of looking down her nose at the Court as if she found it – and all of them – somehow lacking.

'God's Teeth!' Jane Parker, Anne's waspish sister-in-law, stumbled over a spaniel which had been dozing peacefully by the fire and went sprawling, catching her heel in the hem of her gown. She sat up, coif tilted to one side, thin freckled face pink with rage. Then she began to screech like a creature demented while the spaniel kept up an indignant yelping.

'That damned dog! Now my gown is ruined and I'll have to stay behind. I'll wager she did it on purpose.' Glaring, she thrust out a foot to kick the animal.

The others watched, too astonished to speak. It was rare to see Jane jolted out of her composure although there were regular quarrels, even slaps and hair-pullings, among the Queen's younger attendants whenever they were left unsupervised.

'A pox on you, you clumsy slut!' Tiny red-haired Bridget Wilshire sprang forward, scooped the dog into her arms, then rounded furiously on Jane. 'Why don't you use your eyes? You've frightened Druscilla half to death.'

Close to tears, she kissed the top of Druscilla's golden head, murmuring soothingly like a mother whose favourite child has been hurt by the schoolroom bully.

Meanwhile the other girls were making no pretence of going about their business. Jane was almost as unpopular as her sister-in-law and there was more cause to be wary of her. Unpleasant things happened to those rash enough to cross her. A favourite gown would be found slashed to ribbons, a necklace mysteriously broken, the beads scattered every which way. A young woman who had once bested Jane in an argument later discovered that her beloved singing bird had escaped from its cage, the door of which was left swinging open.

Mistress Stonor, the Mother of the Maids, decided it was time to make her authority felt.

'Must you be such a screech-owl?' she demanded of Jane. 'You aren't hurt and the gown can easily be mended. And you, Mistress Bridget, can put that wretched dog outside.'

'Yes, there are too many bitches in here already,' someone called gleefully. This was greeted with squeals of laughter.

Jane turned away, her eyes pale slivers of hatred. She longed to slap Mother Stonor's smug face, but of course that was not her way. Her thoughts were spinning as the little tiring-maid came scuttling over with her work-box.

She was furious with herself for letting the Wilshire girl goad her into that outburst, but she'd known a moment of sickening panic as she fell to the floor and heard her new sarcenet gown tear.

All her life Jane had known the gnawing shame of semi-poverty. That old miser, her grandfather – she and her sister Madge had been orphaned as small girls – had always made her bow and scrape whenever she needed a new cap or nightgown. In the end he would usually give his rare wintry smile and refuse her request. He'd even refused to pay her dowry when she married Sir Thomas Boleyn's only son last year. Jane's spirit had writhed as the tart letters flew between old Lord Parker and the mercenary Sir Thomas. In the end, the King had generously interceded and paid the £300 that Sir Thomas insisted on.

'You see!' Mistress Stonor was holding up Jane's skirt in her pudgy hands, like a cook examining a joint of beef. 'It was hardly worth all that squawking.'

Jane scowled at her, but the scowl went unnoticed. Mistress Stonor's eyes were now fastened on Anne Boleyn's slender back and her jaw was set with unmistakable hostility.

'Not dressed yet, Mistress Anne?' She spoke jeeringly. 'Do you think her Grace has nothing better to do than wait for the likes of you?'

'Why not?' Anne swivelled round on the stool, a cool superior smile on her lips. 'Others are happy enough to do so.'

The other woman blew out her cheeks. 'Be careful, mistress,' she hissed, after a moment.

Unconcerned, Anne beckoned to the tiring-maid. Then, moving across to the tall mirror beside the window, she began dressing.

For the first time Alicia was able to study her at close quarters. She was puzzled by this insolent young woman's fascination. Anne, though very striking, was no beauty. Her mouth was too wide, her neck long and thin like a crane's, and she lacked the soft confiding curves that men set such store by. Yet the flood of thick black hair shone like liquorice and the huge, slightly tilting eyes were alive with mischief and intelligence. Although dark looks were disparaged in England – as were most things that smacked of 'foreignness' – Anne carried herself with the confident ease of a woman who considers herself to be a great beauty. Beside her, the fair-haired pink-and-white English girls seemed as insipid as almond-custard and it was for this reason, more than any other, that they resented her.

Someone had picked up a lute and was plucking out the first few notes of a new dance tune. The other girls, sensing that the drama was over, began putting the finishing touches to their *toilette*, talking in low, earnest voices like subdued starlings.

Margaret Wyatt, a cousin of Anne's and one of the few women who genuinely liked her, drifted over to talk to her.

'Old Mother Stonor is right, Nan, you must be careful. They might send you away again.'

'Don't be a goose, Meg. People will have to learn that I'm no meek little milk-sop. Besides, they can't send me anywhere unless I choose to go. I have a protector now. Pass me the gown, Nell.' She waggled her fingers at the maid.

At last she was ready but still seemed dissatisfied with her appearance, her fingers plucking invisible creases out of her orange silk skirts. She bent close to the mirror, examining her teeth for food particles, then straightened up. Then she spotted Alicia and her eyes began to sparkle with amused curiosity.

'Kathryn Standish's sister, isn't it?' she enquired, tapping one foot on the floor while her gaze raked Alicia's figure from gauze cap to little square-toed silver shoes.

Alicia coolly lifted her eyebrows but didn't answer. All at once Anne burst into laughter, a shrill, almost metallic sound that caused heads to whip round in her direction.

'How sweet you are, like a cuddly kitten. The bitches here will eat you alive.'

'On the contrary, everyone has been most kind!' Alicia snapped, tilting up her chin.

Anne gave an impatient click of her tongue, then, without warning, her bright black eyes narrowed into slits, and when she spoke again her voice seemed to crackle with venom.

'Those simpering sluts! See how kind they are when their lovers come sniffing round your tail.'

She turned away in a fluster of skirts, pausing to call tantalizingly over her shoulder: 'Take my advice, mistress; find a strong man to protect you, as I have, or you'll find yourself lacking a maidenhead.'

The others were filing out of the room. Anne swooped after them like a cruel, brilliant humming-bird. Alicia stood up, her face scorching.

Margaret Wyatt, who was usually the peacemaker in these situations, suddenly appeared at her elbow.

'My cousin didn't mean to be uncivil,' she began awkwardly as they walked together along the narrow corridor.

'Perhaps not, but she has a nasty tongue,' Alicia retorted, staring straight before her. 'And the manners of a Southwark whore.' (She had always known that the years of eavesdropping on Joanna's quarrels with the other servants would stand her in good stead one day.)

'Then you must forgive her. She was badly hurt once and it has hardened her – made her distrustful of people.'

'You mean Lord Percy, don't you?' Alicia was interested in spite of herself. 'Lots of people have been disappointed in love, but they got over it. Your cousin Anne must be very feeble.'

They were descending a sharply twisting flight of stairs, skirts held carefully above their ankles. Two giggling pages came hurtling past, recklessly taking the stairs three at a time. Margaret hastily backed against the wall to avoid a collision.

'It was different for her,' she continued presently. 'The humiliation was more – more public than usual. And Nan is so proud – proud as a sultan. She hated it when people sniggered and pointed at her. God forgive them, but they were very unkind. And so now she wants to prove to them that they didn't break her.'

'Who is her protector?' Alicia asked suddenly. 'The man she mentioned?'

'Who knows?' Margaret said with a show of casualness. 'But try not to think badly of her. She may have a sharp tongue but underneath she is kind and generous.'

Alicia snorted insolently.

By now they had reached the Queen's presence chamber and the conversation ended abruptly as they went to join the other women. Alicia glanced over at Mistress Boleyn, perched on the edge of a rosewood chest like a haughty cat. She decided that she could never like her.

The older ladies-in-waiting were there, their poise sharply contrasting with the shrill vivacity of the maids-of-honour. Alicia suddenly spotted her sister standing beside a window, a tall, graceful figure in a pearl-frosted gown, her fair hair gleaming like a coronet of pure silver in the firelight.

Somehow the sight of Kathryn Standish never failed to evoke thoughts of a chivalrous, bygone age. Alicia could not look at her without being reminded of Joanna's ballads.

The slightly slanting blue eyes, framed by heavy brown-gold lashes, lit up with a rare glow of pleasure as her young sister came hurrying towards her.

'The gown looks charming, Lissa,' she said warmly, after they had exchanged kisses. 'How clever of you to alter it so well.'

'It's the prettiest I've ever owned,' Alicia gloated, smoothing down a silvery fold.

'Then I must look out another for you.'

Alicia began to protest – not too vehemently – but Kathryn silenced her with a flutter of long white fingers.

'Oh, come now, I have dozens of gowns. Giles has always been very generous, as you know.'

Her voice tightened on the last words, and a strange expression flitted over her face.

Sir Giles Standish lavished gowns and jewels upon his wife so that she might mirror credit on him, but he never showed her any affection and rarely made love to her unless he was drunk.

Alicia couldn't think of anything to say, so she squeezed Kathryn's hand. Inside she wanted to cry; it hurt her heart to see Kathryn so unhappy.

She had always thought that her sister's beauty would win her an enchanted life. In romances, the beautiful maiden was loved simply because she was beautiful, but that hadn't happened to Kathryn – her husband preferred the earthy charms of the sewing-maid. Moreover, he considered Kathryn wholly insipid and hadn't hesitated to tell her so. No doubt she accepted his estimation of her, for she had never valued herself very highly.

The ladies went down in a rainbow welter of skirts as the bedchamber door opened and Queen Catherine emerged, closely followed by her beloved Maria Willoughby who had come with her from Spain all those years ago.

Her Grace looked tired. A short, stumpy woman approaching forty, her face was lined and careworn beneath the old-fashioned gabled headdress. The intelligent light-grey eyes protruded slightly and there was a ruffle of fat beneath her chin. Nevertheless she carried herself with a calm unhurried dignity that was part of her proud Spanish blood.

She paused, her eyes skimming the kneeling bevy of females. Heads dark and russet and gold were bent like meadow flowers before the wind, brightly coloured skirts billowed over the grimy rushes, half-bare shoulders gleamed creamy-white in the candlelight. A sudden movement beside her caught her attention. She moved her head and found herself looking into the gentian-coloured eyes of Lady Standish's sister.

The girl was a beauty and, she recalled now, soon to be married. Catherine told herself wryly that she was unlikely to make a satisfactory wife, for there was something restless and driven about her. The small, slightly cleft chin suggested a stubborn will, which displeased the Queen – young women should be docile.

Fortunately the girl – in her mind she groped for her name – would not be at court for long.

Her gaze shifted from Alicia to the dark feline figure of Anne Boleyn, kneeling straight-backed in a cloud of flaming silk. Her nostrils twitched at the scent of French musk on warm skin. Then she glanced away, irritated and uneasy. Anne had proved her wayward nature three years ago, suffered the disgrace of banishment and had now returned, apparently unchastened. Catherine could only hope that she brought no more scandal to her household.

The wide red mouth was curled in what was almost a smirk, suggesting all the brashness of the Boleyns. Perhaps that was why Catherine, the most charitable of women, could never like her. Then honesty forced her to admit that, even if Anne had been modest and gentle as a young novice, she would still loathe the sight of her because her sister Mary had once romped in the King's bed.

The banqueting hall was lit by hundreds of wax torches in iron sconces which sent shadows leaping over the tapestries fluttering at the walls. Faces old and young were flattered by the mellow light. Jewels blazed like scarlet and green dragonfire. A juggler was practising in the shadows, an expression of intense concentration on his face as the balls spun in a golden fountain between his hands. High up in the gallery the King's musicians were playing, the sound of lute, viol and sackbut filling the room with piercing sweetness.

And there was the King, instantly recognizable – a red-gold giant in tawny brocade stamped with jewels, sitting on the dais at the far end. He was bent slightly forward in his chair, hands resting on his parted knees. The torchlight seemed to set his cropped auburn hair ablaze while at the same time casting the rather girlish rosy face into shadow. He was laughing at some remark of his brother-in-law, Suffolk, yet his eyes kept darting anxiously through the crowd.

As the Queen came into view, followed at a respectful distance by her ladies, he went swiftly to greet her. Despite his thickening girth, he was as agile as a lad of eighteen – a lifetime's passion for riding and tennis had seen to that.

'Are you feeling better this evening, Kate?' His voice was unexpectedly thin and high-pitched. 'Your headache has gone?'

There was polite concern in his voice but it was obvious that the subject bored him. Like most outdoorsy men he was repelled by bodily ills, although he coddled his own infrequent ailments shamelessly. He didn't even listen to his wife's reply as his small blue eyes briefly scanned each lady's face, resting just a fraction longer on that of Anne Boleyn. Alicia was startled to see the round handsome face flush red as fire, then a hot hungry light sprang up behind his eyes. He looked at once confused, uncomfortable and desperately eager, like a schoolboy at his first grown-up party. However a moment later he was leading

Catherine towards the dais with such a courteously attentive air, Alicia wondered if she had been mistaken.

Thomas Wolsey, whom some people sniggeringly called 'the Shadow King' – though never to his face – bent to press his thick lips to Catherine's hand with the faint air of one who is conferring a favour. The Queen's plump little figure appeared to stiffen. Henry noticed nothing. He was smiling abstractedly, rapt in a private dream. Wolsey, massive in scarlet taffeta, was also smiling, his pale eyes hard and shrewd as a cobra's.

Long trestle-tables flanked three sides of the hall. Alicia found herself sitting between her sister and the baleful Jane, eating capon in lemon sauce. It was one of her favourite dishes, but tonight nervous excitement had furred her tongue and the food turned to chalk-dust in her mouth. She listened to the clamour of voices, swooping and falling around her, and for the first time felt a heady thrill of belonging. If only Lady Bess could see her now!

From the high table his Grace's boisterous laugh rumbled forth from time to time. His face was flushed with heat and wine and a kind of taut excitement. Alicia watched transfixed as he coaxed the Queen with a piece of heron, glistening in aspic, from his own plate. Catherine was smiling and shaking her head. For a moment she looked almost pretty.

Anne Boleyn was eating her food with an air both delicate and greedy as, between mouthfuls, she talked to the young man on her left.

'Another admirer,' Alicia mused, not without envy. For the man was extraordinarily handsome, his curly hair and beard tinged with dark gold, his eyes glowing tawny-gold as a glass of cider. They were fastened upon Anne's face as if she were some fabulous mythical creature, both beautiful and strange.

Slowly Alicia became conscious that someone was watching her. Glancing along the table she met a pair of amused dark eyes, dancing in a pale-olive face. Their owner, having caught her attention, winked naughtily.

She drew in her breath. It wasn't a classically handsome face but it was vividly alive and somehow familiar. Feeling a tell-tale blush simmering up her face, she quickly looked away.

'It would seem that the gentleman in the yellow doublet admires you,' Jane murmured silkily. Those dagger-sharp eyes missed nothing. 'Don't you think he's charming?'

Alicia, warned by something in her voice, was instantly on her guard. She turned to look at her but the freckled face was innocently enquiring. She sipped daintily from her glass before replying carelessly: 'He looks as if he could be amusing.'

Jane gave a terse unpleasant laugh.

'Oh, George could easily have been his Grace's fool. He takes nothing seriously, least of all women.' She stabbed rather viciously at the slab of mulberry tart in front of her.

'I presume he doesn't amuse *you*, madam?' Alicia said drily.

As Jane turned to her again there was a spark of malice in her eyes, and something else that Alicia couldn't decipher.

'One would hardly expect him to – he's my husband.'

So the audacious young man was Anne Boleyn's brother. That was why the snapping black eyes and mocking, reckless air seemed familiar. Helplessly Alicia turned to look at her sister but Kathryn was deep in conversation with Lady Brereton. She began to stab about for a more comfortable topic.

'Who is the fair-haired man talking to Mistress Anne?'

Jane laughed again to show that she wasn't deceived by the ploy.

'That's Margaret Wyatt's brother, Tom. They say he's the finest poet in England, though his verses always sound like drivel to me. Isn't it sad the way a family's good looks always go to the male side?'

Alicia sent her a hard stare, but Jane was unabashed. She went on. 'My sister-in-law has a taste for men who aren't free to love her. First Percy, a yellow-livered dog if ever I saw one – he was betrothed to Mary Talbot even before his voice broke, but it didn't stop him hankering after Nan. Now Tom Wyatt has turned his back on his wife and their baby son while he chases *sweet* Nan, but she won't have him. She has her sights set higher than a poet.'

Alicia was tempted to question her further but the servants had started clearing the tables, darting back and forth behind the buttery screen with the greasy, high-stacked dishes, and the dancing was about to begin.

King Henry, his great rosy height dwarfing most of the other men, led his sister Mary of Suffolk on to the floor for the pavane. How solemn and graceful the dancers were as they circled the diamond-patterned tiles, the women's gowns a medley of crimson and buttercup, tawny and rose and green. Alicia saw her sister with Sir Harry Norris, the King's groom of the bedchamber. She thought how well they complemented one another – Norris dark and steady, Kathryn looking more than ever like a troubadour's lady in her pale glistening gown. Yet she knew there was little hope of a love-affair flowering between those two. Norris, one of the few genuinely kind people at court, wasn't the type to be unfaithful to his pregnant wife. Kathryn, also, was stubbornly loyal to the husband who gave no loyalty to her.

Anne Boleyn had abandoned her poet and was dancing with red-headed Will Brereton, another of the king's attendants. Alicia caught a flashing glimpse of her face and decided that if Kathryn was the loveliest of the dancers, Anne was the most vivacious – with good reason, since most of the courtiers appeared to be spellbound by her.

The Queen, who no longer enjoyed dancing – nor had the energy for it – sat alone on the dais, her expression doggedly cheerful as she watched the nimble figures go gliding past in a jewel-coloured fan. Nonetheless she had an air of having been deserted. Alicia felt a tiny dart of contempt, though she hated herself for it.

'Will you partner me in the galliard, Mistress Alicia?'

She started at the sound of a smooth masculine voice close by. George Boleyn was standing beside her, casually smiling, one hand fidgeting with the little jewelled dagger at his belt. In that moment Alicia realized that he wasn't as airily at ease as he appeared. Before she could answer he went on. 'You see, I've taken the trouble to learn your name from my cousin Meg.'

'What about your wife?' Alicia flung back, rather more tartly than she'd intended. 'Shouldn't you ask *her* to partner you?'

'Jane?' He glanced carelessly towards the blue-clad figure leaning against one of the pillars. She was staring at them, an aggravating little smile on her lips, as if they were actors in a play that she'd seen so often, she could mouth the lines before they were spoken. 'I doubt if she will care. Besides it's only a dance, not an invitation to my bed. Please, Alicia.' Suddenly all the mockery fled from his eyes and he looked younger than his twenty-two years – vulnerable, too, with those shaggy walnut curls lying like petals on his bare neck.

He was undeniably attractive. Alicia liked his wide sensitive mouth, which gave the impression he was permanently on the brink of laughter; the vaguely impatient grace with which he held his tall body. Somehow she was smiling up at him.

Above in the gallery the musicians struck up a jaunty tune. Alicia dropped a curtsy. George lifted her hand to his lips, kissing the tips of her fingers. All at once a vital charge seemed to rush through her body, making her feel happy and reckless and tinglingly alive. She was conscious of nobody else as they leapt and twirled, bobbed and capered in time to the thumping music. Each time she turned to face him, each time his hand brushed against hers, her heart seemed to bounce on her ribcage.

All too soon the galliard was over, yet still they stood as if rooted to the floor, barely conscious of the breathless laughing crowd pushing past them. George was the first to speak, his voice an indolent caressing drawl that made the skin tighten across her breasts.

'You must think me shockingly rude. I haven't even introduced myself.'

'There was no need,' Alicia replied rather shakily. 'I already knew your name.'

Those bold eyes were dancing mercilessly as they went over her face.

'Nevertheless, one should always observe the rules in the game of courtly love.'

She stared, for once stunned into silence. Was it just a game to him, after all?

A glossy strand of her hair had escaped from her cap. With a baffling little smile, George lifted it to his lips before gently tucking it into place, as if she were a helpless small girl. The cool, mocking light had returned to his eyes, but some-how it was as if he was mocking himself as well as her. Curse his bones, why did he have to be so damned superior! And why did she feel like a gauche cottage-girl, standing before the squire in a greasy apron? After all, he had asked her to dance.

The sense of being subtly ridiculed swelled inside her like a ball of hot dough.

'George takes nothing seriously, least of all women,' Jane had said. Jane, his sly little wife who was now gliding towards them, lazily swinging the topaz pendant at her throat. It occurred to Alicia that she had been the butt of this pair's bitter humour. Between them they had made her look a fool – the green girl from Hertfordshire who was too silly and naïve to understand court ways. Her eyes were hard and slanting as she raised them to George's face again.

'You have me at a disadvantage, sir. I've never played at courtly love and am quite unfamiliar with the rules.'

She bobbed a curtsy and turned to go, coming face to face with Jane. She thought she detected disappointment in the ice-blue eyes but it seemed oddly irrelevant. All she could think of was the need to escape before she collapsed in a humiliated – and humiliating – torrent of weeping. Her face was burning as she stumbled blindly towards the doors.

A cool hand on her wrist halted her progress. Through a stinging mist, she saw Kathryn's face.

'Is something wrong, Lissa? You look distressed.'

Alicia shook her head. The music was still playing; it sounded like a mad, whining tumult in her ears. The reek of unwashed bodies was making her faintly queasy and she thought her skull might burst open if she didn't get away. Meanwhile Kathryn's eyes were anxiously searching her face and she knew she must think of some plausible excuse.

'It's just that I have started my flux.'

'Poor poppet!' Kathryn smiled, relieved and sympathetic. 'Let me take you back to your dormitory. It's easy to lose one's way in the corridors.'

'No, Kathryn!' She heard the sharp note of desperation in her voice and quickly checked it. 'Stay and enjoy the dancing. I shall be fine after a good night's sleep.' She forced a bright careless smile, then fled before Kathryn could insist. She felt slightly guilty, for she hated lying to Kathryn, but she felt that she couldn't endure anyone's company just now.

Twice she lost her way in the dark warren of corridors, and half-wished that she'd accepted Kathryn's offer, but at last she reached the little dormitory that she shared with Bridget Wilshire and Lucy Talbot.

Some of the candles had been left burning and were melted into fat little stubs, so that the room was dotted with smoky amber light. Wearily Alicia reached up to remove her coif, shaking her hair free. She moved towards the bed, unfastening her gown as she went. Then she saw that several of her gowns lay in a bright heap of rags on the counterpane.

Catherine of Aragon knelt at her prie-dieu and crossed herself before the little gilt-and-alabaster statue of the Virgin.

She began to shiver in spite of her fur-trimmed robe, huddling deep inside its silken folds like a sick animal burrowing for warmth. Sweet Jesus, but she was so tired!

Weariness had soaked into her bones and she was unutterably thankful that the banquet was over. No one knew what an effort it cost to nod and smile when you felt old and drained of looks, energy, even your femininity. The greying head sank lower.

As a girl she had been pretty enough — tiny and plump with apricot skin and a wealth of auburn-gold hair that flowed as thick as honey past her waist.

Some of the older courtiers could still remember the sixteen-year-old bride of Arthur Tudor, stepping ashore at Plymouth on a drizzly October day. Her face beneath the wide-brimmed velvet hat was pale with seasickness but when she smiled that shy, slightly bewildered smile for the first time, she unknowingly reached into their hearts.

That Arthur should die of lung-fever just six months later, she mercifully could not have known. Nor that she would live out the next seven years as his father's impoverished hostage while he and Ferdinand of Aragon bickered over her dowry like two old pawnbrokers and her homesick servants plagued her daily with their childish grievances. It had been a miserable existence for a Spanish princess but she never once complained. Then, when the skinflint Tudor died one pink and green April, it appeared that her quiet courage would at last be rewarded.

Seventeen-year-old Henry, the late King's only remaining son but no more resembling him than a kingfisher did a petulant old raven, dashingly succeeded him to the throne. He was determined to marry without delay, and swore that he'd have none other than Catherine.

How her heart had swelled at the sight of him in her rooms — a laughing young giant with hair the colour of an Alhambra sunset and merry blue eyes that looked at her as if she were a saint in a stained-glass window. He was at the age when it was easy to idolize, and the poised Spanish girl had fired his imagination ever since he'd danced as a boisterous ten-year-old at her first wedding.

It seemed as if they would be happy, despite Catherine's seniority and the numerous contrasts between them. Different as black from white, it was said of them, but in those early years life was golden.

The marriage was blighted by their dead children. It foundered in the cold ashes of miscarriages and stillbirths. There was a baby prince, born one New Year's Day and dead before Easter. Even now the thought of him could threaten to tear the living heart from her body.

Mercifully she had Mary, a pretty well-behaved nine year-old. Catherine could have felt no more pride in her daughter if she had been a boy. A clever, serious child, yet with a sweet-tempered gaiety bubbling behind her solemn little face, Mary was adored by her father, who called her his 'pearl of the world'. But for all his furious pride in her, she wasn't a son to quell the gnawing unease of a nation that, only a generation before, had begun to recover from the ravages of three decades of civil war. Small wonder that Henry, son of the conquering Tudor and his Yorkist queen, raised on tales of treachery and bloodshed, was more fearful than any of his subjects as the son-less years wore on.

Catherine knew that he blamed her. He'd never said so directly but sometimes she had caught him watching her, his eyes so cold and accusing that she had been struck by a strange, creeping terror. These days he was hatefully smug, though once he had been almost childlike in his self-doubt. For hadn't he proved to the world that he could have sons with a healthy woman? Six-year-old Harry Fitzroy, his bastard by a flighty maid of honour, now lived permanently at court – a daily reminder and a daily reproach.

Bessie Blount was a silly, vapid creature who would have long since faded from memory had she not borne the king's son. Now snugly tucked away in the country with her kind but unexciting husband, she could no longer threaten Catherine's peace. Strange, then, how the smart of betrayal lingered. And yet Henry, compared to King François or even Catherine's own father, Ferdinand, had been remarkably constant. So far as she knew, there had been only two lapses.

She had never been entirely certain when Henry first noticed the Blount girl, yet she could recall, with aching pungency, a cold spring evening some five years earlier when, in a moment of irritable boredom, his eye had alighted upon the dancing figure of Mary Boleyn. It was a scene eternally tattooed upon her mind – the fresh-skinned girl of seventeen pirouetting in the long gallery, dusky curls bouncing, golden-brown eyes shining like great lustrous berries while she giggled so inanely, the Queen had wondered if she were a half-wit. And all the while Henry was watching her with hot blue eyes.

She hadn't been too disturbed at the time. Mary was newly a bride and said to be in love with her quiet husband, Will Carey. Moreover, her reputation was already tainted, her name no more than a stale, lewd joke at the French court where she and her sister Anne had grown to young womanhood. Catherine assured herself that the prig in Henry would be repelled by such a wanton. Yet Mary, for all her lush sensuality, had a disarmingly sweet way with her. Tender and pliable, she was inclined to fall in love very easily. Men had tricked her into bed with words of love, then later snickered about her to their friends over a jug of wine. A stronger woman would have developed a hard skin, taught herself not to care, but Mary felt only bewilderment, and eventually blamed herself. And so when the King began to flirt with her, she was flattered but expected nothing.

Henry found her as soothing as rose-water. Women had always bargained with him, however circuitously, but Mary seemed content with so little. It was a comfortable, undemanding relationship that had lasted for three years, to the court's cynical amazement. Now it was over, but Catherine had no sense of triumph.

Last year he had decided that they should occupy separate bedchambers – a blow so wounding, so shameful, she felt as if he had publicly beaten her. His affection remained undiminished but now that her monthly flux had ceased, he had no further use for her tired, flabby body.

Catherine had never lacked courage but sometimes it was hard to maintain a calm, cheerful countenance in the face of despair. After sixteen years she felt that Henry was lost to her. His respect, his liking, she had always had, but without his love, life held little flavour.

CHAPTER FOUR

1525

Alicia enjoyed living at court. She loved the bustle and the brilliance, the raw pulsing energy that seemed to emanate from the peach-red walls of the palace. More than anything, she was drawn to the sense of drama that stalked the rooms and galleries like a dangerously attractive man whose love would bring rapture, chaos and, at the last, heartbreak. And though she sensed the chord of violence pulsating beneath all the feasting and the love-songs, she was too young to be dismayed by it.

Foreign visitors to the court were appalled by the vulgarity which they found there. They considered the women too brazenly confident, the men conceited and volatile, quick to draw a dagger for an insult – whether real or imagined – only to vanish into the nearest alehouse minutes later with a comradely arm around the offender.

The English court lacked the chilly elegance of Amboise or Les Tournelles but it had, nonetheless, a solid splendour that was impressive. Led by a shrewd monarch who was greatly respected as an athlete and a scholar, it was fast gaining a reputation as a centre of learning.

Alicia, no longer overawed by her sumptuous new surroundings, found it preposterous that anyone could become disenchanted, although she was aware that there were men and women who disliked the court while continuing to live there in increasing disillusionment and, worse, boredom, as if in a sour marriage. Alicia didn't understand how anyone could be bored at Greenwich.

There were numberless diversions to blot out the dismal thought of her impending marriage – music and dancing in abundance, card-playing, bowling, riding in the great park that lay to the south of the palace. Sometimes she and a handful of other young people went to watch the King playing tennis. It was almost a physical pleasure to watch his Grace, who moved his big body so surely, putting verve and gusto into the game every time.

Alicia had made several new friends; Harry Norris whom she liked if only because he was in love with Kathryn, Will Brereton who had once worn her favours in a jousting tournament – he had sunk to one knee before her and pleaded so comically, she had laughingly agreed to cut the ribbon from her sleeve; also, Meg Wyatt and her brother Thomas. Thomas was one of the few men who made no attempt to flirt with her, for his poet's heart belonged to Anne Boleyn.

Alicia could smile now at her feud with Anne; could think of her without irritation or mistrust. For Anne, who had at first seemed a cold-hearted, jeering enemy, was fast becoming a friend.

The morning after the banquet Alicia had gone in search of Jane Boleyn, whom she eventually found sitting by the fire at one end of the gallery, among a cluster of chattering ladies. The weather had turned bitterly cold and most of them were wrapped in thick, fur-lined cloaks as they sat drinking spiced wine out of tall pewter cups. As Alicia drew closer, she felt her nerve suddenly stumble. They belonged here while she was a stranger. Who was she to make such shocking accusations against one of their number? Yet a quick glance at Jane's face told her that she was not about to make a ghastly mistake.

'I'd like to speak to you privately, Mistress Jane.' It cost her an effort to keep her voice level, for she longed to bury her fists in the bright-blonde hair and tear it out in clumps.

Jane, looking politely bored, bent to lift a handful of sugar-leaves from the dish at her feet, then dropped them into her mouth one at a time.

'It's too cold to stir from the fireside,' she drawled at last, licking a sticky thumb. 'Why don't you tell me what's troubling you – not breeding sickness, I hope?'

Someone giggled and Alicia's temper snapped.

'If I am troubled it's because you have ripped four of my gowns to ribbons, though I've never done you any wrong.'

'I assume you have some proof?' Jane lifted her eyebrows a fraction.

Alicia smiled rather unpleasantly. 'I know of your reputation, mistress.'

There was a long pause while each tried to outstare the other.

'When did this happen?' Jane was the first to break the silence.

'Last night during the banquet, but you know that, so why—'

'Then it couldn't have been me. I never left the hall except to use the privy.' Suddenly her lips curled back in a sneer. 'I shall give you some advice, mistress. Put a stop to this slanderous talk or her Grace will think you're a troublemaker. Remember, you're a newcomer to court.'

It was true, Alicia told herself grimly as, half an hour later, she stalked up and down the deserted garden which was still glassy with early-morning frost. To complain further would avail her nothing. She was aware that the Queen for some reason disliked her and might pack her off to Greenthorpe if she made trouble. Then she thought of Kathryn but dismissed the idea with an impatient click of her fingers. It would be as useless to appeal to Kathryn Standish as to Catherine of Aragon.

She stopped beside a leafless pear tree, horrified at the thought which seemed so mean and disloyal. And yet it was true. Since the day she'd arrived at Greenwich, she had found her sister changed.

Sometimes she wanted to cry when she thought how she'd looked forward to this visit. For she had half-expected that everything would be the same – sharing all her secrets with Kathryn, giggling over the baffling moods and quirks of their elders, yawning and toasting their toes in front of the fire every evening. Yet the truth was, they seldom spent any time together and when they did Kathryn seemed distant and preoccupied.

Alicia had learnt by now that it was Kathryn's own choice to be always in attendance upon the Queen. She had noticed, too, how some of the flighty young women with impatient lovers exploited her devotion. Useless to point it out to Kathryn, for she knew what the reply would be – 'she needs me.'

A high-pitched female voice was calling her name. Darting round, she was amazed to see the sleek figure of Anne Boleyn hurrying across the lawn towards her. She was wrapped in a cloak of carnation velvet, her face glowing pink with the cold.

Alicia stiffened. Had Anne heard about the scene in the gallery and come to taunt her? Yet as Anne drew nearer, she saw that her expression was eager and friendly.

'Alicia, I'm sorry about your clothes,' she said without preamble. 'Jane Parker is a nasty, vindictive bitch – always has been. No wonder my brother can't abide her.'

At the mention of George Boleyn, Alicia reddened, but Anne didn't appear to notice. She went on. 'Enough of curd-faced Jenny! I was wondering – I have some red silk for a gown, if you'd care for it.' The words came out in a breathless rush, as if she was uncertain how her offer would be received. To Alicia's astonishment, she looked almost shy.

'You're very kind,' Alicia said at last. 'But – well, red isn't my colour.'

'Then it should be,' Anne replied briskly. 'Anyway, it's a very dark red. I promise it will be wonderfully becoming to your complexion.'

Alicia was touched. She knew that she herself would never have been brave or generous enough to make such a handsome peace-offering. Suddenly she felt a surge of warmth towards the older girl, whom life had taught to be chary of people.

Anne was right. As she stood in front of the mirror, swathed in twelve yards of shimmering garnet silk, she looked dramatic and arresting. Her skin seemed to glisten like spun sugar, her loose-tumbling hair was lit by hundreds of tiny violet-and-gold fires. Even her eyes looked bigger.

'You see!' Anne crowed, suddenly appearing in the mirror behind her. 'Really, I should have more sense than to deck you out so fine. Still, I mustn't be selfish, it's time there was another goddess at court.'

She flung back her head and gave that startling wild laugh, but this time Alicia laughed with her.

She had gladly accepted the gown and now she and Anne were fast becoming friends who'd discovered that, once all the prickly female defences were broken down, they liked and admired each other.

Yes, life at court was just as stimulating as she'd always imagined. And even though there was a pronounced coolness between George Boleyn and herself, Alicia was determined that nothing was going to threaten her happiness. She was hurt and puzzled when he spoke to her in that distant, courteous voice, or nodded coldly to her in chapel, but she gave no sign. And if Anne was aware of any tension between her beloved brother and her new friend, she said nothing.

Then one morning early in April, Alicia learnt that Sir John Houghton had arrived at Greenwich with his eldest son, Gervase.

Alicia sat alone in the pond garden, her black velvet skirts overflowing on the little stone bench. Her lips were clamped in a tight line as she fidgeted with the silver pomander at her waist and brooded over her miserable lot.

Damn Gervase Houghton! Just as she was enjoying the upswirl of gaiety that her life had become, he had to appear, casting his skinny shadow over her horizon, fixing her with those reproachful eyes so that she felt inexplicably guilty.

She glanced about her, her face as tense and desperate as it had been on that rainy afternoon at Greenthorpe which now seemed half a lifetime ago. The flower-beds were gaudy splotches of colour behind their white-painted railings. Overhead in a cherry tree a Jenny Whitethroat was singing cheerfully. The bright tender beauty of the spring morning seemed to mock her unhappiness, and once again she was conscious of that sick, swivelling panic. For she knew that she had no power, no weapons, against her father's authority.

A pair of lovers came strolling along the path, oblivious to everything except each other. The young man held the girl protectively in the circle of his arm, her bright brown head was tipped back against his shoulder. Alicia watched sourly as they disappeared through a cluster of trees, the girl's skirt a tantalising splash of pink darting in and out of the foliage like a flamingo.

Suddenly a tall figure came loping through a gap in the hedge, paused, then started towards her. Alicia sighed and shifted her buttocks irritably on the hard stone. She had been dreading this moment since he had first arrived at Greenwich.

'Alicia.' He was standing in front of her now, his face apprehensive and wary, as if she were a wild boar whom he had encountered in the forest while temporarily off his guard.

Alicia continued to ignore him, thinking that it might discourage him. It didn't. Instead he sat down beside her, as close as her billowing skirts would permit.

She stared coolly ahead, incensed that he had the effrontery still to be alive. Suddenly she gave the little pomander such a vicious jerk it was a wonder that it didn't snap from her girdle. She was thinking that Gervase Houghton had changed very little in three years. If he was taller, he was also as thin as a quill and, apart from the sparse beard nestling on his chin like a scrap of brown lace, his face was untouched by manhood. If anything, he resembled a page who has borrowed his master's clothes and expects a beating for his impertinence.

'I've been at Greenwich for three days now and it's obvious you've been avoiding me.' His voice reminded her of a sulky little boy.

'Why did you come?'

He thrust out his legs, tilting his head to admire them, long and narrow in delicate white-silk hose.

'Sir Richard wrote to my parents that you were visiting Lady Standish. And as Father had some business to attend to in London, I thought I might as well come with him. After all, we're to be married in the autumn – why shouldn't I visit you?'

At his last words Alicia lapsed into silence. After several moments she flung him a quick haughty glance and caught him peering sidelong into her bodice. Her skin began to prickle with outrage, yet at the same time she felt alarmingly vulnerable and exposed. Somehow his furtive lust was more offensive than other men's blatant ogling.

'You'll like Ryland Place, Alicia,' he was saying, his eyes shifting to her face. 'Of course with my brother Tom away in Italy – I should have gone too, only I had the measles – it's very quiet. There's only Mother and the little girls, Molly and Isabel. Oh, and Cousin Lucy – Father's ward. Lucy is only a year younger than you so you should be good friends, even though you're so different.'

'How do you know what I'm like?' Alicia swung waspishly towards him, violet eyes slitted, chin thrust out belligerently.

Vivid alarm showed in Gervase's face. He put out a hand as if to still her, but evidently thought better of it. He wasn't going to risk a cracking blow across the head from this young hellcat – he'd had enough of such treatment from his bitch of a mother.

'You're practically a stranger, yet you think you know everything about me.'

Her voice rose almost to a screech. 'Well, if you think I'd want to be friends with any of your beastly relatives, you're even more of a numskull than you look.'

Gervase's face had turned the colour of congealed porridge. He didn't speak but those pale-blue eyes were sorrowful and accusing. Alicia watched, disbelieving, as they welled up with tears. Slowly, disbelief turned to disgust. It was as if a sick dog were reproaching her for making no effort to alleviate its suffering. In another moment she would vomit – yes, all over his shiny red-leather shoes. That would jerk him to his senses! Yet in spite of herself she felt a tiny jab of guilt.

His next words promptly quenched it.

'Your father won't be pleased when he learns of your rudeness.'

Alicia glared at him, conscious of the hatred and contempt washing over her like a sickness. She thought how unappetizing he was with his greasy white skin, teary eyes and that wet pink ribbon of a mouth. Suddenly she had a swift horrifying vision of being in bed with him; of feeling his flesh clamped stickily to hers, his hands roaming over her in the dark. A vein began to flicker in her throat. She couldn't marry him – the very thought was unendurable. Let him marry Lucy, his orphaned cousin. Let him marry anyone – God knew, there must be dozens of girls available to the heir of a large Sussex estate – but don't let it be her! She would throw herself in the Thames before accepting him into her life, into her bed.

For some reason an image of George Boleyn's face began to dance before her, dark and teasing as a devil. Tears sprang to her eyes, and she dashed them away with the back of one hand. What had possessed her to think of *him*?

Gervase's eyes were sliding up and down her body, coming to rest on her slender thighs, but she paid no attention. Her mind was working at a frantic pace.

'It's getting late,' he said sullenly, piqued because she seemed to have forgotten that he was there. 'I have to go now – Father's expecting me for dinner.'

He started to get up but Alicia suddenly grabbed his arm.

'Before you go, there's something I must tell you,' she said.

He bumped back down again, then turned to her so eagerly that for a moment she almost hated herself for the deception she was about to play, but there was no help for it. She bent her head, then curled her hands in her lap, the picture of girlish modesty.

'Some time ago I was thrown from my horse. Oh, I wasn't badly hurt,' she added quickly, glancing up in time to catch his perplexed frown and answer it with a sweet wistful smile. 'And Blondel is really gentle. Something must have frightened him – perhaps a hobgoblin.' She saw that she had gone too far and dropped her lashes again. 'Anyway, the doctor told my mother that I would never be able to have children. So you see, Gervase, it would be very wrong for me to marry you.'

It was a scandal, spat Sir John Houghton through a mouthful of sack.

It was an abomination, thundered Sir Richard, who had arrived on horseback less than an hour ago and whose legs were splashed to the thighs with mud. Privately he resolved to make the little bitch pay for *that* particular indignity as he recalled his nightmare progress through the crowded rooms and galleries.

Alicia's eyes darted from one grim face to the other as they stood like a pair of snarling mastiffs on either side of the hearth. Although, she mused with a frightened titter, Sir John was more like a bantam – an angry little bantam, strutting indignantly about the farmyard.

'Snigger would you, girl? You won't snigger when you feel my riding crop across your arse!'

Her father was every bit as frightening as she remembered – a great golden oak tree of a man, towering and glowering above her. Nervously she began lacing the points of her sleeve through her fingers, feeling as if her cantering heart would burst right through her bodice. She knew that she could expect precious little mercy from him. In fact, in his present mood he might even decide to beat her in front of Sir John and that sly dog Gervase who was sitting on the settle looking decidedly pleased with himself. She shot him a vicious look through her lashes.

May God forgive you, you vile sneaking reptile, because I won't! She thought.

Alicia's sense of humour sometimes got the better of her, Richard was explaining. (She was startled by the faint note of pleading in his voice and for the first time in her life almost felt sorry for him.) She would, of course, be beaten for her stupid, tasteless joke, let them have no doubt about that! However she was a good girl who knew her duty.

Without a word, Sir John moved to the side table and refilled both glasses. He was more troubled than any of them could guess. He disliked the idea of girls being given a thrashing, however well-deserved. His wife, Agnes, always complained that he was too soft. As he strolled back to the hearth and handed the other glass to Richard, his expression was sombre. His brown eyes, bright as juicy figs, went suspiciously over Alicia. In that moment it struck him that she was rather delicately built – an unlikely breeder if ever he saw one. Maybe there was fire behind the smoke, after all.

To John Houghton, women were like brood mares, the glossy, high-stepping full-bloods beautiful enough to stop your breath but nervous and unpredictable, especially when in foal. You were better with a sturdy, placid animal – one you could rely upon. He thought of Lucy, his dead cousin's child, with a stab of regret. Now *there* was a dull little hill-pony, timid and plodding, but dependable as leather. Reared in the nursery at Ryland Place, trained and moulded by Agnes, she was tractable enough even for Gervase, whom she seemed to understand better than the rest of them. Were it not for a promise given long ago, he would put an end to this wretched business right now. The Westbrooke girl was vain and flighty, unlikely to be tamed by his puling son. They would make each other miserable. And yet, what was to be done? They were lawfully betrothed, the ink on the contract long since dried. Nor would Agnes let Alicia's dowry slip from her paws without an unholy battle! Anyway, Lucy was promised to Tom, whom she had loved since she was a small girl.

The thought of his younger son was as warming as a glass of brandy-wine on a raw December evening. He could not look at the lad without feeling the pride catch in his throat, along with a dim sense of wonder that he and Agnes had produced this splendid male creature. It was hard to compare Tom with the snivelling craven who was his heir. He looked across at Gervase, who as usual avoided his eyes, and realized, with a small shock of dismay, that not only did he sympathize with Agnes's dislike, he shared it. It was an uncomfortable thought. For the first time, he almost pitied the girl; she seemed a bright little thing. Lively too – Agnes wouldn't care for that. Though of course she might enjoy the task of crushing that audacious spirit like an anthill beneath her shoe, just as she had crushed Gervase and the girls. But not Tom – never Tom!

And so she was travelling home to Greenthorpe on a frost-tipped morning with Gervase's betrothal ring on her finger and the knowledge that before the summer was over, she would be his wife.

The crazy lie, told in panic and a perverse sense of devilment, had gained her nothing. If anything it had only served to hasten her sentence. For in the light of her erratic behaviour – now dismissed as nothing more than a fit of greensickness – it had been decided that the wedding should be brought forward to July. The sooner she was married, the sooner she would lose her silly ideas; the responsibilities borne by a wife and mother were guaranteed to teach common sense to even the most frivolous of young girls.

The carriage gave a violent judder as it ran over a loose stone in the road. Grimly, Alicia clung to the edge of the seat, bracing her feet against the floor. Her father rode ahead on his tall bay gelding, his cloak a disdainful flutter of scarlet in the distance. He hadn't uttered a word since ordering her inside the carriage at daybreak but she knew the moment would come when he'd unleash the full force of his anger and frustration upon her. Strange, but she felt only weary indifference, as if nothing could pierce the numb hopeless apathy that had settled over her spirits.

'Won't you have some wine, mistress?'

Alicia jumped. She had forgotten about the little maid sitting so quietly beside her. She turned to find the girl holding a leather flask towards her. She was smiling, the way one might smile at an unpredictable lunatic with whom one has had the misfortune to be shut up alone.

She was a pretty girl, no taller than five feet, with a cloud of hazel-brown curls and a lively little face spattered with freckles which gave her the look of a precocious child, though she must have been close to twenty.

Alicia was convinced that to drink anything would choke her, but she didn't want to hurt Nanty's feelings. After a moment or two, she felt the Rhenish stealing deliciously through her veins, warming the chilled pit of her stomach. She handed the flask back, then settled against the cushions with a faint sigh.

Poor Nanty! She would find Greenthorpe as dull as a nunnery after living at court. She'd said as much to Kathryn last night, when they were saying their goodbyes. Kathryn, usually the most tender and compassionate of women, was oblivious to any hurt or pique which Nanty might be feeling.

'I think you should take her, darling.' She offered her servant as if she were a woollen cloak to keep Alicia warm on the journey. 'She's sweet and cheerful and will keep you amused. Besides, every married woman should have her own maid.'

Richard had made no comment when she explained about Nanty and this brought home to her the leaden inevitability of her wedding as threats and insults had not. If Richard had accepted the expense of another servant it was because he didn't expect her to be part of his household for long.

The carriage gave another dramatic lurch; the two girls were flung up against each other, uttering little shrieks of fright. Nanty was the first to regain her composure.

'Are you all right, mistress?' Again that nervous little smile.

Alicia nodded, reaching up to set her coif straight. 'This must be the most barbaric way to travel. Luckily the roads aren't too foul right now, or we'd probably be lying in some muddy ditch. Still, if I'd had my way we'd go on horseback and reach home in half the time.'

Then she remembered how she dreaded the journey's end with Greenthorpe a great stone mouth waiting to swallow her up, and sank into gloomy silence.

Nanty peeked curiously at her. She knew something of her story for it had enlivened many an evening in the servants hall that week.

'A proper hellcat,' one of the women had remarked, pulling a face. 'If she were one of mine she'd get such a whipping, she wouldn't sit down before Whit Sunday.'

There was no sign of fire now, not a spark.

On the Essex farm where Nanty had grown up there had been a young girl – a ploughman's daughter – given to roaming over the fields in her sleep. Nanty had seen her one night when she'd crept out of her parents' cottage to search for a pet kitten. She could still remember that pale face, glossy and stiff as if it was coated with egg-white; could still remember the sense of eerie, rushing terror. She thought

Alicia looked a little like that girl – blank-eyed and remote, a frozen ghost of a girl.

The day grew old as the carriage crunched up the miles and the sky changed from rose to creamy-gold to damson. At dusk Sir Richard reined back to speak to the driver.

'We'll spend the night at that inn up ahead.'

Beyond the leather curtain they heard his voice, crisp and authoritative – a voice that always made his peers bristle with annoyance but sent servants scampering to carry out his orders.

The driver murmured obediently, the hoofbeats clopped smartly ahead. Alicia stretched her cramped legs and gave a mighty yawn.

The late afternoon sun had turned the pale walls of Greenthorpe a warm glinting coral. Alicia, looking out sullenly through the curtain, felt her spirits lift ever so slightly. Wars of pride and fury and bitter desolate love had thundered beneath its roof for nearly a century, yet Greenthorpe remained as calm and beautiful as a benediction.

Richard came to help her out of the carriage. His fingers were like the clamp of steel on her wrist as he jerked her to the ground, so roughly that her curls bounced and she nearly lost her balance. As she stood blinking at him in the sudden glare of light she saw the hard thrust of his jaw and guessed that he would have liked nothing more than to send her spinning across the stones. She had a sickening vision of her skull splattered over the courtyard, sticky with hair and blood. She swayed slightly and was thankful for his steadying hand. Sweet Jesus, she was getting to be as morbid as Joanna!

'Go straight to your room and see that you stay there.' Richard's voice was a slap in itself, but otherwise he made no move to strike her. 'I don't want to see your face till the day you leave here to be married.'

Alicia curtsied and turned towards the middle doors just as her mother came out, Alban like a grizzled old hound at her side. Dorothy paused at the top of the steps, a joyous smile breaking over her face. It vanished, however, as soon as she saw the expression on her husband's face.

Alicia felt a hard little knot of pain tighten under her ribs, as if she had been running. She hadn't expected support from her mother, who dwelt so fearfully in Richard's shadow, but she might at least have called out a greeting.

She started up the steps, Nanty close behind her, and would have swished insolently past Dorothy had it not been for Alban. His near-toothless grin, radiant as a sunburst, went directly to her heart.

'You look well, Alban,' she said pertly, after a quick glance over her shoulder assured her that Richard was safely out of earshot. 'I hope you haven't been seducing the maids again.'

'Alicia!' Dorothy was horrified but Alban flung back his big silver head and guffawed. He'd always had a soft spot for Mistress Alicia, because she reminded him so vividly of her grandmother.

Alban had been little more than a boy when Alice fled, a shocked and wounded child beneath her flouncing defiance, but he'd never forgotten her. All laughter, witchery and grace, she'd dazzled him from the first. Brighter than the jewel-tinted oriel that dominated the great hall, elusive as a rainbow, yet her heart had melted like a wax torch at the sight of a homesick lad sobbing in the orchard on that hateful first evening.

'Never show that you're scared.' Those great violet eyes were brilliant and compelling as she gripped both his hands and brought her face close to his. She had looked like a young sorceress watching for the effect of a new spell. Alban, crouched beside her under the mulberry tree, couldn't take his eyes off her.

'The steward is a fearful bully,' Alice went on. 'If he sees you crying, he'll make your life a misery. Pretend you don't care a fig for him and his threats and he'll leave you alone.'

She'd tossed him a well-gnawed green apple, then raced off in the direction of the house as her nurse started to bawl her name from one of the numerous windows.

Alban, still squatting on his haunches in the damp grass, had stared after the swift-running figure, his heart already lost.

Upstairs in her old bedchamber, Alicia tore off her cloak and threw it over a stool. She paced the room, skirts whistling over the rushes, drumming her nails on her teeth. Nanty watched her uneasily. What if she became hysterical? Nanty dared not slap her and every instinct told her that the usual soothing platitudes wouldn't work. She thought of Lady Kathryn's gentle stoicism with a stab of regret. Why, why had she ever thought her dull?

At last Alicia sank down on the edge of the bed, buried her face in her fists and began to cry softly, making little whimpering sounds in her throat like a frightened puppy. Suddenly Nanty remembered how young she was. Without a word she went and gathered the weeping girl in her arms.

'Dorothy!'

The unfamiliar use of her name had made her start up fearfully from the supper table, though for once his voice was soft and low. Dumbly she stared at him, her head spinning. It was as though his eyes could probe her brain, pick out the rebellious thoughts.

'You will *not* go to her – not yet. She thinks herself ill-used as it is. I won't have you cramming her head with more nonsense.'

His eyes shone as hard as agates in the pale yellow candlelight; shrewd, clever eyes that saw her every weakness. After a moment he went on more reasonably. 'Left to herself, Alicia will come to see the folly of her ways, as others have done before her.'

As I have done, you mean. But she didn't say it. She sagged down again and lifted the wineglass to her shaking lips.

Yes, she had been foolish. Like a silly schoolgirl, flouting him, taunting his proud temper to violence and then, after he had trampled her last defences, realizing she loved him if only because she needed his strength.

His low-pitched laughter rumbled down the length of the table, freezing her blood. Once again it was as if he had some demonic power over her – as if even her thoughts belonged to him, though she could claim no part of him. And so for once she decided to defy him.

At nightfall Dorothy braved her husband's wrath and stole up the dark stairs to Alicia's room, even though he had expressly forbidden it. It had been so long since she'd disobeyed him that the thought of his reaction fascinated as well as terrified her. As she skimmed along the gallery, her velvet slippers sounding softly on the wooden floor, his voice seemed to echo inside her skull.

'Other mothers don't slobber over their children like mawkish spaniels. Stop acting like a peasant and leave the girl to her women. They understand her – you don't. The truth is you hardly know her.'

Yet when you have carried a child beneath your heart, felt her turn in your womb, laboured through a whole night to give her life, she can never be a stranger, even if you delivered her into another woman's care as soon as the cord had been snipped.

She found Alicia sitting on the bed, legs tucked up beneath her. In her soft lawn nightgown, with her hair tumbling down her back, she looked like a defenceless child.

Fifteen, Dorothy mused with an odd little pang. It was so very young. *Yet I wasn't much older than her when I married Richard. My mother was seventeen when she gave birth to me. She is no child.*

'Madam.' Alicia had risen warily to her feet.

Dorothy laid a hand gently on her shoulder. 'It's all right, Alicia. I just want to talk to you.'

The little curly-haired maid was folding garments away in the panelled clothes'-press. Dorothy signalled to her to leave them, then she and Alicia were sitting side by side on the bed, studying each other guardedly like a pair of opponents in the tiltyard.

She must learn how to cry prettily, Dorothy told herself wryly, noting the shiny red-splotched cheeks, the tear-stiff lashes. Yet even in tears, Alicia's face was beautiful.

She found herself groping for the right words. With her elder daughter it had somehow been easier. Kathryn was like Dorothy — docile and yielding, always hopeful that obedience would win love. Alicia had been defiant ever since she'd taken her first wobbling steps across the nursery floor.

She sighed, then glanced at the door through which Nanty had just left.

'Are you pleased with your little maid?'

'Oh yes, madam.' Alicia smiled for the first time, her eyes suddenly bright with mischief. 'But I don't think Joanna's very pleased. She looked fit to burst her stays when she saw her.'

'Joanna is getting old,' Dorothy said, with a sharp glance at her daughter. 'She worries that soon we'll have no use for her. Age is rarely kind to any of us, Alicia.'

A dim sense of loyalty to the past prompted her to defend the woman who had loved and then cruelly betrayed her. It was a warning — no one was allowed to poke fun at Joanna.

Alicia peered slyly at her. She knew that despite the reproof, her mother hated Joanna, though she had never learnt the reason. Once she had tried to wheedle it out of Joanna and received a resounding slap that had made her eyes water.

'You have made your father very angry,' Dorothy was saying, her tone almost severe. 'And no wonder — embarrassing him in front of the Houghtons and causing such trouble for everyone. It was very wrong of you — and very foolish.'

'I didn't ask to be betrothed to that dog.' Alicia scowled, her fingers pleating a corner of the counterpane.

In spite of herself, Dorothy nearly laughed out loud. Although the girl looked like her, she had many of Richard's ways. She wondered if the thought had ever occurred to him, but it seemed unlikely. Between siring his daughters and finding them husbands, he'd seldom given them a thought except for those times when they had displeased him. Then he had administered swift punishment and as swiftly forgotten them. Yet he wouldn't easily forget the disobedience of his younger child. She had made him look a fool, the deadliest insult of all.

Dorothy felt terror soar in her heart at the thought of this bright young thing being hurt by Richard. And yet he would crumple Alicia like an oak-leaf in his palm if he thought that it would carve another wound across Dorothy's heart. When she spoke again, desperation lent a harsh edge to her voice.

'Alicia, few of us get to choose our own husbands — you've always known that. But if you yield quietly there is a chance you'll find happiness one day.'

'As Kathryn has?' Alicia sounded very bitter. *And you, madam*, she added silently.

Dorothy caught in her breath, almost as if she could read her daughter's thoughts. She turned her head so that her face was half-hidden in the shadows.

'I can't speak for Kathryn, though it grieves me to see her so unhappy. But if

I had been more reasonable when I married your father, things might have been very different between us.'

Down the years she heard a door slamming and the sound of her own voice, sharp with fear and resentment. *Keep away from me!* She saw Richard, not much more than a boy, glowering at her from the foot of the bed. Stung by her shrewishness, he was too young to hide it. How he must have writhed at the sly looks, the sniggers that were soon rippling through the household. Richard wasn't the only one who had been cruel.

Alicia was startled. It was the first time her mother had ever mentioned the aching misery of her marriage. Indeed, it was the first intimate conversation they had had. When she was a little girl growing up at Greenthorpe, she had often thought that her mother was a little like the Blessed Virgin – beautiful, sweet-faced, but remote. She had never been close to Dorothy as she had been to Lady Bess.

'Madam,' she began awkwardly, but Dorothy was tugging a ring from her finger and didn't seem to hear her.

'I'd intended to give this to Kathryn when she had her first child but – well, now I think you should have it.' She turned the pale glowing object over in her palm so that Alicia might see it.

It was the precious rose ring, sent as a birthday gift from Queen Elizabeth of York when Dorothy was sixteen. She seldom wore it for fear it should become tarnished or chipped but Alicia knew that it was a mystical link with some life-dream now dead.

She was slipping it on to Alicia's middle finger, a strange little smile flickering round her mouth.

'See how well it looks, yet you always used to complain that your hands were ugly. Why, this ring was once worn by Queens – it doesn't belong on an ugly hand.'

Alicia gazed dreamily at the fat pearl enfolded in curving emerald leaves. She stretched her hand towards the bedside candle, noticing how the soft flame reflected rosy apricot and green against her skin.

'It's probably treason to say so, but in their hearts my family always remained loyal to the House of York. I had an uncle and a great-uncle who died fighting for their cause – at Barnet and St Alban's. And my mother . . .' Dorothy bent her head, her voice dropping low. 'My mother died after giving birth to me, soon after King Richard was slain at Bosworth.'

Alicia could feel the tears digging behind her eyes. She had been taught, like others of her generation, that Richard III was a murderous tyrant whose black heart was crusted with the blood of his brother's sons. Yet her mother and her grandmother had felt bound to him in some way, while in the North they still honoured his name. She blinked, then continued staring at the ring, trying to picture it on the hand of the fair-haired queen whose portrait hung downstairs in the hall. It was awkward and old-fashioned, the pearl faded from lack of wear. Nonetheless it was very beautiful. It struck her that Queen Elizabeth must have thought very highly of her mother.

'Madam, I can't take it from you.' The tears came at last, sweeping down her face.

'Don't be silly, child.' Tenderly, Dorothy wiped the tears away with her thumb. 'And no more crying. I'd hoped that my gift would please you.'

'It does, only . . .'

'Perhaps one day you will have a daughter and pass the ring on to her. It's a tradition that was started long ago by another queen.'

Alicia found herself wriggling closer to her mother. Legends had always thrilled her and it seemed as if she would be a part of this one.

Dorothy smiled at the eager little face beside her. Then her green eyes grew misty as she reached back into the past – the romantic, glittering past that had betrayed her.

'Elizabeth's mother, the unbelievably beautiful but meddlesome Elizabeth Woodville – a commoner chosen by Edward the Fourth to be his bride because of a lust so powerful he couldn't withstand it. So history has it, but it's my belief he was in love with her. They were married nearly two years before their first child, Elizabeth, was born. The court held its breath that day, for Edward's rages were famous. However he accepted the news of a daughter quite cheerfully and to show his Queen – and her enemies – that he bore her no ill-will, he presented her with the rose ring. Some years later the Queen gave it to her eldest daughter, with instructions that she pass it on to her own daughter in the fullness of time. She had some notion that it possessed healing properties which would sustain a woman in trouble or turn disappointment to triumph. Elizabeth of York ignored her mother's wishes for she sent the ring to me when I was still a girl.'

'But she had daughters.' Alicia was almost indignant on behalf of the Princesses Margaret and Mary.

'Maybe she thought it all a piece of superstitious nonsense. Likely enough she had much grander jewels to give to her children. And she was always kind to me because my mother had been her dearest friend. She knew that I had very few beautiful things in those days.'

Dorothy's face had lost its misty, faraway expression. Suddenly she stood up, walked over to the hearth and prodded a falling log with her foot. Then she stood for a moment, staring into the flames, a tall slender figure framed in rosy light.

It flashed across Alicia's mind that there was something almost noble about her mother –something in her stillness, the graceful set of her head, the fall of her brown taffeta gown which gleamed like a great copper bell in the firelight.

With piercing clarity she realized that Dorothy was not the timid, feeble milksop people thought her. Her life might be lonely and cheerless, her husband might pummel her body and spirit mercilessly, but there was a part of her that was indestructible, perhaps because a Queen had once loved her.

CHAPTER FIVE

1501

Hot September sunlight pierced the bedchamber windows, spilling over the tapestries and the bulky oak furniture, the garments that lay heaped upon every surface. A silver bowl stood in the middle of the mantelshelf, crammed with late summer roses that had already started to droop. A lute lay abandoned in the corner, gathering dust.

Sixteen-year-old Dorothy stood at the foot of the bed, hot and irritable in her kirtle. Perspiration slipped down her face and neck, between her breasts, in tired little rivulets, yet she was almost dancing with impatience, balancing first on one foot then the other, then twisting round to catch a glimpse of herself in the long curved mirror at the far end of the room.

From this distance she could only make out a restless glimmer of white – white face, white throat, white lawn kirtle that cloaked her to the knees. But the hair flowing over straight bare shoulders glowed like foxfire in the sunlight. She smiled, thinking she looked like a candle flame. Then her eyes swung to the two middle-aged women sitting at the littered worktable and the smile vanished.

Hurry up! she urged them voicelessly. *Why in God's Name can't you hurry for once?*

The women, sisters who resembled nothing so much as twin mice with bright glancing eyes set in sharp-boned little faces, were bunched over a mass of buttercup velvet. Silver needles poised in mid-air, silver heads almost touching, they were enjoying a rather ghoulish discussion of their niece's confinement last month and had forgotten all about Dorothy.

She began nibbling a long strand of hair. It was just as well for them that Joanna wasn't in the room – she would never have approved of such a conversation in Dorothy's hearing and no doubt would have treated them to a venomous tongue-lashing. Dorothy only wished that they'd finish the gown and she could be done with the tedious, pin-jabbing business of being fitted out for her visit to court.

'You will need new clothes,' Lady Cicely had announced tersely, on the morning of Dorothy's birthday. She seldom spoke to her in any other tone and never used her name if she could avoid it.

'Yes, madam.' Dorothy had stood, arms dangling at her sides, miserable and awkward, the way she always was in her grandmother's company. She bent her head, waiting for the inevitable rebuke – her skirt was creased, her posture clumsy, her expression sullen. The strange thing was, she usually *felt* creased and clumsy when she was with Cicely. However Cicely was not looking at her granddaughter but at the letter spread before her on the table.

Dorothy was tempted to ask if she might read it – after all, it concerned her. Then she sighed, so faintly that Cicely didn't hear. Best not risk a scolding – not today, when she was so happy. She fingered a fold of her old green gown. It was perilously tight at the bodice and armpits and covered with dull, bald patches where the pile had worn away. Still, her grandmother had promised her new clothes.

'There's no money to waste on baubles!' Cicely's impatient voice slashed across her day-dream like a blade and she started nervously, as if expecting a slap. The old lady must have seen the panic leaping into her eyes for she went on more gently. 'You may have a couple of new gowns and I've kept some things that belonged to your mother. I daresay they can be altered, though you are rather taller than she was.'

Neither her tone nor her expression altered when she mentioned her dead daughter and before Dorothy could stammer her thanks, she was waved testily out of the blue-and-silver bedchamber where Cicely had slept alone for many years, even before her husband had died a pitiful, broken drunkard.

That very day the great cedar coffers were dragged down from the loft. Dorothy watched enraptured as each garment was carefully lifted out and laid upon the bed. There were voluminous nightgowns, ribboned cloaks, gowns of chestnut velvet, corn-coloured sarcenet, bronze satin embroidered with gold thread. Clearly Alice Marsh had had her daughter's passion for vibrant autumn colours.

At last she gathered up a richly embroidered white velvet, then, ignoring Joanna's amused snort, threw it down again as her eyes alighted greedily upon the sea-green taffeta.

Joanna was holding a heavy brocade gown at arm's length, her head tilted to one side and a thoughtful expression on her face. Dorothy quickly drew in her breath.

It was the colour of clotted cream, with a high gold-cinctured waist and miniver-fringed sleeves. Tiny seed-pearls were spattered like raindrops over the skirt and the long formal train. It was easily the most beautiful of all the gowns, yet the sight of it speared her heart with a swift, unfamiliar pain so that she wanted to bury her face in the gleaming folds and cry.

There were no portraits of her mother at Greenthorpe and though Joanna had described her as best she could, Dorothy had carried only a pale fuzzy image in her mind all these years. Now for the first time she saw a picture, bright as a sword, of a slender young girl dressed in foaming cream brocade, her face a lively oval beneath a mass of terracotta curls. Saw her smile and drop a sweeping curtsy to a man hidden in the shadows – King Richard? Dorothy glanced rather slyly at Joanna, who had babbled 'the secret' to her long ago, after one of Cicely's stern rebukes had reduced the child to tears.

Joanna was fingering a green velvet cloak, her mouth twisted to one side. Now in her thirties, she seemed to have passed straight from shambling, bulky girl to matron with no ripe period between, yet she had a solid dignity in her middle years which suited her; she appeared far more at ease with herself.

'Everything will have to be made over,' she grumbled. 'And we all know who'll have to do it. Jesus, this fur looks as if the rats have chewed it – aye, and spat it out again.'

She wore an aggrieved, put-upon expression for the rest of the day until she learnt that Nell and Emma were to be brought up from their cottage on the estate to do the sewing.

Dorothy eyed them now with mounting exasperation. Nell – or was it Emma? – was casually unpicking a stitch while Emma – Nell? – gleefully recounted how baby Tom was finally born after twenty hours of tearing agony.

She wondered at their enthusiasm for the subject, for both were spinsters. She herself had not reached the stage when pregnancy and childbirth were absorbing and, though aware that one day she would probably bear a child, it was something which belonged in the nebulous future and she seldom gave it a thought.

One of the sisters looked up with a mock-sympathetic grimace.

'Nearly done now, mistress. You'll go to court looking as fine as Princess Meg, thanks to us.' Both women tittered, baring no more than eight pointed teeth between them.

Dorothy gave a haughty toss of her head, not bothering to answer, and they promptly forgot her again. Bored with standing still, she strolled over to the window. Below, the park was spread like a bright green kirtle, sliding down on the west side to the lake, which was hidden by a screen of tall, languid willows. Even so she could picture it, cool and glossy as Italian marble, streaked with reflected green-gold light from the trees and sky.

She leaned her elbows on the ledge, propping her chin on her fists. After a while her thoughts trailed back to another sunny afternoon, when Alban had taken Joanna and her out in the rickety little boat which they'd found hidden among the reeds. They had sung songs, laughing helplessly at their lack of harmony, and feasted on pork pies and ale. Somehow Lady Cicely had got to hear of the outing – and of Dorothy's truancy from the schoolroom. She had vigorously scolded the two servants, even threatened them with dismissal, but said not one word to Dorothy, though she ignored her for nearly a month. She had made her dislike and disapproval felt ever since Dorothy was a small girl, too young to understand her crime.

Without Joanna, Dorothy felt that her spirit would have shrivelled up inside her like a wet little bird, so worthless did her grandmother make her feel. But Joanna was always there, her strong arms a refuge from eyes that were hard and unforgiving as mossy stones whenever they looked at Dorothy.

'You're the prettiest poppet there ever was,' Joanna would often declare, her eyes glistening with fond pride. 'Pretty as a honeypot and as good as may-butter. Small wonder I love you so.' And she would drop a smacking kiss on top of Dorothy's head or a strawberry sucket into her mouth while the child wriggled close to her, feeling safe and happy. She knew that Joanna would always protect her. Nor was Joanna the only one who loved her. Each birthday brought a gift from court – a kite, a gilded hobby-horse, a white coral bracelet, a length of turquoise satin to make a gown. Elizabeth of York, now mother to a growing family, had never forgotten the little girl born during her lonely exile in Yorkshire.

'I will take care of you and the little one,' she had promised Alice all those years ago.

She had been unable to save Alice from that blood-soaked death most feared by women, but she would always do her best for Alice's daughter.

The sun dipped low in the sky, glowing like a bruised orange above Greenthorpe's twisted chimneys. At last the gown was finished and Nell and Emma suddenly became very attentive, fluttering round her, tiny hands plucking, twitching, smoothing each fold into place until she couldn't bear it any longer and broke away to the mirror.

'You look as pretty as a bride, mistress.' Emma ran up behind her to brush away a stray thread.

'Except she hasn't got a bridegroom!' Nell shrieked. For some reason this reduced the sisters to hysterical giggles.

Dorothy studied her reflection shyly. Joanna had often told her she was beautiful, but she hadn't really believed it until this moment. Now for the first time she saw the delicate sculpturing of bones beneath her pale skin, the full tender curve of her mouth. She had her grandmother's slender height, her bright green eyes, though in Cicely's face they glinted icily shrewd while her own betrayed a slightly wistful eagerness.

'That's enough talk of bridegrooms and the like.' Joanna had arrived without any of the three noticing. She was standing just inside the door, arms folded over her bosom, her face as red and cross as a laundrymaid's.

'Take off that heavy gown, hinny.' She spoke wearily to Dorothy. 'You'll swoon in this heat.'

Dorothy turned away from the mirror and ran to give the nurse an impulsive hug.

'Let me keep it on, Joanna – just till suppertime. You know I never swoon.'

Joanna looked at the happy innocent girl standing before her in her yellow gown and felt her insides suddenly clench with pain. She was so lovely; the yellow had brought out unsuspected amber specks in her eyes and the flood of bright hair shone almost violet in the September sunset. Not for the first time Joanna was reminded of Dorothy's mother – self-willed, spirited Alice who had snatched at happiness so greedily and paid for it with her life. Yet there was an almost childlike fragility in Dorothy which had not been in Alice, and it was this which gave the nurse her misgivings. She would fight like a vixen, only to capitulate at the most critical moment which meant that people – men! – would be able to hurt her savagely.

'Take the gown off,' she repeated. 'Anyway, it *is* suppertime, or soon will be, and this room looks like a bearpit.'

She glared accusingly at the sisters who, as usual, were blithely impervious to criticism. Nonetheless. they cleared the table within minutes, somehow managing to convey that they acted upon their own whim rather than Joanna's disapproval. Then they danced out through the door, giggling like a pair of boisterous children escaping from the schoolroom.

Staring after the wiry, energetic little figures, Joanna suddenly felt very old.

'Be very careful.'

Cicely Marsh stood at the foot of the stone staircase, regarding her granddaughter critically. The pin-sharp eyes raked Dorothy's figure from beaded cap to narrow satin shoes, but they found nothing to offend them. The girl was well turned out, even a credit to her, though naturally she would never dream of saying so.

'I will, madam.' Dorothy wondered why her grandmother was looking at her so strangely. Perhaps she was thinking of her daughter; Alice had also ridden out from Greenthorpe on a glittering autumn morning, only to meet with disgrace and tragedy. Yet Dorothy couldn't find it in her to pity the old lady – she had been rebuffed by her too often. Hands coiled together in the folds of her new crimson cloak, she felt only a springing impatience to be gone from the house that had never welcomed her.

'You must do nothing which might displease her Grace.' Cicely's voice was crisp with warning. 'Remember, it is thanks to her that you're being given this chance.'

She knows! The thought seemed to vault across Dorothy's brain. Her heart began to thump so hard it made her feel slightly sick. *She must always have known – about my father.*

Green eyes searched green eyes, but if Cicely had any secrets they were folded away behind her old, cold face and she met Dorothy's gaze unblinkingly. Even in this moment of parting there was no hint of tenderness or concern and there was nothing else to say.

Dorothy glanced towards the open doorway where the sunshine was pouring through in a brilliant yellow stream, beckoning her outside. But first she must take her leave of the woman who had given her shelter since babyhood, albeit grudgingly.

The hand that she raised to her lips felt as dry and brittle as old satin. She had a sudden mad impulse to sink her teeth into the knuckles and quickly smothered a laugh. It was a thought more worthy of Alice than her well-behaved daughter. She curtsied, then, without another word, turned and hurried out to the waiting carriage.

A groom stood at the horses' heads while they danced and pawed at the cobbles, like children impatient to set off on an outing. Alban, now a tall, strongly-built man in his early thirties, helped her inside. He winked at her, his big rosy face as merrily impudent as ever, but she knew he was sad to see her go.

'Don't stay away too long.' Dorothy suspected that those words were really meant for Joanna.

'Mawkish fool!' Joanna plumped down on the cushions beside Dorothy with a grunt. She didn't even look at the steward but there was a faint smile quivering round the corners of her mouth. Alban grinned, then let the curtain fall on them.

The carriage sprang forward with a clatter of hoofs and an eager jangling of harness. Impulsively, Dorothy gripped Joanna's hand. Neither of them thought to look back for a last glimpse of the woman standing alone on the steps and presently she went back inside the house.

At thirty-four Elizabeth of York was still beautiful but she had lost that luminous quality which made people think of candles glowing through a bank of white flowers. No trace remained of the girl who had giggled and wept and dreamed of forbidden love – she was buried deep inside a passive shell where no one could reach her.

Last year she had buried her sixth child, the baby Prince Edmund and, four years before that, the frail little girl who was her namesake. She rarely mentioned them any more but sometimes in her dreams she felt their tiny fingers plucking at her gown, gently tugging at her hair, and would wake in a blanket of chill sweat, feeling as if her heart had stopped.

As she came face to face with the daughter of Alice Marsh on that coral-tinted afternoon at Greenwich Palace, she looked as if she might burst into tears. Then, like a little girl remembering a scolding, she swiftly composed herself as the years with Henry Tudor had taught her to do. Smiling, she stretched out one hand and Dorothy crossed the room, knelt and kissed the long, ring-studded fingers. As she did so she caught a delicious whiff of vanilla perfume.

'You are very welcome, child.' Her voice was light and delicate as Spanish lace. An indulgent murmur rippled among the watching ladies. Dorothy began to feel slightly drunk on the fragrance, the kindness. Why, the Queen was her cousin, though naturally she must never mention it.

Elizabeth inclined her head, indicating that she might stand. Dorothy obeyed, then her eyes began to glide curiously round the room.

A tiny russet-haired girl was sitting on a pile of cushions nearby, playing with a striped kitten. It was impossible not to stare for she was an exquisite child who combined Elizabeth's cameo-fine features with the vivid colouring of the Tudors.

'The Princess Mary,' Elizabeth said, following Dorothy's gaze. She added rather wistfully, '*She* is my baby now.'

Upon hearing her name, the child tumbled the kitten from her lap and ran to bury her face in her mother's skirts. Elizabeth's hand reached out to stroke the mop of burnished curls. As she looked up, she caught Dorothy's round-eyed stare and smiled tenderly.

'We must find you a husband, my dear. It's my belief that no woman knows what real happiness is till she holds her first baby in her arms.'

Dorothy returned the smile rather shakily. She would choose her own husband and she was certainly in no hurry to have babies!

Mary clambered up on to the Queen's lap. Elizabeth's arms closed around her small daughter. Then she bowed her head and said in a sad little voice:

'Children are the greatest comfort in the world.'

As she spoke a great tear plopped on to the little girl's hair but fortunately only Dorothy noticed.

In leafless November Prince Arthur married the King of Aragon's youngest daughter Catherine.

At fifteen he was a pale, listless sapling of a boy with tired mauve shadows under his eyes and none of the bouncing zest of the Tudors. Yet he touched Dorothy's heart as his brother and sisters could not, for he was quiet and gentle, lit by an inner grace.

The sixteen-year-old bride had won England's heart in the first moment. Not only were the people captivated by her clear-skinned prettiness, they were quick to glimpse the rather forlorn, homesick child beneath the buckram-stiff Spanish dignity and were ready to love her. It was a love that was to endure until her lonely death thirty-five years later.

Gowned in apple-green and silver, with her hair spilling in a coppery tempest to her thighs, Dorothy knew that she looked no less beautiful than the royal bride and she danced at the wedding feast with a buoyancy almost rivalling Prince Henry's. The ten-year-old boy, sweating from heat and excitement, had flung off his doublet and was prancing bare-chested through the crowd like a sturdy pink cherub.

Men's eyes followed Dorothy that night as once they had followed her mother. Their admiration was as sweet as hippocras to the young girl who had been virtually ignored for most of her life. She tossed her head, laughing at the compliments and the increasingly lewd suggestions. (At least she assumed they were lewd from the way her partners leaned forward to whisper slyly in her ear.) But as she sped past the canopied dais where their Majesties sat, she dropped her eyelids demurely. She was instinctively afraid of the King – though he had been most gracious on the few occasions he'd noticed her – for she sensed in him a core of disciplined coldness that reminded her of Lady Cicely. To the end of her days she would dread emotional coldness above all things. And yet she was to fall in love with a man whose heart was as cold and unyielding as a lead box.

'None of the men can take their eyes off you,' Bess Ashby said teasingly as they sat together during a lull in the dancing.

Dorothy giggled. She knew that no barb lay behind the words. Bess, a jolly, ruddy-skinned young woman in her mid-twenties, was completely ignorant of feminine rivalry, for she had been surrounded by love and security all her life. Also, she was her friend – the only woman friend Dorothy had ever had, apart from Joanna. She watched sympathetically as Bess, who was eight months pregnant with her fourth child, reached behind her to rub her aching back.

'You'll have to guard your maidenhead, Dorothy,' she added naughtily, after a couple of minutes. 'You've cast a spell over all of them.'

'Not quite *all*.' Dorothy grimaced. Automatically her eyes shifted to a sullen-looking young man who was standing by the doors as if he meant to escape at the first opportunity. He was about twenty and taller than most of the other men – more handsome, too, with a waving mass of blond hair and the vigorous, hard-boned physique of one who spends most of his time outdoors. However, his surly expression was guaranteed to keep women at arm's length. Now as his gaze linked with Dorothy's across the stuffy, brightly lit hall, there wasn't a flicker of admiration or interest in the rock-grey eyes.

'Oh, don't fret over Richard Westbrooke – Cleopatra couldn't have melted *his* heart. He's a handsome devil, though – or would be if he ever learnt to smile. Why, I'd wager he glowers and glares even when he's in bed with a woman.'

Dorothy squealed with laughter. Richard, guessing that she was laughing at him, reddened with annoyance and tried to outstare her. She was the first to look away with a careless tilt of her chin, airily dismissing him.

The dancing was about to resume. Dorothy was immediately claimed by a plump little courtier whose head barely reached her eyebrows and whose breath smelled of greasy meat, yet she threw him a flashing smile, convinced that tonight nothing could dampen her high spirits. For the first time in her life she was being admired and sought after. It seemed to fill the dull, aching void that her grandmother's indifference had left inside her.

All at once the whirlpool of festivities was over and Arthur took his bride off to Ludlow Castle so that the people of Wales might see their new princess. No sooner had the young couple set out with a meandering train of servants, men-at-arms and luggage-carts than a mood of weary petulance seemed to settle over the court, like that of a child who has stayed up too late at a party.

That February of 1502 was uncommonly mild, bringing cool soft showers and a sprinkling of violets and purple and gold crocuses. Already the evenings were longer, indolently sinking into a bed of pale strawberry light. Dorothy moved happily through those pastel days, unaware that her life was about to be irrevocably and disastrously changed.

It was the King, his mind still brimful of weddings, who ordered the marriage between Dorothy Marsh and the youngest son of Sir Cuthbert Westbrooke.

In fairness to Henry, his intentions were kindly. He was aware of his wife's concern for Dorothy – a concern which had fermented into sharp anxiety since news of Lady Cicely's death had reached them early in the year. The old lady had sat down to her usual solitary dinner and then, without a hint of warning, suddenly slumped across the table with an eerie grunting sound. She was dead before Alban reached her side.

What was to become of sixteen-year-old Dorothy, illegitimate and now quite alone in the world? Elizabeth had settled a handsome dowry upon the girl and for once Henry hadn't protested – he had never succeeded in curbing her extravagance, though he still treated her to the odd scolding. As soon as she confided her fears, he reached one of those shrewd, unemotional decisions that had earned him respect throughout Europe. A suitable husband must be found, to bring honour and stability to Mistress Dorothy's life.

If the King had known of the storm of tears that passed in Dorothy's chamber that night he would have been displeased but unsurprised and certainly unmoved. One did not expect women to show good sense, even when their own interests were at stake. Meanwhile Dorothy wept and raged in her nurse's arms until daylight greyed the palace windows.

'They can't make me marry him! I'm King Richard's daughter, I won't be tethered to that – that clodhopper!' She flung herself against Joanna in a fresh torrent of weeping even though she had thought there were no more tears inside her.

Joanna smoothed back the hot tangled skeins of hair, her mind groping for the right words.

'Calm yourself, hinny,' she said at last. 'When you look at this in a clear light it's not so bad. You'll be mistress of Greenthorpe all your days and can still visit the court when you've a mind to. And – and he seems a quiet lad, I doubt he'll give you any trouble.'

Dorothy slid her a baleful look from beneath puffy red eyelids. It might have given her some small satisfaction to know that twenty-year-old Richard was no more eager than she for the match.

'A bastard!' he yelled, aiming a vicious kick at the bedpost. 'You want me to marry a silly, simpering bastard with the brain of a pigeon!'

'She's a very beautiful girl,' Sir Cuthbert snapped. 'And be careful of that wood, you'll mark it with those great hoofs of yours.'

God's teeth, but whoever had said that children were obedient couldn't have had any of his own! He strode across to the hearth and spread his hands over the auburn blaze, silently praying for patience.

Richard glared at his father's broad back. He could feel the anger, as thick as hot cream, filling his throat until he thought it would choke him.

He didn't like Dorothy Marsh; those airy, fragile-as-spun-glass women had never appealed to him. If anything they made him vaguely uneasy, for it was as if they had some unseen advantage over him. He liked his women broad-hipped and placid-tempered, with no silly pretensions or vanity – loving and humble enough to pamper *his* vanity. Moreover, that red-haired chit did not strike him as a lusty bedfellow. Like as not she'd be bleating to her maid of bruises in the morning and tearfully dabbing her white skin with witch hazel! Anyway he couldn't stand her infernal giggling. She was always giggling with that fat Ashby sow – giggling at him, no doubt! At the thought his skin began to prickle and a tight red mist rose up before his eyes.

'She's a bastard!' he shouted again, slamming his fists against his thighs as if he wanted to hit out at someone. 'No one knows her father's name. And you expect me to marry her, take her to bed – have children by her.'

Sir Cuthbert finally lost patience and came swivelling round on his heel.

'Now listen to me, Richard. The girl will bring you a knighthood and a manor in Hertfordshire. Not to mention – are you listening to me, boy? – a dowry of six hundred marks. His Grace has given me his promise and he'll not go back on his word. Furthermore,' he went on in a hard voice that clearly told Richard he was not going to change his mind, 'I've pissed blood to get on at court and won't have you ruin everything with your accursed temper. God knows you've killed any chance of a better match. I tell you it sticks in my craw to see the way you treat women. I've seen a couple of them close to tears because of your nasty tongue. Well, now there's an end to it. You'll marry Dorothy Marsh or beg your bread in the streets. Anyway it's time you were wed and getting sons, great hulking wastrel that you are.'

It was the promise of the knighthood – and the manor – that decided Richard. It had always been a canker in his heart that his brother Nick – stupid, shiftless Nick with his fat, sprawling buttocks and his whining voice – was their father's heir. Richard was the one with the good looks, the energy and determination, the shrewd agile brain, but sour fate had seen to it that Nick was born first.

For as long as he could remember, Richard Westbrooke had dreamed of being lord of the manor. He had a most gratifying vision of himself cantering over wide green acres on a glossy-necked stallion while his tenants came rushing out of their cottages to bow the knee to him. Somewhere in the vision there was a woman, smooth-skinned and smiling, who sat beside him at the high table, listening eagerly to all his plans and refilling his glass without being prompted. Her face was prettily rounded, submissive and yet sensual, unlike the pale doll's face of Mistress Dorothy.

He came to with a jolt to find himself alone in the room. It was Sir Cuthbert's way of letting him know that if he disobeyed him, he would be abandoned to his fate. He stared scowling at the floor. A cockroach was shifting through the dirty rushes and without thinking he cracked it savagely beneath his shoe. Never had he known his father to be so ruthless. Sir Cuthbert was not like Richard's mother, easily swayed by a son's tantrums or sulks, fearful of losing his love, but he had always prided himself on being fair.

'I am firm with the boys but never unreasonable,' he had often said to his wife, 'whereas they know they can do with you as they will, Cat.'

But it was Sir Cuthbert who did with her, and everyone else, as he willed – Sir Cuthbert, who ruled and planned and, if it fitted his purpose, destroyed their lives. Richard could go to his mother and win her sympathy by being sullen, cajoling or, God forbid, humble, and Lady Catherine would cradle his head against her bosom, stroke the guinea-bright hair tenderly as if he were still her little boy. But just when he thought he'd won her over she would tell him that he must do his duty.

'I cannot defy your father, Richard, and neither must you. It would break his heart.' And the gentian-blue eyes would sparkle with tears while the soft mouth quivered like that of a little girl who dreads a scolding.

There was no one, Richard fumed, to stand beside you when trouble reared its head. You were alone in this world whether you were an orphan or one of a great rambling family. The only person you could trust or depend on was yourself. It was a lesson which younger sons learnt early.

He had reached his decision. To achieve his ends, he'd marry a dozen simpering sluts like Dorothy. And yet, like her, in his heart he was praying for some respite.

Respite came without warning when Arthur Tudor died at faraway Ludlow Castle that April, with no member of his family at his bedside. There was only Catherine, his plump little Spanish bride, to hold his hot damp hand in hers, her eyes dark rings of anxiety in her pretty face.

'You will get well, Arthur,' she told him, her voice husky and pleading, still halting in a tongue which she feared would never become familiar. 'You must – for my sake.'

Arthur smiled feebly, as if the effort hurt him. He loved her, she was his sister and his friend – in time he would have made her truly his wife.

Impossible to believe at fifteen that there was no more time!

'Forgive me,' he wanted so say. 'Forgive me for leaving you all alone.'

But he didn't have the strength to whisper her name.

News of Arthur's death sent the country plummeting into deep mourning. It was as if they too had buried a favourite son. He had been their prince, their sweet white hope, and they had loved him. While England burgeoned into sleek green springtime, her people bent their heads and grieved.

When they'd done grieving, their thoughts swung towards Prince Henry. A tough athletic child, he already bore a startling resemblance to his Plantagenet grandfather, Edward IV and the sight of him fired them with fresh courage. It was a time of sorrow and seeping darkness but they knew that one day the sun would come out and young Hal would make them laugh again.

The Queen, who had come perilously close to losing her reason, looked sick and worn. *She* would never be done grieving. In the first wildness of grief she had shown the strong spirit that flamed beneath her gentle heart, for her husband had needed her. For the only time in sixteen years, he had needed her. She remembered that afterwards when Henry had forgotten – remembered, too, how swiftly he'd recovered. But Henry had lost an heir – she had lost her child.

By midsummer she was pregnant again and if the knowledge filled her with numbing despair, no one guessed it. She smiled placidly when her ladies congratulated her and secretly wondered at the stupidity of people who hinted that a new baby would help her to forget Arthur.

'Children can't be replaced like clothes or furniture,' she wanted to scream. But as usual she swallowed her frustration and everyone thought she was contented.

Dorothy passed those dark summer days in a state of leaden misery. She ate only the morsels of food that Joanna managed to force upon her and slept scarcely at all. Above all she avoided Richard Westbrooke, which was easy enough since he seemed none too eager to seek her out.

She knew that if she pleaded her case to the Queen, she would receive sympathy. Elizabeth herself knew the anguish of a loveless marriage. Yet the sight of that pale-blonde head bent so patiently over her needlework stopped her in her tracks. Her problems seemed absurdly petty and selfish beside Elizabeth's terrible suffering.

One night she was lying in bed, on the dusky boundary between consciousness and sleep, when an eerie image seemed to flicker before her. Two black-clad figures were kneeling beside a tiny coffin. One was a little girl clutching a doll, her chin wobbling with the effort not to cry. The other was Lady Cicely as she must have looked some twenty-five years ago. Cicely resembled a sleepwalker with her green eyes staring out hopelessly from a chilled white face.

The two figures crossed themselves and stood up. As they started to move away the little girl seemed to hesitate, then she turned back and went to lay the doll inside the coffin. Cicely gave a slight shake of her head. The child looked mutinous and at the same time close to tears.

'Don't be silly, Alice.' Cicely spoke wearily though not unkindly. 'The doll cannot be buried with your sister.'

'But I want her to have it.' The tears came at last, raining unchecked down Alice's small face. 'What if she's lonely?'

The image faded like a snowflake and died. Dorothy came to with a start, staring petrified into the darkness. *Had* it been a dream? And if so, why was she left with this feeling of desolation and loss, as if someone very dear to her had died? She hadn't loved her grandmother nor, in her heart, did she mourn her. In fact Cicely's death had brought nothing but a sense of guilty relief.

'I want to go home to Greenthorpe,' she announced abruptly next morning as Joanna was helping her into her clothes.

Joanna, reaching for the plain black velvet gown, stopped and planted her fists on her hips.

'Have you forgotten you're going to be married? You can't just . . .'

Then she noticed the dark-red rings under Dorothy's eyes.

'My grandfather had lovers, didn't he?'

'Well, I . . .' For once Joanna was at a loss.

Dorothy gave a tight little smile. 'It's all right, I've known about it for years.' She began walking restlessly about the room, almost as if she were trying to retrace a path back to that troubled childhood. 'It was one night when I couldn't sleep. I went down to the kitchen for a piece of gingerbread and heard some of the servants talking and laughing. They were teasing the new kitchen lad, telling him how no pretty boy was safe in the house with my grandfather. They didn't know I was there,' she added quickly, suddenly catching Joanna's eye. Then she stopped in mid-walk, dropped her head and began to cry.

The nurse was shocked, not by Dorothy's disclosures, for she'd long known all about that sorry business, but that she had learnt of it in such a way. She wondered what had brought it to mind now.

'There was only one lover,' she said briskly, crossing the room and taking both Dorothy's hands in hers. 'Your grandfather loved him very much. There was nothing ugly in it, just a heap of misery for everyone.'

Joanna had heard the whole bitter story from one of the stable grooms soon after she'd arrived at Greenthorpe with the baby Dorothy. Old Will had had a certain wry affection for his master, who was always courteous to the servants even when reeling drunk, and could charm whomsoever he chose.

'Always feckless, even as a lad, but likeable,' was Will's verdict. 'Even my lady liked him at first. Maybe she even loved him, poor lass.'

But how could love survive in the face of Henry's obsessive passion for the flaxen-haired lute-player who had strolled into Greenthorpe one brilliant summer morning and stayed till Christmas Eve – long enough to tear and snare his heart. When the young musician was sent away under a pall of snickering and disgrace, Henry wept wrenching tears as he would never weep for the girl he married a year later.

'In time you will forget,' his mother told him, her heart thawing a little now that the cause of the furore had removed himself. 'Many young men go through – through this sort of thing and go on to make successful marriages. And Cicely is a sweet child who will make you happy if you give her the chance. Believe me, Henry – I know that I'm right.'

Privately she thought him vain and shallow enough to be distracted by a new companion who obviously adored him. He had been petted and indulged all his life, for neither Lady Anne nor the servants could withstand his bright charm. Now Cicely's love would heal his pride and eventually they would all be able to live down the distasteful affair.

She misjudged her son. He didn't forget, even when hope finally died and he knew that no word would ever come from Adrian. Like many a lover before and since he tried to swamp the pain with strong wine until he was too befuddled to feel anything, even self-pity. Yet dying he would cry out for Adrian, though nearly forty years had passed and he didn't even know if Adrian was alive; if he had really ridden out of his life so uncaringly on that icebound afternoon, with never a backward thought, or if some calamity had struck him soon afterwards. It was the doubt, the not knowing, that had eventually destroyed him.

Joanna looked at the strained white face of Henry's only grandchild and wondered what she was thinking. Clearly the girl needed gentle handling just now.

'Perhaps,' Dorothy said slowly, her eyes growing big and solemn, 'he would have loved me if we'd known each other.'

'Assuredly he would, hinny.' Joanna beamed in relief.

She decided then that the love she felt for Dorothy was the best kind – pure as bread, solid and dependable as oak. Fortunately she had no inkling that one day soon Dorothy would break her heart.

Dorothy lay huddled under the covers in the principal bedchamber at Greenthorpe. Although it was a parching August night, her hands and feet were like chunks of ice. Even the sheet beneath her felt chilly, as if it hadn't been aired properly. Her heart was thundering, she could hear it pounding in her ears. It was galling to admit, even to herself, that she was afraid. She couldn't have been more afraid if she was on her deathbed.

The thick powdery scent of lavender drifted in through the open window, sprigs of dried lavender lay strewn among the rushes. Her head began to swim with a dull sickness. To the very end of her days she would hate that scent.

After a while she dragged herself up on to one elbow, listening for sounds in the adjoining closet where Richard was being undressed by his manservant. They had been in there for some time – obviously Richard was no more eager than she for what lay ahead. She stared at the bedpost, her face growing tight and sullen as in her mind she relived the events of the past week.

They had been married in the crumbling old chapel at Woodstock Palace, whither the court had repaired for the summer. To Dorothy's relief it had been a very sedate affair with none of the usual bawdy roistering. The Queen, still grieving for Arthur, was fretful and ill as she had not been in her previous pregnancies. (The baby's birth was to cost her her life, nor would it survive her.) And so Richard and Dorothy rode away from Woodstock on their wedding day, relieved to escape the pervasive gloom of a court in mourning but loath to be alone together. Every night they slept at an inn along the way. And every night she forestalled him with female excuses. It had been childishly easy for, like most men, he had a lively distaste for women's functions and, though she caught him frowning at her suspiciously once or twice, he would as soon have knelt and kissed her hem as questioned her on the subject.

Now on their first night at Greenthorpe, she knew that she would not be able to hold him off any longer. Joanna had hinted as much while she was getting her ready for bed.

'It's nothing, sweetheart, if you just relax.' Bess Ashby, now recovered from the birth of a fat, sunny-tempered baby girl last Christmas and growing daily more convinced that she was pregnant again, had tried to comfort her. But it was different for Bess. She had loved her Walter since they were children. Dorothy didn't even like the curtly spoken stranger who had been thrust into her life. Nor had she felt able to explain that it was outraged pride that ailed her and not the fearful squeamishness of a young virgin, for Bess knew nothing of her Plantagenet blood.

Her eyes began to wander about the room, seeing as if for the first time the faded gilt rosebuds on the ceiling, the dull gleam of the twisted silver candlesticks. The thin amber flames bobbed and swayed, sending shadows dancing over the furniture like giant moths. The bedside table was piled with fruit and honeycakes and a selection of cold roasted meats. A single loving cup stood coyly beside the wine-jug – a romantic touch of Joanna's. Dorothy pulled a face, yet it occurred to her that a draught of wine might steady her nerves. But before she was able to pour it, the closet-curtain swished back and Richard emerged, regally wrapped in a cinnamon-velvet robe edged with fur. He glanced quickly towards the bed but didn't speak. Dorothy held the sheet modestly to her breasts.

Toby, a small fox-faced man in his late twenties, followed behind Richard, a pile of discarded garments flung across his arm. He and Dorothy had already cultivated a hearty dislike for each other. With Toby the feeling was impersonal – he despised most women.

Dorothy frowned. She felt strangely small and vulnerable, sitting up in bed with only the sheet to cover her nakedness, but Toby's expression held no acknowledgement that she was even female. He hesitated, looked questioningly at his master who responded with a terse nod. Dorothy wondered irritably if they always acted in mime whenever a third person was present. It shot through her mind that their dour performance would be greeted with guffaws at the court's Christmas revels.

As soon as they were alone, Richard began strolling round the room, snuffing all but two of the candles. He seemed pleasantly preoccupied – not in the least discouraged by Dorothy's hostile silence. At last he turned and casually approached the bed. Her control suddenly snapped.

She had intended to stay haughtily composed and aloof but the sight of him coming to claim her body as if it were a trophy he didn't particularly value but accepted as his due set her teeth on edge. She knelt up in the bed, her hands still gripping the edge of the sheet and shouted: 'No!'

He stopped half-way across the room. The sheer bewilderment on his face was almost comical, but Dorothy had never been further from laughter.

'What did you say?' At last he'd found his voice.

'Keep away from me.' Dorothy's face suddenly hardened into a cold mask. In that moment she looked remarkably like her grandmother.

'We are husband and wife,' he reminded her with a sardonic little smile, planting one hand on his hip.

'Not by *my* choosing! If you want your sport, ask the maids. Who knows, you might find one of them willing.'

'Yes, and a heap more appealing than the frozen slab of cod in front of me,' Richard retorted. 'But I never shirk my duty, madam.'

He continued towards her, then took off his robe and tossed it across the foot of the bed. Dorothy gasped. It hadn't even occurred to her that he was naked beneath it. He was grinning maliciously because he had set her at a disadvantage. The grey eyes glittered with cunning, suddenly reminding her of the wolf in the fairytale that used to thrill and terrify her as a little girl. Her bemused stare took in the wide shoulders and the solid-looking chest covered with dark-gold curling hairs, the long heavily muscled thighs with that gross appendage of flesh lying between them. She looked up very quickly into his face, saw the smugness that he rarely bothered to hide, and cold primitive rage swamped her.

'Don't touch me.' The words emerged in a savage hiss between her teeth.

Richard felt the quick anger flare inside him, but for once it was tinctured with amusement. So the whey-faced little bitch wanted to fight! Arms folded on his chest he regarded her, as arrogant in nakedness as he was in full court-dress.

'Why, are you still unwell?' His mouth twisted into an ugly sneer.

Dorothy smiled as if he were an ignorant ploughboy who didn't know any better. 'You've no idea who I am, have you?'

'I know that you're a misbegotten bastard, but I don't know why you give yourself these airs, nor will I tolerate them for much longer.'

He was about to fling back the covers and climb into bed beside her when she recoiled to the far edge, panting like a woman in childbirth.

'I won't lie with you. Not tonight – not ever. I – I am more nobly born than you. And I won't have you in my bed.'

For the first time Richard felt vaguely uneasy. He noticed the way her eyes were burning in her chalk-white face. Her hair had swung forward like an orange curtain, swirling around her bare shoulders. Outlined against the dim candle-light and a swag of violet shadows, she looked like a creature not quite of this world.

He found himself mentally retracing the past few days. Ever since they'd left Woodstock she had done nothing but belittle him with scornful looks and those spiky little remarks, made all the more lethal by the almond-sweet voice in which they were delivered.

A small part of him wanted to laugh now as she stared up at him with such hatred and desperation, but something restrained him. He even wondered if she were completely sane. Certainly her boast that she was of illustrious birth suggested derangement or at least a fevered imagination. Everyone knew that her mother was a whore who had lifted her skirts for any man who smiled at her and, what was more, he would prove it to her. He would enjoy smashing her pretty, little-girl illusions. Yet for the moment he wanted nothing more than to get away from her.

He reached down for his robe and, as an afterthought, gave the mattress a hard punch. Dorothy let out a sharp, startled cry.

'Keep your virgin bed, then – for now. Anyway, I'd as soon lie with a toad.'

He was gone then, the door banging behind him, to sleep in another part of the house – she didn't know where. She waited, every nerve tensed, but he didn't return and after a while she slid down between the sheets, then pressed both fists to her mouth. She felt far too miserable to enjoy her victory.

'I'll still have to face him tomorrow. There'll be thousands of tomorrows. Sweet Jesus, why didn't you let me die with my mother?'

Then she thought of Cicely, who had lain in this very bed as a bride. Thought of her not as the terrifying old woman who had overshadowed her childhood but as the girl she must once have been – proud and lonely, lying beside a husband who wept for another man when he thought she was asleep. Small wonder that Cicely Marsh had feared vulnerability above all things.

Early next morning as dawn tinged the sky with rose and lemon hues, she woke to the sound of Richard's voice shouting impatiently for Toby. His boots pounded along the gallery, going straight past her door without stopping, then faded in the direction of the staircase. Meanwhile the dogs were yelping in demented chorus and there was a mighty crash downstairs in the hall as the household came to life.

Slowly Dorothy drew herself up in the bed, pushing the pillows into a mound behind her. Almost at once last night's dread came creeping back, filling her throat and sticking to her ribs. She began to pray – not very optimistically – that she wouldn't have to see him.

It seemed that her prayer was answered. Before she was up and dressed for Mass, Richard and Toby had gone down to the stables, chivvied the grooms and ridden away in a spluttering cloud of dust.

He was gone for three weeks and in that time no word came from him, nor did it occur to Dorothy to worry. In any case, she considered him a match for the most vicious assailant, was convinced that a tougher, more self-sufficient man than her husband had never breathed. Besides he had Toby, who looked capable of coolly slicing any would-be robber or murderer to collops.

And yet, though she didn't love Richard, his absence gave her no peace. He wasn't the man to ride meekly out of her life simply because she wanted him to. Like a leopard he would rest for a while, then stalk her down without pity. She had seen the hard blaze of malice in his eyes that night and now realized that this was no petulant schoolboy but a wily vindictive man with an instinct for his own survival.

Meanwhile, as the new mistress of Greenthorpe, she was expected to shoulder her responsibilities and, aided by Alban and Joanna, she was quick to learn.

At first the prospect of running her own household terrified her and she was convinced that she'd bungle things hopelessly, but as the days passed she became more sure of herself. Her fears that the servants would exploit her youth and inexperience also proved groundless. They had always had a rather casual affection for her and now they came to respect her, for she drove herself as hard as she did all of them. Moreover, she had Joanna as her mainstay. By now, most of them had learnt the folly of pitching themselves against Joanna.

Every morning after breakfast she went directly to the little office next to the winter parlour, to plan the day's work with Alban. Then she visited the kitchen and the pantry, the bakehouse, brewhouse and dairy. She checked the accounts, supervised the laundry and cleaning, ordered the meals and the household supplies. As token of her new status, she wore the great bunch of household keys at her girdle. Secretly she rather enjoyed the feeling of bustling capability and importance which they gave her.

Her favourite hours were those spent in the stillroom. Surrounded by the rich scents of hanging clusters of herbs, spices and dried pumpkins, she would pore frowning over her grandmother's recipe book. Here lay the secret of Lady Cicely's lilac soap and rose-water, her remedies for a variety of ailments, all penned in that familiar spiked hand that, even now, could make Dorothy's stomach flutter nervously. In years to come, Dorothy Westbrooke would be sought out for her herbal recipes but as a seventeen-year-old bride she was like a little girl solemnly playing with her mother's cosmetics.

One cool, windy afternoon in September she was in the little downstairs storeroom with one of the maids, sorting through a chest of bed-linen, when she heard the smart clatter of hoofs outside in the courtyard. Her heart jerked, then seemed to swell in her chest, tightening the edges of her bodice until it hurt to breathe. She knew that it could only be Richard.

Muttering something to the girl, she caught up her skirts, turned and ran up the three steps into the passage, then up the curving stone stairs. On and on she ran till she reached her bedchamber.

Joanna was sitting beside the open casement, crooning a doleful love-song to herself as she sewed a button on to one of Dorothy's shoes. She looked up in alarm as the door burst open.

'Why, hinny, what is it? You look as though you'd been chased by a bull.'

'He's back,' Dorothy panted, slumping against the door as if all the strength had been poured out of her muscles. 'Richard's back and I know he's going to send for me.'

But he didn't – he sent for Joanna.

The hours crawled by, mercilessly slow. Dorothy swept up and down the length of the room, frantic as a caged squirrel. Suppertime passed and still Joanna didn't come. Nobody came. It was as if she had died and they had already forgotten her.

What if that monster had hurt Joanna? The thought wheeled around in her brain like a seagull, yet it made no sense. It was she, Dorothy, whom he hated. Keeping Joanna from her was just a spiteful ploy to make her seek him out. Or perhaps Joanna was enjoying a 'thimbleful' of ale with Alban and both had forgotten the time.

By nightfall her nerves were frayed to exhaustion and she felt swimmy-headed with hunger. Silently cursing Joanna, she undressed in the dark, her fingers tearing irritably at buttons and laces. Still telling herself she was foolish to feel so uneasy, she slipped naked between the cool lawn sheets and, in spite of everything, fell asleep within minutes.

An hour later she woke, her heart cantering, as the door slammed with a deafening crash that seemed to shake the walls. She started up, pushing the hair out of her eyes, then saw Richard standing inside the door, holding a candle. He looked dirty and dishevelled and this shocked her even more than his violent entry. There was a claret stain on the front of his shirt, his red-silk hose was streaked with dried mud. He apparently hadn't shaved since the day he'd left. And even from this distance Dorothy caught the reek of wine and stale sweat.

He began to sway on his heels while a crafty smirk slowly spread across his face. Dorothy was terrified that he'd drop the candle on to the rushes.

'So,' he drawled, his eyes shifting to her face. 'You want to be a virgin wife. That's very unkind of you, sweetheart. Don't you care for my feelings?'

'And don't *you* have any pride – coming here when you know you're unwelcome? Or have you had enough of drinking and whoring – in London?'

For a moment he appeared nonplussed and she knew her guess had been accurate. Then his expression changed and his lips stretched back in a snarl.

'That's enough!' He started heavily towards the bed, set the candle down on the table with exaggerated caution, then turned to face her. 'The time for playing the high-born bitch is over.'

One hand reached down and quickly jerked the covers from her. She let out a sharp protesting cry, burrowing into the sheet in a futile attempt to hide her nakedness while his eyes trailed tauntingly over her body.

'What a bony nag we have here!' He slapped her thigh roughly, making her jolt like a puppet. 'Still, you'll serve to give me a son. Come, Dorothy.'

He leaned half-way across the bed, his hot sour breath searing her face. Then he seized her beneath the armpits and began dragging her towards him. She dug her nails into the sheet, her whole body tensed, resisting him. Her face was still haughtily forbidding even in that moment of terror, and the sight of it maddened him. Without warning he drew back his arm and hit her viciously on the cheekbone.

'Keep still, you little whore. I know you for what you are.'

Dorothy stared uncomprehendingly, her pupils dilated like glossy black beads. Then she began to weep with the pain and shock of the blow. One hand cupping her face she rocked from side to side, the tears pouring ceaselessly into her neck.

'Such a high-born lady.' Richard loomed over the bed, jeering like the nursery bully who has just smashed his playmate's favourite toy. 'Too good to lie with a Westbrooke. Who are you really, Dorothy – the spawn of some peasant archer in Richard Plantagenet's army, or worse? Maybe we shall never know.'

Then he turned and went stumbling from the room, but she didn't even lift her head to watch him go. She could only lie there in the ashes of her pride, the tears growing cold on her cheeks.

Minutes later he was back, half-dragging a protesting Joanna. Dorothy began to think that she was trapped in a nightmare – senseless but insistently terrifying.

The two figures stood framed in a pale frizz of candlelight, Richard big and powerful as a devil, Joanna looking somehow shrunken and defenceless, her shoulders sagging, her cheeks mottled with crying. But Joanna never cried!

'What is this?' Startled out of her self-pity she sat up, dragging the sheet about her. 'Joanna, what's happened?'

'Tell her.' Richard gave his companion a slight push in Dorothy's direction. 'Tell my wife the enthralling tale you told me this evening. As you can see, she's in need of amusement.'

He looked like a man about to settle down to a satisfying meal after a day's hunting. Dorothy's eyes swung from him to Joanna, but the nurse refused to look at her.

'I beg you to leave us, sir.' Joanna made a pitiful attempt to recapture her dignity. 'This will be easier if you aren't here.'

'But I wish to stay.' Richard leaned back against the door, barring the way for both women if either decided to flee. For once he was smiling almost pleasantly.

'Please, sir.' Joanna sounded as if she might start crying again. Suddenly Dorothy couldn't bear it – couldn't bear to see Joanna so humble and helpless. It was like watching the walls of Greenthorpe crumble to dust before her eyes. Still wrapped in the sheet, her hair trailing down her back in a snarled red mass, she rose and walked towards the big broken doll that was Joanna.

'Come, Joanna, tell me.' She laid a hand on the thick, brown-sleeved arm that used to rock her to sleep. She even managed to smile, thinking that now she was the nurse, Joanna the child. Still Joanna wouldn't meet her eyes.

'I lied to you, hinny.' Her voice sounded blank and dull, the way a dead woman's might have sounded. 'I lied all those years ago – about Mistress Alice and the King.'

'What are you trying to say?' Dorothy was surprised at how cool and clear her own voice sounded. In her mind she was thinking: I must ask her to get some witch hazel for my face, it feels bruised.

'I had to do it. My Lady Cicely – she was so hard on you. I wanted you to think you were special. God save me, I never meant to hurt you, hinny. You were like my own child.'

'Joanna, of all the gibberish. . . ! You told me—'

'I was wrong.' At last the red-rimmed grey eyes looked directly into hers. The lashes were clumped into wet brown spikes, giving her the look of a sorrowful rabbit. 'I should have said nothing, then it wouldn't have come to this.'

'She means that the slut who gave birth to you didn't stop to ask your father's name before opening her legs,' Richard crowed. 'It's really very simple.'

Dorothy ignored him. Her eyes were still fastened on Joanna's face, searching – pleading – for some sign that this was a preposterous joke.

'He threatened you, didn't he?' she said very softly. 'He forced you to come here with this wicked lie.'

'It's no lie, hinny. And I'm sorry for it.' Joanna turned away and began to cry silently into her cupped hands, the tears dribbling out through her fingers.

'Who can we trust if not those who are supposed to care for us?'

Again Dorothy gave no sign that she'd heard him. Her brain was reeling in a crazy broken galliard as it tried to make some sense of Joanna's words. However, only two things seemed clear. She was a nobody and Joanna had lied to her.

She opened her mouth to speak but no sound emerged. It was like one of those nightmares when you tried to scream but your voice was trapped in your throat.

As she stood there, the rushes digging into the soles of her bare feet, the room seemed to heave, then tilt upon its side. The shadows curled like lazy snakes before her eyes and she could hear Richard's low-pitched laughter. It sounded muffled and dim, as if he were in the next room. Then she stretched out one arm as if to clutch at something solid and fell forward in a dead faint.

CHAPTER SIX

1525

The great hall at Ryland Place in Sussex was festooned with greenery and fat white garlands. The tapestries, well-scrubbed with orris and sprinkled with lavender-water, barely stirred in the mid-July heat. The long tables, grouped in the shape of a horseshoe, looked as if they were sagging beneath the weight of Lady Houghton's best silver. There were no fewer than sixty dishes, including baked swan, sturgeon, peacocks stitched back inside their gilded feathers, pheasants and chickens cooked in spiced wine, cinnamon-custard tarts, jellies and fruit pies drenched in honey. Most impressive of all was the moated castle, made from glistening spun sugar, which formed the centrepiece.

An army of servants had toiled throughout the night, for the most part uncomplaining – after all, there hadn't been a wedding at Ryland Place for more than twenty years. Lady Agnes Houghton, sweating inside her tightly laced lemon-taffeta gown, reached for a chicken wing and began to chew rather greedily, her expression unmistakably smug. So far everything had gone smoothly –more smoothly than she'd dared hope. It had been worth the weeks of headaches and raging tension, the bitter quarrels with her steward when the excitable little man, reduced to tears by Agnes's chivvying, had threatened to pack his bags and leave Ryland Place for ever. Now at last she could relax and silently congratulate herself on the day's success. Gervase hadn't disgraced her by weeping or vomiting. (His nervous stomach was a curse and one of the numerous grievances she bore against him.) And the Westbrooke girl had been unexpectedly docile – Agnes had feared trouble from *her*!

Guests from all over England had swelled the little chapel and were now enjoying the feast that she'd spent so many tedious, quill-chewing hours planning. Most of them belonged to the enormous Houghton clan, but no matter – tonight Ryland Place would be packed full with them, with the great barn converted into a makeshift dormitory for the extra servants.

Eleven-year-old Molly was still sulking because she had to share a bed with two strange cousins. Agnes frowned at her eldest daughter, her annoyance returning like a tidal wave. The girl had already received a stinging slap across the head that morning for actually daring to mutter some complaint not intended for her mother's ears.

'We will all have to suffer some inconvenience,' she'd told the weeping child. 'Now stop blubbering unless you want a good whipping.'

Agnes herself was to sleep in the bed that she'd shared with Sir John ever since her own wedding night and would suffer no inconvenience whatsoever, but that was beside the point. One had a duty to crush the smallest hint of rebellion in one's children. She wiped her chin with a fur-trimmed cuff, lifted her wine-glass to her lips, then settled back to study her guests. In spite of their rich clothes and jewels, their air of well-bred confidence, she believed that she knew most of their secrets almost as well as they did themselves. Certainly this was true of the family that had become allied to hers today. There was Giles Standish, red-faced and petulant beside his wife, the beautiful Kathryn. At the sight of them, Agnes nearly burst into laughter. They were an incongruous pair, Kathryn so smooth and elegant beside her plump, balding, belligerent little husband whose head barely reached her ear. Giles's glass had been refilled several times but he was loudly declaring that he was 'damned parched'. Kathryn was staring at the table-cloth, the delicate pink tinging her cheeks. She looked tired; shadows stained the skin beneath her eyes like fresh bruises and her mouth had a pinched look. Agnes wondered if she were pregnant, then scornfully dismissed the idea. God's blood, but these Westbrooke women seemed a barren lot – Kathryn of the empty womb and Dorothy of the many dead babies. Would it be the same story with Alicia – Alicia who looked like a younger version of her mother?

Agnes's kohl-ringed grey eyes were narrowed into hard slits as they suddenly shifted to Dorothy. People were always gushing about her charm and beauty even though she had long since passed that luminous girlhood. Agnes, who was neither charming nor beautiful, saw only a weak fool.

Sir Richard, alert as ever, raised his glass to salute her. In anyone else the gesture might have seemed a friendly courtesy but Agnes knew better. She was the first to look away.

Today she had finally admitted to herself that she hated Richard Westbrooke. Somehow his presence had managed to cast a mocking shadow over the festivi-ties while his very elegance was a taunt in itself. The smooth-brushed hair, the splendid blond height, even the plain cut of his jade silk doublet and high-necked shirt, all seemed contrived to make the Houghtons look overdressed, even faintly ridiculous. But there was another reason – one that she scarcely dared to contemplate for it rankled like a red weeping ulcer on her soul.

A secret, shameful part of her had always wondered what it would be like to be in bed with him; to feel his hands moving over her body, his thighs hard against hers while she gasped and writhed beneath him and learnt what it was to yield to a will stronger than her own – something she had never experienced and would only tolerate in bed. Many years ago she had tried to find out.

She stared into the distance, feeling the surging tide of humiliation, as fierce and relentless as it had been on that crisp winter night almost nineteen years ago. Every detail was still etched upon her memory, clear and sharp as a diamond.

She and her husband had left their baby son Gervase at home with the servants while they set out on a visit to Greenthorpe Manor. When they arrived, Agnes was furious to learn that their hostess was in labour and the entire household in a flurry of panic. Standing on the stone steps in their riding clothes, they could faintly hear Dorothy's cries.

'The baby wasn't due for another three weeks,' Richard fretted. Agnes guessed that his anxiety was for the unborn child rather than for Dorothy. She herself wasn't surprised – that simpering ninny had probably miscalculated her dates!

'There's nothing you can do except wait,' she said firmly, making it clear that baby or no baby she expected to be invited into the house. John was frowning at her but as usual she ignored him.

They were just sitting down to supper when a maid came to tell them that Lady Dorothy had given birth to a daughter. Agnes noticed that Richard looked very glum at the news, and was unaccountably pleased. He didn't even go to see his wife and their newborn child and eventually an indignant Joanna brought baby Kathryn downstairs, thickly swaddled against the early December cold. Richard barely glanced at the tiny mewing creature before ringing for more wine.

'You have a fine daughter, Richard,' Agnes remarked as the door closed on Joanna's stiff, offended back. 'Next time it's sure to be a son.' She spoke in a forced, bright tone which indicated that she thought it highly improbable. Richard glowered at her.

'I hope you give me a daughter as pretty next year, sweetheart.' John laughed uncomfortably. 'I've always wanted a little girl to pet and spoil.'

Later Agnes lay restlessly beside her snoring husband, sleep eluding her. Perhaps it was the strong wine or her own unsatisfied yearnings that prompted her to abandon all prudence, for minutes later she crept out of the guest chamber – which had been the solar in Lady Cicely's time – and went padding down the dark empty gallery, clutching her robe close about her. A ribbon of light glimmered beneath one of the doors. She hesitated for barely a second before turning the handle.

Richard was lying on top of the rumpled counterpane, still in his shirt and

hose. An empty glass lay overturned beside him but she saw at a glance that he
was far from drunk. That made it harder to forgive him for what happened next.

Not in the least flummoxed by her sudden appearance in his bedchamber, he
looked up and gave the chilly impersonal smile that both maddened and
intrigued her. She felt her nipples harden while her skin began to prickle with
longing under the thick blue robe.

'How is poor Dorothy?' She advanced towards the bed with a predatory
expression which might have alarmed a more timid gentleman. One hand
reached out and began stroking the bed curtain while she waited for his reply.

The handsome face below her darkened. He was idly twirling the glass stem
in one hand but every muscle was tensed with alertness. Agnes wondered if he
was ever off his guard, even when he was asleep. She remembered the blissfully
snoring oaf in the bed that she'd so hastily vacated and felt her eyelids grow
heavy with passion.

'Dorothy's well enough. It's not her first lying-in, as you know.'

'Ah yes,' she purred silkily. 'Your little sons. I'd almost forgotten.'

Richard scowled but made no reply. Meanwhile Agnes was slowly removing
her robe, talking to him all the while.

'It is a tragedy that you have no heir, Richard – a lusty man like you. Why,
there can't be a woman in England who'd be left with an empty belly after a
tumble with you. But to what avail?' She looked directly into his eyes, then smiled
rather cruelly. 'That little milksop will never give you a boy and you know it.'

The robe slithered to the floor in a heap. Richard's eyes went over her body,
noting the heavy pendulous breasts streaked with blue veins, the dimpled thighs,
the ruffles of fat round her stomach. Still he said nothing. Agnes began to shiver
deliciously. She bent down to kiss him, one hand lightly caressing his cheek. It
was only then that she realized he was almost choking with laughter, the tears
streaming from the corners of his eyes and running down his face.

How she got back to her own bed she could never afterwards remember but the
sound of Richard's laughter haunted her for years. She had insisted on leaving
Greenthorpe the very next day without a word of explanation to her bewildered
husband. Several weeks after that visit she became pregnant with her son,
Thomas. As her belly burgeoned and she grew tired and unwieldy and everything irritated her unendurably, she often thought how very nearly this child had
been sired by Richard Westbrooke and the stark horror of that night would rush
over her again like a sheet of icy rain.

Thoughts of bed had reminded her of her eldest son. She looked across the
table at him. As always the sight of him made her spine stiffen with loathing.
What ailed the boy? This was his wedding day, the day for which she had worked
like an ox to make a joyous occasion, and tonight he would take his pretty young

bride to bed. Yet there he sat, crouched miserably over the table, his eyes fixed on the sugar castle as if it might contain an asp. Sheer anxiety had produced a livid crop of pimples on his face. Worse still, he looked as if he might dissolve into a puddle of tears at any moment.

He wouldn't dare! Agnes's fat, ring-clamped fingers clutched the table-edge. Rage tightened her face until she thought it would burst. Wedding day or no, she would box his ears and a pox on what people thought!

As if feeling the intensity of his mother's gaze, Gervase looked up. All at once his face turned white beneath the purple spots. He swallowed, then hastily looked away.

Agnes smiled grimly. He could never look her directly in the face for long but she'd seen the light of fear in his eyes and was mollified.

The girl seated beside him was white and silent, picking at her food. She looked bored rather than nervous – Agnes might have forgiven her *that*! – and gazed into space as if oblivious to her surroundings.

'A fine pair we have here!' Agnes snorted to herself. Disgusted, she turned to talk to the brother-in-law on her left.

Alicia's head was swimming in a haze of unreality. Certainly Gervase didn't seem real. As they'd knelt together before Father Charles, the family chaplain, at the Altar, he'd slipped her a look of pure dread, then proceeded to ignore her for the rest of the day.

Paul, the resident player-fool, was singing a ballad about a knight's love for an unattainable lady. His voice was rich and clear, pulsing with strong emotion.

Involuntarily, Alicia began to shiver. Despite the summer sunshine beating in through the windows she suddenly felt so cold, her silver wedding gown might have been made from cobwebs.

As the song died on a quivering note, there was a tumult of applause. Then all at once the hired musicians in the little gallery overhead struck up a gusty tune. They had been instructed to keep playing until the last guest stumbled off to bed at daybreak. Gervase led her on to the floor where they were soon joined by other couples. He danced surprisingly well but Alicia didn't bother to compliment him. She was watching Lady Bess who, rosy with rich food and wine and none too steady on her feet, was weaving a path through the crowd. Her eldest son Roger had come as her escort, for Sir Walter was busy overseeing the sheep-shearing and had been unable to leave Ashby Place. At twenty-eight, Roger's face was as impudently boyish as ever. He held his mother gently by the elbow so that no one would notice he was supporting her.

Lady Bess had grown very fat, her face showing all the signs of good living. However, as the dancing began she suddenly became very dignified, like a child on her best behaviour. Alicia wanted to giggle as she dropped a curtsy, her face as solemn as an abbot's. She was glad that Bess was here – at least *she* was real.

Later – much later – they put her to bed in a hot stuffy room heavily scented with damask water. Women were clustering and flustering around her, plucking at her hair and her clothes until she wanted to scream with annoyance. Her eyes picked out Lady Bess, who was strumming on a silver hairbrush as if it were a lute. She wondered if Bess was remembering her own wedding night.

Nanty was laying out her new satin robe, her face pink with excitement as she draped it carefully across the foot of the bed. To Nanty, all weddings were joyful occasions and for the moment she had completely forgotten all the tears and rages that had preceded this one. Meanwhile Alicia stood wearily in the middle of the room while the women stripped her of her ivory-damask kirtle, her stockings and silver-buckled garters. Someone bundled her nightgown over her head and there were shrieks of mock-dismay when they saw how flimsy it was.

'Come Lissa.' Kathryn took her hand and led her over to the *toilette* table in the corner. Alicia sat down, numbly obedient, then Kathryn began brushing her hair. Her hands were as deft and gentle as if they were arranging a bowl of roses. Suddenly she bent down, pretending to smooth a wayward curl.

'You're the most beautiful bride I ever saw,' she whispered encouragingly.

But Kathryn, with her moonlight-coloured hair and spun-glass features, was more beautiful than Alicia – she always had been.

She stood up and was about to approach the bed when a plump little fair-haired girl came over and shyly pressed something into her hand. She was Lucy Vernon, Tom Houghton's betrothed. Tom was the only member of her new family whom she hadn't met yet, for he was still completing his education abroad. Before Alicia could thank her, Lucy darted away in a swirl of pink silk and dark-honey hair.

Father Charles, a rosy-faced dumpling of a man, had blessed the marriage bed and now the room was beginning to fill. Alicia, sitting up in the big bed, felt something close to terror as the drunken crowd stumbled towards her. Their grinning faces, hot and glistening with sweat, looked almost evil in the light from the dripping candles.

And now Gervase, blinking like a tall, bashful rabbit in his linen nightshirt, was being pushed into bed beside her. She thought that everyone would leave the room then, but they seemed to be waiting for something. For some reason her thoughts went back to an afternoon when she'd gone to a bear-baiting with some of her friends at court. There was the same glee, the same hungry, taut excitement that she'd sensed in the crowd just before the dogs were unleashed upon the wretched roaring creature staked out in the middle of the pit.

Sir John Houghton, who was rather drunk by this stage, started to sing a bawdy song but a warning glare from his wife brought it hiccuping to a close.

At last they all tripped away, laughing and calling advice as they went, to finish their revelling downstairs. Suddenly Alicia was alone with the nervous boy who was now her husband. She found that she couldn't look at him.

The candles had guttered into waxy little puddles. Beyond the window the indigo sky was faintly streaked with silver, promising that dawn wasn't far away.

'What have you got in your hand?' Gervase spoke to her for the first time.

Alicia started. She had forgotten about Lucy's gift and now she let out a little cry of pleasure as she examined the square of delicate white silk embroidered with pansies and fleurs-de-lis.

'Ah yes,' he said in a bored voice when she'd explained. 'She told me she was making something for you, so that you'd feel welcome.'

'She's very gifted.' Perhaps if she could keep him talking about Lucy's needlework skills, he might forget the reason why they were both here! Then she saw, with a sinking heart, that he was already reaching across the bed for her.

It was as she had so often imagined it, only worse. The wet lips, the hands slippery cold as twin haddocks crawling beneath her nightgown, over her naked body. A strong wave of revulsion rushed over her but she dared not protest. After all, he had the right to handle her in any way he chose, and they both knew it. His fingers were digging into her breasts, pinching the soft flesh under her armpits, and she willed herself not to cry out. It was as if he wanted to remind her that she belonged to him now.

But I belong to nobody except myself.

It was that thought alone that kept her mind from toppling into blackness. By shielding her innermost self from the touch of another human, she would always be strong and complete. That was the bitter secret her great-grandmother Cicely had learnt all those years ago – it was the essence of Cicely's strength. But she would be even stronger than Cicely, for Cicely had given herself to Greenthorpe.

She could faintly hear the whining of music, the odd gust of laughter downstairs in the hall. She gulped back the sharp little knot of tears that had risen into her throat. If she started crying now, she knew she wouldn't be able to stop.

Breathing noisily, Gervase rolled on top of her, banging his elbow hard against her jaw so that this time she nearly *did* scream aloud with the pain.

'There is usually some pain the first time but it doesn't last,' Kathryn had told her. 'And afterwards comes the most exquisite pleasure imaginable.'

There was no pain, no pleasure – there was nothing. After a few minutes of agitated jabbing between her thighs, Gervase suddenly flung himself to the far side of the bed.

Alicia lay very still, her brain swimming. She didn't know what to think. Inexperienced though she was, she knew that the act had not been completed. Was it because he found her unattractive? She pouted to herself in the dark, her vanity piqued. Then she remembered how he had pestered her, hungered for her, all but stripped her naked with his eyes. No, there was no doubt about his desire.

There was the sound of a gasping sob beside her, then all at once the mattress began to shake.

'Gervase, what is it?' Alarmed, she propped herself up on one elbow to look at him. Perhaps he was ill. She wondered whether she should call for help.

'Nothing!' He was lying face down on the pillow, pale brown head burrowed into his arms. Then: 'It's always like this for me. I thought it might be different with you but – maybe I wanted you too much.'

'So I am to blame?' Her voice was an icy whiplash.

'No – I mean, I don't know.'

He rolled on to his side, curling up like a miserable puppy in the rain.

Alicia stared at the thin heaving back in disgust. A beggar in the street would have more pride! She couldn't pity him – his snivelling and snuffling were an insult to her. Suddenly she couldn't bear it another moment. Reaching across for her robe, she slid quickly out of bed and, without a word or even a backward glance at the weeping boy, went to sit at the window.

The house lay blanketed in silence, all the guests having at last gone to bed. Down in the courtyard one of the musicians was relieving himself in the fountain. Normally the sight would have had her giggling hysterically but now she barely glanced at him. She felt nothing but emptiness – the ash-grey emptiness that later brings despair.

To the end of her days she would be entombed in Ryland Place with a weak, self-pitying husband and his dreary family. She saw the long years stretched before her in a dark, plodding trail that led only to the grave. There would be no warmth or laughter in her life, only sterile loneliness. No one in this rambling vault of a house would care what happened to her, or whether she was happy. Not quite sixteen, her life was over.

The musician, having finished at the fountain, was returning briskly to the hall, tugging at his codpiece as he went. Alicia glanced over at the bed but no sound came from it. Like a little boy, Gervase must have cried himself to sleep. He lay sprawled on his back, his mouth slightly open and one arm flung out across the pillow beside him. He looked so young and defenceless that, for the first time, she felt a tiny flicker of compassion. She turned back to the window, dragging her knees up under her nightgown and resting her cheek on them.

The morning grew soft with bird-song as the sun climbed steadily higher in the sky. She was so tired, her body felt like a dull, sagging weight but still she sat there, arms wrapped round her knees, staring out at the brightening dawn.

It was a garden much like other English gardens at that time. Embraced by cherry-brick walls, it lay crouched beneath the terrace at the rear of the house. There were fruit trees splayed along the southern wall and the lawns, fringed by neatly paved walks, sparkled like sheets of green glass in the sunlight. The rectangular flower-beds were bordered with rosemary, thyme and marjoram. The flowers were drooping now, crumpled like dirty napkins on their stems.

Armed with a leatherbound volume of *Aesop's Fables* which she had filched from John Houghton's library, Alicia hurried down the path to the pretty little yew arbour that she had marked as her own. Already she thought of it as her sanctuary, the one place she could go for solitude and peace.

The morning was as warm and pale as butter-milk but there was a heavy stillness in the air. A faint bruising of cloud had gathered above the timbered roof of Ryland Place, threatening a late-summer storm. She settled herself on the bench, tucking her skirts beneath her. Yet even as she opened the book in her lap, she knew she wouldn't be able to concentrate. Still, it was quiet and restful here and perhaps the storm would hold off till late afternoon, for the thought of being cooped indoors was depressing.

There were many things to depress Alicia these days. Her marriage was six weeks old and already it was clear that something was very wrong. She never saw Gervase during the day, for he rode out on his stallion, Black Ruby, soon after breakfast and seldom returned before dusk, his face tired and streaked with dust. He evaded all her anxious questions and now what little concern she'd felt had died. She knew he was avoiding her and was secretly relieved.

At night, in the dark humid cave of their bed, it was a different story. As soon as the candles were doused, he would fall upon her like a ravening beast, clawing at her breasts and thighs while he tried to plunge himself into her body. Lying beneath him, tense and silent, Alicia would feel sick with humiliation. It was as if he regarded her body as a complex puzzle that could be solved if only he persisted. Always, always it ended in stark failure with Gervase rolling away to his own side of the bed without a word. Then they would lie staring into the darkness, the tension stretched between them like a sword. Only when she knew he was asleep could she relax.

How she'd come to dread those nightly assaults on her flesh – the striving and heaving, the grim, dry gasping that cloaked sheer despair. At first she'd hoped that some vestige of pride would make him desist but he seemed driven to prove himself and now they were both growing raw-nerved under the strain.

Almost as bad as Gervase's fumbling were Lady Agnes's coy hints. She had gleaned that all was not well with the pair and was determined to rootle out the cause.

'It's to be hoped that you soon prove with child. That is the *real* purpose of marriage, Alicia.'

'You look pale, child. I hope my son isn't tiring you out.' This was said with a coarse snigger that set Alicia's teeth on edge.

'I've never known a bridal couple spend so little time together. You mustn't neglect Gervase, my dear. A wife's first duty is to make her husband happy.'

There was menace behind the playful tone and this was not lost on the fifteen-year-old girl.

How can I get pregnant or make him happy when he's impotent in his mind and body! she wanted to scream. But she said nothing, merely smiled with infuriating sweetness at all the gibes. Besides some instinct told her that Agnes, despite her claims that she wanted a grandson, would gloat.

'Oh, I'm sorry. I didn't think anyone would be here.'

She jumped at the sound of a light girlish voice. Lucy was standing some three feet away, a plump little figure nervously fingering the strand of coral beads at her throat. She looked even more timid than usual, as if undecided whether to stay or to run back indoors.

Alicia smiled and patted the space beside her.

'Come and sit beside me. We may as well enjoy the fine weather while it holds.'

For a while the two girls sat in wary silence. Since the wedding, they hadn't exchanged more than two dozen words. Alicia, brushing a stray leaf from her skirt, realized guiltily that she'd barely given Lucy a thought. Now for the first time she found herself wondering what her life had been like as an orphan at Ryland Place – one of the family and at the same time an outsider. In some ways their positions were very similar.

'You must find Ryland Place very quiet after living at court,' Lucy ventured, with a shy glance through her lashes.

Alicia was about to agree airily, giving the impression of a worldly creature hurled into a life of rustic boredom, but there was a certain wistful sweetness about Lucy Vernon that made her change her mind.

'I was only there for a little while, visiting my sister.'

'I should like to go to court,' Lucy said. There was an almost dreamy note in her voice as she spoke. She leaned forward, hands clasped around her knees and an eager expression on her baby-round face. 'It must be very exciting – and a little frightening. They say his Grace is the most handsome man alive and there's no lady kinder than Queen Catherine. Uncle John has promised to take me there after my wedding next spring.'

'Is Tom like Gervase?' Alicia was secretly piqued by the last remark, for there had been no suggestion of *her* going to Greenwich. She was also curious about the son whose name could bring a light even to Agnes's dour countenance.

As Lucy turned towards her she was startled by the flood of emotion in her face. The grey eyes were shining like big silver buttons and when she spoke again there was a decided lilt to her voice.

'Tom is very handsome. And so full of life. He loves to laugh and joke and set the house a-flurry with his fun. Everyone loves him, even the servants.'

'And so do you,' Alicia mused with a little jab of sympathy. It occurred to her that Lucy would always live on the crumbs of love. Plain and shy as a red squirrel, she lacked the fire to captivate a wilful, dashing young man who had evidently been raised to consider himself a great prize.

Almost as if she had guessed her thoughts, Lucy hurried on.

'Of course, I've known him since we were in the nursery together, so we're good friends. Indeed, he's always treated me just like Molly and Isabel,' she finished with an uneasy little laugh that sounded more like a sob.

'If you are already fond of each other, your marriage should be happy enough,' Alicia said gently.

'He has been away for nearly two years and must have changed a great deal. Perhaps he'll find me dull.'

She sounded so hopeless and defeated that Alicia wanted to shake her. Why was she so humble? It was as if all the wit and spirit had been squeezed out of her like pumpkin-seeds.

It now dawned on her that Gervase and his sisters were just the same. Gervase she had long since dismissed as a lily-livered dog who'd scamper for cover at the first clap of thunder, but why were the girls so timorous? She realized that she had never seen them playing outside on the lawns, never heard them laugh aloud.

One evening last week she had met Molly in the long gallery and, prompted more by boredom than any compassionate instinct, had invited her to her room for a game of backgammon before bedtime. The younger girl had appeared almost vivacious for a moment, her sallow little face turning pink under the cloud of mouse-brown curls. Then before she could reply a swishing of silk heralded Lady Agnes's approach – she seemed to have appeared from nowhere – and Molly's thin little body bristled like a frightened hedgehog's. Muttering something about an unfinished cushion cover, she scurried away downstairs, leaving Alicia to stare after her in bewilderment.

'My daughter is a very diligent girl.' She'd turned at the sound of Agnes's amused voice. The woman was smiling unpleasantly, her hands cupped before her as if she had caught a spider. 'I don't believe she has a frivolous thought in her head, unlike so many of these silly young things nowadays. Come Alicia, or we'll be late for supper.'

It's Lady Agnes, she thought grimly. They're all afraid of her and she's like a black slug growing fat on their fear. Well, she doesn't frighten *me*!

'Tom isn't as gentle as Gervase.' Lucy, still in a confidential mood, broke into her thoughts again.

'Gervase gentle!' Alicia gave a terse laugh, slapping at a bee hovering perilously close to her cheek.

'There *is* gentleness in him,' Lucy persisted. 'Kindness too, if you look for it. Tom has great charm but he never learnt to be kind.'

'Maybe *you* should have married Gervase.' Alicia sounded very bitter. 'You might have pleased him better.'

Lucy eyed her uncertainly; now it was her turn to feel pity. She had admired Gervase's bride from the first, and longed to be like her. An imperious, vital beauty with the glamour of the court fresh upon her, it had appeared that nothing could daunt her, but Lucy had studied her young goddess covertly and glimpsed the insecurity lying like a fresh wound beneath the burnished curls and dainty manners.

'Alicia, are you very unhappy?' Her voice suddenly dropped an octave. Then, seeing Alicia's startled look she grew flustered. Cheeks flaming, she looked away into the distance. 'Forgive me, I didn't mean to pry. But − well, sometimes you look sort of far away, as if you're thinking of happier times. Oh dear, now I've made you angry.'

Her face was screwed up as if she were about to cry, so that she looked more like a little girl than ever.

'Don't be a goose.' Impulsively Alicia leaned over and kissed her cheek. 'Of course I'm not angry − you're the only one at Purgatory Place who has been civil to me. I'll never forget your beautiful wedding gift. But now it must be dinnertime, so we'd better go indoors.' A fresh thought struck her. 'Perhaps this afternoon we can find some pretty cloth to make you a gown for when Tom comes home.'

She laughed then, recalling that day at Greenwich when Anne Boleyn had given her the red silk. She wondered what Anne was doing now − practising her beloved dance steps, no doubt, or teasing some young man to distraction in the long gallery. She sighed. It would be good to see Anne and her other friends at court again.

As the two girls started back towards the house, the skies suddenly crackled, then split open. A cold sheet of rain swung down, instantly soaking them. Laughing helplessly, they broke into a run, each trying to drag the other up the terrace steps.

'You can go straight upstairs and take off those wet things,' Lady Agnes said, taking one look at Lucy. 'Your food will be sent up to you.'

'But Aunt Agnes, I'm fine—'

'I think that I'm the best judge of that, Lucy. And you will spend the rest of the day in bed. I won't have you catching a chill just because you were too stupid to take shelter from the rain.'

She ignored Alicia, making it clear that she blamed her for putting Lucy's health at risk.

Lucy looked as if she were about to burst into tears. Sent to bed like a naughty child! Nonetheless she had no choice but to obey, just as she always did. She curtsied and, without looking at anyone, went stiffly from the room.

Alicia felt that she should say something, even though the situation seemed unutterably absurd to her.

'It couldn't be avoided, madam – the rain came down so suddenly.'

'I must ask you not to meddle in the running of this household as long as I am still mistress here,' Agnes snapped. 'You'd do better to concentrate on your own affairs – your husband, for instance, who has once again chosen not to join us. Truly it's beginning to look as if he's avoiding you.'

'Perhaps he doesn't find the atmosphere to his liking,' Alicia said pertly, and sat down at the table.

There was a spiteful little silence. The two young girls, Molly and Isabel, seemed to shrink on the wooden bench as if willing themselves to disappear. From the corner of her eye, Alicia saw that Molly's hands were trembling.

'You *do* fuss over Lucy.' John Houghton must have been making free with the malmsey that morning, for he wouldn't normally dare to criticize his formidable wife.

'I'm anxious for her frail constitution,' Agnes snapped.

Her husband guffawed, unaware of the danger he was courting. 'God's teeth, but I never clapped eyes on a hardier creature. I don't know where you get this notion that she's delicate.'

He saw her face stiffen with fury and, too late, realized his mistake. Turning puce, he began to choke on a piece of bread and hastily gulped some wine. Eventually he was able to gasp: 'Although I know you must have your reasons.'

'Indeed I do,' Agnes said icily. 'Women, being mothers, are better at judging these matters. Perhaps when Alicia bears a baby of her own she'll understand – if she survives the ordeal with those puny hips. Sweet Jesus, Isabel, how many times must I remind you not to slouch across the table like a peasant!'

Isabel started violently; her knife went clattering to the floor. Alicia could not believe the look of terror on the child's face. Eyes bulging with panic, she was staring at her mother like a fawn cornered by a starving bear. Agnes sighed irritably.

'How did I ever come to have two such ungainly daughters? It will be a miracle in Heaven if I ever find men stupid enough to take them off my hands. Isabel!' Her voice soared up the scale. 'Go to your room. I'll attend to you later.'

Isabel pushed her plate aside, untouched. The sight of her dead-white face as she got up from the table was to haunt Alicia for weeks.

All this because Lucy and I were a couple of minutes late for dinner! she mused. God, how I despise her.

After dinner she went upstairs to her bedchamber, feeling sickened by the scene she'd witnessed. She had planned to look through her chests for some material for Lucy's new gown but found that she could think of nothing but Isabel. Restlessly she paced the length of the room, drumming her nails on her teeth, her skirts streaking over the dirty rushes. Outside the rain was slashing across the courtyard and the sky looked muddy above the rose-red chimneys. Suddenly she kicked a footstool from her path with unwarranted viciousness and went to sit on the bed.

Why had Isabel been so frightened? Did Agnes beat the children? She had a flashing vision of the small girl, cowering and twitching under a hazel switch and for a moment the room seemed to rock around her. Somehow she had the unpleasant feeling that the whole wretched business was her fault. She knew that was exactly what Agnes intended but it made no difference. She couldn't bear the idea of scared little Isabel being used as her whipping boy – or girl, she quickly corrected herself. There was nothing for it but to apologize – and hope that Agnes was satisfied her apology was sufficiently humble.

There was an unpleasant, gritty taste in her mouth as she went in search of her mother-in-law. As she neared the staircase, she heard Sir John's angry voice directly below.

'You won't lay a finger on that child, Agnes – not this time.'

'If it were left to you, she'd lie in bed all day eating roast venison and syllabub. But I'll brook no more disobedience.'

Alicia, hovering at the head of the stairs, pictured the sneer on Lady Agnes's mouth and pulled a face.

'God's teeth, madam, she's only a little girl!' Could it really be meek John Houghton bellowing like a pain-maddened bull? 'All this pother because she dropped a damned knife! I tremble to think what would have happened if it had been a gold cup!'

Alicia waited to hear his wife's reply but it never came. After a moment or two she sped back to her room on feet that were as light as puffballs, her heart singing because Isabel was not going to be punished.

And because, just for once, someone had got the better of Agnes Houghton.

Autumn's red fingertips had brushed across the land. Already the air was drenched with the clean feathery scent of freshly cut grass. In the park yellow leaves fluttered ceaselessly down from the giant elms. The days were shorter, the nights often crisp with frost. At daybreak the mists hung as heavy as cream over the lake until the pale sunlight came limping through the clouds like an apologetic guest arriving late at the breakfast table. There were sulky showers that left every blade of grass glittering like tiny jade swords. Half-way through October they grew tumultuous – swirling white curtains of water that beat against the walls of Ryland Place and thudded on the windowpanes like furious fists.

The apples had been stored away in the loft and at supper all the talk was of the killing season soon to begin. Alicia said very little as she pushed her food around on her plate. For once the thought of fat joints of beef being briskly salted down in tubs and pale slabs of pork hung to cure in the gasping chimney smoke made her feel queasy. She was as well aware as the rest how essential it was to have a bountiful store for the winter months but she was so low in spirits, she hardly cared if she ate another meal. Cold misery lived with her every waking moment, prodding at her heart with iron pincers. Her life was so lonely and joyless, and she didn't know how she could change it.

She felt trapped and helpless, cut off from her old life, not knowing if she would ever again see the people she loved. She even missed surly old Joanna and, somewhat to her surprise, missed Greenthorpe, which she'd taken so carelessly for granted, like having pretty clothes to wear, a feather bed to sleep upon, a fire to warm her in winter. During those rain-sodden weeks she often found her thoughts turning hungrily to the autumn-tinted house with its cool little orchard and the gardens that were primly beautiful as a bride. So many times in her mind's eye she rode up the wide lime avenue that in summer yielded pale, creamy-scented blossom. When the longing became almost a physical pain, she would draw the rose ring into her palm, holding it as if it were a lifeline to Greenthorpe. Whether the ring really had magical powers she didn't know but she found it a soothing ritual.

Gervase still came to her bed every night – he continued to avoid her and everyone else during the day – but he no longer tried to make love to her and was usually gone by the time Nanty came to wake her in the morning.

There was nobody in whom she could confide. She still felt like an intruder in this tense, uneasy household. Molly and Isabel seemed to regard her with awe, which should have been flattering but wasn't. As a married woman, she supposed she must seem almost middle-aged to the two girls who were still in the school-room.

Agnes, watchful as a hungry vixen, had noted her glossy-eyed pallor, the way she started at every sound, and would give her no peace.

'No sign of a baby yet?' There was a hard disapproving look when she spoke to her daughter-in-law these days. It was obvious that she believed Alicia remained barren out of sheer perversity. And yet, for all her apparent eagerness to see her belly swell, the girl had an inexplicable feeling that Agnes was pleased. The thought would not leave her, though it made no sense.

Lucy was the only one who seemed to care about her. Yet even to Lucy she was loath to confess her troubles. Pride and an obscure sense of loyalty to Gervase kept her silent.

'I'm fine,' she said firmly when the younger girl questioned her. 'Sometimes I sleep badly but it will pass.'

Lucy decided in the end that nothing worse than homesickness ailed her new friend. She herself was more fortunate than most girls, for she would continue living at Ryland Place after she and Tom were married. Although it wasn't a happy house, it was the only home she had known since she was a small girl. Change always disturbed Lucy and the very thought of going to live among strangers made her turn clammy with fright. When visitors came to the house she felt sick and miserable, and it was only her fear of Lady Agnes that stopped her from hiding in her room until she heard them ride away. She could well sympathize with Alicia, but didn't know how to comfort her. Meanwhile it seemed kinder – and decidedly more tactful – to let the subject rest. Nonetheless she was puzzled because Alicia seldom mentioned her husband. She wondered if all newly wed couples were as casual with each other. How lucky she was to have Tom! The thought of him made her want to hug herself with pleasure that was faintly tinged with apprehension. Lord, how she missed him! She couldn't remember a time when she didn't love him, didn't strive in her quiet way to win his heart.

Lucy had no conscious memory of her parents. Her father had been killed at Flodden when she was three years old and her mother, too young and childlike herself to cope with the responsibilities of a large estate, a houseful of bickering servants and a small daughter, sickened and died inside a year.

'I don't want her here. Can't you send her back?' Tom Houghton, not yet seven, had scowled at the chubby little girl sitting on his father's knee, her face half-hidden in his neck.

From that moment she had adored him, set herself to win his approval. Now he was hers in as much as they were pledged to marry next April. She had no way of knowing how he felt about it, for they had never discussed anything serious, but she hoped he was pleased. She had decided that she would make him the happiest man in England. She would never harangue him, as she'd heard Aunt Agnes harangue Uncle John. She wouldn't complain or sulk if he lost too much money at cards or overspent on his wardrobe. Like his brother Gervase, he loved to deck himself out in finery, yet in Lucy's eyes it made him seem more human, like a boastful boy instead of the charming but rather superior figure of her memories.

Perhaps they would spend part of the year at her childhood home which she'd inherited upon her father's death but had never returned to visit. She liked the idea of showing him the home of her birth – she wanted to share every part of her life with him. Above all, she wanted to give him children.

I must have a son.

The thought now possessed Alicia as it had women down the centuries; as it had Queen Catherine and her own sister. However, unlike those good women she was driven not by maternal urgings or the desire to please her husband, but by vanity. The birth of a male child, besides making her life at Ryland Place more tolerable, would give her status. It would also shake Agnes from her sleeve.

Without a son, or even a daughter, she could expect nothing but condescending pity and scorn, and she would be viewed as that most useless of God's creatures, a barren wife.

She toyed with the idea of writing to Lady Bess but it was easy to guess the reply. *Blessed Jesus, why such haste – you're still a baby yourself.* Besides, Alicia brooded as she looked out across the leaf-tossed landscape with a sharp little frown cutting between her brows, there was no point in asking people for advice. They would give you their opinion, which might be helpful but often wasn't, yet in the end the problem was still yours to solve. She would have to tackle it alone.

One night shortly after her sixteenth birthday she was sitting at her *toilette* table, wrapped in her favourite turquoise robe. Nanty was standing behind her, brushing out her hair in long, languorous strokes. For once, neither of them spoke. Nanty had an uncanny gift of sensing her mistress's moods and knew when merry chatter was likely to amuse her and when it would be unwelcome.

As Alicia gazed into the little metal mirror, her brow was creased in a frown that made her look remarkably like her father. Tonight she would have to speak to Gervase about the state of their marriage. She would be calm and reasonable, give him the chance to discuss whatever it was that disturbed him. Perhaps once the air had been cleared he would be able to be a proper husband to her, at least until she knew for certain that she was carrying his child. Whatever the outcome, they couldn't continue living together under this pall of festering silence.

At the memory of those cold, clutching hands, something stirred and writhed deep inside her, but she steeled herself to face it. There could be no girlish shrinking on her part.

She watched while Nanty went to slide the copper warming pan between the sheets, thinking how deft and sure all her movements were. It was a bitterly cold night, even for November. Outside the wind snapped and tore at the naked elm branches like an angry dog. Alicia took off her robe and slipped quickly into bed.

As Gervase opened the bedchamber door a draught shook the tapestries and put out some of the candles. Alicia stretched her toes out as far as she could reach, then curled them back towards her. They greeted each other politely, though with little enthusiasm, then Gervase went through to his closet.

'Can I get you anything, mistress?' If Nanty was embarrassed by the frigid atmosphere, she gave no sign. 'A glass of brandy-wine or another blanket, perhaps? It's fearful cold tonight.'

'No thank you, Nanty.' Alicia smiled lazily over the furred edge of the counterpane.

'I'll be away downstairs then.' Nanty bobbed a curtsy and went off to fortify herself with a glass of ale in the hall. Alicia stared after her almost wistfully. Lucky Nanty, with her uncomplicated, husband-free life!

Gervase returned, clad in his long white nightshirt. He doused the remaining

candles and got into bed beside her. As he lay there flat on his back, the covers
tucked under his chin, Alicia found herself studying him the way a stranger
might. A thin streak of moonlight probed the chink in the bed curtains, flickering over his checkbones, tipping his lashes with flecks of white. She found herself
thinking how vulnerable he looked, like a timid animal that wants to hide in the
depths of the forest. If he had been anyone else, she might have felt sorry for
him.

'Gervase, I have to talk to you.' She chewed her lip, thinking how cold and
terse her voice sounded. She had meant to be so sweetly reasonable – at first,
anyway.

'There's nothing to be said.' Gervase slid further into the bed.

'There is much to be said!' Alicia snapped, her noble resolutions instantly
crumbling. 'I am your wife yet you constantly avoid me. We've been married
nearly four months and—'

'Do you think I choose for it to be like this?' He sounded tired and bitter
beyond his years.

'I don't know. Your mother keeps telling me that I must bear a son for Ryland
Place but you've never bedded me in the true sense and I know of no other way
to get one.'

'You had little wish to be bedded before,' Gervase jeered.

Angrily she answered the gibe with one of her own.

'Most wives have a full belly before their first anniversary. No wonder your
parents are worried.'

'Why listen to them?' He stretched yawning between the sheets. 'I don't.'

'Am I so hideous in your eyes?' It cost her all her pride to ask that, despising
him as she did.

'You know that you're not.'

'Then why—'

'Leave it be, Alicia.' He turned over in the bed so that, as usual, his back faced
her.

Alicia stared in disbelief. He was going to leave it at that! The lily-livered dog
had dismissed her as if she were of no more importance than a laundress who
had mislaid one of his shirts. Cold primitive fury shook her, blotting out all finer
feelings so that she no longer cared what she said.

'Gervase, I care as little for you as you do for me, and if you left my bed
tomorrow I'd be as happy as a morris-dancer. But I'm being taunted day and
night by your damned mother because I'm not pregnant, and it's humiliating.'

Wearily he turned towards her again like a man returning to a tedious task.
Then his lips twisted into a sneer.

'Why don't you take a lover, then?'

Without pausing to think, Alicia slapped him across the mouth with all the force in her body. The sound seemed to crackle through the dark room like a whiplash while they stared at each other, startled.

All at once tears of self-pity began to roll down his cheeks, but she felt no remorse, only a weary sense of satisfaction. For a moment she thought he might hit her back, but she didn't care. She wondered if she would ever care about anything again.

'You're a vixen,' Gervase whimpered, dabbing the sheet to the corner of his mouth where one of her rings had cut him. 'No man would want to bed such an ill-natured slut. You – you're worse than my mother.'

'And you are the most contemptible creature this side of hell! Stop wiping your mouth on the sheet – the maids will think it's my virgin blood,' she finished spitefully.

Gervase was shocked, not by the words but by the sheer venom behind them. He looked at her apprehensively. The pretty mouth that had once tempted him beyond reason was pressed in a tight unyielding line, the violet eyes were as hard and bright as metal.

She was a bitch, he mused, sniffing; a cold, unfeeling bitch, just like every woman he'd ever known, except for Lucy and his small sister Isabel. Those two alone had his heart, for they gave him theirs so trustingly. They loved him as he was, never expecting him to be like his brother or any of the other swaggering hearty males whom he secretly envied and hated. Gervase returned their love unstintingly – there had been little enough affection in his life. He thanked all the saints in Heaven that he'd never loved Alicia.

A pox on women! He thought sourly, and went to spend the rest of the night in his closet.

Left alone, Alicia slowly closed her eyes, listening to the sound of her husband muttering and twisting unhappily under a mound of cloaks in the little curtained recess. This was one of those rare occasions when she felt tired and defeated, filled with morbid self-doubt. She knew that she had bungled the whole business. Kathryn would have been more delicate in her approach. Would have had him agreeing that the fault was all hers, but that with his help and understanding they could put it right.

Alicia gave the sheet a sudden sharp kick. Would she never learn? She recalled Sir Walter's advice during her early struggles with Blondel, the gelding he had given her last year.

'Easy, little one! You must give him time to trust you. A quiet word and a gentle hand will win him sooner than tears and temper.'

Perhaps, she mused, curving her body into the mattress, all men were like horses and needed to be patted and coaxed into eating sugar from your palm. Instead she had been sharp, obstructive and, worse, cruel.

Damn Gervase! He was turning her into a shrew.

*

'My son is unhappy.'

Agnes Houghton drew herself up to her full height of five feet eight and glared at her daughter-in-law, who gazed back at her almost serenely.

A great shaggy hound lay stretched before the fire where apple logs sizzled and spat like giant sausages. He raised his head to fix them with a reproachful eye, farted unceremoniously and went back to sleep.

Alicia wrinkled her nostrils for the windows were shut fast against the pinching cold of a December day and the hound was old and smelled horribly.

Agnes saw her wince and was amused. The daughter of an upstart and a bastard *would* give herself dainty airs! God's blood, what had she been thinking of, letting John persuade her that the bitch would be a suitable bride for Gervase! Tonight she would give him a tongue-lashing that would make him writhe.

Her foot began to tap on the rushes, her thinly plucked brows were slanted in a severe frown. As she stood there, she felt resentment tightening around her ribcage like a clenched fist. It displeased her to have to pitch her wits against a will that she sensed was as steely as her own. The girl was, after all, Richard Westbrooke's daughter – and therein lay Agnes's mistake, for which she now conveniently blamed her husband. During that visit to Greenthorpe four years ago, she had seen only Dorothy in her.

Her eyes went searchingly over the graceful figure before her. Like most fashionable young women, Alicia usually wore a corset. Indeed, the current style made it possible for a woman to conceal a pregnancy for several months if she wished or needed to do so. However it was startlingly clear that Gervase's wife had *lost* weight. Also, she looked white and strained, and the brilliant sheen in her eyes would have told a more intuitive person that she was fuelled by brittle nervous energy alone. Agnes merely thought her stubborn.

'My son is unhappy,' she repeated slowly, as if she were addressing a half-wit.

'I'm sorry.' Alicia's expression didn't alter.

'It is reassuring that you feel shame, but what will you do to remedy matters?'

'You misunderstand me, madam.' The small chin suddenly jerked upwards, the violet eyes turned dark with defiance. 'I'm sorry that he is unhappy but it isn't my fault and I feel no responsibility to do anything.'

'No responsibility!' Agnes's entire body seemed to swell to twice its size. Her cheeks were bulging as if they were crammed with hot sweets. 'Sweet Jesus in Heaven, he's your husband! If he is troubled, it's your duty to comfort him.'

She paused for a moment, regarding Alicia thoughtfully.

'Is it – intimacy?' Her voice had dropped to a hushed confidential note quite unlike her usual strident tone. 'Maybe all is not well in bed?'

'Madam!' Alicia could feel her face scorching. But perhaps Agnes did not intend to sound lewd. She peered at her through her lashes, trying to read her expression. The red-painted mouth was curled in an unmistakable leer.

'If there's trouble in a marriage, it's usually to be found between the sheets.' Agnes was like a large tenacious dog, gnawing at the bone of Alicia's anguish. 'Do you deny him his pleasure? I said from the first that you were a haughty snip and now—'

'I have never denied him.'

The slut was stubborn. Agnes decided to change tack. She walked across to the window and stared out at the winter afternoon that had swathed everything in a salty grey light. When she turned round again, there was a look of piety spread across her features. Alicia thought she resembled nothing so much as a fat, scheming abbess and quickly smothered a giggle.

'Alicia, I only want to help you. Above all, I want to help my boy. You have been married five months now and he's growing more miserable by the day. Does that indicate a normal marriage?'

'Gervase was miserable before he married me,' Alicia said. 'I think he has always been miserable – like your daughters.'

'What impertinence is this?' The pious expression and the syllabub-sweet tone had vanished as if by magic.

Alicia smiled. She realized that she was beginning to enjoy herself.

'Madam, you say you have noticed my husband's low spirits. Well it hasn't escaped me that Isabel and Molly creep about the house like frightened field-mice. And Molly's hands shake whenever you're in the same room.'

Agnes came to stand in front of her, her face like a cloudy red sun looming above her. For a moment Alicia's heart quailed before the murderous hatred in those grey eyes, but she willed herself to stand firm. Instinctively she knew that if she recoiled now, she would be in the woman's pudgy grasp for ever – like the others. And yet there was something unnerving about her. For the first time in her life she felt as if she were in the presence of true evil. Tiny diamonds of ice seemed to be dancing all over her body. Suddenly she felt as if she were choking and had to gulp for air.

'You little bitch, to speak like that to me!' A fleck of spittle had appeared at the corner of Agnes's mouth. 'I've a mind to have you flogged till you can no longer stand. You are just like your scurvy father.'

'Gervase says I'm like you.' Alicia's eyes were sparkling with reckless inso-lence. She had a tendency to act perversely when she felt threatened and was beginning to feel light-headed, even a little crazy. 'I think he meant it as a compli-ment,' she added sweetly, watching for the effect of her words.

She saw the puffy white hand rise through the air, only to flop down again at the sound of approaching hoof-beats outside. As one person, both women turned towards the window and saw two riders cantering round a bend in the avenue in a flurry of yellow dust.

Agnes tossed her daughter-in-law a look that boded ill for the future and went rustling from the room, all the keys and scissors jangling at her waist.

After a moment, Alicia followed her into the hall. Life at Ryland Place was so dull that even the most ordinary visitor was a welcome distraction.

She arrived in time to see a young giant go striding across the floor, encircled by a storm of leaping, excited dogs. Laughing, he pushed them away and went to clasp Lady Agnes in a bone-crushing embrace. The sullen little steward was beaming all over his face as he took charge of the saddlebags while two serving maids leaned against a pillar, mouths agape.

'Tom!' Agnes disengaged herself with a weak, protesting little laugh. Her eyes were as bright as polished coins and, to Alicia's amazement, she looked almost vivacious. 'I thought it was you but I – oh, this is wonderful! I wasn't expecting you so soon.'

She wheeled round, snapping her fingers at the maids. 'Fetch wine and cakes – and more wood for the fire.'

Pink-cheeked, they scurried away, erupting into excited giggles once they were safely behind the buttery screen.

'I couldn't stay away from home another day, Mother.' Tom Houghton went to spread his hands over the fire. Although Agnes was taller than most women, he towered over her by several inches. 'Jeb is seeing to the horses – I told him to go round to the kitchen for some food when he's done. I hope that's all right.'

'Of course,' Agnes replied mechanically. Her eyes were flickering almost wonderingly over her son as if she couldn't believe that he was actually here in the flesh.

The servants returned with a jug of cold Rhenish, two tall glasses and a platter stacked high with honey-cakes. Fresh logs were flung on to the fire. Agnes filled the glasses while Tom helped himself to a cake. A couple of dogs squatted hopefully at his feet.

Alicia stood in the shadows, still unobserved. She thought that she had never seen such a disturbingly attractive young man.

Tom Houghton was a striking figure, with hair the colour of highly polished chestnuts, falling over his collar in a gleaming mass of curls. His skin glowed clear and faintly golden with good health. Even a broken nose – the result of falling from the stable roof when he was eight – did nothing to mar his looks. A bright green cloak bordered with black fox swung carelessly from his shoulders and he exuded an air of happy confidence as if he were on excellent terms with himself and everyone else who had the good taste to admire him.

'Where is everyone?' He took a long draught of wine, regarding his mother over the rim of his glass.

'Your father had to go to one of the cottages – a leaking roof or some such nonsense. The girls are having a dancing lesson. As for poor Gervase . . .' She let out a regretful sigh, as deep as her tightly laced stays would permit. 'I'm afraid you will find him greatly changed.'

Then Tom spotted the solitary figure standing some feet away. His sudden grin was like a sunburst and as he started towards her there was frank admiration in his eyes.

'There's no need to introduce this pretty lady, Mother,' he drawled, though Agnes had had no intention of doing so. 'My new sister-in-law, isn't it?'

Agnes smiled icily. 'This is Alicia – Gervase's wife.'

Before Alicia could make her curtsy, he had taken both her hands in his, holding them in a warm, strong clasp. All at once she found herself wishing that she had changed out of her plain grey gown. Meanwhile Tom's eyes, darkly green as the sea with intriguing flecks of amber swimming close to the pupils, were sparkling with audacity as they roamed over her face and body.

'If I'd known you were so lovely, I wouldn't have stayed away for so long,' he breathed. And, before she could reply, he bent forward to kiss her full on the lips.

There was nothing improper about the kiss. In court circles, the most casual acquaintances greeted each other in the same way, yet it left Alicia shaken. As she briefly felt the warm insistence of his mouth against hers, a little shock of pleasure ran up her spine and across her shoulder-blades. She was dimly aware of Agnes glowering at her. That lady wanted more time with her favourite before surrendering him to the rest of the family, and didn't care to have him pay attention to the daughter-in-law who was now her acknowledged enemy. Alicia didn't care. Laughter was bubbling up inside her like a fountain of rare wine. It was as if she had been imprisoned in a cage of ice and steel all these months and had just been released into a warm, brightly lit room where lively music was playing. For the first time since she had ridden out from Greenwich Palace on that April morning, she felt completely alive.

CHAPTER SEVEN

1526

There was a feverish energy about Alicia as she danced with her brother-in-law on New Year's Night. All the guests sensed it, but none of them guessed the reason. To them, she was just a happy, high-spirited young bride, excited to be at a party.

For once Ryland Place radiated cheery warmth and welcome. Supper was long since over, but the hot greasy aroma of roasted boarmeat and peacock still lingered in the air. The hall had been magically transformed into an eastern temple, brilliant with sunset hues, from the scarlet of holly and Christmas roses to the lion-gold blaze in the hearth. Even the dancers looked faintly exotic, leaping and twirling in the orange torchlight. Some of the women were panting in their tight stays, their cheeks glowing pink, their eyes bright with laughter and, in some cases, belladonna. Paul the fool darted among them, his mournful dark beauty hidden behind a grotesquely painted mask.

Alicia danced on, slim and vivacious in her red-silk gown. It was the same gown that Anne Boleyn had given her nearly a year ago, and was her favourite, for it set off her charms quite dramatically. Tonight there was no mistaking its effect on Tom Houghton.

She smiled as they turned to face each other, hands briefly touching as the dance dictated. Not only was he the most handsome young man she had ever clapped eyes on but his admiration was sweet salve to the vanity that Gervase had wounded.

Tom read the message in those bright, slightly tilting eyes – reckless, defiant, daring him to love her – and returned the smile lazily. A crisp white bud of a girl, she would open like a gaudy sunflower to meet him with a passion as urgent as his own.

Tom Houghton had never questioned his power to charm any woman into bed. It was his boast that, although he didn't fall in love with his mistresses, he had never made any of them cry. If they wept over him, they did so in the arms of their maids, or their sisters, or alone. And so he went on his way, jauntily oblivious to any heartache he might have caused.

As he danced in a haze of candlelight, passion and wine, he couldn't help but be aware of Lucy, helplessly penned into a corner by a pompous aunt. The aunt was explaining the intricacies of an embroidery stitch, her beaded hood bobbing vigorously each time she stressed a point.

Another girl would have muttered some excuse and fled. And certainly any other man would have gone to his sweetheart's rescue, he mused with a grin. However he could not, would not, tear himself away from Alicia just yet, and if Lucy was growing desperate she gave no sign. She sat, hands folded quietly in her lap, embroidered slippers peeping out from beneath her skirts. Her expression was gravely respectful and she appeared to be listening attentively to every word. Suddenly he felt a ripple of warmth towards her. Lucy, his little brown rabbit!

Ever since he'd come home to Ryland Place she had been awkward and shy with him, but neither he nor anyone else was blind to the love that glowed like Advent candles in her eyes whenever he was in the room. Of course he had always been casually aware of her love, even when they were children. Like a tiny emperor, he'd accepted it as his due – and still did. He in turn was quite fond of her. The thought of their approaching marriage didn't dismay him, for he didn't expect it to change his life significantly. He would continue to indulge his every fancy, his every hunger, even if that hunger burned and raged like a plague-boil for the sister-in-law who gave every appearance of being in love with him.

Alicia didn't know if she was falling in love with Tom, but the thought of him possessed her. Somehow her dreams of him helped to ease the living mockery of her marriage.

'You're dancing on burning logs!' Gervase hissed, after Tom had led her back to his side and gone to claim a dark-eyed little girl of about thirteen who peered up at him like a saucy kitten and giggled when he bent to kiss her hand.

Alicia flung her husband a haughty look but didn't bother to answer. She no longer felt such desperate loathing for him, only lazy contempt. Twirling the miniature golden slipper that hung from her girdle, she stared out across the hall, her mouth pursed in a superior smile.

Taking her silence for assent, Gervase pressed on. 'My brother is going to marry Lucy in the spring – and perhaps you should remember that *you* are married,' he added reprovingly.

'Not in any real sense!' Alicia retorted, stung. She was about to move away when he caught her wrist in a pinching grip that made her wince.

'Keep away from him, Alicia. He'll only hurt you.'

'I don't need your advice – let me go.'

The dawning truth of Gervase's words merely infuriated her; in her present mood she had little regard for common sense. She glared at him, at the same time managing to jerk free with a violent twisting movement that caught him unawares. Then she whirled round, ruby skirts snapping, and went swiftly from the hall. Neither she nor Gervase was aware that Lady Agnes had seen everything.

'A pretty state of affairs,' Agnes mused, fanning herself indolently with a gilded peacock feather. She told herself that she shouldn't really be surprised. Alicia Westbrooke – never would she think of her as Houghton! – was as undisciplined as a gypsy brat. And yet even Agnes hadn't expected that she would quarrel crudely with her husband in public. She was debating whether to follow her and give her a piece of her mind when she caught sight of Molly vomiting into the rushes.

Gervase had rushed to the scene and was now tenderly holding the little girl's head. A small knot of women had gathered round, cooing like anxious pigeons. One of them produced a handkerchief.

Grimly, Agnes shouldered her way through the crowd. God's blood, how many times had she warned that wretched child not to gorge herself at parties!

Molly raised her head, saw her mother lumbering towards her and began to tremble. Her face, already as pale as an onion, turned even paler. Instinctively she groped for her brother's hand.

'Poor little moppet!' cried the woman who had provided the handkerchief. 'My Margery is the same – no stomach for rich food.'

But Molly wasn't listening. She was wishing desperately that she was upstairs in her safe, quiet bedchamber with her old nurse, Mother Luke, to take care of her. She pictured Mother Luke's comforting little figure next to Agnes's large menacing one and burst into tears.

Tom, watchful for his chance, decided to steal the moment and went off in search of his quarry.

It was cold on the terrace, the ground thickly spangled with frost. Stars glittered like frozen blade-points against a blue-black sky. Below in the orchard the trees loomed, mournful black giants that looked strangely humble in their nakedness.

Alicia, sitting on the topmost step, hugged her arms, shivering in her thin silk gown. The tears felt as cold as sleet on her face.

Behind her Ryland Place soared like a house of burnt seashells, smoky-red in the starlight. To Alicia it was a gloomy, hateful prison from which she would never escape. At Ryland Place she would never find love, only its bastard sister, lust. For Tom didn't love her and she must not love him.

She wrapped her arms tightly about her body as the night air, sharp as a rodent's teeth, gnawed through her clothes. I mustn't cry any more, she told herself dully. But the tears came anyway.

From inside the house came the high, throbbing wail of music. She pictured them all, drinking and dancing in the torchlight, and was suddenly seized by a violent longing for Greenthorpe.

If a house could speak, Greenthorpe would tell of heartache and betrayal; of men and women who had bled upon the broken stones of love. Yet still it stood, calm and gracious, welcoming as a mother.

The sound of light, hurrying footsteps coming round the side of the house suddenly alerted her. She swung her head round and saw Tom walking towards her.

As he drew nearer, she felt her heart tighten painfully under her breasts. She hoped her face wasn't red and puffy from crying.

'Ah, there you are. I was worried about you.' His quick, lopsided smile reminded her unexpectedly of George Boleyn. Then she remembered that other wintry night at Greenwich, when she'd fled the banqueting hall in misery and confusion, and smiled ruefully to herself. Perhaps she hadn't changed that much, after all!

Tom hesitated, peering at the slender arched throat, the half-bare shoulders – no wonder she was shivering! – and last of all at that tearstained face.

'I'm sorry,' he said gently, stepping close, cautious as a groom approaching a temperamental young mare.

'Why?' Alicia stiffened. She couldn't bear to be pitied, and certainly not by him.

'Because my brother can never make you happy.' He squatted down on the step beside her, then reached for her hand.

As always, physical contact with him turned her body to liquid. His closeness, his restless vitality, the smell of crisp air and rose-water on his clothes made all her senses scream out with longing.

'And I doubt if I'll make Lucy happy,' he added, after a long pause.

He found himself staring at the white hand lying in his and smiled with tender amusement. Small and uncompromisingly square-shaped, it looked both strong and vulnerable, like its owner. Swiftly he raised it to his lips, brushing the palm with a feathery kiss that made Alicia draw in her breath. Confused, she snatched her hand away and started to gabble.

'Why won't you make Lucy happy? She asks for so little and—'

'In time she'll expect me to love her.'

At that, they both fell silent.

Alicia could never remember afterwards how long they sat there, with the frosty night spread around them like a sea of black crystals. It was as if time itself had frozen and they were the only two people left in the universe.

At last Tom curled a finger beneath her chin, slowly turning her head towards his. She could no more have resisted than willed herself to stop breathing. For a wild moment she thought he was going to kiss her. Even as she was trying to decide how she should react, he gave a low harsh laugh that sounded like ice crunching under heavy boots. Then his finger reached up to trace the soft outline of her mouth. She sat, still as marble, wondering what would happen next.

'Oh Alicia,' he groaned, from some deep place inside him, 'they should have married me to you.'

Towards the end of January it grew savagely cold. For weeks the Sussex countryside lay numb beneath a shroud of ice and snow. Yet nearly every day a host of pinch-faced villagers gathered at the iron gates of Ryland Place, to wait with terrible patience for the food which was so grudgingly given. Listening to Agnes's irritable muttering, Alicia was sickened. Her own father, the least sentimental or generous of men, had never shirked his responsibility to the local people during a bad winter, nor had he complained about it.

While the family sat huddled in the winter parlour, seldom stirring from the fireside unnecessarily, Alicia stalked back and forth through the icy-cold rooms, unable to settle. Her emotions were in such turmoil, she sometimes thought that her skull would explode. Tom continued to pursue her with warm eyes and teasing remarks that veiled a hungry longing. She wanted Tom. She liked and pitied Lucy, even though there were times when the girl bored her to distraction.

I mustn't hurt Lucy, she told herself frantically.

Gervase's feelings weighed upon her scarcely at all. He had boorishly, insultingly spurned her and, in any case, she blamed him for most of her problems. However, she shrank from hurting the gentle creature who had befriended her during those early weeks at Ryland Place when she was so lonely and homesick.

One afternoon she was kneeling at the window, staring across the barren, snow-bleached park. The elms arched, wetly black and desolate, each branch circled with a garland of ice. Their shadows cast glossy pools of violet on the snow. Everything was sombre and still, like a frightened heart that suddenly stops beating.

She gave a shivery little sigh and turned away.

'God's blood!' Lady Agnes frowned at her from behind her embroidery frame. 'Of all the jittering, jumping Joans! I vow it makes my eyeballs ache just to look at you.'

Tom, seated across the chessboard from his father, looked up with a sly grin. Purposely avoiding his eye, Alicia went to sit on the settle beside Isabel. Then she pleated her fingers together in her lap and looked round the room in near-desperation.

There were the two men crouched over their game, their faces fierce with concentration like two generals studying a map. Old Melchior lay stretched out beside them, his head pillowed on Sir John's shoe. He smelled more vilely than ever and his legs were so stiff with rheumatism, he could no longer climb the stairs. It would be a miracle if he survived the winter and, Alicia mused with a tweak of dark humour, a blessing if he didn't.

Agnes, still frowning, stabbed at the mound of silver cloth in her lap as if she were performing some diabolical ritual. Her black brows cut into her skin like twin quill strokes, her mouth was pinched and set.

Alicia, watching her mother-in-law's frustrated struggles, smiled maliciously to herself. Young Isabel would have made a better job of it. Agnes Houghton was a hopeless needlewoman, yet she seldom sat down without a piece of mending or embroidery in her lap. She hated sewing but felt that it gave her a genteel air – and an excuse not to talk to her husband!

Molly was also frowning as she pretended to learn some Latin verbs. She sat straight and prim with the heavy volume lying open in her lap, thinking about marriage.

Molly longed most of the time to be married, although she was barely twelve years old and no one had yet been suggested for her. To Molly, marriage promised a calm, secure refuge from her mother. Whenever Agnes looked at her in that mock-despairing way, whenever she shook her head and announced loudly that there was no man in England so stupid that he could be duped into marrying her, Molly felt sick with fear in case it should prove true and she would have to live out her life beneath the raw flick of Agnes's venom.

Isabel was gazing into the fire as if she could read a secret message for herself in the flames. She had lost interest in her game of cat's cradle, especially as Molly refused to play, and was content to sit there, wrapped in her childish dreams.

Only Lucy and Gervase were absent. Lucy was in bed with severe menstrual cramps and Gervase . . . Alicia's lips curled at the thought of her husband. No doubt he was in the stables, spilling out his woes to that dumb beast whom he treasured above all living creatures. Restlessness began to tug at her like a gust of chill wind until she could no longer keep still.

'Let's go sliding on the lake,' she said suddenly.

Agnes looked as if her worst fears about her daughter-in-law's mental stability had just been confirmed, but John was smiling approvingly.

'An excellent idea – for the younger folk, of course,' he added nervously, catching his wife's eye.

Agnes hesitated, reluctant to sanction any suggestion of Alicia's. And yet, if she were truthful, having them around her day after interminable day was beginning to rasp on her nerves.

'All right, but you'd better go now, before it's dark. And Tom, look after your sisters. Keep them away from the middle, where the ice is thinnest.'

It was one of Agnes Houghton's inconsistencies that, although harsh, critical and at times even brutal with her daughters, she would sometimes slather them with a shower of fierce affection. To Alicia, those demonstrations spoke of possessiveness and a desire to control, rather than tenderness. Perhaps in her heart Agnes felt guilty because she couldn't love them but if so, it never extended to Gervase whom she detested and didn't care who knew it.

She rose now to her feet and went to gather Molly and Isabel in her arms, kissing each curly head in turn. Alicia thought they looked like two brown birds caught helplessly in the claws of a large, malevolent cat.

'Run along, poppets, and put on your warmest cloaks – not that flimsy thing you usually wear, Molly. And remember to keep moving or you'll catch a chill.'

Isabel's small face was pale and frightened. It disturbed her when her mother behaved unpredictably. Molly merely looked resigned.

'Don't fuss so, Mother.' Tom teasingly set all the keys jangling at Agnes's stout waist as he went past. 'Anyone would think we were going to Scotland.'

Alicia, pulling on her gloves, held her breath, waiting for the storm to erupt. Damn Tom! Now they would be forbidden to go. Then she looked at Agnes's face and saw that she was beaming indulgently.

'Silly boy!' she muttered fondly, and took a mock swipe at him.

The lake shone like a bridal cake under the pale red sun as they stood at the edge, hands linked, the icy wind whipping their faces. All around them the white world rolled and dipped, reaching out to nudge the mother-of-pearl skyline.

Tom was the first to break away. They watched as he went scrambling across the ice, his cloak fluttering out behind him like a proud green banner. His curls glinted warm and vital as claret in the dull winter light.

'Come on, you snivelling milksops!' He looked back over his shoulder at the others, his cheeks crisp and pink. His eyes were sparkling with devilment.

'Damned braggart!' Alicia muttered. 'I hope he falls on his arse.'

There was a shocked silence, then Molly giggled and Isabel joined in. Alicia grinned. For the first time she felt a surge of real affection for her sisters-in-law. And yet even their laughter sounded frightened, as if they half-expected Agnes to emerge scowling from the shadow of the trees. She felt the prickle of exasperation tinctured with pity that she so often experienced with Lucy. As always, it made her feel guilty. She tersely let drop their hands and began to fidget with her hood.

Like an arrogant schoolboy, Tom was still shouting rudely to them across the frozen air. They were lily-livered rabbits, baby girls who should still be in swaddling.

Alicia was about to reply with even choicer insults when a shriek from the usually sedate Molly pierced the air.

'I'll show him who's a baby girl!'

Before Alicia could stop her, she went tearing off across the ice. Tom greeted her with a cheer as she came panting up to him.

Out in the middle of the lake, the two figures began to dance. They looked so beautiful, so innocent and young – the tall wide-shouldered lad and the thin little girl, bobbing and swaying on the ice – that Alicia felt a great lump form in her throat. Then Tom seized Molly's hands and began to spin her round until she was breathless with laughter and collapsed in a soggy welter of skirts.

Isabel clung to Alicia's hand and wanted to stay close to the edge.

'I feel safer here,' she confided in the babyish voice that always annoyed her mother. Alicia glanced at the earnest little face. For some reason she tried to picture her as a grown woman, tall and stately with her hair pinned up, but it was no good. She could never see Isabel as anything but a child – a solemn-faced child who wants only to be safe.

'What's wrong, sweetheart?' Tom came sliding up to them. Molly, in a silly mood, clung to the tail of his cloak, pretending that he was a duchess and she was carrying his train. 'This was your idea, remember. Why aren't you skating?'

'Lady Agnes said you must keep the girls away from the middle.'

Too late, Alicia realized that she sounded like a priggish schoolgirl. She stared at the ground, feeling suddenly foolish. Meanwhile Tom was grinning at her, his eyes crinkled mischievously.

'Lady Agnes will forgive me anything.'

'Brat!' But she smiled in spite of herself.

'You mustn't speak to her Grace like that!' Molly squealed.

'Maddening child!' Tom swivelled round with a mock scowl. He was already bored with the little girl but too good-natured to say so. Then he noticed Isabel watching them with a sort of wistful hunger as she stood shivering in her berry-red cloak, her small hand curled trustfully in Alicia's. All at once his expression softened.

'Why don't you play with Molly, my love? It will put roses in your cheeks and bluebells in your eyes.'

Isabel peered at him through snow-tipped lashes, doubt registering in her face. She was dazzled by this glamorous brother but only too aware that, unlike Gervase, he had little time for her.

Everyone thought Gervase was a stupid, surly oaf. Only Isabel knew how clever he was, what magical stories he could tell of hobgoblins and unicorns and beautiful yellow-haired princesses. Only the wisest and kindest had any power and anyone who was cruel was instantly cast out of Gervase's enchanted kingdom.

'Are you really a duchess?' Owl-eyed, she decided to test Tom's humour. At nine, she had already learnt that adults' moods could erupt into something dark and ugly without any warning.

'No, I'm a big fierce lion who eats little girls up!' Tom growled, baring his strong white teeth.

At that, both children squealed and fled across the lake, gloved hands locked, hair fluttering out in long brown frills from beneath squirrel-bordered caps. Tom, snarling and grunting ferociously, gave pursuit.

Alicia decided not to follow them. Watching the brightly cloaked figures grow smaller in the distance, she was suddenly struck by a strange terror, like a snow-ball hitting her in the chest. She had an inexplicable urge to call Isabel back to her side but it was as if her throat had closed and she couldn't get the words out.

'I'm growing as maudlin as a drunken old cottage-wife,' she told herself impatiently, as the moment passed. She pulled her cloak tightly about her, then stamped each foot in turn until she felt the blood returning.

The sight of Molly and Isabel playing reminded her of Kathryn and herself as little girls. Like the Houghtons, they had clung together in fear of a grim parent. Although Sir Richard had never tormented his daughters as Agnes did, each had sensed his chilling indifference and the violence that lay coiled beneath its surface. Yet it was Richard who had rescued Alicia that day, so long ago, when she was lost in the woods.

She stared into the distance remembering . . . a day so different from this one, it might have been another world. A hard blue day in summer, with the midday sun beating down on Greenthorpe's golden walls and lozenged glass windows. Alicia was six years old and had just been scolded by Joanna for some piece of mischief.

Fractious with the heat and resenting the nurse's hectoring tone, she answered back pertly and – she congratulated herself – wittily, though Kathryn was making frantic warning gestures behind Joanna's back. Meanwhile Joanna, hot and exasperated, was in no mood to be lenient with the defiant little girl. She sent her to bed with the threat of a sound beating as soon as she had energy enough for it.

Alicia took to her heels as soon as she'd closed the nursery door behind her. Once safely out of the house, she made for the woods beyond Greenthorpe. It was so cool and dim and leafy there that her hot heart was instantly soothed. She would build herself a tree-house, she decided, setting off down a rutted path, and live on nuts and berries. Perhaps she could teach herself to snare rabbits, as Alban had done when he was a boy.

It was nearly dusk when Richard Westbrooke rode into a clearing and found his younger daughter crouched under a beech tree, her face scratched and tear-streaked, her gown torn in several places. Although he had been searching for her for nearly three hours, he didn't say a word as he reached down and lifted her into the saddle before him.

Cradled against her father's chest, Alicia's terror began to subside until she felt drowsily peaceful and contented. Richard smelled of rose-water and horse-leather and fresh sweat – reassuring smells to the child. There was no sound anywhere except for the flutter of birds settling into their nests for the night, the solemn, rhythmic clop of hoofs and her father's heart beating steadily beneath her cheek as they rode home in the twilight. She sighed happily, nuzzling her face against his stiff satin doublet.

It was the first time he held her and the only time. When they arrived home he spanked her. His hand was far heavier than Joanna's but Alicia made no sound – the sense of betrayal was too deep. After that she often dreamed of being lost in the woods. In the dream it was different for instead of running away she had been left there and though she sobbed and screamed for her father, he never came.

'You look pensive, my love.'

Alicia jumped. Tom was standing in front of her, watching her curiously.

All at once she was on the defensive. She had never told anyone except Kathryn about the nightmare that, even now, could make her wake sweating and panting with fright. Gervase was never disturbed by her night-terrors and it didn't occur to her to seek comfort from him for, though they still occupied the same bed, the emotional gulf between them was as wide as ever.

Tom seemed to be waiting for an explanation.

'I was thinking – Isabel and Molly seem very close,' she said quickly.

Tom shrugged his shoulders. He wasn't thinking of his sisters, those stiff pallid little girls, but of the wilful young woman standing before him. For the first time it occurred to him that she might still be a virgin, but of course the idea was absurd. Even Gervase, his gangling boor of a brother, wouldn't be able to keep his hands off her at night, for all that he ignored her during the daytime. Besides he sensed the turbulent vein of passion in her; it was unlikely that Gervase had been the first to enjoy her. He made as if to move away but something in her eyes caught and held him.

Her face, framed in the white velvet hood, was almost eerily beautiful in the fading light; the features so fine and delicate, they might have been carved from the snow. A stray tendril of hair fell across her temple, red as a garnet. To Tom, she appeared both fragile and dangerous – a disturbing combination.

'You remind me of a vixen,' he said, half-mocking, half-wondering. 'A slightly crazy but beautiful vixen who has just rolled wantonly in the snow.'

'I'm sorry you think me wanton,' Alicia breathed, letting her eyes slant warmly at him.

'No, Alicia – only in my imaginings.'

For a moment they stood as if transfixed, then his hands reached out to clasp her shoulders and draw her close, and his head bent swiftly over hers. All thought of Lucy and Gervase, even of the two children playing so unconcernedly in the distance, was blotted from her mind as her mouth opened beneath his and she felt the hot probing of his tongue. Just for an instant she leaned into him, savouring the delicious friction of his lips on hers, the hard, agile warmth of his body. Her head was swimming, her whole body trembling like a tapestry in the wind.

'I want you.' Tom raised his head to look at her. There was a hot, greedy glow in his eyes as his hand reached up to cup her face.

Not *I love you* but *I want you*. Alicia, her legs still shaking, could have wept with disappointment. Then she glared at him and pulled away.

'You are the crazy one!' She spat. 'Do you think your sisters are blind?'

'I couldn't help myself.' Tom was breathing hard; a little ribbon of vapour curled up between them. 'And never tell me you didn't like it, dear sister-in-law.'

The sun had almost disappeared behind the thick spidery mass of trees, the sky had turned a pale, sullen grey. For the first time Alicia realized how cold she was.

'Come, darlings!' Tom's voice sounded so normal as he called to his sisters that she shot him a suspicious look. 'It's time we went indoors.'

Turning back to Alicia he said carelessly, 'They saw nothing. Anyway, they're as innocent as goslings. Like as not they'd see nothing wrong in my kissing our brother's beloved wife.'

Alicia felt swift scalding hatred, like an arrow plunging into her side. Unfortunately it wasn't quite potent enough to kill her infatuation. He didn't mean to sound cruel, she told herself as they made their way silently through the still, grey-lit park – at least she was silent. Tom laughed and chatted as if nothing were amiss, tweaked Molly's hair, then chased Isabel up the slippery avenue.

He was only joking.

She had to believe that. And so she forgave him.

It seemed as if the steel jaws of winter would never loosen their grip on the land but almost overnight the weather softened, with the ice and snow melting in sugary brown pools on the ground.

One night Alicia lay in bed, drowsily listening to the icicles dripping from the eaves. For once she had the bed to herself as Gervase was down at the stables, assisting with a difficult foaling. With luck he would be detained there all night, for the mare was young and nervous and Gervase's skill was invaluable on such occasions.

She snuggled deeper into the nest of blankets. For the first time for months, she felt cheerful. Soon she would be able to roam outdoors as she pleased. She would hunt for early snowdrops, go for long invigorating rides on Blondel, maybe even wheedle Sir John into taking her on a visit to court. She smiled to herself in the dark, picturing the lovely riverside palace sprawled around three courtyards in an enormous T-shape. She could almost hear the clinking of the weather-vanes twisting in the wind. Surely one day she would be there again.

Before long it was springtime in earnest. Taut green buds swelled into plump clouds of blossom, the surrounding woodland was blond with daffodils. As far as the eye could see, the hills were bleached white with newborn lambs.

Alicia and Lucy strolled arm-in-arm across the lawns in their spring-coloured gowns, went to peep at the new foals, gathered armfuls of bluebells and giggled foolishly at nothing, like two schoolgirls at a picnic. For all that one was, and the other soon to be, a married woman, they were very young and it was easy to laugh in the pale-gold sunshine.

And then towards the end of April when the orchard was foaming with pink and white blossom, Tom and Lucy were married and Ryland Place rollicked through a day and night of festivities.

Fifteen-year-old Lucy, radiantly pretty in her white brocade gown, her hair shimmering like fresh honeycombs under a circlet of primroses, looked like a shepherdess who has just discovered that she's really a princess. Both her voice and her hands were shaking as she gave the responses, yet happiness streamed from her like a perfume.

Tom, nearly a foot taller than his bride, looked faintly amused by the proceedings, like a good-natured uncle taking part in a children's game. By contrast, his voice sounded almost inhumanly cool and steady.

Father Charles, whose innocent green gaze concealed a brain that was sharp as a sword, felt the vaguest rumbling of unease as he stood over them at the Altar. He had been tutor to both Houghton boys and congratulated himself that he knew them as well as he did his own personal habits. Tom was as mettlesome as a young colt, yet it was difficult to dislike him for he had such a winning way with him. However, Father Charles suspected that behind the genial smiling face there lay a cold heart; that when it came to his own pleasure, he could be utterly ruthless. And the little Vernon girl was in love with him, that was as plain as water.

The priest discreetly stifled a sigh behind a genteel cough. It had always been his opinion that Lucy's nature was not robust enough for married life. She was better suited to the peaceful, orderly world of a convent. Still, he must hope that time would prove him a morbid old fool.

Alicia smiled and chattered like a vivacious humming-bird all through the wedding feast, danced with her brother-in-law – though not with her husband – and drank too much hippocras, even though she didn't usually care for its cloying sweet taste and knew that she would wake in the morning with a dully thudding head.

No one could have guessed at the hurtful jealousy scraping at her heart as she watched the bridal couple being put to bed.

'Now do your duty, Tom!' his father bellowed exuberantly, heedless of poor Lucy's blushes.

'Yes, for Ryland Place needs heirs.' Lady Agnes looked spitefully in Alicia's direction, but Alicia was watching Tom and didn't hear her.

For the briefest of moments, his eyes were locked with hers but she couldn't read their expression. Was he wishing that it was she who lay curled into his side like a trustful kitten? Was he regretting that he had once kissed her beside a frozen lake and told her she looked like a beautiful vixen? Suddenly she threw him a dazzling, careless smile then darted out of the door before she disgraced herself by bursting into tears.

Later as she lay beside the gently snoring Gervase she wept until her jaw ached. Wept with jealousy, loneliness and despair. She still didn't know if she loved Tom. She only knew that he could have brought living warmth and colour into her life.

As Tom turned to take Lucy into his arms, it struck him that she would be his first virgin.

Some men might have found the idea daunting, but not he. After all, he'd never had cause to doubt his prowess, having been complimented by more than one delighted lady.

His first lover had been an older woman, sharp-tongued and plain as wool, but with a body that would have tempted a monk. The fact that she was married to his uncle had weighed very lightly on his conscience. She was the one who had made her vows before God's altar, he'd reasoned, and anyway it was hardly his fault if she was bored with her pompous, middle-aged husband.

At twenty-six, Nan Houghton was clever, amusing, energetic and ripe for a love-affair. She taught the fifteen-year-old Tom how to use his hands and his mouth, how to bring a woman to a climax of pleasure that would leave her gasping and whimpering with gratitude. He had been to bed with many willing females since then but it was Nan he remembered most vividly, perhaps because she had been the first.

Lucy was watching him with that half-shy, half-eager expression she sometimes had. For the first time, he felt his nerve falter. This was his cousin who had been raised in the same nursery with him, who used to trail solemnly after him as he played with the lads on his father's estate, ignoring their disdainful hoots. He had a swift vision of the nine-year-old Lucy, crying because he wouldn't play shuttlecock with her. He remembered her falling off her pony and being in bed with concussion for a week. Sweet Jesus, she was practically his sister! How could he kiss her, fondle her, probe the secret parts of her body?

It was Lucy who curled her arms round his neck now, pressing her soft young body against his. The feel of her breasts straining against her thin nightgown stirred him and, as if by magic, he felt himself grow hard. He began kissing her, his tongue slowly licking her lips, then wriggling inside her mouth while his fingers teased her nipples.

Her naked body was a revelation to him, with breasts that were wonderfully lush and rounded, curving hips and thighs that looked as smooth as white velvet beside that soft triangle of hair. He wondered why he had ever thought her plain, then ceased to wonder as he parted her legs and gently eased himself into her.

Afterwards she seemed rather subdued so he kissed her tenderly on the cheek. He guessed that it had been fairly uncomfortable for her but it was usually that way for a virgin – or so he'd been told – and would get better. Feeling very well contented, he cuddled her close and presently he fell into a light doze.

Daylight was beginning to creep across the room, pale and furtive as a ghost, when Lucy brushed her body against his and whispered, 'Can we do it again?'

This time she was eager and joyous, arching her back as if she could not get enough of his caresses, stroking the rigid appendage between his legs until he was quivering with desire. As he thrust himself into her, Lucy's thighs gripped him strongly, holding him close. Presently her hips began to rotate in rhythm with his thrusts. Never before had she felt such wild sweet excitement; it was coursing through her body like a slow trail of fire and she thought she would weep with disappointment if he stopped then.

Without warning, Tom gripped her by the waist and rolled over on the bed so that she was on top. He recalled that that was how Nan had liked it best – how it had never failed to send her into a frenzy as she writhed and twisted above him, tearing at his arms and his chest with her sharp nails. He began to gyrate his hips slowly, deliberately, bringing Lucy to a shuddering climax.

Minutes later as they lay cuddled beneath the blankets, their bodies warm and moist with sweat, he gave a low chuckle.

'I had no idea you were such a wanton, sweetheart,' he said lightly, his eyes crinkled with amusement.

Lucy's face crumpled – for a moment he thought she was going to cry. Lord, must she take everything so seriously? Life would go very hard for her if she didn't learn to laugh but now was not the time to tell her. He laughed instead and gave her a hearty slap on the bottom.

'If you are always such a saucy piece, marriage is going to be fun,' he said, and tweaked her nipple.

Lucy smiled at him uncertainly; it wasn't quite what she wanted to hear but for now it would have to suffice.

Two weeks later Sir John went to London on business and it was decided, almost at the last moment, that Tom and Lucy would accompany him. The trip would be a honeymoon of sorts. John owned a house in the pretty little village of Chelsea, not far from the City, and had already hinted that he might give it to the pair as a wedding present.

It was better that they went, for Alicia could hardly bear to look upon Lucy's happiness. Love – and, no doubt, Tom's expert lovemaking – had given the girl a fresh, peach-blossom radiance that had quite transformed her.

'I think he must love me,' she confided to Alicia, the night before she left Ryland Place. 'He is so – passionate.'

She ducked her head to hide the blush that was creeping up her face like the stain of ripe fruit. She was sitting at the foot of the bed, bare toes curled under her nightgown, the candlelight throwing lilac shadows over her hair. She smelled of apples and violet soap, and looked very young in the demure, high-necked garment – virginal, too, despite all the prattle of love and passion.

Alicia, sitting up in the bed twisting her hair into a fat plait, silently willed her to go away. The girl must be half-witted, she thought sourly, to mistake primitive male desire for love.

Yet even as she thought it she was ashamed. She must be truly wicked to begrudge Lucy her happiness.

'Of course he loves you,' she said with forced heartiness. 'How could he help himself?'

'But I'm not beautiful.' Lucy nibbled her thumb, the old self-doubt naked in her eyes like a wound too painful to be concealed.

'Men don't fall in love with beauty.' Alicia thought of Lady Bess, coarse and fat, frequently drunk – and a goddess in her husband's eyes. Then, fearing that she might have sounded churlish, she added, 'You are very pretty, Lucy. Why, I'd commit a murder to have hair like yours.'

Lucy smiled bleakly, unconvinced.

For once it was a relief when Gervase appeared and Lucy finally took up her candle and padded back to her own room.

Alicia slid down between the sheets, her thoughts working. With Tom and Lucy gone, she would be able to relax. She hadn't realized how tiring it was to have to sparkle and flounce, always pretending to be as blithe as a swallow when her heart was aching. Nonetheless it irked her to think of Sir John taking them to London. As the first bride, she should have gone. Her face was set in bitter lines when Gervase lifted the covers and got into bed beside her. He shot her a look which seemed to be full of gloating triumph. She scowled at him, then flopped on to her stomach like an offended seal. Then he quenched the bedside candle between his thumb and forefinger – a habit of his that had always annoyed her.

After a moment she heard him chuckling to himself in the dark. She jerked the sheet pettishly and turned her back to him.

*

Ryland Place seemed as grey and desolate as a winter orchard after Tom had gone away. There was no more laughter, only that stiff brooding silence that Alicia had noticed when she first came here as a bride. The little girls remained closeted in the schoolroom even on the brightest summer days and Alicia only saw them at Mass and at mealtimes.

In June Isabel had her tenth birthday. Alicia gave her a cap of pale-yellow satin that she'd made from a worn-out gown and though the child seemed pleased with the gift, she never wore it.

Alicia filled in the long empty hours as best she could, embroidering her old kirtles and nightgowns, practising her lute and going for long rides on Blondel. There was something rich and bracing about the green Sussex countryside that never failed to lift her spirits. Riding across the downs, she would sometimes stop and sit for a while in one of the numerous hollows while Blondel grazed blissfully nearby. The view spread before her was heartstopping. There were numerous mossy copses, and hills whitely dotted with sheep. Water voles romped along the banks of the glittering green-brown river that dawdled towards the Thames.

There was little risk of her meeting Gervase. With Sir John away in London, his elder son had been forced to take over his duties and was too busy to enjoy those long meandering rides.

And then one morning she did meet him.

She was riding across a meadow where some plump cattle were grazing when Blondel suddenly shied, very nearly unseating her.

Alicia quickly gathered up the reins, murmuring soothingly to the little horse. Then she spotted Gervase in the shadow of the twin poplars.

'God's blood!' She muttered furiously beneath her breath.

She half-expected him to pretend that he hadn't seen her, but he was riding towards her at a steady trot. As he drew closer, she noticed the slightly sheepish expression on his face. Suddenly it struck her that this was no chance meeting, though he usually avoided her like the French pox!

'I didn't mean to startle you.' His eyes went over the slim figure in the tawny velvet riding-gown, noting the jaunty white feather curled in her hat. She was a wife of whom any man would be proud, yet his desire had been numbed by whatever private terrors had come to the surface on their wedding night.

Alicia smiled carelessly. 'Blondel is just being silly.'

However, she patted the horse's arched satiny neck as she spoke and for the first time since he'd known her, Gervase saw her eyes mist with a look of fond pride. He felt a tiny thrust of irrational jealousy but it was quickly gone.

For a while they rode along in silence, Gervase skilfully holding in the great prancing stallion. The sky overhead was the pale, greenish-blue of beryls, dabbed here and there with wisps of cloud. Alicia stared straight between Blondel's ears, enjoying the cool breeze on her cheeks. After a moment or two, Gervase glanced curiously at her. Her body no longer tantalized him as it once had, but he found himself approving of her light hands, her easy graceful seat. So many women looked like soggy woodpiles in the saddle, and sawed on the reins as if they were carving a pheasant but Alicia rode as if she and the silver-grey horse were one.

'He's a fine little gelding,' he remarked, breaking the silence.

She gave a slight frown but there was no trace of mockery in his tone.

'He has a sweet nature and goes smoothly for me – at least most of the time. I could never manage a horse like Black Ruby.'

'He just needs to know who's master. I've had him since I was sixteen. You should have seen him when he first came, he was as savage as a wolf. We thought he'd kick the stable walls down.'

Alicia laughed, picturing the scene.

By now they had come to a little stream, banked with golden kingcups and straggling rushes. An ancient willow trailed green lace into the water while nearby a trout was lazing in a pool of sunlight. Gervase suggested that they stop for a while and, almost without thinking, she agreed. It was a pretty, peaceful spot and so far he'd managed not to irritate her.

He dismounted, then came to lift her from the saddle. As she came lightly to the ground in his arms, their eyes met and locked in confusion. His hands dropped from her waist as if he had unthinkingly clutched a bunch of nettles. He turned away, his neck glowing red, and went to tether the horses to some low-lying branches.

'So gallant,' Alicia said teasingly as he spread his cloak on the damp grass for her.

At those words he looked wary, stern and vaguely alarmed all at once, like a very young priest listening to a startling confession. Alicia was amused. Dear God, surely he didn't think she was flirting with him!

She sat down on the bank and took off her hat, shaking loose the thick mass of her hair. It blazed like foxfire in the bright sunshine, heightening the chalky pallor of her skin. Gervase, fidgeting with the open neck of his shirt, found himself spitefully hoping that the hot sun would spatter her face with freckles. She might not be quite so insufferably pleased with herself if she saw a boiled thrush next time she looked in the mirror!

The thought made him smile and Alicia looked up at him questioningly.

He sighed, wondering why she always brought out the worst in him. In his heart he knew that he resented her; felt threatened by the beauty that she seemed to flaunt like an ermine cloak. Gervase merely saw it as another weapon in the silent war between them.

He squatted down on his haunches, fixing his eyes moodily on the stream curving below. The water seemed to spin with tiny silver lights, the pebbles at the bottom shone like new-minted coins.

Alicia rolled on to her stomach, cupping her chin in her hands. The sunshine felt deliciously warm on her back, making her feel peaceful and contented. She had almost forgotten that Gervase was there when she heard his voice again.

'Does Ryland Place seem like home to you now?'

'It will never be my home.' She snapped a thin blade of grass between her teeth, her face growing sulky.

'Even so, you'll probably spend the rest of your life here.' He gave his rare, uncannily mirthless laugh. Alicia turned her head round to glare at him. Sometimes he seemed to take a perverse pleasure in depressing her.

'If I thought that, I'd drink a cup of poison and put an end to it,' she said sharply.

'Don't be a fool, Alicia. How can it be otherwise? You're a Houghton now.' The light-blue eyes were gleaming with sly amusement as he went on: 'Anyway, I thought you'd managed to find consolation – of a sort.'

'You're talking in riddles as usual,' Alicia said coldly, but her mouth had turned dry as tinder. Was it possible that he had seen her and Tom embracing at the lakeside that snowy afternoon? His next words seemed to confirm it.

'I'm talking about Tom – Lucy's husband,' he added for good measure, like a sarcastic tutor emphasizing a point for his none-too-bright pupil.

'What about Tom?' She tried to coolly outstare him but her heart had quickened and she could feel a pulse leaping wildly in her neck. She hoped that Gervase hadn't noticed.

He looked scornful and, unless she imagined it, slightly hurt, although it might only have been his vanity that was hurt – the thorny vanity of a man who doesn't want his wife but can't endure the thought that another man might.

'If you must play the whore, look elsewhere than my brother.'

She felt the swift surge of fury, like the roar of the sea in her ears, and made a move as if to hit him but something checked her. It was so unlike him to make a direct accusation, she decided he must be genuinely disturbed. She knelt upright on the grass, flinging a long curl behind her, and faced him steadily.

'I've no wish to be any man's whore, least of all Tom's.'

In her mind she saw his bold bright face with the sea-coloured eyes laughing down at her, the golden skin tinged pink with the stinging cold. Involuntarily, her fingers bunched themselves into fists. Why did it still hurt to think of him?

'Yet there must have been men at court,' Gervase persisted.

Her eyes swung back to him reluctantly.

'I'm still a virgin, Gervase,' she said softly. 'You yourself have seen to that.'

'A virgin who prances and flaunts herself like a tavern slut! My mother told me it would be like that.'

It sounded so dramatic and absurd, yet she believed him. The words didn't sound like his. She sensed also, without knowing why, that they held some deeper meaning, perhaps even the key to their bitter marriage.

'What else did she say?' She was still kneeling as if nailed to the ground, scarcely daring to breathe while she waited for his reply.

The old evasive look had crept into his eyes. Suddenly he turned his head and viciously wrenched up a clump of daisies by the roots.

'Nothing – only that you would probably play the slut.'

'And yet she thought me a suitable bride for the heir of Ryland Place,' she said wryly.

'No, she would rather that I was dead and Ryland Place passed to Tom. She thinks you're probably barren anyway.'

'Then why the devil does she pester me day and night about babies?'

But she knew. Her old instinct that Agnes privately gloated over their miserable fruitless union had been accurate. As she knelt there, other puzzles began to clear like clouds shifting away from the sun; Agnes's violent aversion to her eldest son, coupled with her possessive love for his brother. Her exaggerated concern for Lucy's health. It was all part of her plan that Ryland Place should eventually pass to Tom and his heirs, and not to any son of Gervase and Alicia. For if Agnes could possibly prevent it, they would have no son.

Gervase glanced uneasily at his young wife. Seeing the stricken look on her face, he knew an instant of pity. Then he caught the flame of temper as it sprang to her eyes and he felt himself recoil. He could cope with a woman in tears, but not one in a spitting fury.

'Why don't you prove her wrong and give me a son?' she demanded, her voice shrilling up the scale.

'Because I – I can't. She told me I'm not like other men and—'

'And you believed her?' Alicia stared at him, torn between astonishment and contempt. 'Gervase, your mother isn't God. How can she—'

'Don't blaspheme!'

'Against God or Lady Agnes?'

She saw that she had genuinely shocked him and was a little ashamed. She had no wish to bait this unhappy boy. Her lashes fell, casting dark shadows on her cheekbones.

When Gervase spoke again his voice sounded tired and defeated.

'Whatever your opinion of my mother, she was right. I've never been able to take a woman – any woman. Maybe I should have joined the Church,' he added with a grim little chuckle.

'Gervase, why does she hate you?' The words had spilled out before she had time to consider them.

He turned on her a look of such anguish, it went straight to her heart. Silently cursing herself for being so thoughtless, she bowed her head. After a moment she murmured, 'I'm sorry.' And thought how futile those two words always sounded, especially to the person who had been hurt.

Without a word, Gervase scrambled to his feet and, ignoring her startled protest, walked quickly towards his horse. Alicia rose also, started towards him, but he had already swung himself into the saddle. She could only stand helplessly as he cantered off down a sandy little slope, leaving her coughing and blinking in the cloud of dust kicked up by Black Ruby's heels. It wasn't until he was a mere smudge in the distance that she remembered today was their wedding anniversary. She turned away, wiping a piece of grit from her eye.

Had Gervase also remembered, and was that why he had waited for her in the meadow? She would never understand him – she wasn't even sure if she wanted to.

As she bent to examine a grass-stain on her skirt, she noticed the broken daisies scattered at her feet, their hearts torn out.

CHAPTER EIGHT

1526

'The green taffeta gown!'

'Mistress?' Nanty blinked, her face sweetly innocent as a baby's, but Alicia wasn't deceived. The small figure standing before her was almost bristling with disapproval, and they both knew why.

'The one I wore last week when Lady Houghton's sister was visiting. I want to wear it now.'

'Now, mistress?' Again the bland tone, the politely puzzled stare.

Alicia stared almost defiantly at the maid, trying to remember when she had been so obstructive. Although they had never enjoyed the close, almost sisterly relationship that many mistresses shared with their maids, and rarely confided in each other, she had always regarded Nanty as an ally, if only because she was paid to be.

'Yes now! God's blood, can't I even change my gown without all this pother?' she cried, exasperated.

Nanty knew when to retreat and went stiffly to the clothes press. Alicia frowned, tapping a small white-shod foot on the floor. Then she glanced impatiently towards the window at the torpid August evening outside. The sun dangled low in the sky like a great copper pendant. The treetops, already flicked with russet, barely stirred in the dusty heat.

It was three months since she had seen Tom and now he and the others were home again. Only Alicia had not been downstairs to welcome them, for she had more pressing matters on her mind. Like the green gown!

She whipped round but Nanty was already returning, the garment draped over her arm like a mass of trailing ivy.

There was just enough time to brush her hair and change her plain velvet coif for a frivolous little halo-cap of white gauze. Ignoring Nanty's indignant stare, she recklessly splashed lilac-musk on her shoulders and breasts. Then she picked up the mirror to give her face a final anxious scrutiny.

Excitement had brought a vivid glow to her eyes. Her carmine-painted mouth glistened smooth and bright against her pale skin, like a scarlet jewel on a wedding gown. Satisfied, she stood up and, snatching up her skirts, turned and ran lightly from the room. A thick scented cloud hung in the air behind her. Nanty sniffed, her freckled nose twitching like a hare's, then went to gather up the discarded garments which had been carelessly flung across a stool.

The winter parlour sounded like a singing hive of voices with everyone trying to make themselves heard at once. As she paused in the doorway, Alicia could feel her heart tapping against her tight bodice. For once she felt almost shy, rather as if she were intruding on an intimate scene.

Tom was the first person she saw, her eyes going directly to him as he lounged against the chimney breast, arms folded, obviously enjoying the commotion which his arrival had caused. The sunlight pouring in through the window picked out bronze glints in his hair. His face was tanned a deep golden-brown. After a few seconds he turned his head and saw her standing there. All at once he straightened to attention, a happy grin breaking over his face. Fortunately no one appeared to notice except Gervase, who was smirking in that sly, hateful way. Not that she cared; Tom was home and she felt alive again.

She was pleasantly surprised at the warmth of Sir John's greeting.

'How pretty you look, my dear!' he exclaimed, coming to take her hand and lead her into the room. 'It's good to see your sweet face again.'

His wife snorted like an irascible old war-horse.

Lucy sat apart from the others, gazing silently out of the window. Several tendrils of hair had escaped from her coif and clung about her face like strands of coral. As she turned her head Alicia saw the smudges, dark as Lenten ashes, under her eyes. She returned Alicia's greeting with a stiff little smile but didn't speak.

Alicia, her heart suddenly gripped by ice, wondered if she were pregnant. How she dreaded the moment when Lucy, blushing and simpering, drew her to one side, whispering that she had wonderful news to share. Yet surely pregnancy wouldn't leave her looking so wretched, as if all the hope and energy had been sapped from her. Something terrible must have happened to her while she was away.

Father Charles joined the family for supper that evening. Alicia wondered if anyone else noticed the sharp, searching looks he sent Lucy along the table, but they were engrossed in swapping all their news and seemed to be scarcely aware of the sad little figure picking at her food.

The priest excused himself as soon as the table had been cleared. As he headed towards the door, he paused for a second to lay a hand that was as soft and white as a woman's on Lucy's shoulder.

'You know where to find me if you need me, my child,' he said gently. Privately Lucy was his favourite.

'Thank you, Father.' Lucy's eyes were bright with tears as they followed his plump, oddly comforting figure from the room.

Alicia stared at Tom, wondering how he could be so blind.

Because it was a festive occasion, Paul the fool was summoned to play for them as they sat in the gallery after supper. As that rich golden voice flowed across her senses, Alicia found herself studying him curiously. The great mournful eyes, legacy of a French-born mother, glistened like rare dark pearls in his pale face. And yet, for all that he could act like a half-wit when the occasion called, she suspected that Paul was far shrewder than any of them. She reflected also, with a wry little grimace, that if an artist were to paint the family group now, they would make a deceptively loving and harmonious picture for posterity. Sir John and his wife, flushed and slightly drowsy with rich food and wine, sat beside an open casement, a doll-faced daughter on either side of them. Alicia and Lucy sat on fat pink cushions at their feet – like a pair of spaniels, Alicia told herself crossly. Tom had thrown himself down on a stool and was drumming his fingers on the edge, keeping time to the music. (Gervase had curtly excused himself and gone to bed.)

A crescent moon peeped coyly through the glass, teasing the indigo shadows, while a single candle dipped and danced like a harlot in its silver bed.

'*Adieu*, mine own lady,' Paul sang wistfully, his fingers curved around the lute as if it were a woman's body.

It was one of the King's songs. And it was of the King's affairs that Sir John spoke as the song faded on a shivery note and Paul went straight into a lively French air.

'His Grace had young Harry Fitzroy created Duke of Richmond in June.' The words were intended only for Agnes's ears but everyone heard and was instantly alert.

'Bessie Blount's brat!' Agnes was satisfyingly horrified. She stared for a moment into the dusky half-light, considering this piece of news, then snapped: 'Why?'

'Who knows?' John swatted lazily at a moth. 'The King has no heir except for Princess Mary. The next step may well be to have the lad legitimized by Parliament. There's even talk of him marrying Mary, though I—'

'Incest!' Agnes's nostrils quivered as if they had just detected a foul smell. Molly glanced up curiously at her mother's face, but Agnes ignored her. 'Incest,' she repeated, and gave a disgusted click of her tongue.

'Agnes, the Queen can have no more children. His Grace is frantic to secure the succession. And in case you've forgotten, Mary is only a girl.'

'Yet they say she's clever.' Agnes privately believed there was no logical reason why a woman should not rule – as she herself had proved. Yet even Agnes shrank from voicing such heresy.

Sir John kept his prize titbit until his daughters had been sent to bed.

'Perhaps I shouldn't mention this,' he began awkwardly. 'But er – well, I thought his Grace seemed greatly taken with Boleyn's girl.'

'You must be in your dotage, John Houghton! Mary Carey was poured out along with the chamber pot three years ago. Though I must say Tom Boleyn managed to fatten his purse on her.' She gave a coarse laugh and went on. 'Maybe we should dress Molly up like a slut in a year or two and pack her off to court! Who knows what riches it might bring us!'

'My dear!' John viewed his wife with mild reproach. Then he continued placidly. 'I meant the younger girl – the thin, dark little thing with a cat's face and eyes like black cherries. Not pretty but . . .' his voice tapered off as for a moment he dwelt on the wildsprite charms that had disturbed even his stolid heart.

'Her name is Anne, sir,' Tom called helpfully, cramming walnuts into his mouth.

'Anne.' Sir John bent his head, gracious as a bishop. 'Anne, of course. He hasn't taken her to bed yet, of that I'm certain, but when he does—'

'When he does he'll spit her out like a mouthful of sour ale and there'll be an end to it. Eyes like black cherries indeed!'

Agnes pettishly shuffled her buttocks along the seat until several inches lay between her and her husband. He stared at her, innocently perplexed. What the devil had he said now!

Alicia's thoughts sped back to that frosty February night at Greenwich; to a brightly lit banqueting hall and a big tawny lion of a king who had stared at a girl with midnight hair as if she were a kingdom he planned to conquer. So she had guessed rightly. King Henry, who had enjoyed and then heartlessly discarded the sweet, empty-headed Mary Boleyn, now hankered after her sister.

'His Grace is only a man.' Agnes was now in full spate and was clearly going to brook no argument. 'He has a man's appetites, some of them base – to his shame. But for all that, he's devoted to Catherine. He is never serious about any of his strumpets – never!'

For some reason this brought a low hoarse cry from Lucy. Almost in the same movement, their heads whipped round in her direction. Paul gave his lute a final startled twang then gently laid it aside as if he were paying tribute to her distress.

Lucy clambered awkwardly to her feet, muttered something which might have been an apology, then went scuttling off down the gallery.

'What the. . . ! Tom, what's the matter with her?' Agnes's eyes were bulging like marbles.

'Just weariness, Mother.' He threw her his flashing smile. 'Lucy hates travelling. She'll be fine after a sound night's sleep.'

If he was disturbed by his wife's behaviour, his face gave no sign. Instead he stared at Alicia, sitting so still on the cushion, her face pale and serious, her half-bare breasts gleaming creamy-white above the tight green bodice. She was the virgin-whore of all his fantasies, with the added fillip of being out of bounds. He could feel the desire singing in his blood like an anthem.

But Alicia wasn't even looking at him.

'I'll go to her,' she said quietly.

And rather to her surprise, none of them tried to stop her.

The bedchamber was a black and silver grotto of moonlight and shadow. Alicia, crossing the room as stealthily as if an invalid were resting, nearly tripped over a pair of shoes lying upturned on the floor. Gowns and hats, kirtles and stockings were strewn across the bed, indicating that someone had been disturbed while unpacking. And in the midst of all the havoc Lucy lay huddled on her side, quietly sobbing, both fists pressed to her mouth as if she were anxious not to disturb anyone.

Alicia sat down on the edge of the bed and began stroking the soft fair hair. After a long moment Lucy lifted a tear-splotched face.

'I really thought he loved me at last,' she choked. 'But now – now I know that I'm not enough for him.'

The sad little tale came tumbling out, of flirtations and daily trips to the Queen's presence chamber where the maids of honour were like succulent plums, ripe for the picking. Lucy, her heart hurting as if it had been repeatedly punched, had tried to ignore it, telling herself that it was just another of those flippant courtly games that she didn't understand. And then one afternoon last week she had been taking a turn about the palace gardens, her footsteps eventually leading her to a wild, secluded part. There she had found Tom sitting on a fallen tree trunk, a small blonde girl on his knee. Her skirts were spilling over his hose like a blue fountain and his hand was dipping inside her bodice while Lucy stood less than five yards away, frozen in shock.

'They didn't see me. They were too – absorbed.'

And so she had run back inside the palace to cry.

She was crying now in Alicia's arms, her eyes as small as berries in her hot face, her shoulders twitching under the weight of grief.

Alicia held the girl tenderly, her face impassive. When Lucy had first started to tell the story, Alicia had been angry and indignant, almost as if Tom were her husband and had so uncaringly deceived her. Now she felt only a weary sadness for this young girl who was too gentle and trusting to protect herself. And beneath the sadness she was conscious of her own guilt throbbing like a gum boil.

'I don't know what to do.' Lucy's voice was muffled in Alicia's neck.

What would I do in her place – cry, curse him, scratch his face? And then be flung aside like a tiresome puppy while he swaggers off to see his tailor about a new cloak!

For the first time Alicia felt a flash of contempt for the young man who rode across female hearts like a conquering army that cared nothing for the devastation it left in its wake.

'Do nothing,' she said at last. 'What – what happened meant nothing to him, I'm sure. Why, he's like a little boy who breaks into the pantry and can't resist a whole batch of honey-cakes, even though he knows it will make him sick later. I think most men are like that.'

Lucy gave a doleful sniff. 'Gervase isn't.'

'No,' Alicia agreed. 'Gervase isn't.'

And the smile that curled across her lips wasn't very pleasant.

On 30 October Alicia woke feeling gloomy and discouraged. Today was her seventeenth birthday – a reminder that life was tramping past with careless feet. And that, though she had been married for fifteen months, she still wasn't a wife.

A grey shaft of daylight glanced in through a chink in the bed curtains. Beyond them she could hear Nanty singing softly to herself as she built the fire. Still foggy with sleep, Alicia turned her face towards the pillow next to her. As usual it was empty. There was only a small hollow and a wisp of gold-brown hair to show that Gervase had slept there last night.

She told herself that she might as well get up, and called for Nanty.

Although she didn't feel in the least bit festive, she decided to wear her new white velvet gown over a violet kirtle. Her mother's gift, a little curved amethyst and gold brooch, had arrived yesterday. As she sat at the *toilette* table, pinning it to her bodice and thinking how well it looked against her white gown, there was a soft whining sound on the other side of the door, then Gervase came in, carrying a wriggling grey bundle in his arms.

'I thought you might like him,' he said brusquely, and plumped the bundle into her lap.

A pretty deerhound puppy sat looking up at her with liquid honey eyes. She glanced round at Nanty who was standing behind her, hairbrush in hand and mouth agape. Suddenly her face broke into a delighted grin.

'Is he really for me?' And then, as the puppy began pawing at her sleeve, 'Oh, I do thank you!'

Gervase stood watching her with a strange expression. She felt the old creeping unease, reminiscent of the days before they were married, and turned away, making a great show of stroking the little dog's head.

'I – I think I shall call him Hero,' she said at last. For some reason it was the first name that occurred to her.

'I'm glad you like him.' Gervase spoke stiffly, possibly to hide his own awkwardness. 'Your maid will pleased to know he is house-trained.'

With that he swung round and walked from the room.

'Hey ho,' Nanty sang as the door closed behind him. 'Jewellery would have made a better gift. Isn't that just like a husband!' She sounded like a woman with many years' experience of marriage behind her, all of them disappointing.

A messenger appeared during breakfast with Kathryn's gift – a beautiful rosewood workbox filled with bright silken threads and silver needles. To her joy, there was a letter inside the parcel. Otherwise, her birthday was ignored. She guessed that she was in disgrace because of her various crimes in Agnes's eyes.

She spent the morning in her chamber, playing with Hero and reading Kathryn's letter. Her sister hinted at the King's passion for Mistress Anne, so there was obviously some substance in John Houghton's bumbling tale.

Such a brazen young woman. I never cared for your friendship with her and am glad that you are removed from her influence.

Alicia glowered as she read those words. But maybe Kathryn didn't mean to sound so stiff and disapproving. And of course, she would resent any woman who threatened the Queen's happiness.

She flung the letter down, telling herself she would finish reading it later.

The day was fresh and vibrant for the end of October and after dinner she changed out of the impractical white velvet – now covered with dog hairs: Nanty would be peeved – and went down to the stables.

Blondel greeted her with a joyous whinny. He hadn't been exercised for a couple of days and was inclined to be skittish, capering and tossing his head as she rode him into the lane. She held him in until they reached the open countryside, then pressed him into a madcap gallop, laughing exultantly as the wind slashed her hair around her face in thick ruddy ropes. It was several minutes before she realized that another rider was pursuing her.

'Hey ho,' she sighed, unconsciously echoing Nanty. She reined in at the edge of a little copse and waited for Tom to catch up with her.

'You ride like the devil,' he called, swinging down from the saddle with that easy buoyancy that imbued every movement.

Alicia hesitated for a moment, then she too dismounted. She went to stand at Blondel's head, her face apprehensive as Tom approached her across a crackling carpet of twigs and leaves. He took off his cap, swept the rich bronze hair out of his eyes, then he was standing in front of her.

'Why have you been avoiding me?' he asked softly, tilting up her chin with his thumb so that she was forced to meet his eyes.

'I haven't.' She dropped her lashes in sudden confusion. All at once her heart began to thud in thick, rapid strokes.

'Liar!' Laughing, he released her, then leaned back against the tree trunk, one blue-clad knee bent at an angle as he studied her through narrowed eyes.

The sunlight swerved down through the branches to which several autumn-singed leaves still obstinately clung, splashing prisms of red and gold light across his face. Alicia, who had indeed been avoiding him ever since the night of his return, realized she had almost forgotten how handsome he was.

'I didn't buy you a birthday gift,' he was saying. 'I thought it best – under the circumstances.'

Under the circumstances! She stared at him, puzzled. Did he mean that he was afraid to show regard for her when she was at odds with his mother? Or did he merely think it wise – Tom, who always scorned to act wisely if a rash course were open to him – not to lavish money and attention on another woman after his exploits at court?

'Yet Gervase remembered, didn't he?' His voice was like a coil of dark silk, winding itself around her senses.

'Gervase is my husband,' she said haughtily.

Suddenly reluctant to meet his eyes, she turned away and began to fidget with Blondel's bridle.

Tom tossed his cap to the ground, then came and caught her by the shoulders, spinning her round to face him. Blondel gave a protesting little squeal and neatly side-stepped.

'By the living Christ, no husband ever behaved as he does! And as for Lucy—'

'Lucy loves you very much,' Alicia cried. She remembered the hot, moon-flooded room, the girl sobbing in her arms. At the thought her body went rigid beneath his hands. This could not, must not happen!

She tried to jerk free but Tom's fingers tightened on her shoulders, burning through the velvet of her cloak. He shook her – very slightly, yet her teeth began to clatter.

'Lucy's love is a burden,' he said roughly, his eyes fixing themselves upon her face. 'And what's more, I can never return it. Do you know why?'

Dumbly Alicia shook her head. A sense of inexplicable dread was beginning to steal over her, thick and pervasive as a sulphur-cloud. Tom gave a low savage laugh, then shook her again.

'Lucy is a little brown rabbit and I love a beautiful wild vixen with hair the colour of a forest fire.'

'What a poet you are!' Alicia tried to laugh but only a thin, jerky sound escaped from her throat.

'No, sweetheart,' he breathed. 'Just a man who's hopelessly in love.'

He swayed closer, one hand reaching up to stroke the slender white stem of her throat. She saw the warm amber lights swimming in his eyes, like eager fishes splashing in a fern-green pond. He appeared so sure of himself – and of her – that her quick anger sprang up and she gave him a sharp impatient thrust in the chest.

'Name of God, Tom Houghton, you love no one but yourself!'

Even as the words came rushing out, she realized that they were true. It was what Gervase had clumsily hinted on occasion, though she'd paid him no heed. It was what Lucy had always suspected in her heart. For a flashing moment she was back in the garden at Ryland Place, her senses filled with the papery scent of dying roses. Once again she heard Lucy's bleak, discouraged little voice, as vividly as if the girl were standing beside her.

Tom has great charm but he never learnt to be kind.

The face above hers seemed to darken, altering so swiftly and dramatically, it was like watching a reversal of one of the court revels when grown men would sweep aside grotesquely painted masks to reveal their own grinning faces beneath. The green eyes had the glazed bright chill of Flemish tiles, with no hint of compassion. His fingers were like iron pincers as they travelled down her arms.

'Let me go,' she whispered hoarsely, not even thinking how foolish the words must sound.

'No woman spurns me, Alicia.' His voice was as soft and caressing as an April morning yet for some reason it terrified her. The carefree, impudent, laughing young man had fled and in his place was a pitiless, unsmiling stranger.

This is Tom, she reminded herself dizzily. Tom, who would never hurt you.

He drew her up against him, clutching her to the length of his body, and all the breath went out of her lungs. Her face was crushed against his doublet; she could feel the little gilded buttons digging into her cheek. The hard bulge of his codpiece was like a boulder pressing insistently against her belly. She tried to wriggle away but somehow her arms were imprisoned against her sides. He was panting like a winded stag, and some instinct told her that no plea or threat or command would reach him.

One of his hands moved inside her cloak, roughly squeezing her breasts, and she gave a cry of pain. Then, through the whirling white haze of terror, she felt a stab of hysteria.

'This was what you wanted!'

But she had never wanted him like this, mauling and thrusting, heaving like a crazed beast. She had a sense of losing control of her body, her will. Then she pictured him forcing her down on the leaves, dragging her skirts up, and thought she would faint.

'I think I'm going to be sick.' She was surprised how cool and clear her voice sounded, for she was shaking from head to foot.

Tom's hands suddenly dropped to his sides and Alicia tottered backwards. She felt frighteningly giddy, as if she'd been spinning in a game of hoodman blind. When she was at last able to drag her eyes towards his face it was as smooth and merry as ever – slightly flushed but in no way menacing. The cruel panting tyrant had disappeared. She wondered dimly if he had ever been there at all.

'There darling, I was only teasing.' His voice had a light wheedling tone which she'd sometimes heard him use when he was trying to coax something from his mother. 'Say you'll forgive me.'

Alicia gave a thin little smile but it seemed to reassure him. She didn't protest as he slipped an arm around her waist and led her over to her horse.

'You do forgive me?' His fingers were stroking her hip in a way that once would have tantalized her.

Perched in the saddle, she gazed thoughtfully at him. Suddenly she gave a dazzling smile.

'I forgive you.'

Then she leaned across and sharply rapped his mare on the quarters.

'Hey!' Tom shouted, startled.

The mare sprang forward as if she had been singed beneath the tail, and went galloping into the copse in a tangle of trailing reins.

Alicia wheeled her horse round and cantered away at full pelt. Fields and hedgerows blazed past in a flurry of bronze and scarlet and tawny. Evening was prowling across the countryside, turning the sky the colour of frosty plums. The sound of Blondel's flying hoofs echoed like cannon-fire in her brain.

A stooped little groom carrying two brimming water-pails was walking very slowly across the stable yard as she came clattering beneath the arch. He stopped, laid the pails down on the cobbles and frowned pointedly at Blondel's steaming flanks. Mistress Alicia was usually so fussy about that gelding and had plagued him from the start with instructions about his care – as if he needed to be told his business!

Clicking his tongue, he ambled towards her but she was already out of the saddle. At the sight of her glassy white face, the surly retort died on his lips. She looked as if she'd had some shock and could use a cup of brandy-wine, but that was her maid's affair. Without a word he took the reins from her and led the heaving animal away.

Alicia swiftly entered the house through a side door, praying that she wouldn't meet anyone. Then she remembered that the family would be getting ready for Mass. Well, she wouldn't be joining them this evening – she couldn't face anyone just yet. Tomorrow was soon enough to do battle with Agnes.

The steward glanced curiously at her as he passed her on the back stairs, but fortunately the little man was preoccupied with his ever-pressing duties. In any case he rather disliked her, thinking her a silly young snip who gave herself too many airs. It was one of the few things in which he was in agreement with his mistress.

As she opened the bedchamber door, Hero leapt down from the window seat and came panting to meet her. She bent to lift the puppy into her arms, pressing her face against the warm mass of fur. Luckily there was no sign of Nanty – she would have known at once that something was wrong.

Moving very slowly, as if her bones had turned to wood, she went to sit beside the fire, now burning low in the hearth. All at once her body gave way to a violent trembling. Again she saw the light, coldly brilliant as cathedral glass, swinging down through the trees; felt Tom's hard body crushed against hers. She gave a low soft moan, as if she were bleeding from an internal wound.

Hero was lapping at her hand with a wet pink tongue. Absently, she tickled his ears and he snuggled his head into the crook of her arm. Slowly, the cold sick trembling began to subside.

Surely she was making too much of the whole affair. Tom loved a joke and that was what it had been – a cruel, vulgar joke.

I let him think I was willing, so I am to blame.

She recalled the innumerable glances and smiles, the words richly spiced with innuendo, the kiss beside the frozen lake. In her tormented thoughts she saw now that the smiles, the looks, the stolen kiss had woven a thorny trail towards this day. And yet he had no right to handle her so roughly, to use his physical strength as a weapon of force and terror.

It was almost dark outside. The fire sank lower and finally went out. Still she sat there in her riding clothes, her hair a snarled red wilderness about her shoulders, staring blankly at the cold dead ashes.

CHAPTER NINE

1526–1527

The December day carried the tang of snow but Lady Agnes had announced in her forceful way that there would be none. And, Alicia mused, jabbing viciously at her embroidery as she sat in the solar with Lucy and Molly, the old bitch would probably be right as usual.

She let out a faint cry as the needle pierced her thumb and a bright bead of blood appeared. Raising it quickly to her mouth before it could drip on to the yellow silk, she looked across at the other two but they didn't appear to have noticed. Molly was gazing mistily into space, her sewing lying in an abandoned heap beside her on the stool. Lucy was also absorbed in her own thoughts as she sat close to the fire, blue hood bent over her needlework, lips tightly pressed as if she was determined to let no secret pass them.

Ever since that night when she'd unburdened her heart to Alicia, there had been an invisible chasm between them. Lucy was as sweet and agreeable as ever, but in her passive way she kept Alicia at arm's length. Also, there was a barely perceptible change in her, as if she really did have a secret – one which she had decided not to share with anyone, not even Tom. Alicia snapped off the thread between her teeth. She didn't want to think about Tom. Since that awful birthday, she had taken care never to be alone with him.

The terror of that afternoon had begun to fade and she no longer tortured herself with images of what might have happened. She was now able to view his behaviour as the clumsy cruelty of a spoilt boy who had never known what it was to be denied anything. Nonetheless, it had been cruel – cruel and degrading – and it had left her with a strong instinct to avoid him. And whether from some sense of shame or because his desire had passed elsewhere, Tom never sought her out.

Thirteen-year-old Molly suddenly rose and went to kneel at the window. Tucking her skirts under her knees, she pressed her flat little nose against the glass.

'I hope it doesn't snow,' she sighed.

Lucy raised her head and smiled vaguely, like an absent-minded old lady, then bent over her sewing again.

'It won't.' Alicia looked mischievous. 'Your mother promised us it wouldn't.'

Molly opened her mouth to protest, then caught the spark of mirth in her sister-in-law's eyes.

Alicia shrugged her shoulders. Her Agnes jokes were always wasted on Molly. In fact she sometimes thought that the girl had no more sense of humour than the stable cat.

Molly went back to her stool by the hearth, across from Lucy. She began drumming her fingers on the sides, her expression restless and bored, while the black and silver clock on the mantelshelf ticked away earnestly like a metallic heart.

Lucy's fingers darted in and out of the colourful silk square in a ceaseless dutiful rhythm that seemed like a reproach, but for once Molly didn't feel guilty. Like her mother, she hated sewing. To Molly, the hours spent stitching along interminable hemlines and getting rough fingers into the bargain would be more usefully spent in reading. Molly loved books and greedily devoured every volume she could lay hands on. Yet today her mind wasn't on history and poetry.

She was thinking of Oliver Jennings, the London cloth-merchant who had visited her father last year. A twenty-five-year-old widower – his wife had tragically died two years ago after choking on a fishbone – there was nothing handsome or dashing about him. In fact he looked very ordinary with straight fawn-coloured hair cut bluntly beneath his ears, and instantly forgettable features. And yet there was a mellow brown twinkle in his eyes that had made Molly think of sun-speckled leaves, and he had a gentle low-pitched voice that had sent a warm little thrill dancing down her back every time she heard it.

Thirteen and twenty-five!

'Yet if we got married it wouldn't be for a couple of years, and when I'm twenty-five he will be thirty-seven. No one will think that such a great gap.'

Her lips were puffed out almost mutinously. If only Master Jennings was invited to Ryland Place this Christmas, she would find a way to make him fall in love with her. The seamstresses had nearly finished her pale-blue taffeta gown and perhaps Lucy would lend her her coral necklace. She felt a rare tingle of pleasure as she pictured herself transformed from a prim schoolgirl into a wholly delightful young lady. Who knew, Oliver might even be tempted to ask for her hand!

She wanted Oliver Jennings as she had never wanted anything before. For not only was he good-natured and kind, if they married he would take her to live in London, far away from her mother.

As if Molly's thoughts had mystically summoned her, Lady Agnes came sweeping into the room, panting slightly for she had grown rather stout and found the stairs a trial. As she paused by the door, the three girls rose and curt-sied dutifully, their skirts billowing out like clouds of spring blossom. Her eye rolled over each one in turn, not missing the smallest detail. Suddenly she barked, 'Molly!'

Molly jumped, nearly overbalancing to the floor in her fright. She had hardly put a stitch in that cushion cover and now . . .

'Go to Mother Luke, child. The blue gown needs altering.'

The pure relief in Molly's face would normally have alerted her mother, but now she was beaming with happy excitement and looked as if she could hardly contain herself until Molly left the room.

Alicia was instantly on her guard. Experience had taught her that Agnes's spurts of good humour were usually peppered with spite.

'Well, Lucy.' Tilting her head to one side like a knowing old goose, she regarded the girl. 'This is splendid news – splendid. You must be the happiest girl in England.'

'Aunt Agnes?' Lucy stared at her, round-eyed. For some reason, Alicia's heart began to beat so fast it made her feel sick.

Agnes gave a bellow of laughter.

'You sly kitten, you know very well what I mean.'

'No, Aunt, I swear—'

'Your maid tells me you haven't had a flux since September.'

Lucy's face turned crimson, then she ducked her head as if expecting a scold-ing.

'I wanted to be sure,' she mumbled. 'I – I thought there might be some mistake. I've never been regular, so I thought I'd better not—'

'Silly girl, you should have told me. Well, you shall have the best of care.' Agnes shot a triumphant look in Alicia's direction. 'At least one of my son's wives has done her duty.'

Alicia lifted her eyebrows mockingly, but inside she was screaming with hatred and frustration.

You evil old witch! One day I'll make you squirm. One day. . . .

But for now her only weapon against Agnes – against all of them – was her pride.

Somehow she forced a smile to her lips and went to kiss Lucy. The girl instantly drew back, as if dodging a blow. Alicia froze, too shocked to protest, while Lucy stared down at the floor.

'We shall have a celebration supper,' Agnes was saying. 'For I know Sir John will be as delighted as I am. You must wear your prettiest gown, sweetheart. You too,' she added, with an acid glance at Alicia. 'It's obviously your destiny to be an ornament, so you'd best look the part.'

It was all Alicia could do not to slap that fat, gloating face with all the force in her body.

John Houghton's eyes glistened at the sight of eel pie. (It was Advent and no meat could be eaten until Christmas Day.) Without hesitation, he lifted his knife and plunged it into the thick golden crust, grinning like a greedy schoolboy.

'What I don't understand,' he kept saying between mouthfuls, 'is why you kept it from us. Such wonderful news, after all.'

And Lucy kept replying in a slightly dazed tone: 'I wanted to be sure.'

Alicia, her heart hot and sour with humiliation, thought she sounded like a drunken minstrel who can't remember more than the opening line of a song. She reached for her glass and drank deeply while the plate of food turned cold in front of her.

'You could always be sure of me, sweetheart.'

Tom, already more than half-drunk, squeezed his wife's thigh under cover of the tablecloth. He laughed, then copied Alicia's gesture and took a long draught of claret, sloshing the glass across the table. A dark-red splotch slowly spread across the white damask, but Agnes didn't rebuke him.

'Yes, but I wanted to be entirely—'

'How could you doubt it after our tumbles? Didn't I rut like a—'

'That's enough, Tom.' Sir John looked stern, remembering his young daughters. Isabel's eyes were as big as florins.

'Don't be such a prig, John Houghton!' His wife, mountainous in ruby satin, her pale doughy breasts threatening to pop from her bodice, scowled down the table at him. 'If there were more such ruttings and tumblings under this roof, Ryland Place would have a nursery full of boys.' The scowl deepened, slanting towards Alicia. 'And as for you, Mistress Grand Airs, aren't you ashamed – married all these months and yet to tell us that you are carrying a baby under your girdle?'

Alicia drew in her breath. From the tail of her eye she could see Gervase squirming with embarrassment. For some reason the sight fired her courage. She smiled coolly at the snarling crimson colossus.

'I think it best to leave such things to God, madam.'

'Bah!' The thick fingers, studded with a flaming array of gemstones, clicked through the air. 'I've a mind to have you examined by a midwife.'

Suddenly Gervase pushed his plate aside and sprang up from the table. He didn't look at any of them as he rushed from the room but Alicia caught a glimpse of his dead-white face and was alarmed.

'Sulking!' Agnes pursed her lips, but Alicia could tell that she was pleased. She leaned over to pat Lucy's wrist. 'You must remember to beat your boy often so that he learns good manners.'

'Oh Aunt Agnes, I couldn't!' Lucy simpered.

Alicia stifled a groan. Somehow she pushed the thought of Gervase from her mind and steeled herself to get through that nightmare supper. Slightly tipsy from the strong claret, she even managed to rally her spirits a little. She congratulated Tom and Lucy so prettily, not even Agnes could have accused her of jealousy. She almost – but not quite – flirted with her father-in-law. Sir John refilled her glass, fairly purring under the glow of her vivacity, while Agnes's face turned as red as her gown.

When at last everyone had retired for the night and the house was dark and still, Alicia lay tossing fretfully in bed, unable to sleep.

She pummelled the pillow, then turned on her side, but it was no use. The memory of Gervase's still white face continued to claw at her brain. Eventually she gave an exasperated sigh and kicked back the covers. Her feet groped for the leather slippers under the bed, then she pulled on her robe, shivering and muttering with cold.

Hero was curled up in front of the hearth, making little snuffling noises. As she drew back the curtains, he looked up at her with sleepy questioning eyes, but seemed to understand that he wasn't to follow her.

Alicia crept through the gallery and down the black, curving staircase, praying that she wouldn't lose her balance. She remembered Nanty telling her once that one of the side doors was usually left unlocked at night, so that the steward could slip out to visit his sweetheart and be back before breakfast, his employers none the wiser. It didn't take her long to find it.

Out in the courtyard, the freezing air hit her lungs, making her eyes water. The sky was a smoky tangle of clouds, rushing across the face of the moon as if they had a pressing appointment. The frost-coated cobbles stung her feet through the soles of her slippers as she hurried in the direction of the stables, where there was a thin band of light shining beneath the doors.

She found Gervase sitting on an upturned pail, his face burrowed in his hands. He glanced up wearily as the door opened and she saw the sheen of dried tears on his face.

A horn lantern flicked shadows against the walls, where mounds of hay and straw lay in straggling heaps. Faint snickering noises were coming from some of the stalls. Black Ruby, sensing an intruder, thrust back his ears and snorted suspiciously. Alicia glanced at him warily. She had never liked the horse and thought he had a silly wild look in his eye. However, at a word from his master, the big ebony stallion quietened.

'You didn't come to bed.' Alicia stood cloaked in her robe, staring almost accusingly at her husband.

'No.' He studied his fingernails, refusing to look at her.

'Gervase—'

'I am a failure. As a son, a husband – in every way, I have failed.'

'You've made your own failure,' she said sharply.

His head shot up then and he looked at her as if seeing her for the first time. She reminded him of a young warrior-queen, proud and unyielding, in spite of her soft turquoise robe and tumbling curls.

'Alicia, is there no pity in you?'

'I don't know – perhaps. You can't help being – incapable. But you should have more pride than to snivel and whine.'

'It's all very well for you,' he said bitterly. 'You don't know what it is to have your heart cut to collops by your own mother.'

The tears came again, running into his collar like rain. Alicia, watching him apprehensively, felt her exasperation melt away. It seemed as if all the anguish and despair of his troubled young life were streaming from him in those tears. She found herself creeping closer and somehow she was sitting on the icy floor at his feet. Without forethought, she reached out a hand and laid it gently on his knee. Somewhat to her surprise, he didn't slap it away.

'Tell me,' she said softly. 'Whatever it is, you can't keep it to yourself any longer.'

Agnes Clifford was already twenty-three years old when she married John Houghton. Consequently, her only emotion on her wedding night was chill relief.

As the daughter of a prosperous Suffolk farmer she might have made a good match long ago, but for some reason it had never happened. Perhaps men were dismayed by her violent and destructive temper – a trait she seldom troubled to conceal.

Of course, shrewish women were commonplace enough, in cottages and mansions alike. There were high-born ladies who would scream into the pillow if their wishes were flouted, hit their maids and bicker savagely among themselves, but in the presence of men they were always sweetly submissive, at least until they were safely married. And so when John Houghton – *Sir* John Houghton – slid the gleaming gold ring on to her finger, Agnes came as close as she was capable to feeling grateful now that the dowdy grey shawl of spinsterhood had been lifted from her shoulders.

Even as a young woman, Agnes had had no charms to speak of, but that didn't bother John. At seventeen he had fallen frantically in love with his pretty young cousin, Jane. She was gentle and innocent, slender as a candlestick, with a shower of buttercup hair and a happy disposition – as different from Agnes as any woman could be. John was captivated by her creamy-rose skin, the tiny mole on her shoulder, the quick gliding movements of her body. The very sound of her voice, soft and slightly breathless, could make him feel quite dizzy. Yet in spite of his blushing and stammering, Jane was quite oblivious to his powerful feelings, nor did he ever mention them, for she was betrothed to his younger brother, Thomas. Now John no longer looked for beauty or romance in his life. He chose Agnes for her robust constitution and her hips – those ripe, childbearing hips – nor did she disappoint him. When the marriage was ten months old she gave birth to a son, William.

As soon as the midwife had wiped the baby of birth-slime and laid him, red-faced and bawling, in her arms, Agnes lost her heart, though she would never have believed it possible. Women of her class – or the class into which she had married – brought forth their young and promptly dispatched them to the nursery, only to visit them at prescribed times, yet Agnes couldn't bear to have William out of her sight. She would have suckled him herself but met with such a clamour of horror from her new relatives that she sullenly yielded.

A few months later, when William was growing into a strong flaxen-haired infant with Agnes's high colour and John's placid temper, she was faintly surprised to learn that she was pregnant again.

'We've made another fine boy, sweetheart,' John said jubilantly, patting her belly.

Agnes nodded, but said nothing. As the months went by and her body began to thicken, this second pregnancy seemed almost unreal to her, like a hazy dream. She simply could not imagine loving another child the way she loved William.

Early in May when William was just over a year-old, she was delivered of a second son – a sickly-looking scrap who lay whimpering feebly on the pillow beside her. Agnes looked at the splotched face, the sticklike limbs, and thought him a very poor specimen.

'Take him,' she said faintly as the midwife bent over the bed, an anxious little smile pinned to her lips. Then she averted her face as if from a foul odour.

In high summer both babies caught heavy colds. At first there seemed no cause for alarm but when they grew fretful and feverish, the doctor was hastily summoned.

Nobody expected the frail snuffling Gervase to survive, nor did they much care. It was a hard cold world where weaklings were nothing more than a burden. Yet that night it was William, Agnes's golden child, who went into convulsions and died in her arms.

'You have another son,' her in-laws told her as she stood numbly before them, her face like grey glass in the shadow of her hood.

When she didn't answer they wondered if their words had been a lance in her wound, since the poor little mite looked as if he would follow his brother within hours.

They were proved wrong, for the very next day, almost as if he wanted to spite them all, little Gervase began to recover.

'She never forgave me for not dying.' Gervase's face looked white and drained, as if all the blood had been squeezed out of it. 'William would have inherited Ryland Place. She loved him. Maybe he was the only person she ever loved – except Tom.'

'It wasn't your fault,' Alicia whispered.

'I never wanted her love.' Gervase went on as if he hadn't heard. 'An unloving mother – it's not that uncommon. And I had my nurse to care for me; she was a darling. But *she* hates me – because I lived and William didn't.'

Alicia stared at the floor. She could think of no words that wouldn't sound hopelessly banal.

'She tried to drive out her grief afterwards by travelling all over the country, visiting everyone she knew. She was at Greenthorpe the night your sister was born. Did you know that?'

Dumbly, Alicia shook her head.

'I was seven months old and she couldn't bear to be under the same roof as me.'

With sudden venom he scraped his shoe on a stray wisp of straw and cried, 'I hate myself! Because of her I shall always hate myself.'

As Christmas drew near Alicia's spirits began to lift, for Sir Giles and Lady Kathryn Standish were among the guests invited to spend the holiday at Ryland Place.

'I haven't seen Kathryn since my wedding day,' she said excitedly to Lucy as they walked along the gallery to their bedchambers one freezing December night. A high wind had risen earlier in the evening and was now screeching down the great chimneys, making the tapestries flap like frightened birds. The torches were swaying drunkenly in the iron wall-sconces.

Lucy smiled benignly but didn't bother to answer.

Alicia shot her an irritable look. One might as well try to make conversation with one of Isabel's wooden dolls! Why couldn't Lucy be pleased for her? And why did her indifference hurt?

Pride dictated that she ignore these constant rebuffs, and yet not so long ago they had been friends. It hurt to have Lucy turn away so uncaringly when once she had clamoured for her opinion on everything, even to the choice of which shoes she should wear with her gown. Yet in spite of everything, she was still fond of the girl.

'I'll say goodnight now.'

By now they had reached Lucy's chamber. Her fingers were curled round the doorknob and there was an expression of near-panic on her face, as if she were afraid that Alicia might invite herself inside.

Alicia hesitated, even though she knew her presence was unwelcome.

'Lucy, have I done something to offend you?' she asked quietly.

At first Lucy looked taken aback, then her grey eyes glazed with politeness. She smiled the way one might smile at an eccentric but harmless stranger.

'Of course you haven't. It's just that I've been a little distracted lately.' She touched the slight velvet-covered mound beneath her girdle with an air of fulfilled womanhood that was infuriating.

Alicia lost patience. It was not for her to ingratiate herself into this silly girl's favour and she was livid with herself for trying. She swallowed the caustic remark that had leapt into her throat and turned to go. At that moment she saw Tom strolling in their direction.

He looked inordinately pleased with himself, having just won twelve guineas from his father at primero. Sir John was an enthusiastic but clumsy card-player, yet his son felt no shame in exploiting his weakness. Now he could settle with his tailor.

Alicia, in no mood for idle chit-chat with the likes of Tom Houghton, hurried on her way.

'If ever I find myself with child, I hope I don't turn into an insufferable bore who can talk of nothing else,' she remarked waspishly to Nanty some minutes later as she stood shivering by the fire, naked except for her slippers.

'You could never be boring, mistress.' Nanty quickly dropped her nightgown over her head. 'You've too restless a way with you.'

Alicia regarded her thoughtfully. Nanty was given to making these double-edged remarks that could easily be taken as a compliment or as a veiled reproof. She decided to let it pass.

A week later on a drizzly Christmas Eve, Kathryn arrived at Ryland Place, accompanied by a small mounted escort. There was no sign of Sir Giles.

'My husband sends his apologies, madam,' she said politely, curtsying before Lady Agnes in the hall. 'He has toothache and felt too wretched to travel, but insisted that I didn't miss the pleasure of seeing you again.'

For a moment it looked as if Agnes was about to deliver one of her famous tirades as she received this unlikely tale but something – possibly the quiet poise of the young woman standing before her – held her in check. She remembered that Kathryn was a favourite of the Queen and smiled, though the smile was closer to a feral snarl.

'He should get the surgeon to pull it before infection sets in. Welcome to our home, Lady Standish.'

Kathryn looked thinner and more delicate than ever. As she gathered her in her arms Alicia could feel the fine bones protruding through the narrow shoulders. She peered worriedly at the smooth heart-shaped face, blue-white with fatigue. Perhaps it was just fatigue that ailed her, she thought with a little flutter of relief. She remembered how, when they were little, Kathryn rarely caught colds or any of the usual childhood ailments. It could be that those frail-as-gauze looks concealed a wiry strength.

The sisters went arm-in-arm up the stairs to Alicia's chamber where a cheery fire crackled and glowed and a jug of spiced wine rested invitingly on the hearthstones.

Nanty, who had been trying on one of Alicia's quilted satin caps, leapt up guiltily from the *toilette* table as they came in.

'Living in the country seems to agree with you, Nanty.' Kathryn smiled kindly at the girl as she handed her her cloak.

'Yes, my lady.' Nanty dropped her eyes.

Now how the devil could she know that! These fine ladies were all carved from the same wood, treating you as if you were an old gown to be passed along – *It no longer fits me but I thought* you *might care for it* – then trying to convince you that they only had your interests at heart. Nanty's face was mutinous as she took the cloak away to be brushed of mud-stains.

'Lady Houghton didn't believe me.' Kathryn sagged down on a stool. 'She must think I'm a shocking liar.'

'A pox on her! Here, this will warm you through.' Alicia poured wine into two tall pewter cups and handed one to her sister.

'But she's right!' Kathryn's face crumpled like an unhappy child's as she lifted the cup to her lips. 'He refused to come. He said that, as Father's heir I should have pressed for an invitation to Greenthorpe – that it was my duty.'

Alicia pictured Giles Standish pouting in his empty mansion this Christmas because he had been denied the chance to look over his future home. Then she wondered what her father would have made of it, and nearly exploded into laughter.

'Did the Queen mind your coming here?' In spite of herself, there was a tart note in her voice.

A tiny cloud rippled over Kathryn's features.

'No, she is a kind mistress and knew how I longed to see you. Besides, she has other things on her mind nowadays.' She paused to swallow another mouthful. 'I expect you've heard all the talk of a divorce.'

Startled, Alicia stared at her sister, then slowly shook her head.

Kathryn's hands were folded tightly round the cup, savouring its warmth.

'It's supposed to be a secret but even the palace spit-boys have heard by now. People are saying that his Grace intends to put her aside and take a younger wife

– one who can give him a son.'

'But who—'

'Princess Renée of France seems the most likely choice. She's only in her twenties and said to be pretty and highly educated. Cardinal Wolsey is in favour of it. Of course, his sympathies have always lain with France.'

'But I thought . . .' Alicia was still staring, her eyes round as platters. 'The King seemed so fond of her. And what of their daughter?'

'He loves her dearly, but she *is* a daughter – his joy and no doubt his torment. And I think in his heart he still loves the Queen, but not the way a man loves a woman. Not since he's grown so smitten with Mistress Boleyn.'

There was no mistaking the irony in Kathryn's voice when she spoke of Anne. The beautiful face had turned pink with indignation.

'But wouldn't a second marriage put Anne's nose out of joint?' Alicia argued. 'Especially if it's to a young and pretty princess.'

Kathryn bent her head, remembering Abigail, the blowsy seamstress who held her own husband in such thrall, it rent his heart to be away from her for more than a day. Some women had a power – a *witchery*, much as Kathryn detested the word – which had little to do with beauty or even personal charm. Neither Anne nor Abigail was considered to be pretty and in times of stress both could display the disposition of a hellcat.

A single tear slipped down her cheek, falling on to her wrist where a sapphire bracelet sparked blue fire – another of Giles's presents. His wife must always be seen to reflect the glory in which he held himself. Seeing Alicia's dismayed expression she swallowed the hard little node of tears in her throat, but the pain didn't leave her eyes.

'Oh Lissa, if only you could see her – how she tries to pretend that everything's normal. And yet sometimes she forgets herself and sits staring at the door as if she still believes he'll come to her. It's so wrong.'

Stark emotion had darkened her eyes to indigo and her mouth was wobbling as if she might start crying again. After a moment she went on. 'Whatever his needs or desires, it's wrong to treat another human being like that.'

Alicia, watching her, wondered whether she was thinking of the Queen, or of herself. Perhaps somewhere in the alcoves of her mind the two were in some strange way interwoven, even though Kathryn had never been in love with her husband. As a sixteen-year-old bride she had been chaste but not naïve – one could not have survived at the robust Tudor court without acquiring at least a veneer of worldliness. Common sense had told her that a husband was unlikely to behave like a courtly lover. She had however hoped for loyalty and some degree of affection, but received neither at Giles's hands. He had surprised her on their wedding night by unleashing in her a flood of sensual feeling that she had never suspected. Yet the very next day, just when she had managed to persuade herself that there was a chance they might be happy, he'd returned to Abigail's beefy arms.

Alicia brushed a crease from her skirt, struggling for the right words. In her heart she knew that she felt no more than casual sympathy for the Queen, yet Kathryn's unhappiness dug into her heart like a steel spur. As always she felt that she could bear anything in the world except to see her beloved sister in pain.

'Perhaps it is just a rumour and nothing will come of it,' she said briskly, trying to lighten the atmosphere. 'Why don't I take you to your chamber now and you can rest till suppertime. You'll need all your strength to face my mother-in-law,' she added with a brittle little laugh.

To her surprise, Kathryn stood up and came to kiss her on the cheek. She looked dangerously close to tears again.

'Oh Lissa, nothing has turned out the way we planned when we were children,' she said with a sigh.

Because it was Christmas Eve, fish still dominated the meal, which was served in the great hall.

Paul the fool sat alone in the minstrels' gallery overhead, soothing them with the liquid sorcery of his lute. Tonight his romantic soul was fired by the moon-tinted beauty of Lady Kathryn Standish. She was Guinevere to his Lancelot, the chaste, pale-haired lady of every troubadour's song he had ever sung, and he played that night as never before because he was playing to her alone. Meanwhile his muse sat below, surrounded by crude mortals and quite unaware of the tempest thundering in his heart.

Even Alicia had to admit that the cook had surpassed himself. There was baked sturgeon and salmon, succulent prawn pasties and plump puffins. She had never understood why these last were classed as fish but they were delicious in their bed of sour cream.

Molly sat beside her, her small face for once pink and glowing with happiness. She looked almost pretty in her new beryl-blue gown, her hair shining like brown satin in the firelight. Every now and then she peeped timidly at Master Jennings, but only when she thought nobody was watching.

Oliver had also heard the rumours of the royal divorce. His pleasant face looked grave as the conversation turned to it.

'To put aside a good and virtuous wife – and a princess of Spain no less!' Agnes's three chins were wobbling with indignation. 'It's unthinkable.'

For once Sir John dared to contradict his wife.

'I believe the Queen has a duty to step aside in favour of a healthy young woman who can give the country an heir. No doubt his Grace will deal honourably with her if she's prepared to be sensible.'

'Of all the gibberish. . . ! Where is the honour in being flung aside like a worn out blanket? I'm sure Master Jennings agrees with me.'

Oliver, uncomfortable at being drawn into a dispute between husband and wife, stared at his plate.

'Indeed it is most distressing,' he murmured, dabbing the napkin to his lips. 'And yet . . .'

'And yet *what*?' Agnes's brow darkened ominously. Surely this tradesman wasn't going to range himself against *her*!

'Well, they say his Grace now questions whether the marriage was ever legal. The Queen *was* married to his brother.'

'They say!' Agnes snorted rudely, reaching across the table for another pasty. 'That business was all settled long ago. The whole world knows that the Pope granted a dispensation at the time, so there can be no question of its legality. Why, if this disgraceful mummery is allowed to continue we'll have every man in England deciding that his wife is really his whore and every lawfully begotten child declared a bastard.'

'Any man wed to a honeypot like you would be a fool to wish it otherwise, my love.' Sir John tilted his glass to salute her.

For once Agnes was stunned into silence. Was it her imagination or did some barb lie behind those words? She decided not to pursue it.

John drained his glass and sighed so faintly that no one heard. He knew that it was foolish to bait Agnes, and that he would pay for it later, but tonight some perversity had him in its grip. He wondered if it had anything to do with Lady Jane, who had been his boyhood love. His only love, he reminded himself with a rare wave of self-pity as he looked across the table at her.

The years had wrought their change upon the enchanting girl with the butter-cup hair. The bearing of seven children had thickened the once candle-slim body, the fair tresses had dulled to the grey-gold of a summer twilight. Mauve veins inked the pink-and-cream complexion which used to glow so sleekly that his sisters would laughingly accuse her of stealing out of the house at dawn to wash her face in meadow dew. Yet she had retained her guileless blue gaze, her happy gurgling laugh. She was speaking now in the low breathless voice that used to enthral him and now briefly did again.

'Well I for one pity her Grace. It must be mortifying to have the whole court whispering and smirking. I suppose she has heard the gossip?' Hands steepled under her chin, she turned to Kathryn.

'She couldn't help but hear, madam, but she's too proud to let anyone know.'

'Her Graish is a magnifishent woman!' Jane's husband, Thomas, had a weak head for wine and had now reached his sentimental stage. 'A jewel among her shex. And I shay let the Boleyn whore be damned to hell!'

'What do you mean, Tom?' Agnes shifted round to face her brother-in-law. 'Surely the King's divorce and his passion for that – that creature are separate issues?'

'Maybe.' Thomas belched comfortably, his chin sinking into his collar like a weary pigeon. 'But I'll wager she's at the root of it all.'

'If you please, madam.' Lucy, who so far hadn't spoken a word, looked up from her plate where she had been listlessly toying with a little mound of fish bones. 'May I go to bed? I feel rather queasy.'

Agnes nodded brusquely, annoyed at the interruption.

As Lucy went from the hall the conversation veered to the ever-absorbing theme of pregnancy. Alicia felt all her muscles knot with foreboding, but for once no vicious little thrusts were aimed at her.

She winked mischievously at Kathryn. Her sister smiled back at her, though whether with sympathy or amusement she could only guess. Backache, nausea and tender nipples were recalled with gusto while the two sisters sat, forgotten for the moment. After all, they had failed in their function as wives and were considered by the rest to be something lesser, more contemptible, than female.

Later they sat together on Kathryn's bed, wrapped in their chamber robes, a little silver dish of walnuts lying between them. Alicia felt a sudden stab of nostalgia for their childhood. She could almost hear Joanna's testy 'come now, are you going to sit up all night when sensible people are asleep? You can cackle and clack tomorrow.'

Kathryn was giving her hair its customary 200 strokes, a task she liked to perform herself. Alicia lay curled on her side, lazily crunching nuts. She watched her sister curiously.

'Do *you* think Anne put the idea in his head – about the divorce?'

'No.' Slowly Kathryn drew the hairbrush through the fall of silver that shimmered from head to thigh, frowning slightly, for the muscles in her arm had begun to ache. 'But she has hardened his heart against the Queen. I know you like her, Lissa, but she is . . . cold. And ruthless. It is she who keeps him away from my poor mistress with her singing and witty remarks and entertainments.'

'Yet she can be kind.' Alicia remembered the red-silk gown.

'So can the King, until someone stands in his way. Then he can strike out like a trapped bull, smashing things and trampling over people. I've seen the rage – and the hatred – in his eyes if he thinks himself challenged in any way.'

'Who would challenge the King?' An image of the great striding Tudor monarch suddenly blazed before Alicia's eyes. 'Anyway, he needs a son.'

Kathryn laid down the hairbrush, her face thoughtful and serious.

'Is there any chance that you are with child yet, Lissa?' she asked softly.

'No, nor ever likely to be.' Alicia spat a flake of nutshell into her palm.

Kathryn continued to regard her gravely and somehow it seemed unfair not to explain those bitter words. Alicia drew a deep breath. For the first time it was a relief to unburden herself.

'Poor Lissa.' As the delicately boned hand reached out to caress her cheek, Alicia felt tears smarting behind her eyes. 'But you mustn't despair. It sounds as if you've won Gervase's confidence.'

'He had to confide in someone!' Alicia hissed. 'Who better than a stranger – for that's all I am to him. A stranger who just happens to share the same bed. Why, we're no more intimate than the Queen's maids who sleep three to a bed and like each other no better for it.'

'No, he's beginning to trust you.' Kathryn patted her cheek. 'You must continue to encourage that trust.'

'But Kathryn . . .'

Her sister rose up and crossed the room, her robe a glistening slither of coral on the rushes. She paused in front of the *toilette* table, then began arranging the phials and boxes and combs in neat rows.

'You haven't always been kind to him. Oh, I realize how galling it must have been for you – you've always been so proud. Proud as Lucifer, Joanna used to say.'

Alicia giggled as an image of Joanna's glum face floated across her mind.

Kathryn came back to sit beside her. Then she began to stroke the brilliant tumble of hair, the way Alicia had stroked poor Lucy's hair on that parching summer night.

'Patience will win him in the end – patience and sympathy. He has had little of either, if I am any judge.'

Alicia smiled dubiously. Sympathy of a sort she could manage, but she'd had little patience with Gervase's fears and inadequacies from the outset. Perhaps it simply wasn't in her nature to gently coax another's confidence.

'And what about you, Kathryn?' Even as she spoke, she felt a cold little flutter of apprehension. She knew that Giles Standish's loutish behaviour had left a deep ugly scar upon Kathryn's spirit, for all that she tried to conceal it beneath a mantle of pale dignity.

Kathryn smiled rather shakily. 'Giles isn't – Giles isn't impotent but – well, I have never conceived. I don't know why.'

'Perhaps you should spend more time at home with him,' Alicia couldn't refrain from pointing out.

'Lissa, I can't possibly abandon the Queen at this time. Why, I shouldn't even be here now.' Then, seeing her sister's crestfallen expression, 'I didn't mean it to sound that way. I'm so happy to be with you, it's been a long time since we've really talked but – I worry about her Grace.'

'Kathryn, she has other ladies to attend her,' Alicia protested. 'It's hard to blame Giles for neglect if you are never there.'

As Kathryn's face slowly turned towards her she was dismayed to see that it wore the same look of raw desolation that had been on Gervase's that night in the stables. When she spoke her voice was cracked with the pain that she had carried inside her like a canker for nearly four years.

'He doesn't want me there.'

The house seemed like a vast echoing shell after Kathryn had gone away. Alicia stood at her window, wrapped in a cinnamon velvet cloak thickly edged with black lamb's fur – a New Year's gift from her sister. Kathryn had taken such pleasure in giving it, her face sparkling as she draped it across Alicia's shoulders, then stood back, smiling, to admire the effect. Now she was being borne away in her carriage through the leafless countryside, back to the court and the brave, sad Queen.

Alicia tilted her head, nestling her cheek against the silken fur collar. Who knew when she would see Kathryn again? It might not be for several years.

Winter gave way to a crisp spring that turned the landscape green and white – the Tudor colours. It was as if Nature herself had written a poem to celebrate the King's great love. And while Henry pursued his mocking dark-eyed nymph and the court held its breath, the family at Ryland Place also seemed to be waiting for something to happen.

Lucy's small body burgeoned with the child but her spirits drooped and trailed in a mire of apathy. She spent most of the day lying on her bed, nibbling sweets and staring blankly into space. Her fresh young face grew pale and puffy, the dark-honey hair hung in oily strands around her shoulders, but she didn't seem to care.

Alicia, moved to sympathy, would have invited her for a stroll in the park but one day when they were sitting together in the solar she happened to glance up from her sewing and caught Lucy watching her with hard, narrowed eyes.

She hates me! The thought was like a blade plunging into her brain. *She hates me even as Lady Agnes does – perhaps more so, for Agnes hates everyone.*

Her fingers began to shake until she thought she would drop the needle. Tears pricked her eyes; she swiftly bent her head to hide them.

Tom was as restless as a caged animal these days. His wife's pregnancy, though gratifying, had long since lost its novelty, especially since she'd turned into a flopping sack of hopelessness before his eyes. Moreover, her condition prevented any real intimacy as sexual contact with a pregnant woman was considered to be unhealthy.

He took to riding into the village every day, seldom returning before nightfall, and soon there were rumours of a mistress. The landlord at the Red Stag inn had three nubile daughters, the eldest of whom was known to be bold and pretty. She boasted that Master Tom was so smitten, he bought her rich gifts – a pair of musk-scented leather gloves, a little amber ring, gorgeously sequinned hair ribbons, petal-pink taffeta to make a gown.

On Sunday mornings the Houghtons usually attended Mass in the village church, not from any feudal sense of duty to their tenants but because it gave them the opportunity to meet and gossip with their neighbours afterwards. Alicia hated those weekly excursions, for she was forced to ride in the bumpy carriage with Agnes and Lucy. The others went ahead on horseback; even Molly and Isabel were allowed to ride into the village demurely seated on their ponies.

One Sunday towards the end of April Lucy complained of a headache and was given permission to stay at home.

'And see to it that you rest,' Agnes commanded, in the half-solicitous, half-threatening tone she often used with her younger daughter-in-law. 'There's barely two months to go now and we want no tragedies at this stage.'

Lucy, looking white and dispirited, meekly agreed.

As usual, Alicia found the service dull and monotonous. Kneeling between Gervase and Molly in the Houghton pew, she began to wish that she'd followed Lucy's example and pleaded illness – not that any ailment of hers would ever be met with sympathy!

She gazed at the dust motes twisting in the shaft of sunshine slanting across the altar. Her attitude towards religion had always been rather detached – she gabbled the responses to the Mass as mechanically as the French verbs that Madame had made them recite long ago at Ashby Place.

Afterwards the congregation stood dotted about the churchyard, exchanging news, enquiring politely about weddings, pregnancies and deliveries, and complimenting each other on their clothes.

Bored, Alicia wandered off by herself and went to lean against a tall head-stone in the shade of a yew tree. It was uncommonly hot for April and she was longing to get home and drink a long cool glass of ale, but the family appeared in no hurry to depart. Her heart sank when she saw that they were talking to Sir John's cousin, Ralph Waters, and his fat, spaniel-faced wife. She told herself that they'd be lucky to be home before nightfall, for Anne Waters was a voracious gossip.

Suddenly she spotted Tom standing by the gate, deep in conversation with a dark-haired girl in pink.

The girl was laughing up at him, all pertness and vivacity, as if they were equals. Alicia watched, astonished, as she slapped his arm playfully in response to some quip.

The others were coming slowly down the path, John and Agnes at the head of the procession like a king and his consort. Tom muttered something to his companion, then turned on his heel and went to meet them.

Once inside the carriage, Agnes spread her skirts over the cushions, then began drumming her fingers on her thigh.

'That son of mine has an appetite for trouble,' she muttered angrily.

'Madam?' Alicia looked up with an abstracted little frown.

Agnes surveyed the girl thoughtfully. After a moment a look of amusement crept into the cold grey eyes.

'Remember never to give your heart to a man, girl,' she said tersely. 'You won't get it back.'

'I'll remember,' Alicia promised, bemused.

The brief moment of intimacy passed. Agnes seemed to recall that the girl seated beside her was her sworn enemy – as troublesome as a boil on the arse, and as difficult to crush. She lifted the little mirror which hung from her girdle and spent the rest of the journey studying the spidery veins on her face.

April trickled into May. One sparkling warm day Alicia was sitting in the courtyard with her mending. Her beaded velvet cap lay beside her on the bench and her hair fell unbound to her waist – a sight which would have undoubtedly offended Lady Agnes.

'Only virgins should go bareheaded,' she had scolded on more than one occasion. 'Virgins and unmarried girls, it's one and the same – or should be.'

What about married virgins? Alicia had longed to ask, but had curbed her levity.

She paused now, leaning back against the sun-baked wall, her needlework lying in her lap. Nearby Hero was playing with his shadow in the sunlight. Alicia found herself grinning at the puppy's antics. He had grown to gangling proportions but was as clumsy and boisterous as ever. Round and round he circled and capered, first pausing, now pouncing, like a small child trying to grab at his mother's pendant. Suddenly he spotted the kitchen cat, a gaunt striped animal with fierce yellow eyes. With a joyous yelp, he went loping towards her. The cat stiffened, then seemed to hesitate as if it offended her dignity to retreat before such an unworthy assailant, but at the last moment she streaked off in the direction of the stables. Hero went bounding after her.

Alicia started up to fetch the puppy back, then changed her mind. Hero would return in his own time, probably bearing the marks of his rashness. She settled back against the bench, lifting her face to the sunlight. Both Dorothy and Joanna had often warned her that the hot sun would give her freckles, but it never did.

Presently she heard voices coming from an open window overhead.

'You think I'm ugly!'

It was meek, gently spoken Lucy, yelling at the top of her lungs.

'Sweetheart, you're imagining things.' Tom sounded bored.

'You do, you think I'm ugly because I've grown so fat and clumsy. You'd rather I looked like Alicia or one of your other whores.'

The girl sitting below in the courtyard froze as if someone had tipped a pail of icy water over her. Part of her felt she shouldn't stay here, eavesdropping on what was after all a private quarrel. And yet with Lucy screeching like a frustrated housewife, the quarrel wouldn't remain private for long.

'I can't talk to you while you're in this wild state.'

Never before had Alicia heard him speak in that cold, peremptory tone. It was as if Lucy were an incompetent serving-girl whom he was about to dismiss from his household. What had become of their affection for each other, their joy and triumph in the coming child? Alicia began nibbling her thumb. She thought she knew the answer to that. All the love in their marriage had come from Lucy, and now that it was foundering in fear and suspicion, Tom wanted none of her.

Lucy broke into wild sobbing that had a high jerky sound, like that of a wounded animal. There was the crash of a door slamming, then the sobbing tapered off into discouraged little whimpers. Someone – probably Sir John – must have spoken to Tom because after that he went less frequently to the village and was always home before dusk. If anything went wrong with this pregnancy, no one would be able to lay the blame at his feet.

Meanwhile Alicia could not get Lucy out of her mind. She kept hearing her voice, harsh and shrill as a night bird's – *you think I'm ugly!* An image of the dull face bent over the awkward, cumbersome little body had burned itself into a corner of her brain. Lucy's spirit was dying before their eyes, yet they could only think of the child her body sheltered. Even Gervase, who had always been fond of his cousin, seemed to shun her nowadays, as if her unhappiness was as infectious as the sweating sickness – and as deadly.

'I have my own troubles,' he said ungraciously, when she accused him of being unkind. 'And don't talk to me about kindness when your own is nothing but sugared guilt.'

Sugared guilt! She glared at him across the length of their bedchamber, feeling as if she would choke on her rage. He was smiling unpleasantly, silently daring her to deny it. Instead she turned back to the mirror, her fingers shaking as they reached up to unclasp the locket at her throat.

I did nothing wrong, she told herself later, lying beside him in the dark, only half-listening to his slow, steady breathing. That time he kissed me – they weren't even married. Anyway, I never meant for it to happen.

Nonetheless Gervase's words stung like a whip because they held some grain of truth. Somewhere at the root of her concern for Lucy was a sense of shame for the wrong she'd done her. There was, in the end, only one person whom she could approach.

One clear golden morning as Tom arrived at the stables for his daily ride, he was amazed to find his sister-in-law waiting for him. Alicia's heart was bounding as she watched him hurrying across the yard, his green cloak swinging with every step. He stopped dead when he saw her, then his face lit up with the old devil-may-care grin and he continued towards her.

'You're the last person I expected to see.' He greeted her cheerfully. 'Will you come for a ride with me? It's a fine morning and I'd welcome the company.'

She stared, wondering if she had misheard. He must be the most insensitive clod alive to think she'd go riding alone with him again.

'I want you to tell Lucy that we're not lovers,' she said abruptly.

The boyish grin vanished and something like a sneer broke over his lips.

'I'd forgotten how outspoken you are – unlike your sister. She would have been more delicate. You have no more subtlety than that dog you set such store by. And,' he went on in a hard glossy voice, 'I surmise that those pretty ears have been eavesdropping.'

Alica gave an impatient swish of her skirts.

'Will you speak to Lucy – kindly?'

'I'm always kind to Lucy. It is she who's cruel to me – forever nagging, accusing, insisting that I behave like a damned lapdog.'

'It's because of the baby,' Alicia said. She might have added that there was sound cause for Lucy's behaviour, but a dull weariness was crawling over her, making it an effort even to speak. She looked down at the ground where the green weeds were sprouting up between the flagstones.

'If all this moping and squawking is what I can expect every time she quickens, she'll have no more babies by me,' Tom retorted.

She glanced up at his face, saw the green snap of temper in his eye, the obstinate thrust of his jaw. She found herself wondering, almost regretfully, what had happened to the bright, golden lad she had been half in love with. But of course, she knew; he'd disappeared that autumn day when he had mauled her body the way a starving hound might maul a hunk of venison.

In a rare moment of perception, Tom seemed to guess her thoughts. He stared at the top of her head, his face slowly reddening.

'I wouldn't have hurt you – that time,' he mumbled, shifting from one foot to the other with an awkwardness that unexpectedly reminded her of Gervase.

'I had no way of knowing it – at that time!' she flashed back. She was about to walk away but something made her pause and look back at him over her shoulder.

'You *will* speak to her?'

Tom suddenly raised his fist and smashed it against the stable door in a gesture of helpless rage.

'I'll speak to her,' he hissed between his teeth. 'Before God, I'll speak to her, plead with her, tell her how much I love her though the words will probably choke me, but it will change nothing. Lucy has turned into a shrew, like all women once they're married.'

Alicia could think of no reply to that so she gave a mocking little laugh and flounced back to the house, aware that he was still standing there, watching her.

CHAPTER TEN

1527

It is a year now since my heart was wounded with the dart of love...

Anne Boleyn smiled ironically as she scanned the King's latest letter, then folded it away in the little walnut casket along with all the others. She liked to take them out sometimes and review them, especially when she felt her nerve stumbling; when she found herself wondering if this game of passion and power were not after all a deadly mistake which would destroy her in the end. Reading again those words of yearning and tenderness, her confidence never failed to come swimming back, like the flow of blood in a limb once the night-cramp has eased.

Her pale feline face was both amused and determined as she turned the key. Who knew but the day might come when he tired of the chase, was no longer captivated by night-dark hair and light-stepping grace; by a wit that wounded as much as it entertained. If that day should come, those letters might prove her only bargaining point against a dismal future.

Unlike her silly sister Mary, she had little faith in men's promises. For hadn't Harry Percy promised to love her for ever, sworn to make her his wife though Heaven itself should forbid it? Yet he'd deserted her in the end, smashed like a robin's egg by a fat cardinal's temper.

The thought of Harry no longer threatened to slice up her heart, though at the time she'd really believed she would die. How young she had been then – young and rash and undeniably silly. Yet now the memory of that love-burnished spring and summer was so remote, it might have happened to two other people.

A clumsy clumping oaf. That was how her brother George had described young Percy. But it was his very clumsiness that had caught at her heart; the hothead-edness that knew no malice, the eager honest affection that he'd wrapped about her like a sumptuously furred counterpane, making her feel warm and precious.

Since entering her adolescence she'd discovered that men could desire her beyond reason, but love was something she'd scarcely known, having been sent far away from home as a very young child. Most of her life had been spent at courts, where there was glitter and excitement but little emotional warmth. Then she had met Harry and fallen in love, only to have him wrenched away from her.

Nowadays he lived in increasing bitterness with Mary Talbot, the 'Shrewsbury Shrew' as they'd gigglingly named her during those reckless months when they giggled at everything, as if their love was an amulet that could protect them from the ugly bald vulture of reality. If Harry had disliked the haughty, high-nosed Talbot girl before, now he detested her with all the sparse energy left to him. Weeping over his mangled love-affair like a child with a broken kite, it never occurred to him that Mary had also been hurt by the scandal.

Stone-faced in her wedding gown, she'd watched him lower his face into his hands and sob, and in that moment felt a crust of ice harden over her heart. She had known even then that she could never forgive him for that boorish and insulting pageant of grief. Not that he cared. Life –and Wolsey – had broken him.

The thought of Wolsey now made Anne's eyes gleam as hard as black marble.

'A foolish girl at court,' he'd said of her, then dismissed her with no more thought than if she were a butterfly that had landed on his shoe-buckle. Now he was beginning to realize that she was no fool; may even have guessed that she'd never forgiven him, for all that they minced and simpered and sprayed each other with compliments.

When Anne was sent away from court on that dark, rainy autumn day, there had been no room in her heart for anything but driving grief and rage. The chill rain streamed over her riding cloak, mingling with her rebellious tears until she could barely see in front of her, and all the time her mare's hoofs seemed to slap out a sullen dirge along the muddy road – *a foolish girl at court . . . a foolish girl. . . .*

If she had expected the calm and stillness of Hever Castle to soothe her sore heart, she was disappointed. Accustomed to the din and verve and colour of courts, she found the rustic life agonizingly dull, the silence as sinister as the dank green hush that hangs over a churchyard. She loved her mother, she loved her waspish old governess, Simonette, who had taught her to dance and to speak a powdering of French when she was still in the nursery, but she was bored. After several months had creaked past, she grew convinced that if heartache didn't kill her, boredom would. For three years she felt like a prisoner, helping Lady Elizabeth, visiting elderly villagers and struggling to appear sympathetic when they described their odious symptoms, suffering her father's taunts when he made his infrequent visits from court. Until that cinnamon-bright day in September when the King came to hunt in the fertile woods surrounding Hever Castle.

If he remembered the furore surrounding her departure he gave no sign, but

was most gracious, as her mother later remarked. Anne, her skirts spilling over
the flagstones in a wide hoop of taffeta as she made her curtsy, caught the hot
blue glitter in his eyes and unaccountably shivered. In that instant she thought of
Harry and how little their love had counted with this man whose will governed
all their lives. She also thought of her sister, who had rolled like a puppy in his
bed and may even have loved him. Once he must have looked at Mary like this
– eager little eyes slitted, his face like a great orb of red wax about to melt in the
fire of lust. Anne tried to picture his expression the day he told Mary that he was
done with her. Although, she mused grimly, staring at a big square ruby on his
thumb, he had probably sent Wolsey to deliver the bad tidings. The thought
filled her with acid fury that sustained her throughout the royal visit. Seated
demurely beside him at supper, she was unable to resist a few gibes, though she
could see her mother turning pale with alarm.

However, Henry must have construed her behaviour as girlish pertness for he
didn't seem offended. His booming laugh rolled out across the hall time and
again while his thick-muscled thigh nudged hers so frequently, she knew it was
no accident. Through sheer will power, she managed not to kick him viciously in
the shin.

Early next morning before the castle had stirred to life, Anne set off down the
lane with a basket of fruit and cakes on her arm and a malicious half-smile on
her lips. She spent the day with a sick widow in the village, taking care not to
return till it was almost nightfall. Seeing the King's tight dark face, she was
charmingly contrite. All that evening she flattered him, flirted with him, sang so
prettily the songs that he himself had composed – 'I know each one by heart,
sire; they are in my heart' – that Henry's pique thawed like an icicle in the sun
and Lady Elizabeth permitted herself to breathe freely again. Yet when he took
his leave two days later she pleaded a stomach-ache and stayed in bed.

The summons to court came as no surprise to Anne, nor did she mistake its
meaning. Officially she was to serve in the Queen's household. In reality she
would be expected to serve in the King's bed. He'd never been one to retire from
the field until his quarry had been run to ground, and he didn't intend the black-
and-white hind of Hever to be at large for long. Now he had her in his sight but
always just beyond his grasp. Since the day she'd returned, she had continued the
game begun at Hever – enticing and eluding him, encouraging his desire and
then freezing him with a prim little homily about her virtue until he was whipped
to a foam of bewildering emotions. Now he was in love, possibly for the first time
in his life, but Anne couldn't pity him. And in her heart she didn't trust him.

In a few days' time he planned to stage a shallow farce that would deceive
nobody. By his command and under a mantle of secrecy, the chief members of
his Council, headed by the Archbishop of Canterbury, would summon him to
Wolsey's residence of York Place where he would be solemnly accused of living

in a state of sin with his brother's widow. The image made Anne shake with laughter, yet it also disturbed her. Whatever her personal shortcomings, she was always relentlessly honest with herself, though she might lie along with the best of them to others if it suited her purpose. She felt there was something sinister about a man who was able to believe whatever he chose and who, through obscure and circuitous reasoning, could convince himself that his motives were always right.

There was no doubt in Anne's mind about the outcome of the 'trial'. His Grace would be found guilty of immorality and sternly urged to find a remedy. Then the bramble path to marriage with Princess Renée would be clear. But was that actually his goal?

As the thoughts came rushing upon her, Anne's heart began to hammer until the sound filled her ears. Clasping her hands in the folds of her sleeves, she swung round to stare at the window as if searching for symbols in the jewel-tinted glass. She was recalling a conversation she'd had with George a few days ago. Strange, she told herself now, how strange that George should be the one to plant the dangerous, intoxicating thought.

They'd been gossiping about the King's trial, laughing and mocking all the actors involved. No one had her brother's gift for peeling away human pretensions, which was why Anne found these caustic conversations so delicious. Then, as casually as if he were discussing a game of bowls or an excursion on the river, he'd remarked that the King was so deep in love he would probably marry her.

Alicia tried not to wince as Lucy's fingernails dug into her palm.

She sat beside the bed, a thin robe flung over her nightgown, her face still damp with sleep. Outside the moon hung low, like a blob of vanilla about to drop from a black-cherry sky. The June night was drenched with the scent of nightstock and roses but in the bedchamber the air was as thick as curd cheese, for all the windows were shut and a fire had been burning in the hearth since early evening, when Lucy's labour had begun.

She wondered for the thousandth time why Lucy had sent for her. Could it be that all the jealousy and hatred had been swallowed up by pain? Or maybe she simply wanted someone to protect her from Agnes's bullying. She dabbed at the hot face tossing on the pillow with her handkerchief, hating herself for feeling so useless.

The wave of pain slowly died away. Lucy closed her eyes and seemed to fall into a semi-doze.

Alicia shifted her weight on the stool, letting her thoughts drift beyond the stifling room. Only that day she had received a dramatic letter from Kathryn. Somehow, it had been made all the more sensational by her sister's elegant handwriting. There were no blots or smudges; each word was exquisitely penned, as if it had been embroidered upon rare silk. Nonetheless, she had been able to sense Kathryn's anger and shock.

It was now known in every household in the land that the King intended to rid himself of Catherine and had appealed to Pope Clement for an annulment. Yet more horrifying was the news that, after a year of fighting between Catherine's nephew, the Emperor Charles, and the combined French and papal forces over rival territorial claims in Italy, the Imperial army had brutally sacked the Holy City of Rome. Half-starved and on the brink of mutiny, the Emperor's troops had shown appalling savagery, smashing holy relics, butchering priests, raping and beating nuns, stabling their horses in the churches. The Pope was now virtually a prisoner in one of his own castles. Cardinal Wolsey, his heart still set on a French marriage, was making plans to travel in great pomp to France, in order to negotiate a peace treaty and, at the same time, seek to further his master's aims.

A sudden hoarse cry jerked Alicia back to her surroundings. Lucy was staring up at her, her eyes black-rimmed as if they were painted with kohl. Her face and her hair were soaked in sweat. Alicia picked up her hand again.

'I never knew it would be like this,' Lucy said after a while. She sounded almost apologetic.

'It will all be over soon.' Alicia smiled encouragingly. Secretly she was almost as frightened as Lucy. Childbirth killed women all too frequently, even the robust ones. The thought of her grandmother, Alice, sped through her mind like a blood-tipped arrow. So must Alice have sweated and striven, wept and cursed, only to die without ever holding her child in her arms.

'God's blood!' Lady Agnes came rustling into the room and up to the bedside. 'Have a little courage, girl. You're not the first to have a baby.'

Lucy, her bulk twisted at an awkward angle across the bed, slid her a look filled with pure loathing, but Agnes didn't seem to notice.

'I gave birth five times without so much as a squeak and, let me tell you, I suffered worse than – this.' She flung out her hand, sweeping Lucy's pain aside like a film of dust on her *toilette* table, then turned and went away again.

'Do you believe her?' Lucy whispered, as the door closed with a derisive thump.

Alicia smiled wickedly. 'Can you imagine her suffering anything in silence? Why, I'll wager she screamed fit to raise the timbers every time.'

Lucy tried to return the smile but another powerful spasm wiped it from her lips.

Alicia glanced nervously round the room. Shadows hovered in all the corners like frightened ghosts while the tapestried knights and ladies on the walls seemed to take on a life of their own.

What would she do if the baby came suddenly? She had never even witnessed a birth. Moreover, the little serving girl unconcernedly airing sheets in front of the fire looked as if she would be no more use than a six-year-old.

It was a relief when Agnes returned with the midwife, a hearty giantess with vividly rouged cheeks and hands the colour of raw beef. The sight of that lurid yellow wig alone would have alarmed Alicia had she been in Lucy's place; the woman was inordinately fond of it and refused to officiate without it. Nonetheless she had a knack of soothing frightened young mothers and was much sought after for her skill.

'Still here?' Agnes gazed mockingly at Alicia. 'I would hardly have thought a lying-in chamber was the place for a barren wife.'

She glanced at the midwife, obviously hoping for a sycophantic titter, but Mistress Hobbs was regarding her patient.

'So this is the new mother!' She boomed cheerfully. 'You'll do very nicely, sweetheart. You're a fine strong wench, that I can see.'

Agnes frowned at the familiarity but Lucy looked reassured. She even managed a grateful little smile.

Mistress Hobbs beamed like a tutor delighted with an exceptionally bright pupil. 'That's a brave girl. And the baby will be brave too – brave and bonny like his mother. I'll take a look at you now, my love.' She turned and swept the curtains about the bed, unceremoniously shutting out the other two.

'Go to bed.' Agnes's sudden harsh whisper sounded like the tearing of delicate silk. Alicia started, for she was almost rocking on her heels with weariness.

'You can serve no purpose here.' Again that penetrating whisper which managed to sound more vulgar than if she'd shouted the words. 'Mistress Hobbs will take care of Lucy. She doesn't need you.'

Alicia hesitated. She was reluctant to leave Lucy, who seemed to derive some comfort from her presence. Yet it was true that, with experienced help now at hand, she would only be in the way. She curtsied with as much mockery as she dared, then walked haughtily from the room.

The torchlight cast a smoky red haze over the gallery, giving it an almost mystical air. Alicia's footsteps seemed to echo in the stillness. Then she stopped abruptly, her sharp ears catching another sound.

There it was again, an urgent scrabbling and scratching that seemed to be getting closer. She whipped round in the direction of the sound and as she did so a plump black rat hurried across her path, nearly brushing the tips of her slippers. She gave a small, startled squeal. The rat appeared to hesitate before turning its head and looking directly at her. Its red eyes were gleaming as if they'd drawn brilliance from the torchlight. Then, as suddenly as it had appeared it scampered away, vanishing behind the tapestry with a final switch of tail.

Alicia stood stock still, waiting for her frightened heart to quieten. It was then that she noticed Tom, huddled in one of the window seats, his hair like a bright halo in the gloom. As his face swung towards her, she saw that it was streaked with tears.

'Is she going to die?' he asked gruffly.

Her heart gave another wild bound. It was what she herself had been thinking as she sat by Lucy's bed, helplessly watching that raw-lipped suffering, but now she managed a careless smile.

'She will be fine. Mistress Hobbs is the best midwife in the county.'

Privately she was puzzled by this display of grief – if it was grief! Tom had not been kind to his young wife. There might even have been times during this past year when he'd actually wished her dead. She gazed for a long time at the frightened, uptilted face, wondering how to comfort him. Once she might have reached out to touch him but the memory of that cold, bright October day lay between them like a dozing lioness.

Then Tom shrugged his shoulders and turned to stare out of the window at the moon-dappled darkness below. Realizing that he'd already forgotten her, Alicia tiptoed away.

Back in her own room she took off her robe and let it fall in a heap to the floor. As she crawled into bed beside Gervase he grunted and stirred in his sleep, as if sensing her presence. There was no sound apart from the gentle night breeze whispering through the window. Suddenly she remembered the rat, how it had looked at her as if it understood her fear.

Hero rose and softly paced the length of the floor like a sentry before returning to his place by the hearth. Alicia stretched, yawning. Her arms and legs felt stiff and heavy as if they were coated with treacle, and her head was fuzzy with weariness but still sleep wouldn't come. She didn't know what time it was but guessed it must be close to three o'clock. Dutifully she tried to pray but all she could manage was: *don't let Lucy die*, over and over like a weary cartwheel until finally she slid into a heavy dreamless sleep.

When she woke the room was flooded with brilliant yellow sunshine. The first thing she saw was Nanty standing at the foot of the bed, grinning like a minstrel. She was fairly bursting with the news that Mistress Lucy had borne a fine son just before daybreak, and all the servants were to be treated to wine and cakes.

Summer winged to full arrogant splendour, tipping each day with molten gold. Hot sunlight bleached the cornfields almost white. Swallows began to appear, singly at first like bashful young girls arriving at a party, then in threes and fours, weaving in a stately pavane towards the clouds. Still Lucy lay in bed, sick with 'milkleg' and thoroughly depressed.

'Such a wretched complaint!' Mother Luke, overjoyed at having a baby to care for again, was rocking the cradle with the ball of one foot while at the same time sorting a tangle of threads in her lap.

Alicia, watching her, found herself wondering for the hundredth time how old she was. The small heart-shaped face beneath the flat linen cap was as smooth as pink glass, the trim little figure fairly crackled with energy. She might have been any age between thirty and sixty. Mother Luke's life revolved entirely round the secure, orderly realm of her nursery, in fact she had very little contact with the world of adults. Alicia guessed that was the secret of her youthful demeanour, for she even moved like a buoyant young girl.

Isabel, busily dressing one of the treasured wooden dolls which by rights she should have outgrown by now, looked rather woebegone. For as long as she could remember, she had been Mother Luke's baby.

'I'll write to my mother,' Alicia said at last. 'She's sure to know the best remedy.'

She had a sudden vision of herself at four years old, confined to bed with the measles, and Lady Dorothy tenderly cradling her in the circle of one arm while she coaxed her to drink a vile-tasting concoction. It was one of the few occasions she could remember her mother tending to her for Joanna had always ruled in the nursery, yet all these years later she could almost smell the misty white-flower essence on Dorothy's hair and skin, feel the tickling of a cool silk sleeve against her cheek.

'She'd mend a lot faster if her spirits weren't so low,' Mother Luke was saying. 'It's common enough after a lying-in – my sister was the same after birthing her Maud – but it should have passed by now.'

She paused, glancing almost shyly at the girl standing beside her, so slim and dainty in her pale-blue gown, her high-piled hair glowing like a coronet of rubies.

'Maybe you could help, mistress. She's always been fond of you.'

Alicia sighed and stared at the window where a bee was crawling up and down the pane, buzzing furiously. She had visited Lucy twice since baby Jack's birth and each occasion had been a tense ordeal. The old animosity, forgotten during those hours of panic and suffering, had returned threefold. Lucy had looked at her with eyes that were as cold as the sea when she leaned over the cradle to admire the little boy. The air was rancid with the smell of sweat and sour milk, for Lucy's breasts had been tightly bound to stem the flow. It had occurred to Alicia, faintly queasy from the atmosphere, that Lucy would have been uncomfortable even if her legs were not swollen and throbbing with pain. However she said nothing, guessing that any advice she offered would be taken as criticism.

Dorothy recommended a brew of feverfew, vervain and betony, with regular compresses to reduce the swelling. By September Lucy had recovered physically but still refused to leave the bed that had been her sanctuary for so long.

'I'm still weak,' she protested, her voice a fog of tears.

'And always will be unless you bestir yourself,' Agnes snapped. For weeks she had veered between wheedling and bullying the girl. Now she tried blackmail. 'Aren't you proud to have such a beautiful little son?'

Lucy gazed helplessly at the baby who had been unceremoniously plunged into her arms.

Jack was plump and rosy with a crest of yellow hair that gave him the look of a faintly puzzled duckling. He was a baby to delight any mother's heart yet his own mother seemed uncertain what to do with him. Eventually she extended a stubby finger and tickled his chin. Agnes let out her breath in a frustrated hiss and flung up her hands.

Tom spent several hours a day sitting at his wife's bedside, holding her hand and trying to jolly her out of her gloomy despair. His manner was that of a bored schoolboy who has been ordered to visit an ailing, querulous old aunt, while Lucy didn't seem to care whether he stayed or went.

One wet grey morning Tom felt that he couldn't bear it any longer. Rain capered on the windows, spat viciously into the grate. He had been sitting there for over an hour, mouthing half-hearted compliments that plopped like stones into the muddy pond of Lucy's apathy. And all the while she lay stretched flat beneath the covers, inanimate as a gingerbread doll, not even looking at him but staring blankly at the bedpost.

Suddenly he thought of Deborah, the innkeeper's daughter. He hadn't seen her for almost a month and guessed that she must be feeling peeved at his neglect. Next time he visited her she would probably pout and flounce her skirts. She might even fly at him, claws curved and a tumult of abuse on her pretty lips, for she had never been in awe of him, even in the beginning. But in the end she would sigh, wind her arms around his neck and press her body against his, especially if he brought her some gaudy trinket. He decided that he would ride into the village that afternoon. Deborah was exactly what he needed just now – fiercely spiced wine after weeks of soggy bread and milk.

Having reached his decision, he made a final attempt to comfort the defeated doll in the bed.

'It's a long time since I saw you in that yellow gown.'

To his surprise, something stirred in the sullen face on the pillows. Slowly she turned her head towards him, her grey eyes alert, almost pleading. Feeling encouraged, and at the same time guiltily conscious of his intentions, he rushed on. 'You wore it the night you told me that you were pregnant with Jack. You looked so pretty, Lucy. I could scarcely breathe for looking at you.'

Next morning Lucy told her maid that she was getting up. She asked the girl to fetch the yellow satin gown from the press and, for the first time, painted her face with the cosmetics that she'd bought in London but had never had the courage to use.

The mirror reflected back to her a tired face the colour of unbaked dough, with black-rimmed eyes like ashes. Lucy was bewildered. Surely she didn't look like that? Her scarlet-painted mouth, glistening bright as sealing-wax, was the only touch of colour. She shivered – it made her think of a bloodprint on the face of a corpse. As she sat there, twitching a fold of her gown and staring, staring with frightened fascination into the polished bronze-framed oval, her heart banged and heaved inside her body. The sense of unreality that had dropped like a glass curtain between her and the rest of the world since Jack's birth came rushing over her, threatening to suffocate her. She glanced behind her at the unmade bed in the corner. Softly framed by lavender damask curtains, it offered comfort, safety, sweet blessed rest. How easy it would be to crawl between the sheets like an exhausted child and sink deep inside a warm dark womb of sleep. But she must make an effort for Tom's sake – he had said that she was pretty.

'I vow it must have been that scolding I gave her the other day,' Agnes crowed an hour later, watching Lucy playing with her child in a corner of the solar. 'The silly girl needed bracing, not coddling. We'll see no more mopes after this.'

Alicia didn't share her mother-in-law's confidence. She had seen how Lucy's eyes bulged with fear when Mother Luke brought the baby in, swaddled in snowy lawn and making mewing noises like a kitten. She found herself wondering whether it was fear for him or of him.

The summer made its final curtsy in skirts of tawny and green and in October Alicia was eighteen.

'I feel like a withered old harridan,' she wailed to Nanty, who merely snorted and said she had never looked half so pretty. Nonetheless, she stared glumly into the mirror on that dull autumn morning, half-expecting to see wrinkles criss-crossing her forehead, silver skeins in her sunset hair. And yet there was no doubt that face had altered. It had grown much thinner, the skin now so close to the bones that the slant of brows and cheekbones was too sharply emphasized. Also, there were times when her eyes had the wary, hunted look of a young vixen.

A beautiful vixen. . . !

The memory of Tom's voice seemed to pulse like a vein inside her head. She flung down the mirror, muttering a curse.

It seemed to Alicia that the Houghtons' desperate efforts to be jolly made Christmas a strained and rather sad affair that year. The boar's head, pronged with pale gleaming tusks, was carried into the hall on Christmas Day to the accompaniment of carols. Roasted capons and larks, mince pies, marchpane and jellies were consumed with gusto as people recalled the recent privations of Advent.

Little Jack was admired and passed from lap to lap while Alicia soon stopped counting the number of times she was asked if she thought *she* might be preg-

nant at last. She thought longingly of the court revels, with Anne Boleyn the
reigning Yuletide Queen now that Henry had declared his intentions.

For the unthinkable had happened. The King was now heartset on marrying
Tom Boleyn's lively, gypsy-haired daughter and nothing would sway him. It
would be a royal love-match, each year crowned with a healthy baby to compensate for the barren years with Catherine.

There was nobody there tonight who didn't know how the Queen's oaken
calm had splintered into hysterical weeping when Henry, in a clumsy attempt to
be kind, broke the news to her in her rooms. The sound had torn through
Greenwich Palace that hot June day like the scream of a mortally wounded
beast. After the screaming came silence. All that day she knelt at her prie-dieu –
knelt till her knees were numb, her small freckled hands on the rosary beads
white to the knuckles – praying for the courage that had never failed her until
now. She had known adversity before, but now she was older and would have to
fight without the weapons of strawberry-gold hair and a fresh complexion. Yet
fight she would, for her honour and that of her daughter.

The Pope, now released from captivity, was in a highly nervous and tearful
state. Mindful of his recent ordeal, he was terrified of offending Catherine's
powerful nephew, the Emperor Charles. Henry's agents in Rome were
pessimistic in their reports. It was their opinion that such a timid, vacillating man
could not be counted on.

Thomas Houghton, recently returned from London, had an amusing anec-
dote for them. It seemed that Wolsey, still saddle-sore from his mission in France,
had arrived at court with the dust and grime of his journey still thick on his
robes. He'd promptly sent word to the King, requesting a private interview.
Henry would have obligingly trudged off to the Cardinal's chamber but Anne
Boleyn was having none of it. Sitting upright on Henry's knee, her face was
wrenched in a scowl that made it appear almost ugly. How dared Wolsey
summon the King like a lackey, she had demanded. There was no question but
that he should come to his Grace.

'That sounds like her vulgarity,' Lady Agnes said as the snickering faded away.
'The Boleyns may have pushed their way up from the merchant class but no one
can buy breeding.'

'Or marry it,' Alicia agreed sweetly.

There was a shocked silence but she was in a reckless mood and didn't care
what they thought. As she lifted her glass to her lips, she suddenly caught
Gervase's eye. He looked as if he were struggling not to burst out laughing. She
winked naughtily at him.

Lady Jane Houghton quickly plunged into a dull story about her youngest
son's latest prank against his long-suffering tutor and everyone relaxed. Alicia
dared not look at Gervase. She allowed her thoughts to go fluttering back to the

court – and to the dazzling Anne. It was hard not to feel envious. Anne would be Queen of England and everyone would kneel to her as if she were Queen of Heaven. The son whom she would undoubtedly bear was destined to be king, his position assured before he was even conceived. And Anne would be wrapped in the jewel-bright folds of Henry Tudor's love to the end of her days.

Anne the Queen and Alicia the faded virgin! For that was all the future held for her.

Feeling singularly depressed, she decided to go to bed.

CHAPTER ELEVEN

1527–1528

When she reached her bedchamber she was annoyed to find that the fire was sinking low in the hearth and most of the candles had gone out. There was no sign of Nanty – she must be enjoying a private celebration with the other servants.

She sank down on the edge of the bed, easing off her slippers, then reached up to remove her green-and-gold coif, letting her hair pour down over her shoulders. She felt slightly dizzy from the strong sweet wine. No doubt she would wake tomorrow morning with a headache, her tongue as thick as a sable muff, but right now it didn't seem important.

She began idly twining the ends of her hair round her fingers, admiring the way they rolled back into fat curls as soon as she released them.

She glanced up at the sound of the door opening, expecting to see a slightly tipsy Nanty, flushed and giggling an apology, but it was Gervase.

'I was bored,' he said shortly, in answer to her puzzled look. He glanced disapprovingly round the room. 'Jesus, it's as dark as a tomb in here!'

Alicia shrugged her shoulders but didn't answer. She watched as he went to fling a log on to the dying flames, then took up a taper and lit the candles. Then he came to sit beside her.

'You made my mother look a fine fool,' he said, glancing curiously at her.

'I suppose you think I was fearfully rude.' Alicia gave a tiny hiccup.

'No, you only said what everyone was thinking.' He spread his fingers over his knees, then unexpectedly chortled. 'I thought she was going to burst like – like an overstuffed cushion.'

She giggled, sending him a sly look through her lashes. Suddenly they were both laughing helplessly, unable to stop even though they were almost choking, as they remembered Agnes's visible efforts to control her wrath; remembered too the frozen faces around the table.

'Your Aunt Jane saved the moment though!' Alicia gasped at last. 'It was very tactful of her.'

' "My Francis will go too far one day." ' Gervase aped his aunt's breathless, rather girlish voice with cruel but brilliant accuracy. ' "Truly I don't know where he gets his naughtiness from." '

Alicia stared at him amazed, then burst out laughing again. 'I had no idea you were such a mimic,' she sighed, wiping her eyes on her sleeve.

Gervase looked embarrassed, yet pleased. It occurred to him that it was probably the first compliment she had ever paid him. He stood up and went to pour wine for them both.

'I've always had a feeling that my father used to be in love with Aunt Jane,' he said, handing her a glass and sitting down beside her again. 'There's a strange look in his eyes when he's with her – almost a pleading look.'

'Yes, pleading that she won't embark on another dreary tale about her odious son.'

'Alicia!' He raised his eyebrows, mockingly stern. 'Anyway, I've often thought how different my life would have been if he'd married her. She may be a bore, but she has a good heart. And she really loves her children. It's obvious from the way she's always talking about them.'

He was silent then, staring into his glass. In the firelight the claret glowed deeply red as bird's blood. He was thinking that, despite their troubles, Alicia was the only person in whom he could confide. Quite why this should be, he wasn't certain. Perhaps it was because, like him, she didn't really belong at Ryland Place. Or because he sensed that she too was insecure, had her own private wounds. The only thing he knew for sure was that, in spite of her sharp tongue and maddening ways, he instinctively trusted her.

He raised his head to look at her. She was very beautiful tonight, with the warm half-light softening her features and a dreamy faraway expression in her eyes. Her gown was of pale-green velvet that made her skin glow like summer cream and lit her hair with a multitude of coppery sparks. He recalled that he'd always liked her in green. His eyes strayed to the contours of her breasts. It had been a long time since he'd seen them naked. He pictured them now, smooth and white, slightly pointed, with nipples like sharp dark buds.

The claret fizzed in his stomach, making him feel warm and reckless. Presently he grew conscious of a slow fire stealing through his loins as rich desire rose in him, quenching all other emotions. Almost unthinkingly, he reached out to touch her warm, slim throat.

Alert as a hare, she turned to face him. Mild surprise flickered in her eyes but she didn't speak. Not pausing to reflect on his own daring – for he'd come to expect only stinging taunts and obstructiveness from her – he leaned forward and kissed her full on the lips, his hand sliding down inside her square-cut bodice to cup one taut bare breast. Part of him expected her to push him away and leap up in a fury but she merely sighed and swayed towards him. Before he knew it she was returning his kisses avidly.

Somehow they were lying full-length on the bed, still kissing with a kind of greedy impatience while their fingers tore at buttons and laces, pushing aside layers of velvet and satin until their clothes lay in a heap on the floor and they were naked in each other's arms.

Alicia tried to speak but Gervase's lips were on hers again, kissing her with slow insistence before moving to her throat, gently nuzzling the smooth skin that smelled so bewitchingly of lilac-musk. As they slid down to encircle one pale-brown nipple she moaned faintly, burying her hands in his hair.

He began to caress her delicately, his fingertips tracing a path from breast to hip to thigh, evoking sensations of almost unbearable pleasure. She reached for his penis and found a hard column of flesh where before there had only been sad limpness. He paused to look into her face. Eyes half-closed, skin faintly flushed and moist, red lips parted, it was the face of a wanton – eager, unashamedly sensual. By contrast her nude body looked so white and defenceless against the crimson counterpane that for the first time he felt a fierce thrill of power. If he wanted to crush her between his hands, those delicate bones would snap as easily as a starling's. With that thought he slipped his hand between her thighs and found her moist for him.

'I won't hurt you.' His voice was barely above a whisper, yet it sounded unnaturally loud in the warm, quiet room. Alicia knew an instant of blinding panic as the memory of those other nights went spinning through her brain. She remembered the panting and probing, the smell of slow-dripping sweat, the hands that clutched and kneaded and hurt, and she nearly screamed at him to leave her alone.

This time it was different. Perhaps it was the strong wine or the intimacy of their laughter and conversation that had fired him with confidence, for his hands and lips upon her body were gentle and sure.

She gasped as he entered her for, despite his promise, it did hurt – each movement was like a dagger-thrust. Gradually, however, the pain ebbed away and the feeling of pleasure crept back, steadily mounting inside her. Involuntarily, her hips began to sway in rhythm with his thrusts. Her hands closed over his buttocks as if she wanted to draw him deeper inside her. Her breathing quickened as the excitement continued to mount, higher and higher till she thought she would explode into a million fragments. . . .

The very first thing he did afterwards was to kiss her very gently on the lips. His expression was undeniably smug. Suddenly Alicia was struck by a delicious thought.

'We did it,' she said rather breathlessly, then began to giggle while he stared at her in bewilderment. 'We did it, we proved her wrong. I told you your mother wasn't God.'

'Don't blaspheme, Alicia,' Gervase murmured drowsily. Then he kissed her again, this time on the tip of her nose.

That winter of 1528 was a time of rare peace and happiness for Gervase and Alicia as at last they came to know and care for each other.

After that memorable Christmas night their relationship began to blossom into, if not love, a deeper affection and understanding. Alicia's restless temperament grew more mellow, her tongue less astringent, so that she seemed a calmer, more tolerant person, while Gervase rapidly gained in self-confidence.

At night they continued to enjoy their passionate lovemaking and were constantly exploring new ways to delight each other's senses. And, though they rarely spoke of it, the thought that they'd secretly got the better of Lady Agnes was an added fillip.

Sometimes Alicia found it hard to associate the nervous fumbling boy she'd married with the lover who carried her to the heights of ecstasy in bed. In fact when she had woken that first morning in a dull haze, the whole experience had seemed like a crazy dream till she slowly turned her head and saw him lying asleep beside her. Mouth half-open, one hand tucked under his cheek, he had looked like a contented small boy.

'There is gentleness in him – kindness too.' Lucy's words frequently came swimming back to her during those ice-fringed weeks of January and February. She saw for the first time that he *was* kind to those who didn't rebuff him. He had boundless patience with young Isabel who adored him. Watching the two of them huddled together on the settle one evening, Alicia was both amused and touched. Gervase was telling one of his whimsical fairy tales and there was a rapt glow in the little girl's face as she listened, her eyes never straying from his face.

Alicia found that she had a loyal, caring friend in her husband and this meant as much to her as their sexual passion. She often thought of Walter and Bess Ashby that winter. As a child she had thought their happy marriage as miraculous as one of the giants in Gervase's stories. Well, Gervase wasn't like Walter and she wasn't Bess, but after two and a half lonely years their relationship was at last bright with hope.

Sometimes after making love late at night while the rest of the house slumbered, they would lie in each other's arms, talking softly in the dark. Gradually she told him of her fears for Dorothy and Kathryn; of her lifelong sadness because her father didn't love her.

'It's not your fault if he has no heart,' Gervase said reasonably. 'Maybe you should pity him, for it must be like a sickness.'

Alicia was silent as she mulled over this idea, which had never occurred to her.

'As for your mother,' he continued, weaving a long skein of her hair through his fingers, 'no doubt she's contented enough with her needlework and her herb garden. She's probably too busy with the running of Greenthorpe to fret over Sir Richard. Though it's monstrous of him to beat her. I've always thought that men who hit their wives should be put in the stocks. Still, I'm sure he will stop one day.'

'Yes, when they're both too old and frail to stir from the fireside.' Alicia sounded very bitter. 'And what about Kathryn – surely you don't think her life is happy?'

'Kathryn chooses to stay in her Grace's service and is free to do so. Where is the tragedy in that?'

'But Giles doesn't want her. He—'

'Then she should find a lover.'

Alicia was shocked by the forthright words. Then she remembered Hal Norris and the sadness in his warm brown eyes whenever he looked at Kathryn. Kathryn deserved happiness, so why question where and how she found it? Moreover, in spite of her virginal looks, she had long ago confided to Alicia that she enjoyed lovemaking. And yet Alicia knew her sister. Kathryn would no more betray her husband than pick up a dagger and plunge it into his heart.

Like many a host before and since, Richard Westbrooke was beginning to think that his house-guests had no intention of leaving.

Kathryn and Giles had come to Greenthorpe for the Christmas holiday which officially ended in early January. It was now the middle of February with the frog-spawn rising on the ponds and the woods powdered with snowdrops and still they showed no sign, gave no hint, of departure.

It wasn't that he disliked Kathryn, he told himself as he rode his favourite bay horse, Chance, beside the lake one cold clear afternoon. Of his two daughters he found her the least provoking for she was quiet and obedient and had always shown him proper deference – unlike that young hellcat, Alicia. The bald truth was, he couldn't stomach Kathryn's husband. Giles Standish was undoubtedly the most pompous, pretentious and absurd little man he had ever encountered. He had never cared for the fellow from the outset and now several weeks of enforced daily contact had turned irritable dislike into a taut blistering hatred so that every word, every gesture, even the way he unfolded his napkin with that ridiculous flourish as if he were about to perform some amazing feat, made Richard long to smash his fist into the smug pink face till it was as soft and pulpy as a dish of stewed plums.

Giles had made it insultingly plain that he was waiting for his father-in-law to die so that he could take possession of Greenthorpe and its treasures. Those pale-grey eyes would bulge like goose-eggs as they went greedily over the silver cups, the tapestries and Turkey rugs, the splendid oriel that dominated the hall. Giles wasn't a poor man but Sir Richard had gleaned that he only spent money on outer trappings and had sold most of the Standish heirlooms to pay for sleek horses, jewels and fine clothes for Kathryn and himself. His northern mansion was bleak and draughty with few creature comforts, aside from a blowsy mistress.

Not that Richard disapproved of the young man's philandering – no full-blooded male wanted to bed the same woman every night of every year till he was in his dotage. That would be as tedious as eating the same dish at supper every evening. Besides, a man could hardly be expected to moon after his wife like a sick calf. And there was a puzzle. Giles Standish was said to be wholly besotted with that serving-slut, plying her with gifts and fretting miserably when-ever he was away from her. Yet still he stayed on at Greenthorpe that winter, with a wife who appeared to bore him and in-laws who failed to appreciate him. Clearly Greenthorpe had become an obsession with him. He ached to possess Greenthorpe as a man might ache to possess a beautiful woman. Yet obsession or no, he had overstayed his welcome. Richard's face was thundery as he gave a flick of the reins and turned his horse homeward.

'I hope you are still comfortable in the gatehouse wing.' Lady Dorothy smiled anxiously at her son-in-law as he helped himself to a hefty portion of baked carp that evening. She was embarrassed by Richard's glum silence and as a result found herself being especially gracious to her annoying guest.

'Tolerably comfortable, madam.' Giles treated her to his rather condescend-ing smile. 'It could be a very beautiful room but has obviously been neglected for many years. Still, I have noted its possibilities.'

'You speak as though you have plans for it.' Richard spoke for the first time, his voice like dry ice. 'Pray be kind enough to share them with us.'

At that, Giles looked flustered. He quickly swallowed the half-chewed mouth-ful of fish. For the first time he noticed how cold his father-in-law's eyes were – cold as iron, and as unyielding. Meanwhile Kathryn was gently clearing her throat. He guessed that she was about to offer some syrupy explanation, which would only send this ill-humoured bully into a fit of temper. He decided to fore-stall her.

'I must protest, sir – I meant nothing untoward, I vow and swear. It merely occurred to me—'

'That is fortunate, Giles, for I must tell you that I am in excellent health and expect to spend many more happy years as master of Greenthorpe.'

For once Giles was crushed into silence.

Seeing his bluster so neatly punctured, Dorothy felt dangerously close to laughter. Even as she managed to control her facial muscles she could feel her eyes watering. Then she noticed Kathryn's crestfallen expression and was swept by remorse.

'Why do we always feel guilty when our husbands behave badly?' she pondered, recalling in a flash those times when she'd found herself apologizing for a brusque remark of Richard's or nervously striving to make amends for some piece of boorishness.

Later in their bedchamber, Richard still seemed moodily preoccupied. He sat on a low stool, drumming his fingers on his knee and frowning as he stared off into space.

Sitting up in bed in her cream silk nightgown, Dorothy signalled to Joanna to leave them.

'You seem troubled, sir.' She slipped him a timid look as he crossed the room and got into bed beside her. After twenty-six years of marriage, she was still afraid of him.

To her surprise he gave a dry little chuckle.

'It's ironical I know, but I can't help wishing Alicia was my heir. It would be better than having Giles Standish strutting about the house like a fat little sultan when I'm dead.'

'Life can't be easy for Kathryn.' Dorothy spoke wistfully, seeing again her daughter's white stricken face at the table. Giles belittled Kathryn even as Richard belittled Dorothy. She could only hope that he didn't lash out with his fists!

'Christ's holy wounds, madam, must you always miss the point! I'm not talking about Kathryn's comfort, but of the future of Greenthorpe. But if it comes to that, life is hardly a couch of ease for me. There'd be no danger of this place falling into Standish's paws if you had given me sons.'

The cruel taunt, which she had heard countless times throughout their marriage, still had the power to hurt her but tonight, for the first time, she felt hard bitter anger at the injustice of it. It seemed to seep through her veins like a cold poison.

'I did give you sons,' she said in a harsh voice that sounded quite unlike her own. 'I gave you two sons. They died.'

Richard was startled. Most of the time his wife was as meek as a woodland doe, for he had long since beaten the very spirit out of her body. Very occasionally, however, the ghost of that defiant girl he had married would rise up like a thin mocking flame to disconcert him. It was one of the reasons why he could never be entirely sure of her and therefore didn't trust her. His only response now was to give a scornful snort as he turned away and flung the sheet over his head.

At breakfast next morning, Giles unexpectedly announced that he and Kathryn would be starting on their journey home that day.

'Might as well, while the clear weather holds,' Richard agreed cheerfully through a mouthful of bread and honey while Dorothy allowed her face to register polite regret.

'I hope we haven't overstayed our welcome.' Kathryn, radiantly pretty in a soft lilac gown patterned with velvet pansies, smiled across the table at them. 'But it has been wonderful to see you again. You've both been so kind and made our visit so enjoyable, we could hardly bear to leave.'

Richard's stony features melted into a rare smile. To everyone's astonishment, he reached across to pat Kathryn's hand.

She has the charm of an angel and a tongue of pure silver, Dorothy mused. No wonder the Queen treasures her.

She stared at her elder daughter with a combination of pride and envy. Had she been born a boy, Kathryn would have made a superb ambassador.

After the goodbyes had been said and Giles and Kathryn had ridden away in the frosty morning air, thickly swaddled in furs like two large infants, Dorothy was struck by a sense of emptiness which felt both strange and achingly familiar. It was the same feeling she had had all those years ago when the twelve-year-old Kathryn had left home to join the Queen's household. She recalled now how she'd cried in bed that night while Richard slept, picturing her little girl alone among strangers. Wondering if Kathryn would be homesick. Praying that she wouldn't be bullied by the other maids of honour who might resent her extraordinary beauty.

A multitude of chores awaited Dorothy's attention that morning but first she had to compose herself. She went swiftly upstairs to her chamber; at least there she could be guaranteed a few moments privacy before having to face the servants.

A large wooden box lay in the middle of the bed. There was also a letter, addressed to her in an unfamiliar hand. Intrigued, Dorothy opened the box first. She gave a sharp little cry of pleasure as she slowly unfolded a chamber-robe of copper-coloured velvet, thickly fringed with mink. The letter was from Giles.

This is but a token of my deep respect for a great lady and I hope you will not be offended nor think me unmannerly. Please accept this humble gift, dearest, madam, with my heartfelt wish that one day you will be happy.

As Dorothy stood there on that grey February morning, the thoughts were racing through her mind like a snowstorm. First there was pure astonishment that her son-in-law, whom she scarcely knew and had never liked, should want to give her such a beautiful and expensive present. She was struck by the unworthy thought that it had originally been intended for his strumpet, but somehow knew that it wasn't so. And yet who could have imagined that Giles Standish, who had always appeared so loutish and self-engrossed and who treated his wife abominably, was capable of such sensitivity? The brief letter – obviously written in a hurry for the writing was a frantic scrawl and there was a great blob of ink beside the signature – revealed a man who was warm, perceptive, generous of spirit. A man, moreover, who had glimpsed the despair that she strove to hide from the world, and who wanted to comfort her. It seemed to confirm what, even in her darkest moments, she had always believed – that most human nature was a patchwork of light and shadow, and few people were entirely evil. Even Richard, selfish and brutal as he was, had some basically decent qualities for he treated his tenants fairly and would always protect his family from danger.

It was with a glow in her cheeks and a decided spring in her step that Dorothy folded the gleaming robe away in her clothes press before going downstairs.

CHAPTER TWELVE

1528

On a blustery March day Alicia sat at the writing-table in the solar, chewing the end of her quill.

She had been sitting there for more than an hour, trying to compose a reply to her mother's letter, but it was as if a soggy blanket had been flung across her brain so that she was unable to gather her thoughts, let alone express them in a letter to Dorothy.

An icy gust of wind hurled itself against the window, rattling the glass. She wriggled her toes inside her slippers, for it was bitterly cold even with the brazier burning in the middle of the room. As she sat there, she could feel a draught fingering the back of her neck.

Dorothy's letter had been cheerful and affectionate, crammed with details of a new fox-trimmed cloak, a supper party that she and Sir Richard had recently attended in St Alban's, and the news that her sorrel mare had foaled. Then after a few courteous enquiries about the Houghton family, she concluded with the amazing words: *your father sends you his kindest wishes and hopes you are happy and well.*

Alicia smiled ironically at that. Now that she was comfortably off his hands, it was unlikely that Sir Richard ever gave her a thought. She realized by now that nothing she could do would ever soften his heart towards her. She still loved him, but the hurt had long since faded to a dull hollow ache.

Now that she herself was married, Alicia had a better understanding of her parents relationship, though some areas remained fogged in mystery and half-perceived truths. Like so many, Richard and Dorothy had been forced to marry while they were still barely acquainted, and tension had smouldered between them from the outset. Somehow Dorothy – soft, vibrant Dorothy with her life-long hunger for love – had come to love her husband, but it was a feeling that he had never returned.

Alicia sighed, reaching down to scratch her shin. She thought what her mother must have suffered, caring so passionately for a man who had neither gentleness nor kindness in him, only a frozen shard of flint for a heart and a brutal nature that did not shrink from beating her into cowed obedience. Whatever problems she may have experienced in her own marriage, at least Alicia knew that Gervase would never hit her. Nor could he hurt her emotionally, for she wasn't in love with him.

She stared dully at the creamy-pale parchment spread before her on the table. So far she had written: *Dearest madam, my beloved mother.* There was a black freckle of ink after the word *mother* where she hadn't lifted the quill in time, but she knew that Dorothy wouldn't object. She only complained if her daughters neglected to write, and always gently, as if she understood that they had lives and concerns of their own.

Her hand hovered uncertainly over the page. For a moment she was tempted to let her mother know how things really were at Ryland Place. How Agnes and Lucy hated her. How she sometimes longed so sharply for Greenthorpe, it was like a sickness in her bones.

She caught herself up briskly. It would be very wrong to unburden herself to Dorothy, who would worry and grieve for her. Besides, Dorothy wasn't a sorceress who could magically wave away the problems of personal conflicts and homesickness. She must find her own solution, as women down the centuries had always done.

She sighed again, pushed back a stray tendril of hair from her forehead and dipped the quill into the pewter inkpot. It would be best to stick to domestic matters – the baby who continued to thrive, and Molly's betrothal to Oliver Jennings, the London cloth merchant. (She did not add that Molly had changed overnight into an insufferable bore, endlessly twittering about wedding gowns and garlands, feasts and maids of honour till you were tempted to leave the room or shake her into silence.)

The wedding will not take place until after her sixteenth birthday, so she will be hard-pressed to contain her exuberance.

Would Dorothy detect the sarcasm? She continued hastily:

Last Thursday it was unseasonably mild so we went for a picnic by the river. It was very pleasant after being cooped indoors for so long, though my dog Hero stole a whole chicken from one of the baskets and Lady Houghton was rather vexed.

(And that, she told herself, grinning broadly, did little justice to Lady Houghton's outraged bellows.)

However, just as the men decided they would have a game of football it began to rain heavily and we all got soaked to the skin. We are none the worse for it, except for Isabel who has caught a bad chill.

She paused for a moment, her thoughts turning to the little girl who was now confined to bed, where she lay beneath a smothering mound of blankets, sweating and shivering in turn. Mother Luke bathed her hot little body several times a day, dosed her with possets of wine, honey and herbs but despite these measures the fever continued to rage and the infection had now spread to Isabel's lungs. The doctor had called yesterday but was unable to do anything for her, though he recommended mustard-poultices for her chest and plenty of fluids – 'as much as you can get her to drink. She's not a very strong child, is she?' he added accusingly, running an experienced eye over Isabel's puny frame.

Mother Luke, leaning across the bed to straighten the pillows, flushed to the hairline but didn't answer. Three months short of her twelfth birthday, Isabel might have been taken for an eight-year-old. Her appetite had always been birdlike – she ate as if food were some kind of punishment. Moreover she had never been allowed to enjoy the outdoor exercise which Mother Luke believed was essential for growing children. Lady Agnes prized learning above play and had long ago decided that if her daughters could not be pretty they would at least be well educated.

Now Isabel needed constant care and Mother Luke, already preoccupied with the baby, had been beside herself trying to cope with the extra burden when help came from an unexpected quarter.

Gervase, usually so fearful of the most minor ailment that he would rush to gargle vinegar if someone nearby sneezed more than twice, now slept on a pallet at the foot of Isabel's bed every night. The slightest movement or sound would have him instantly alert and on his feet.

Only this morning Alicia, shocked by his haggard face, had offered to take his place that night but he'd rebuffed her with unexpected bitterness.

'No, you might not hear her if she wakes. Anyway, you don't really care about her. No one does, except me.'

Alicia was too startled to answer. And yet even as she stood there, feeling her eyes drop guiltily before his harsh blue gaze, she felt a stab of resentment. It flashed through her mind that if she were sick, he wouldn't give her a fraction of the care that he lavished upon Isabel. If anything, he would keep his distance rather than risk infection.

Then she thought what he must be suffering – the fear and the tension, the moments of despair – and was ashamed. She wanted to tell him that she was sorry – that she was fond of Isabel. But before she could speak, he had turned on his heel and gone quickly from the room.

The cold light moved across the solar, the wind outside gathered speed. Alicia looked down at her hands, saw that they were blotched with mauve. She blew on them, rubbed them together, then bent over the letter for the last time.

We are all hopeful that she will soon mend and be up from her bed, she wrote with a jaunty confidence that she was very far from feeling.

She signed her name with a bold swirl, sanded the ink and sealed the letter with a great globule of purple-red wax.

Motionless as a figure of bleached stone, Dorothy sat staring into the plum-coloured dusk as it settled over Greenthorpe.

Alicia's letter had been closely followed by one from Agnes Houghton which now lay spread open in her lap. The words seemed to shimmer before her eyes like bright black stars against old snow.

Today my little daughter Isabel died and nothing will ever be the same again.

And so she learned of the tragedy that had struck Ryland Place.

Nothing will ever be the same again. They were the exact words that Dorothy had said to herself when baby Richard was taken from her, twenty-four years ago. Three months old and golden haired like his father for whom he was named, but he'd had her slender bones and graceful hands. Would he always have had those hands, she'd wondered as they laid the tiny coffin in the vault, next to that of her mother, close to where Henry and Cicely lay. She'd tried to picture him, a young man grown tall and strong but with those fine, tapering hands. He would have been loving, sensitive, generous – everything that her husband was not.

The pain, buried deep in some inner pit all these years, was dragged up searingly by Agnes's words. She glanced almost fearfully at the creased sheet of paper. It was almost a physical effort to read it again, yet somehow she felt that she owed it to Agnes to do so.

And yet she couldn't help wondering why Agnes, within hours of her loss, had opened her heart to her. Ever since they'd first met more than twenty years ago, Dorothy had had the distinct feeling that the woman disliked her, even secretly laughed at her.

Her thoughts swept back to that frosty December night when she'd given birth to Kathryn. As she lay flat on her back, feeling weak and sore after her long travail, she remembered that her husband was entertaining John and Agnes downstairs. Weary as she was, she nonetheless thought it strange that nobody came to see her. In fact, they hadn't shown a flicker of interest in her or her daughter. It was at first puzzling, then hurtful and insulting. Early next morning the two guests rode away, leaving Dorothy with the sense of having committed some social breach. Later she questioned Richard but found him curiously evasive.

'I think Agnes found the entertainment less than adequate,' he'd said with one of those nasty smiles.

'It's hardly my fault that I was in childbed.' Dorothy hadn't spoken so sharply to him since they were first married, and he looked momentarily taken aback. She went on. 'They have insulted me and our child. Not that I should be surprised – that woman has never liked me though I've always treated her courteously.'

So why, why had Agnes written now? Unless she'd remembered, in the wilderness of grief, that Dorothy also knew what it was to bury a child and found a sliver of comfort in the thought that she would understand.

Yet somewhere inside her doubt continued to gnaw and scratch like a rodent. She had seen Agnes Houghton in the heart of her family seldom enough, but it was impossible to mistake her antipathy.

'I believe she hates those children,' she'd remarked to Richard, the night they returned to Greenthorpe after seeing Alicia married to the elder Houghton son.

As always Richard had shown impatience and contempt for her 'notions'. He'd even hinted that she was approaching the change of life.

Experience had taught Dorothy not to challenge him. He had not hit her for a long time but his tongue was as wounding as his fist and could leave her feeling stunned and crushed as if from a physical blow. Besides, she was sick with fear for her daughter.

'Will Agnes be kind to my Alicia?'

She had tried to push away the memory of those agate-cold eyes; of the rage that seemed to emanate from the woman's very bones. She had told herself that Alicia had enough wit and spirit to defend herself even against Agnes Houghton. Yet the clawing anxiety did not leave her.

'You didn't have any supper.'

Dorothy jumped. The letter rustled to the floor like an elm-leaf. Joanna was standing beside her, breathing quietly through her mouth. She hadn't heard her enter the room.

'I'm not hungry.' The old resentment instantly had her in its grip, plucking at her heart with white-hot tweezers. She raised her head, stared coldly at the servant and wondered, not for the first time, why she stayed on at Greenthorpe.

'You'll get sick if you don't eat.' For some reason the words reminded Dorothy of when she was a little girl and Joanna had always made her feel safe. Her head began to swim. She had a sudden irrational impulse to fling herself into those tough old arms and weep – to be called 'hinny' again.

Just in time she remembered how Joanna had destroyed her life with her cruel, senseless lies. Her lips tightened until they were no more than a slit of rose-quartz against her pale skin. She would never forgive her, never relent.

The old woman was still standing there, her face half-hidden in the shadows. She seemed to be waiting for something. Dorothy turned to look out of the window, silently dismissing her.

Joanna stooped to pick up the letter. Without a word she laid it in Dorothy's lap, then turned and left the room as silently as she'd entered it.

After she had gone, Dorothy lowered her head into her hands and began to cry.

She knew that she should cry for Isabel. As she knelt in the pew between Gervase and Molly she *was* crying inside. Cold tears spattered on her heart like hailstones but they were tears of pity and remorse rather than grief. For she had never really known the quiet child who was now being laid away in the dark – never tried to understand her or win her confidence.

I feel safer here.

Through the suffocating mist of hot candle-wax and incense, she heard again the little treble voice, so piercingly clear that it seemed to drown the bittersweet singing of the altar-boy. In that same moment she saw herself standing beside a frozen white lake while a hand as light as a moth fluttered timidly in hers. She bent her head, recalling how she had tried – and failed – to picture small frightened Isabel as a grown woman.

I feel safer here. The words tapped against her brain like mice's feet. She hoped that wherever Isabel was now, she felt safe at last.

It was a bitterly cold day even for early April. Dirty-looking clouds crouched low in the sky, almost shutting out the sun. The chill seemed to rise from the stone-paved floor like a cloud of vapour, the trees outside cast a dull green light against the windows.

The sound of Agnes's sobbing seemed to fill the little church. In spite of herself, Alicia felt a tweak of annoyance. Never, never could she believe that Agnes's grief was sincere.

John patted his wife's hand, diffidently as if he feared a rebuke. When it didn't come he clasped it firmly in his and she stopped crying almost at once.

From the corner of her eye she caught Gervase's profile. Like her, he still hadn't shed any tears for Isabel but since her death he had retreated into some shadowy place inside himself where Alicia couldn't reach him. His face had the same raw, bleached look she remembered from that night in the stables. *If only he would cry!* For somehow his silence was more disturbing than Agnes's noisy lamentations.

Suddenly Molly gave a tiny hiccup. Alicia glanced at her worriedly. Small and hunched over in her black clothes, she looked like a sick little crow huddled into its feathers. She fumbled for Molly's hand and was dismayed to find it icy cold.

Molly raised her head to look at her, almost as if she were wondering who she was. Her face looked twisted and swollen in the chilly green light. She had wept almost ceaselessly since the night her sister died; wept alone in the little room where the two of them had slept, snuggled close as puppies, often whispering childish secrets to each other long after the candles were quenched.

For the first time Alicia was glad that Molly would be leaving Ryland Place next year. She knew that Oliver Jennings was somewhere at the back of the church among the other mourners. As an image of his amiable face swam before her, she felt a tiny glow spread across her heart so that the draughty village church no longer seemed so cold and gloomy. Although she used secretly to agree with her in-laws that he had no more spark than an empty hearth, she now realized that he was a good man. There was no doubt that he would be a kind and affectionate husband to little Molly.

To her amazement, she felt a small tug of envy.

It began to rain shortly after midnight, tumultuously as if the heavens were angry. Ryland Place stood like a dispirited red beast, flinching under the raw needles of rain as they swerved across the courtyard and the dark, bud-fattened gardens. Cloudy moonlight pricked the windows, sifting through the bed-curtains where Gervase and Alicia lay wide awake, listening to each other breathing. The fire had gone out in the hearth but a few embers still burned, glinting like red beads in the dark.

Alicia arched her neck, letting her head sink deeper into the plump feather pillows. Gervase lay completely still at the far edge of the bed, his hands folded on his chest like a wax effigy on a coffin. Only his lashes moved, flicking against his cheekbones.

Ever since they'd come to bed, Alicia had been stabbing around in her mind for something comforting to say, for she was guiltily aware that he suffered as she did not. She felt only a weary kind of sadness for the girl who had lived on this earth for eleven years, all of them filled with harshness and fear. For Alicia there was a sense of waste but not loss. Yet Gervase had loved his little sister deeply and a part of him would always grieve.

Suddenly she became aware that the mattress was heaving, then there was the sound of a muffled sob. Without hesitation she reached across and curved her arms about him. At her touch he turned swiftly towards her, clinging to her as if he wanted to lose himself in the warmth of her body. Wordlessly, tender as a mother, Alicia stroked the feather-fine hair as he wept into her neck.

At last the sound of his sobbing died away, like the last notes of a mournful ballad. He began kissing her with what seemed like a kind of feverish gratitude. Feeling confused, she lay stiff and unmoving as those desperate kisses drummed on her face and her throat. Gradually his body began to move slowly, insinuatingly against hers. He wrapped his arms round her, gathering her close, and as his lips found hers she felt herself responding – almost reluctantly, for their lust seemed almost sacrilegious after today's events. However as he reached under her nightgown and began to caress her small belly, as his fingertips teased her

nipples into hardness, all thought of Isabel began to fade. Then he was lying
between her thighs, moving vigorously inside her. Alicia flung back her head,
wound her legs about his waist and felt herself being swept up into the velvet
darkness until wave after wave of exquisite pleasure broke over her.

Like an exhausted child, he fell asleep in her arms afterwards, his head
burrowed into the hollow of her shoulder, one leg bent intimately across her
body. She lay very still, scarcely daring to move in case she woke him. The room
was drenched in darkness now, the moon obscured by swollen black clouds. She
could still hear the rain battering against the glass, yet her thoughts were peaceful. As always after the sex-act, she felt completely relaxed, her body warm and
deliciously limp, moist with their mingled sweat. After a long time she fell asleep,
Gervase's tears still damp on her neck.

When she woke it was almost daybreak, with the light outside turning flinty-
grey. Gervase was sitting on the edge of the bed, dressed in his riding clothes,
watching her with a ruefully tender expression. Startled out of her drowsiness,
she propped herself on one elbow to look at him. Surely he wasn't going riding
at this hour?

'Alicia, I have to go away for a while,' he said softly, then added, 'I shall speak
to Oliver today.'

'Oliver?' Alicia stared blankly.

'He said I might stay with him in London for a spell. If I stay here, I . . .' He
broke off abruptly, his chin dropping into his collar.

Alicia caught both his hands in hers.

'It's all right, Gervase,' she murmured gently. 'If you think it will help, you
must go.'

Agnes Houghton stood at the window, watching the first pale thread of light
winding through the clouds.

She had been standing there all night and her body felt stiff with cold and
fatigue but she did not stir from her post.

Behind her her husband lay stretched out in the bed, silent and still as if he
were sleeping, but she knew that he was not. She felt a small flutter of gratitude
that he didn't speak for he was bound to say something that would annoy her.
Besides, she wanted to be alone with her thoughts for a little longer.

As she stood there, staring across the brightening green acres which she'd
always felt belonged exclusively to her – as if John were no more than the bailiff
who managed them for her – her eyes were glossy but tearless. All her weeping
had been done the day before in the little village church. People had thought she
was crying for Isabel and been very kind but as she knelt there, surrounded by
her family and neighbours, all her thoughts were of William, her firstborn. It was
as if the years had fallen away and she, young and stunned by grief, were numbly

clinging to the strands of her sanity.

'She is at peace,' they told her, and she thought how little any of them knew her.

And yet somehow in the grey blur of the past few days, the two children had become as one in her mind. She wondered now why this should be – the blond cheerful little boy whom she had adored and the mouselike girl who had so often irritated her.

Yet I would have done my best for her, she told herself. She was mine. But when she wept it was William's face that she saw before her.

She didn't realize that John had got out of bed until she felt his hand fall softly upon her shoulder. She turned her head and saw him standing behind her in his nightshirt, his face puckered up like an unhappy monkey's.

'My dear,' he murmured, patting the thick shoulder awkwardly. 'This is doing you no good.'

Agnes stared at him as if he was an intruder and she could not decide whether to call for assistance. Then a look of annoyance passed over her face. She struck the hand away as if it was a ladybird, then stomped away to the far end of the room, her body rigid as if he'd insulted her.

It wasn't until Nanty pointed out that her monthly flux was late that Alicia suspected she might be pregnant.

As the two girls faced each other across the bedchamber on that pale-yellow morning late in April, sympathetic concern showed in one young face, stark white shock in the other.

Nanty was the first to move, gently steering her mistress towards the hearth-side stool, then going to fetch a cloak and spreading it over her shoulders. As she went to pour a glass of wine, she cast a wary glance behind her at the stiff, icy-faced figure as if afraid that she might fling herself into the fire or out of the window.

'This will make you feel better,' she murmured like one trying to pacify a lunatic as she returned with the glass.

Alicia clasped it in shaking hands, took a slow mouthful – and then another. Then her paralysed mind jerked into action.

Why hadn't she suspected anything before this? Her courses had always been regular and it had been more than six weeks since the last one. Though of course she had been nervous and distracted and simply hadn't given the matter a thought.

As she sat there, blankly watching the honey-flecked sunshine weaving patterns on the bed curtains, she realized that there had been strange new sensations in her body lately. She often felt drowsy, her breasts were sore and taut and there were swimmy bouts of nausea that might strike her at any hour of the day.

*

The day after Isabel's burial, Gervase had ridden back to London with Oliver Jennings. The two had struck up a friendship of sorts, and so when Oliver in a moment of half-tipsy compassion had suggested that Gervase pay him a visit soon, he'd seized upon it the way a man stricken by a mysterious disease will clutch at a new remedy even though its healing properties have not been proved.

'I'll ride back with you today,' he'd said tersely. 'If I may.'

'Why certainly.' If Oliver was startled he gave no sign, but merely smiled that affable smile which never told people anything. His tall house in Holborn was comfortably furnished, his servants well trained, and a guest could easily be accommodated at short notice.

Nobody could have been more surprised than Alicia by her husband's decision. Awkward and sullen in other people's company, he was usually loath to seek them out. She could only assume that Oliver's kind heart and sturdy common sense provided some kind of anchor for the unhappy youth, and she encouraged the visit.

After Gervase had set out for London on that dark, rainy spring day, Alicia had flopped down on her bed, limp with relief. Away from Ryland Place and its memories, he would surely begin to recover. Yet as the days passed she found that she missed him. Worse still, a heavy sense of guilt began to press upon her spirits.

'I have failed him,' she told both herself and Father Charles in a rare moment of humility.

The old priest gave a mild shake of his head which was almost completely bald now except for a thin frill of white around the crown. Fingers pleated under his chin, he regarded the girl kneeling at his feet, her anguished white face begging for comfort. It was a rare occurrence for her to seek spiritual counsel from him, and yet he had long ago gauged the turbulence that drove her.

'You judge yourself too severely, child. He needed to go away for a time. You must stop torturing yourself. Pray instead that he returns calmer and refreshed in spirit.'

'But if I had been a good wife to him – if I had made him happy . . .'

Father Charles gave her an oddly penetrating look that made her quickly duck her head.

'Alicia, you gave him the few moments of happiness he has ever known. Remember that, and be at peace.'

Neither of them was aware that she carried Gervase's child beneath her heart.

A great wave of pain and longing washed over her all these weeks later. Never had she missed him – wanted him – so much. With his baby growing in her body, she needed him close by. And yet nothing could persuade her to write and ask him to return. She had always despised women who whimpered and begged men to take care of them.

'You mustn't tell anyone.' Her voice was shrill with fear as she turned back to Nanty.

Nanty's mouth flew open, then closed again as if she had meant to protest but changed her mind. Suddenly Alicia's face softened.

'Not yet,' she added gently. 'I have to think. And I know I can trust you, Nanty.'

Slowly a warm light crept into Nanty's eyes. Then she smiled and, for the first time since they'd met, the smile was relaxed and friendly. She reached down to pat Alicia's arm.

'You must take care of yourself,' she said. They were the same words that Agnes had said to Lucy on that far-off winter day.

Alicia's heart plunged at the thought of her mother-in-law. Agnes Houghton had always hated her. She had dreamed and schemed that Tom's son would one day inherit Ryland Place, and believed that she had succeeded. When she learnt how Gervase and Alicia had thwarted her, her malevolence would know no bounds.

Alicia stared straight before her, a worried frown criss-crossing her brow. Although she had always longed for the day when she might taunt Agnes with the knowledge that she was pregnant, she now realized that to do so would be both childish and dangerous. Instead she must play for time as Lucy had done before her, though for a far deadlier reason. For there was no doubt in her mind that if Agnes could find a way to prevent her child from being born, she would not hesitate to use it.

Yet she knew it was impossible to keep it a secret for ever.

Before long she started to retch miserably every morning as soon as she lifted her head from the pillow. Fortunately Nanty always had a glass of tansy-water at hand. Alicia remembered her mother saying that it was a sovereign remedy for breeding sickness.

'Don't tell anyone,' she half-sobbed, as Nanty washed the icy sweat from her face. 'No one must know yet.' The vision of Agnes's dark scowling face seemed to loom larger and closer with each passing day.

And then one morning she fainted during Mass.

The smell of smoking candles, combined with the prickly May heat, made her head swim weakly, the weight of her black taffeta skirts seemed to be dragging her down towards the floor. Swept by sudden panic, she fixed her eyes on the pale pages of her missal but the words were blurred, as if she were looking at them through a haze of tears. Someone – it must have been Agnes – gave her a sharp jab in the ribs as if to remind her where she was. That was the last thing she remembered before slumping forward in the pew.

'I must have swooned,' she said foolishly, soon after floating back to consciousness in her own room, where one of the menservants had carried her. Nanty was leaning over her, vigorously waving a burning feather under her nose. She paused to give a grin of sheer relief.

Alica's nostrils quivered at the acrid smell. Weakly she turned her head, which seemed to be stuffed with soggy linen, and saw Agnes standing at the foot of the bed, like a sinister black toad in her mourning gown. The onyx brooch on her bodice winked like a malicious eye in the sunlight.

Agnes flapped a pudgy hand, indicating that Nanty should leave them alone. Nanty glanced anxiously at her mistress's ash-tinged face. Alicia nodded feebly, for her head still felt thick and fuggy, and Nanty curtsied and scurried away.

'So.' Agnes folded her hands beneath her breasts, fixing Alicia with her most unpleasant smile. 'You fainted. I don't believe it has ever happened before?' Her eyes raked the inert figure on the bed as if it were transparent.

Alicia lifted her eyebrows mockingly. All at once it was as if the fear and tension of the past few weeks had evaporated, leaving only contempt.

'There's only one reason why a healthy young woman should suddenly fall into a swoon,' Agnes continued smoothly. 'But your husband is away, so I must be mistaken.'

'I am with child – by Gervase.' The words came spilling out before she had time to consider them.

Agnes bent over the bed as if she were about to hit her. Alicia jumped, then her entire body stiffened defensively. Then she saw that Agnes was smiling.

'You silly little harlot! Do you think I don't know how things stand between the two of you? Why, I examined your sheets personally for months.'

Revulsion rolled over Alicia in thick waves, so powerful that she thought she would faint again. Yet even as she lay there, utterly mesmerized by the evil face shimmering above her like a great florid moon, sheer hatred came to her aid. It pounded through her veins like rich wine so that she no longer felt so weak and helpless. She thought how this woman had so nearly destroyed her own son. She thought of Isabel. And lastly she thought of her unborn baby, for whom she would fight like a vixen if she must. Her eyes were hard and taunting as she returned Agnes's gaze. At last she gave an insolent little smile.

'It would seem that you relaxed your vigilance, madam. Gervase and I have been truly man and wife for some time now.'

There was no sound in the room except for Agnes's breathing. Alicia, her fingers curled into her sides, watched her mother-in-law's expression change from coarse amusement to an appalled stare as the words slowly registered. The ruddy colour had frozen from her face, leaving it as pale as lard. At last she straightened up, backing away from the bed as if she had just seen a slug wriggling from the sheets.

'That of course would explain my son's eagerness to go away. I must confess I thought it strange at the time but now – now I understand. Oh yes, I understand well enough! It must have been a most distasteful experience for the poor boy.'

With that she swept towards the door and went out, leaving Alicia still lying on the bed, her heart banging so hard the sound seemed to fill her ears. Yet as the moments passed, she was filled with a hot dizzy sense of triumph.

'I've won,' she whispered, wrapping her arms round the pillow. 'At last I've beaten that vicious old bitch.'

She wanted to laugh, dance round the room, lean out of the window and shout the words across the courtyard.

And then, like a shadow prowling across the face of the sun, fear rose up and clamped her heart.

Seven months must pass before she gave birth. Seven perilous months during which anything might happen. A topple headlong down the stairs. (Pregnant women were sometimes known to be clumsy.) Sudden debilitating illness after dinner. *The food was wholesome and well prepared, but she always* was *a glutton,* Agnes would crow. Or a pillow crushed over her face while she slept. . . .

She caught herself up briskly. That last would certainly not happen, for no would-be assassin would ever get past Hero. Yet she knew her fears were not without foundation; knew that anyone as ruthless and determined as Agnes could destroy a vulnerable pregnant woman as easily as tearing blossom from a young tree.

She rolled on to her back, her hands mounded protectively over her belly. Her smooth features hardened into obstinate lines and in that moment she looked very much like her father when he suspected that his authority had been flouted.

Now that her pregnancy was no longer a fearful secret, she could indulge in the normal maternal feelings of pride, hope, excitement, tenderness. But she would need to be vigilant. For the sake of her baby she would be on her guard – every moment – against Agnes.

CHAPTER THIRTEEN

1528

Gervase was riding home through the gold-spangled heat of a June afternoon.

The day had been swallowed up in a hot haze as he passed through bustling market towns and desolate flat fields; along dusty cart-tracks, past meadows thick with clover. The landscape was dotted here and there with a greenish glint of water, the sky was all blue, without a shred of cloud.

As he set his horse upon a lane turning sharply off from the road he was aware that the groom jogging a couple of paces behind him was swearing under his breath, but he ignored him. He would ride on until nightfall and if the fellow couldn't stay the pace it would be *his* worry and he could sleep in a hedgerow tonight. For the first time in his life Gervase was frantic to reach home.

That dreaded scourge, the sweating sickness, first brought across the channel by Henry VII's mercenary soldiers, had returned to London that week, striking terror into the hearts of its citizens. On the first day 2,000 had been stricken, and the death-toll was expected to soar yet higher.

Watching the people flooding through the narrow streets like a panic-ridden army of ants desperate to reach the sanctuary of their homes, Gervase had felt chilling fear knock against his heart. Nothing, not even Master Jennings' easy-going hospitality, could persuade him to stay.

Unknown to him, Anne Boleyn had also set out for her family home in Kent that same day. One of her maids had fallen sick and it was decided that it would be unwise for Anne to accompany the court in its flight to Waltham in Essex.

For once, King Henry did not implore his sweetheart not to leave him and it was with considerable relief that he stood at an upper window and watched her carriage go swaying across the cobbles and out beneath the great curved arch, followed by a straggling train of mounted servants and luggage carts. Utterly intrepid in the tiltyard and the chase, the very thought of the mystery disease could reduce him to a wobbling blancmange of terror.

Gervase could feel his heart thudding in rhythm with Black Ruby's hoofs. His shirt and doublet were soaked in sweat, he could even see the sheen of sweat on the side of his nose, like tiny seed pearls scattered in the sun. A list of symptoms galloped mercilessly through his mind – profuse sweating, a wild heartbeat, pain in the head, the belly, the lungs . . . *Sweet Jesus, don't let me get sick!*

He thought of Ryland Place waiting for him at the end of his journey like a grim but efficient nurse. There would be cool ale for him to drink, cool water to bathe in, cool holland sheets to slide between and rest his sore tired body. For weeks he had shrunk from the very thought of home, yet now his frightened heart strained towards it, longing to be cradled inside its rose-coloured walls.

Alicia had written him that she was pregnant and expected to be brought to bed in December. It was strange to think of that lithe body growing swollen and drowsy with a child. Stranger yet to think he would be a father.

An image of his wife's face seemed to glimmer through the heat haze – proud and sleek with tilting white cheekbones and black-fringed nightshade eyes. He wondered how she felt about the pregnancy – proud? Frightened? Disgruntled that she would lose her slender shape? Her letter had given no indication and he hadn't bothered to reply to it.

The memory of their last night together had become a jarring whirl of images in his mind, all of them lashed by the sound of cold April rain. He could recall very little pleasure, only the heaving grief that had driven him to seek comfort in Alicia's arms. He had often wondered since then how many other men had sunk into a woman's body for the sheer bliss of forgetfulness. Surely it was the way a heartsick man used a whore rather than his wife.

And now, incredibly, they were to have a baby.

The lane dipped and curved before him like a pale stream, flanked on either side by elder bushes aflame with white, as if someone had hung rosary beads upon them. He could see the sun dropping behind the distant smudgy blue hills. Already the day was dying.

Alicia! Why did his thoughts go back and back to her? For so long they had been enemies, locked in a silent war of distrust until that Christmas night when he'd made love to her for the first time. He had come so close to loving her then, for she was warm breathing proof that he was like other men, despite his mother's gloomy predictions. Now she was carrying his child.

'May God send you a lusty son,' Oliver had cried heartily when the news arrived.

Gervase secretly hoped it would be a girl – small-boned, quiet and gentle like Isabel. Already in his mind he had created a fairy-child with Alicia's face framed in his sister's soft brown hair.

The sudden spike of pain piercing the side of his head caught him unawares. He let out a hoarse cry, almost dropping the reins. The huge black horse flung

back his head and gave a shrill, startled whinny. The world became a mad spinning blur of blue and green and gold.

Gervase managed to check the prancing, snorting horse. The pain was reced-
ing, but his eyes were screwed up against the sharp bright glare. His throat felt
as if it was coated with hot ashes.

'Is something wrong, sir?' The servant came jogging up on his tired brown
cob.

'There's a village some two miles ahead, if I recall.' Gervase tried to sound
casual and offhand. 'We'll rest there a while and let the horses breathe.'

'Yes sir.' A smile of sly triumph curled across the sour features.

Gervase kicked his horse forward. Who wouldn't be weary after riding all day
in the choking dust and heat? No wonder his head ached. Good food and ale and
an hour's rest were all he needed, then he would be as hale as a farm-boy.

He couldn't have the sickness! The idea was too appalling to think of.

Alicia stood in the cottage doorway, looking about her with mingled satisfaction
and dismay.

Her hair was bundled beneath a large white kerchief, her figure entirely
covered by a billowing apron. There was a black smudge on one cheek, another
across the bridge of her nose. Her fingernails were caked with dirt but for once
she didn't care what she looked like. No one except Lucy and the two serving
women would see her until the danger had passed and they could return to the
manor house.

She and Nanty had been working all afternoon to put the primitive one-room
dwelling in order and now she felt a small surge of pride as she surveyed their
handiwork. They had swept the beaten-earth floor and laid down fresh green
rushes which Alicia had insisted on sprinkling with rosemary and hyssop.
Fragrant juniper had been burnt in the hearth to sweeten the atmosphere, yet as
she stood there, hands on hips, it seemed to her that only the smoke lingered in
a choking cloud, for there was no chimney in the cottage.

An old wooden press and a scarred, rickety table were the only pieces of furniture left behind by the previous occupants. Nanty and Alicia had vigorously
polished them with linseed oil and now they gleamed like satin in the bronze
evening light which sloped in through the doorway and the tiny square window.

Three stout chests containing clothes and linen were arranged against the
walls. Piles of bright blue and cherry velvet cushions had transformed them into
attractive seats that lent an air of defiant luxury to the drab little room. Jack's
cradle stood in one corner, two straw pallets lay side by side in another. Alicia
eyed them dubiously. They had been left to air in the sunshine all afternoon and
Nanty insisted they were clean, yet she still had visions of fat bugs biting her flesh
while she was asleep. She also wondered if Lucy realized that the two of them

would be sharing a bed. The girl was more withdrawn than ever nowadays but her hostility towards Alicia remained, like a thin candle flame in the fog that cloaked her mind.

Alicia bent to straighten the covers and give the pillows a final pounding. Then she looked round the room again. Despite her and Nanty's efforts, it still looked depressingly cramped and dark. She was struck by an unexpected wave of longing for own bedchamber with the big feather-bed covered in bright taffeta, the mullioned windows that let in plenty of air and light, the tapestries and plump cushions and richly gleaming candlesticks. In that moment she felt a small shaft of respect for John Houghton's tenants. How did they manage to live in these squalid little cages with their tumbling broods of children and still cling to sanity? And how by all the saints was she to manage it, cooped up with the two servants, a baby and a woman who was already half-crazy?

The room seemed to be closing in around her like a muffling blanket. Filled with sudden, inexplicable panic, she ran to the window and stood thankfully drawing in lungfuls of clean golden air.

As she stood there, clutching the narrow ledge, she caught sight of Lucy kneeling in the grass, making a daisy chain. With her head slightly bent and her mouth open, she looked like a child absorbed in some task. For some reason Alicia thought of the delicate altar-cloths and prie-dieu covers, the soft quilted caps and sleeves gilded with golden thread that Lucy used to turn out in abundance. Suddenly she felt the hot sting of tears behind her eyes. How proud Lucy had been of her handiwork, allowing nobody to see it till it was finished, then displaying it with shy but unmistakable pleasure. But she never did any sewing now – it was as if she had forgotten how.

Mother Luke was sitting on a blanket in the shade of a sweet-chestnut tree, cuddling one-year-old Jack against her shoulder. He was screaming at the top of his lungs, his fat little face turning from pink to scarlet.

'There, there, my love-duck,' the nurse cooed, rubbing his back and gently rocking him back and forth. As she caught sight of Alicia she gave an apologetic little grimace.

'It's his teeth,' she called, striving to make herself heard above the din. 'The poor little lamb suffers mightily when they're coming through.'

Alicia smiled weakly. Why had she never realized before that Jack cried so much? At home, she'd scarcely been aware of him but now. . . .

She turned away and went to sit on one of the chests. Leaning back against the wall, she thrust her legs out before her and stared moodily at the tips of her black leather shoes.

'How long?' she groaned to herself. 'How long will we be able to bear this?'

Almost at once she was ashamed. She must be one of the most wicked creatures alive, fretting over a little discomfort when her husband was struggling and fighting for his life.

Last night he had returned from London, grey-faced and soaked in sweat, obviously on the verge of collapse.

'It's the sweat, my lady.' The groom's frightened gaze slid from Agnes's grim countenance to the thin shivering creature who was now crumpled on a stool and looking mighty sorry for himself. Why hadn't he yielded to the cowardly but sensible impulse to flee hot-heeled back to London and let the wretch blunder homeward as best he could? Now *he* would get sick, like as not, and who would look after Ellen and their five little ones?

Alicia was secretly impressed at the way her mother-in-law assumed command. Gervase was speedily put to bed, swaddled in blankets despite the parching midsummer heat, for it was considered vital that the patient be encouraged to sweat out the infection.

'Light a fire in his room and see that it is kept going.' Agnes snapped orders at the terrified servants. 'And don't let him kick the blankets off – he must stay completely covered.'

Molly was sent away that same evening to stay with her father's cousin, Ralph Waters, in the village. As she walked stiffly across the courtyard towards the waiting carriage, a sullen maidservant trailing at her heels, she felt sick with apprehension. Aunt Anne was almost as frightening as her mother; fat and sour and given to making spiteful remarks whenever you were alone with her. There wasn't even the prospect of other young people to brighten her exile, for Ralph and Anne were childless.

Tom had vowed that he wouldn't be driven from his home.

'I'm not a baby or a quaking old greybeard,' he'd retorted, and no one bothered to argue the point.

Naturally concern ran high for little Jack. John was reluctant to impose further upon his cousin, especially as Agnes's hastily scrawled note had been concise to the point of rudeness. In the end it was decided to install the child, with his mother and his nurse, in an empty cottage near the old water-mill, now fallen into disuse. It would be crude and uncomfortable, but at least they would be safe from infection.

'And what about Alicia?' John glanced at the girl who so far hadn't spoken a word. He thought she looked pale and drawn – the baby must be sapping strength from her. Of course, she must be half-distracted with fear for Gervase.

Agnes, impatient to set her plans in motion, looked at him as if he were an irritating small boy bent on gaining a parent's attention with silly questions.

'Women are said to be more resilient to the sweat!' she snapped.

'But my dear – remember she is with child.' Even as he spoke John mentally girded himself for battle. 'Surely it would be sensible for her to take every precaution?'

Agnes savagely rubbed at a grease-spot on the table which her usually sharp eyes had only just detected. The others watched her nervously.

Always that wretched girl! she was thinking. I curse the day I first clapped eyes on her. Such a mealy-mouthed little thing she seemed then – not two words to say for herself – yet I vow and swear she's been more trouble than the whole parcel of them.

'Very well,' she said at last, her tone as grudging as if she had been forced to part with a valuable piece of jewellery. 'But I hope Mistress Grand Airs won't be too distressed by rough living. Mother Luke will be busy enough with Jack, without having to wipe *her* arse for her.'

Alicia leapt up now at the sound of footsteps outside. Nanty came in, almost staggering under the weight of an enormous basket. It had been arranged that they would collect their supplies daily from the home farm, yet the basket appeared to hold enough food to last them for a week.

Alicia hurried across the room to help her but was met with a piercing scream that made her spring back in alarm.

'Careful, mistress, it's heavy! Do you want to hurt the baby?'

Alicia sighed. Would she ever be allowed to forget for a moment that she was pregnant and her body no longer her own!

Later when Jack was asleep, they ate supper outdoors, beside the little stream which ran behind the cottage. Alicia, hoping to raise everyone's spirits, fetched a bottle of Sir John's best claret from the press. It made a fine accompaniment to their meal of cold bacon, soft wheaten bread and cherry pie.

'We're just like gypsies,' she remarked cheerfully, sucking cherry juice from her fingers.

'Gypsies are free!' It was the first time Lucy had spoken. They turned to her politely but her eyes were fixed on some spot on the horizon. For some reason Alicia shivered.

Suddenly there was a furious yell from inside the cottage. A look of resignation slid over Mother Luke's face.

'I'd better go to him,' she said placidly. She stood up, brushing crumbs from her bodice, then picked her way daintily across the grass, a neat little figure in her snowy cap and grey gown, the evening breeze gently ruffling at her skirts.

Without a word Lucy got to her feet and followed her, like a shy calf padding behind its mother.

Alicia and Nanty washed the supper things in the stream. Kneeling side by side on the bank, they worked in companionable silence while the summer dusk settled around them, staining the hills and downs with purple. There was no sound anywhere except for a couple of late birds gossiping and the occasional slither of a night creature in the undergrowth.

Suddenly Nanty gave a whoop of laughter. Alicia looked up, startled.

'I'm sorry, mistress!' Tears of mirth were running down the freckled face. 'But you'd make a poor housewife.'

She pointed at Alicia's wide silk sleeves trailing in the water, already soaked to the elbows.

Dawn had tinted the sky with apples and roses when Alicia woke next morning.

She moved gingerly on the rough straw pallet; her whole body felt stiff and bruised, almost as if she'd been beaten, and there was a dull thudding ache above her eyes which reminded her of those occasions when she had drunk too much brandy-wine. Although she had been close to fainting with fatigue when she finally crawled into bed last night, she had slept badly and felt far from refreshed.

Lying crushed between the wall and Lucy's hot, plump body, her thoughts had instantly fled to Gervase.

What was he thinking now, she'd wondered, picturing him in his sweltering bed, the pain tearing at his arms and legs, the fever rippling through his body like rivulets of fire. He had always been so terrified of illness. She recalled him anxiously brooding over a mild rash on his chest and repeatedly asking her if she thought it might be serious.

'I dread to think what you'll do if you are ever really ill!' she had exclaimed, losing patience with him.

Would he die? For the first time she had allowed her mind to dwell upon the possibility. She tried to imagine her life without him. She would be alone again – alone and friendless in the red-brick prison that was Ryland Place.

With that dismal thought she drifted into oblivion. It seemed that she had no sooner closed her eyes than something – perhaps the sound of an owl hooting in the trees or a gust of wind rattling the wooden shutter – made her wake abruptly, her heart pounding. The room was cloaked in darkness but she was able to discern a small shape creeping across the floor.

At first she thought it was Mother Luke but Jack was snoring softly in his cradle on the other side of the room. Then she noticed that the narrow space beside her was empty.

Silent as a cat, she slid out of bed and padded towards Lucy, who had now reached the door and inched it open. Moonlight sifted in through the slender chink, and she was able to see that, though Lucy hadn't bothered to comb her hair, she was wearing her best yellow gown, haphazardly fastened, and slippers on her unstockinged feet.

'Where are you going, Lucy?' Conscious of the others sleeping nearby, Alicia kept her voice to a whisper.

'This isn't my home.' Lucy was also whispering, as if she'd taken her cue from Alicia. 'I have to go home.'

'There is sickness at home,' Alicia said gently. 'We have to stay here for a little while till it's safe for us to return.'

'Tom!' Lucy breathed the name as if it were a prayer to some powerful saint.

'Tom wants you to be safe.' Alicia was growing desperate, wondering if she would have to physically restrain the girl. 'And you are safe here, Lucy. We are all going to take care of you.'

Something like comprehension stole into Lucy's unnaturally bright eyes. Her hand fell away from the doorknob, then she bent her head like a penitent child. Alicia put an arm around her waist and guided her back to bed. There she lay, motionless as a doll in her satin gown, her head tilted as if she were listening for some signal that only she would understand. Alicia sighed irritably and turned over, her nose flattened against the wall, and went back to sleep.

The cottage was empty when she woke but she could hear voices outside – Nanty's light, sing-song tones blending with Mother Luke's cosy Suffolk burr. She kicked back the covers, climbed out of bed and threw on yesterday's clothes, which had been left in a heap on the cushions. Then she tied a clean kerchief over her head without bothering to consult the mirror, and hurried out into the sunshine.

After a breakfast of cold bacon and bread washed down with ale, Nanty took the basket from behind the door and set out for the farm. At the last moment Alicia suggested that Lucy might go with her and help carry the things back. It occurred to her that a walk might do Lucy some good, but a selfish part of her wanted to be relieved of that unnerving presence for a while.

She stood in the doorway, one hand shading her eyes as she watched the two figures set off across the meadow, carrying the basket between them; Nanty so small and sprightly, deliberately slowing her steps to Lucy's stolid tread.

While Mother Luke was dressing the baby, Alicia washed the breakfast things in the stream, this time remembering to fold her sleeves back. She hummed to herself as she swirled the pewter cups and dishes, the silver spoons and Sheffield knives in the water, then spread them on the grass to dry. Then she squatted down at the water's edge and wrapped her arms round her knees, greedily drinking in the peaceful scene.

The June morning was a lyric of green and gold spread under a cloudless sky. A blackbird was singing throatily in the sweet-chestnut tree. It was hard to believe that something as ugly as the plague could be gnawing its way through England like a maggot at the core of a rosy apple.

The stream looked enticingly cool, curled between the tangled bulrushes in a glittering silver ribbon. Alicia gazed at it longingly. She felt unpleasantly hot and sweaty; her gown was clinging in wet patches to her body, her stockings were stuck to her legs.

The next moment she was peeling off her clothes on the bank. Then, cautious as a baby nymph, she lowered herself into the water, shivering at its icy bite on her bare flesh.

Gradually she grew accustomed to the cold and began splashing recklessly at her arms and breasts, her slightly rounded belly. Fortunately the cottage was situated in a fairly isolated spot. She had a picture of Agnes's face, thunderstruck at the sight of her daughter-in-law romping naked in the open air, and broke into peals of laughter. In that same moment a long shadow slanted across the water, blotting out the sunlight.

Alicia glanced up quickly, instinctively folding her arms across her breasts. She was horrified to see Tom Houghton, mounted on his chestnut mare, on the far bank.

Although common sense told her that he must at least have glimpsed her body, she huddled into a ball, looking up at him imploringly. Why was it that he always managed to catch her at a disadvantage?

Tom was regarding her almost impersonally, as if she were of no more interest to him than a blade of grass.

'I'm glad that anxiety for your husband hasn't deprived you of your sense of the absurd,' he said at last, and this time his eyes went over her with a touch of the old insolence.

Furious, Alicia manoeuvred herself to the edge of the stream and reached for her gown. Half-concealed among the dark-green rushes, she quickly drew it on over her wet naked body.

'Lucy has gone up to the farm with my maid,' she called haughtily, as if to compensate for the undignified picture she'd made. 'They should be back soon.'

'I haven't come to see Lucy.' Even his voice sounded different, as if he were speaking through a muffling veil. He edged his horse forward and continued to regard her with that odd, blank expression. His face was as pale as carved ivory above the black doublet.

For no reason that she could think of, Alicia felt a cold fear begin to crawl through her body. She opened her mouth to speak but no sound emerged. Then she saw Tom's hands suddenly tighten on the reins, the knuckles standing out, the skin white. When he spoke again his voice sounded harsh and flat, as if he wanted to hurt her.

'I came to see you – to tell you that Gervase died last night.'

She lay like a small stunned animal on her bed of straw, just as she had lain these past three days, staring blindly at the thatched ceiling overhead. She felt as if she were lying in a sticky web of greyness yet she didn't want to leave it; she wasn't sure if she could.

She was unaware that during that time the sweat had claimed Agnes Houghton, two housemaids and one of the gardeners. Agnes had insisted on caring for her son personally, for reasons which one could only guess at. It was probably the first noble deed in her selfish life; there was bitter irony in the fact that it killed her. Later Alicia was to feel only a dim sense of wonder that her mother-in-law, who had seemed invincible, was after all mortal – that the terrible disease sweeping the land had crushed that savage strength for ever.

The weather continued hot and drowsy. Now that the threat of a miscarriage had passed, the others spent most of the time outdoors, in deference to Alicia's grief. Yet she felt no grief. She felt nothing, only that empty greyness as if she too were dead.

Sometimes she was conscious of Nanty and Mother Luke bending over the bed, their faces pale anxious smudges swimming out of the gloom as they pleaded with her to eat something. Feeling unutterably weary, she would turn her face into the pillow. She felt no need of food.

At dusk on the third day, Mother Luke sat on the edge of the bed, a tray balanced on her knees. There was an iron glint in her eye that told Alicia she was ready for battle.

'You must eat, mistress,' she said firmly. 'If you want to live – if you want your baby to live – then you must eat.'

To please Mother Luke – or rather, to be rid of her so that she could crawl back inside the painless grey cocoon – Alicia sat up and took the cup of buttermilk in both hands. Her eyes purposely avoided the hearty slices of bread and mutton.

No sooner had she drained the cup than her long-empty stomach rebelled and she was unable to stem the stream of greenish bile as it spewed on to the rushes, spattering Mother Luke's shoes.

The sweating sickness raged through the south of England like a mighty, unquenchable fire, leaving in its wake a pall of devastation and grief.

London suffered the highest mortalities. In the riverside mansions of the great and in the overcrowded stinking slums sprawling out behind the waterfront, people were still reeling from the speed with which the disease had taken their loved ones.

At the Tudor court most of the nobles who had succumbed to the sickness eventually recovered but even there there were fatalities – Sir William Compton, Edward Poyntz and Mary Boleyn's mild-mannered husband, William Carey. Anne Boleyn had also been ill, as had her father and her beloved brother, but in the end all three rallied.

By July the epidemic had begun to subside and people gradually took up their lives again. Their hearts were still heavy but there was the sheep-shearing to be done, the corn to be threshed, winter clothes to be looked over and a multitude of small tasks and dramas to fill their days.

One sultry afternoon Sir John came to the cottage, a sad yet dignified figure in his black mourning clothes. He hadn't bothered to shave during the crisis and the spiky little beard merely emphasized the fresh lines on his face. For the first time he looked like an old man.

'God be praised that I find you all safe,' he breathed, after he had kissed Lucy and chucked Nanty under the chin.

Mother Luke brought his grandson to him. Jack had grown very bonny during those past weeks. His limbs were brown and sturdy, his thick mop of curls blanched almost white by the hot sun. He looked back at his grandfather with golden-brown eyes that were remarkably like Sir John's own, then gave one of those dimpled smiles that always drew cries of delight from the women.

'He has his father's charm,' John said with a sigh. He kissed the little boy and handed him back to his nurse.

He went to stand beside the bed where Alicia lay, inert as a stone. Her hair lay in lank coils on the pillow, yet its redness managed to look almost profane against her black gown.

'I've come to take you home,' he said quietly, his eyes fixing themselves upon the shuttered white face.

'Ryland Place is not my home.' Alicia spoke very slowly, as if she hadn't used her voice for a long time and wanted to see how it sounded.

John drew in his breath sharply, as if someone had punched him in the stomach. For a moment it looked as if he would turn away, then he reached down and took both her hands in his.

'Alicia, there has been much unpleasantness and I know you have been hurt.' He did not mention his wife but her name seemed to hover in the air between them. Seeing no flicker of response in her face he went on. 'What can I say except that you are my son's wife – and I need you.'

Like someone coming out of a poppy-drugged sleep, Alicia slowly turned her head to look at him. She searched his face for signs of mockery but the hazel eyes held only kindness. In that moment she remembered that, while she had lost a husband, he had lost a wife and also a son.

Somehow her hands were locked around his neck and she was sobbing against his doublet – hard, wrenching sobs that seemed to be tearing themselves from her guts. After a time John's arms crept around her.

'There my little one, you're safe now.'

He held her for a long time, letting her weep until she was drained of tears.

CHAPTER FOURTEEN

1528

Stripes of corn-coloured sunlight fell across the long gallery where Alicia sat stitching a coat for her baby.

It was a beautiful garment of rich crimson taffeta looped with irises. She had been working on it for several weeks and was very proud of it. And yet it was almost an eerie feeling, making clothes for someone who didn't actually exist yet and whose presence she still found impossible to imagine even though she often felt it fluttering like moths' wings under her heart.

She reached up to push the window open another couple of inches. The early September heat seemed to hang over the land in a stupefying cloud. Now that she was nearly six months pregnant, Alicia found it oppressive.

The worst part of being pregnant was the way it sapped her energy, making her feel clumsy, slow and, worse, ugly. No longer could she move quickly about the house, romp with Hero or ride her horse at a furious gallop over the ripening countryside.

Yet life at Ryland Place was undoubtedly more peaceful without Agnes's malevolent presence. Yes, there was sadness still, for the memory of sickness and death was fresh in everyone's minds, but that sulphurous pall of menace had been miraculously lifted.

Somewhat to her surprise, Alicia found that she was regarded as unofficial mistress of the household. The servants spoke to her with a deference that had been singularly lacking before, often coming to her for advice or to settle some dispute. At first she was a little disconcerted, just as her mother had been all those years ago when the reins of Greenthorpe were thrust into her inexperienced hands, but her fears proved groundless. The steward was almost inhumanly efficient and had hinted that he would not be browbeaten by Alicia as he had been for so many years by Agnes. In fact he clutched at his new power so enthusiastically, it was difficult not to suspect that he had been waiting all this time for Agnes to die.

Sir John often sought her company in the evenings when the day's business was done and he was able to relax. A warm affection had grown between the two of them and they looked forward to those quiet hours on the terrace, sometimes talking, sometimes companionably silent while the twilight gathered about them and birds called to each other as they settled into their nests.

John's favourite topic was Ryland Place. He made Alicia think of a besotted mother, eagerly recounting the smallest deed or quirk of her child. Nonetheless there was something soothing about those conversations, if only because they were so simple and undemanding.

'When I am dead, all of this will belong to your son,' he told her more than once, with a casual wave towards the rolling green acres that surrounded them. Alicia struggled to look pleased and grateful. She did not share his passion for Ryland Place, though she wasn't blind to its beauty. To her, there was still something cold and austere about the house. Sometimes she thought that, if it weren't for the child curled helplessly inside her body, she would have gone home to Greenthorpe and done her best to forget the unhappiness of the past three years. Yet for the time being life was pleasant enough, if a little dull with each day an exact replica of the one before.

No longer did she see danger around every corner she turned, or start up fearfully at the sound of approaching footsteps or the rustling of a tapestry in the breeze. No one would harm her now. Agnes was dead and with her had died the threat of violence. Tom treated her with the courtesy usually reserved for the most formidable matrons. With her puffy face and distended belly, she guessed that she held little charm for him nowadays. Besides, though it was never spoken of, she suspected he still secretly visited the dusky-haired beauty at the Red Stag.

She raised her head now to look at Lucy, sitting alone at the far end of the gallery. She was bent over the chessboard which had not been cleared away since before the plague struck, her fingers moving the carved figures across the squares in a sort of hypnotic dance.

Alicia pushed her needle through the yellow heart of an iris. She no longer had any doubt that there was something terribly wrong with Lucy. That dull apathy was sometimes broken by bursts of restlessness when she would march up and down an invisible path like an agitated sentry, head bent low, furiously twitching her skirts from side to side.

Alicia had suggested to her father-in-law that Lucy should be examined by the local doctor but he proved surprisingly obdurate, refusing to admit that there was a problem.

'She has had a difficult year. I'm told that she had a hard time birthing Jack and of course she still grieves for her aunt and cousins. But she'll rally, my dear. Given time, she'll rally. She comes of hardy stock.'

Alicia had stared at him in disbelief. Hardy stock! Had he forgotten Lucy's mother, brought to the grave by grief and worry when she was still little more than a girl?

Your kindness is nothing but sugared guilt, Gervase had once taunted her.

Gervase, Gervase! As long as she lived at Ryland Place his memory would haunt her, even though he lay silent in the musty black bowels of the village church.

Because of the virulent nature of the sweat, it had been necessary to bury its victims without delay and so she had been spared the ordeal of another funeral. Instead she had attended the requiem mass last month, in the little chapel at Ryland Place where she and Gervase had been married just three years before.

Bars of hot sunshine had burned through the windows, dusted with vermilion and sapphire from the tinted glass. Alicia held her white-coral rosary as if it were a flower, wishing that she shared her father-in-law's faith. He looked so peaceful kneeling beside her, his grey head lowered in prayer. Alicia's thoughts were not of God, but of Gervase and their pitifully short marriage. They had been strangers for the most part; it was only at the end that they had come to know and care for one another.

She thought of his lifelong despair, his occasional acts of kindness, the birthday gift of Hero. She recalled the rapture they'd shared every time their bodies merged, and for the first time was gripped by a sense of pungent loneliness. She realized how much she would miss him; that a part of her would never cease to mourn. In that moment she found herself fiercely hoping that their child would be a boy. He would be Gervase's only legacy.

A commotion below in the courtyard tugged her back to her surroundings. Her curiosity aroused, for visitors seldom called at Ryland Place these days, she leaned out of the window, resting her elbows on the sill. A small party of riders, one of them female, came prancing across the cobbles. A slender young man clad in slashed claret and silver, was the first to dismount. Alicia watched him go to lift the girl from her white palfrey, wondering what it was about him that seemed so familiar.

There was a ripple of laughter and the flutter of forest-green skirts as the girl came to the ground, then swung round to look up at the house. It was Anne Boleyn.

Alicia turned and started towards the stairs with more alacrity than she had shown in a long time.

'We have visitors,' she called to Lucy, still hunched over the chessboard in the shadows. 'Won't you come downstairs and meet them?'

Lucy looked up with a sullen glare but didn't answer. Alicia shrugged. 'Stay up here and sulk then!' she muttered under her breath, and bustled on her way.

The house appeared to have woken from its long sleep. Servants and dogs were scurrying every which way, haphazardly crossing each other's paths. Sir John, who had been enjoying a nap in his office, was greeting Anne and her brother in the hall, his face moist and pink like a morning-fresh baby. He seemed both flattered and bemused at the arrival of such illustrious visitors.

'I hope you won't think us unpardonably rude,' George Boleyn was saying in the velvet drawl that, for Alicia, kindled memories of a February night glowing with torchlight and music and rainbow-coloured jewels. 'We have no wish to intrude on your grief, Sir John. It's just that we are visiting our grandmother in Horsham and Nan had a hankering to call here.'

'Not at all, you are very welcome.' John turned away, signalling to a servant to bring refreshments.

Alicia, awkwardly conscious of her bulk, hung back shyly but Anne had already spotted her. Scooping up her skirts she ran across the floor and the next minute Alicia was being wrapped in a cloud of French musk and ebony hair.

'How fine you look – and in full bloom too, I see.' Eyes sparkling with fun, Anne stepped back to survey her old friend. She added slyly, 'It suits you.'

'I feel like a bloated old sow,' Alicia replied, pulling a face. For the life of her she couldn't bring herself to look at George but she was burningly conscious of him.

'What brings you to Sussex?' she asked as they sat down to cakes and wine.

'I've been sent into exile.' Anne sank her teeth into a saffron bun. 'Pope Clement is at long last sending a legate to try the King's cause, so I've been packed off like a naughty child.'

'Don't exaggerate, Nan.' George leaned back against the wall. He looked completely at ease, like a favourite nephew who could always be sure of his welcome. 'His Grace simply thought it best if you weren't exactly prominent when Cardinal Campeggio arrives. He's only trying to be discreet.'

A look of lively amusement danced between the pair – a look that mocked King Henry and possibly everyone at his court.

'What news of my sister?' Alicia asked quickly. 'I heard that she kept well during the sweat, thank God, but she hasn't written to me for ages.'

'She is fine.' Anne's smooth brow had clouded at the mention of Kathryn. She'd never really had the knack of winning female friends, nor had she felt the need to acquire it, but it was galling the way so many of the court ladies remained stubbornly loyal to Queen Catherine. Kathryn Standish was among those who treated Anne with a stiff-backed courtesy that was somehow more insulting than if they'd slapped her.

'You say the Papal Legate has started out from Rome?' John looked eagerly from one dark Boleyn face to the other. Unlike most people, he was in favour of the divorce, though he privately believed that Henry would have been wiser to choose a bride from one of the royal courts of Europe – Princess Renée would have been an excellent choice. Still, the sophisticated young woman drinking Rhenish at his table looked healthy enough to bear a crop of lusty sons and that was all that mattered in the final count.

He reached across to refill her glass, taking the opportunity to study her closely. Yes, she was every whit as dazzling as he remembered, the ever-changing expressions playing like sunbeams on her face, her vitality a flame to draw bored or disillusioned men. And yet it struck him that there was something hard and unapproachable about her. After all, you couldn't hold a flame in your hand. He felt a sudden stab of pity for his Sovereign – marriage to Agnes had taught him to recognize a shrew.

'Yes, the gouty old dog is limping towards Paris at last and will go thence to Calais, from where he will sail – if his health permits.'

John's eyebrows lifted a fraction. The girl seemed to have no notion of propriety.

'God help his Grace!' he prayed silently and with feeling.

'I can't help but wonder if all this dithering is part of their plan.' Anne's eyes flashed dark fire across the table. 'I think Pope Clement is playing a delaying game, hoping his Grace will get tired of me and crawl back to his wife like a whipped spaniel. Well, it's not going to happen.'

At that moment Tom came sauntering in through a side door, whistling a snatch of a song. He stopped dead when he saw the Boleyns, the tune dying on his lips. Then his face broke into a grin and he crossed the room in four strides, bent and kissed Anne's hand. Alicia noticed the rush of pink to his cheeks and was amused. Like most full-blooded males, he was ready to lose his heart to the King's darling.

John asked if they would excuse him.

'Those wretched accounts! I vow since my dear wife died they've been woefully neglected.' With that he returned thankfully to the sanctuary of his office like a rabbit scuttling back to its warren.

Presently the four young people made their way out on to the terrace and down to the gardens. Tom led the way, with Alicia and Anne trailing behind him, arms linked. George brought up the rear.

Splashes of sunlight lay on the impeccably cut lawns, turning them a sparkling emerald. The cherry-brick walls glowed as if they were on fire. The fruit trees splayed against the southern wall sagged with ripeness, the air was heavy and moist with the scent of plums.

'It's like a miniature Eden!' Anne looked about her, her expression for once peaceful and contented. 'And those plums look most succulent.'

She sank down beside a rosemary bed, her skirts a tumbling green waterfall on the grass.

Eager as a schoolboy bent on impressing his first love, Tom started to tear fruit from the branches, recklessly braving a cluster of drowsy wasps. Soon he was fill-ing Anne's lap with fat purple-red plums.

Alicia settled herself on the low bough of a cherry tree, slightly apart from the others. No longer could she fling herself down on the grass like a carefree young hoyden. She tried to compose her features into sweetly serene lines, though she was conscious of a little jab of envy. She told herself she was being foolish. After all, she was a widow and soon she would be a mother.

To her surprise George came to sit at her feet. He threw his cap to the ground, then quickly raised his bright dark eyes to her face.

'I was sorry to hear of your husband's death,' he said quietly. 'It must have been a hard blow.'

'Yes, it was.' Alicia curled her hands in her lap and stared down at the ground. She could feel her face starting to burn under his scrutiny. Her breathing quick-ened, though she tried to steady it. She had almost forgotten how handsome he was and now that quicksilver charm of his had taken her unawares. If only she didn't feel so ugly and cumbersome! Was he comparing her in his mind to the light-stepping girl who had once danced with him, all grace and enticement in a white-and-silver gown?

'I missed you when you left court.'

Alicia wondered if she had misheard him.

'You were most uncivil to me.' The words burst out before she had time to consider them.

'I know.' For once his face was serious. Suddenly he placed one hand on her knee. 'The truth is, I was afraid my bitch of a wife might do you some harm if she suspected that – well, that I gave you more than a casual thought.'

Alicia stared at him in amazement. So that was the reason for his coldness towards her after the banquet – the chilly glances, the air of bored indifference.

In a flash she saw her gowns lying in a bright pool of ribbons on the bed, saw Jane Boleyn's smirking face. A sharp retort sprang to her lips but something in his face held her silent.

He was regarding her through half-closed eyes which seemed to gleam like chips of quartz. The sun had sprinkled his dark hair with flakes of red and gold and she had a sudden compulsion to run her fingers through it. After a moment she saw a slow smile curl across his mouth, telling her that, pregnant or no, he found her a richly desirable woman. A ripple of pleased vanity made her shiver, in spite of the September heat. For the first time for months she felt sleek and attractive again.

'You should come to court,' he said, opening his eyes again and leaning closer. 'My sister needs all her friends now.'

'I can't travel until after the baby is born.'

'And then?' The hand tightened ever so slightly on her knee.

Alicia gave a humourless little laugh. 'I haven't made any plans. No doubt I shall stay at Ryland Place and become a withered old crone before my time. Oh, but how I would love to go home, if only for a little while.'

'Home?' He looked at her, one eyebrow swung up at an angle.

'To Greenthorpe.' Her eyes swept over him, then stared away into the distance, seeing not the formal Sussex garden but a honey-glazed house set in a bright green jewel of parkland. Almost unthinkingly, she touched the rose-ring on her middle finger. It was her only link with Greenthorpe now.

'Yet one day you'll come back to court and dance with me again.'

'I can't dance.' There was a ragged edge to her voice, as if she was about to cry. 'I have probably forgotten how.'

'Nonsense, a witch never forgets how to weave a spell.'

Before Alicia could think of a reply to that, they saw Tom and Anne walking across the lawn towards them. Tom was swaggering even more than usual. Anne, her head barely reaching his armpit, was swinging her skirts and laughing up at him; flirting the way she did with every man whether he interested her or not.

'Thomas refuses to introduce me to his wife,' she called to the other two. 'I think he's afraid to have her meet me.'

She turned back to Tom, head tilted to one side, black eyes glinting.

'Am I really so dangerous?'

'Never, madam.' Tom raised her fingers to his lips, holding them there a fraction longer than was proper. 'But Lucy can't meet anyone. She is in poor health.'

Seeing the curious light in Anne's eyes, Alicia came to Tom's aid.

'It's true that Lucy is delicate,' she said as George helped her to her feet. 'She had a difficult confinement last year and – and never really recovered.'

'Not recovered after a year!' George looked sceptical. 'She must be delicate.'

'Will you stay for supper?' Alicia decided it was time to change the subject.

'No, it's a good two hours ride to Horsham and old Agnes is likely to box our ears if we're late,' Anne giggled.

Alicia had a vision of the Dowager Duchess of Norfolk – whom she had never met – with jewel-studded claws and a wrinkled yellow face like old parchment. Her very name filled her with horror.

The sun was dropping behind a bank of carnation cloud as they crossed the stable yard. Tom kissed Anne, then slapped George on the shoulder with a comradely air that didn't quite ring true.

'I hope next time we meet you will be Queen of England, Mistress Anne.' He gave the boyish grin that had torn so many female hearts, then walked quickly back to the house, tossing his hair as he went.

Alicia waited with her friends while their servants were summoned and the horses saddled.

It had been a golden afternoon – one which had lifted her out of the torpor of pregnancy and reminded her that there was another world beyond the confines of Ryland Place.

I have friends, she told herself now. Good friends who would welcome me at Greenwich. I needn't fear the future whatever happens.

In that moment she knew with ice-cold certainty that she would dance again beneath the vaulted roof of Greenwich Palace. There was a dreamy little smile on her face as Anne turned to embrace her.

'I hope all goes well with you and your baby.' Anne spoke in a low, tender voice which would have startled many of those who thought they knew her. 'I envy you, Alicia – children are a great joy.'

George lifted his sister into the saddle then went to mount his own tall chestnut hunter. He was about to kick the animal forward when he appeared to hesitate.

Then he leaned down to speak to the girl standing beside his stirrup.

'I shall see you again, Alicia, never doubt it,' he said softly.

Then they were gone with a sharp ringing of hoofs upon the stones, the snaffles and spurs a blaze of silver in the rays of the dying red sun.

Alicia was more tired than usual that evening.

Sitting in the gallery after supper, her beloved *Aesop's Fables* lying face down in her lap, she found herself struggling to stay awake. The plaintive sound of a lute drifted along the gallery from the propped-open door of Molly's chamber. The notes seemed to quiver like raindrops, forming no recognizable tune. It was as if Molly had picked them out of the air at random, like plucking berries from a tree.

The music died on a mournful little note and Alicia smothered a yawn.

'I think I'll go to bed,' she said at last.

Sir John, his fingers absently scratching the chin of his favourite wolfhound, smiled at her affectionately.

'Of course, my dear. It has been a long day, and I expect our visitors tired you.'

'It was pleasant to see Anne again.' For no reason that she could think of, Alicia was unable to meet his candid gaze. Blushing to her hairline, she rose, gathered up the book and shook out her skirts.

'Indeed, indeed.' John sounded wistful. 'Sometimes I forget that you're young and need other young people about you. I'm a selfish dog.'

'You are a poppet.' Alicia bent to kiss his cheek. As she turned to go, she caught Lucy glowering at her from the shadows. Her heart gave an odd little flutter, even though she had grown used to the other girl's animosity. Yet it was unpleasant, knowing that someone who had once cared for her now resented and despised her.

Minutes later she was sitting at her jumbled *toilette* table, clad only in a silver gauze nightgown. She found herself staring almost impersonally at her reflection in the mirror. Violet-grey shadows stained the delicate skin beneath her eyes, giving her face an oddly bruised look. Her breasts swelled above the low-cut nightgown, lush and creamy. However, Mother Luke had told her that they would return to their usual size after she'd had the baby.

Nanty suddenly appeared in the mirror behind her. As she picked up the hairbrush, Alicia snapped:

'You can leave the brushing tonight. I'm too tired.'

Nanty's eyebrows swooped up at her mistress's terse tone, but she didn't answer. Instead she went to turn down the sheets. Unrepentant, Alicia fingered a scrap of silver lace which had once been a garter, irritably wishing that the girl would hurry.

Suddenly Nanty gave a click of her fingers, remembering something.

'I'd better take Hero for a run – he hasn't been out this evening.'

'That would be splendid, Nanty.' Alicia forced a grateful smile. She knew that the household was still a-buzz with the visit of the notorious Anne, and Nanty must be looking forward to the lively gossip in the hall.

Nanty went off in search of Hero's leash and soon Alicia was alone in the room that, not so long ago, she had shared with Gervase. Although her whole body was sagging with weariness, she decided that she might as well wait up till Nanty returned.

She went to sit at the window where there was a mild breeze fluttering in. A chapel-like stillness hung over the house at this hour. Some of the windows overlooking the courtyard stood partly open to the cool evening air. Others were filled with candlelight that struck thin showers of amber against the glass. It was a velvet drowsy night with both a faded sun and a crescent moon showing in the sky.

Almost inevitably, Alicia found her thoughts turning to George Boleyn. In her mind she was already reliving every moment of that enchanted afternoon; recalling everything he'd said, searching for nuances of emotion and hidden meaning in his most casual word.

'Fool!' she muttered to herself after a while.

For even if she did return to court one day, what hope was there of a relationship between them? He was married to an unhappy, embittered woman who'd already proved that she would make short work of any rival, while she would be a widow with a young child. And yet the memory of that magical hour in the garden was as warm and satisfying as lying in a perfumed bath.

She didn't bother to look round as she heard the door open quietly behind her, then close again; she wanted to be left alone with her delicious thoughts for a little longer. However as the seconds crawled past, she began to feel a little uneasy. At last she turned to see Lucy standing just inside the door.

There was a peculiar glazed look on her face which reminded Alicia of that night in the cottage. For some reason her heart began to gallop erratically, making her feel slightly sick. Her fingers clutched the edge of the seat and the baby seemed to bounce in her womb.

Lucy didn't speak but continued to stare at her, grey eyes gleaming in a rigid white face.

Summoning her courage – and her common sense, for the girl wasn't dangerous, merely sad and confused – Alicia rose and started towards her.

'Is something wrong, Lucy?' She stopped half-way across the room, her nerve unexpectedly failing her. 'Did – did you want to talk to me?'

Lucy's eyes dropped to Alicia's swollen belly.

'What will you name your bastard?' Her voice sounded unnaturally loud in the quiet room.

Alicia was too shocked to protest. She could only stand there, her heart still racing frantically, watching a smile cut across Lucy's mouth like a knife wound. Then she spoke again, still in that hard bitter voice.

'That is my husband's brat you're carrying.'

She stood straight as a spear, shoulders erect, hands curled into the folds of her gown. Only her eyes and her lips were moving – eyes that glinted with hatred, lips that were now spewing out a stream of venom.

Alicia felt terror mounting inside her – terror such as she had never known – as the ugly words spattered out. She was a bitch, an imp from hell, a whore who rolled in bed with other women's husbands in order to get herself a bastard. Some instinct told her not to speak until Lucy's rage had spent itself.

Why did I never realize how angry she is! Her head began to swirl; she felt her arms and legs turn to ice-water while the weight of the child seemed to be dragging her whole body down. Oh Nanty, Nanty, where the devil are you?

'You're wrong, Lucy,' she said at last, and was dismayed to hear her voice shaking. She could only hope Lucy hadn't noticed. 'It is Gervase's child that I'm carrying and no bastard. You have insulted my husband's memory.'

'Whore!' The word was like a slap. 'Do you really think I had no idea about you and Tom? I used to watch you preening and giggling, making slut's eyes at him. I'll wager you thought I was too stupid to notice – silly little Lucy with her needlework and her childish dreams! How the two of you must have laughed!'

She paused then but only, it seemed, to recapture her breath.

'You think I'm a fool, don't you?' she screeched, all the veins straining at her throat.

'No, Lucy.' Alicia's mouth felt hot and dry. She swallowed and went on: 'I think you're unhappy and it has made you imagine things.'

Oh Jesus, I shouldn't have said that!

She glanced quickly behind her at the window, praying that someone had heard the commotion and realized something was wrong.

'I've imagined nothing!' The round grey eyes were bulging like marbles. 'Even Aunt Agnes warned me about you. She said you couldn't wait to lift your skirts for Tom because your own husband was incapable and you'd go to any lengths to get a son.'

She began to laugh then, a high, unnerving sound that made Alicia's flesh prickle. 'Your vanity couldn't bear for me to succeed where you had failed. Why, you would have killed Jack if I hadn't had him guarded so closely.'

For the first time Alicia began to feel irritated by the shrill voice, the fantastic accusations, the sight of Lucy's hate-shrivelled face.

'You're wrong,' she said again, and this time there was an edge to her voice. 'You know full well that I would never harm you or Jack. Why, you and I were friends once.'

'Yes, until you betrayed me – whore!' Saliva flecked the corner of Lucy's mouth. Then she smiled, a smile full of cunning and cruelty, and when she spoke again her voice was almost eerily quiet.

'I'm not quite as stupid as you think, Alicia. I won't let any bastard of yours cheat my son out of his rights.'

She took a step closer, then stopped. Alicia, rooted to the floor, saw her hand move quickly against the side of her gown, then there was the cold metallic gleam of a pair of embroidery scissors.

At first she was numb with disbelief but as Lucy advanced towards her, the scissors clutched in her fist, she started to back away.

'Lucy – please.' A sob came bubbling from her throat. 'You have misunderstood – everything. There is nothing between Tom and me. We – we don't even like each other.'

But Lucy was too far gone in hate and madness to listen.

Alicia could feel the blood thundering in her head. She stepped further back and further until she felt her shoulder blades brush against something soft and bulky. She clutched the tapestry behind her as if it were a lifeline, suddenly recalling that it depicted a hunting scene. Through the clammy mist of fear she tried to focus her mind on each minute detail, as if doing so could somehow save her.

Green-clad figures on sleek horses pranced against a woodland background. A swarm of hounds bounded joyously after a huge golden stag who plunged ahead, his antlers almost brushing the ground. And last of all the curved hunting knife, dripping triumphant rubies of blood over the broken carcass. . . .

Sick and trembling, her skin wet with sweat, she sagged to her knees. She lifted her face, ready to plead for her life and that of her baby but the words seemed to be stuck in her throat. Lucy was standing over her, her face a glistening savage mask. She seemed to grow larger and more powerful with each slow-passing second. Whimpering low in her throat, Alicia leaned forward, at the same time curving her arms protectively around the bigness of her belly, and in that moment Lucy struck. Alicia let out a high jerky scream as the shining points of the scissors plunged into her arm.

Dimly she heard someone shouting in the distance. There was the sound of swiftly running footsteps and suddenly the room was full of people.

'Lucy!'

At the sound of Tom's voice, Lucy twisted round; the scissors went clattering to the floor. Then she bowed her head submissively, the frenzy dropping away from her like a shawl.

Tom streaked across the floor, gripped his wife by the shoulders and roughly shook her. She slumped against him and started to cry but he thrust her into the arms of a gaping servant as if she were a sack of cornmeal. Then he turned to stare, appalled, at the sobbing terrified figure crumpled against the wall. Damp wisps of hair lay against her temples like streaks of blood. Her face was washed of colour, she looked close to fainting. Then he saw the dark-red patch seeping through her sleeve. At the sight his heart seemed to roll over in his chest like a snowball.

'Sweet Christ!' Sir John was standing beside him, shaking his head like some sorrowful animal. 'Sweet living Christ!'

'Get Lucy out of here, Father.' Tom spoke through clenched teeth. 'And send for Dr Hill at once.'

It was the first time he had ever given orders to his father but as John silently led the weeping Lucy away he didn't even raise his head to look at him.

Tom sank to his knees beside Alicia, who was staring at him with huge, petrified eyes. At that moment Nanty came flying into the room, her cap twisted to one side. She took one look at Alicia, then burst into hysterical sobbing.

'Be quiet girl, or I'll slap you,' Tom snarled.

Nanty gave a small hiccup, then was quiet.

At a word from Tom, the other servants trailed away, some glancing back sheepishly as they went.

Very gently, Tom eased Alicia's sleeve back. It was wet and sticky with blood, and he tried not to wince at the ugly crimson gash. She was whimpering softly, her pupils dilated with shock.

'Try to keep calm, Alicia.' He spoke to her as if she were small Jack, sobbing in his arms after taking a tumble. 'Luckily it's not a deep wound.'

He tore a wide strip from his shirt-sleeve and proceeded to bind it tightly about the wound. He worked silently, frowning with concentration, his fingers deft and gentle. Nanty was weeping quietly into her fists but he paid her no attention.

As he lifted Alicia into his arms and carried her towards the bed she gave a low, shuddering moan. She could feel a bolt of fire tearing through her belly, closely followed by another. Through a scalding mist of pain, she heard Nanty's voice, sharp with panic.

'It's the baby! Sweet Blessed Virgin, she's losing her baby!'

Then she went down into a rushing river of blackness.

She had never known a night like that night. A hot swollen night filled with shadows and harsh urgent whispers and hurrying footsteps that seemed to lead to nowhere while she lay helplessly snared in a pit of suffering.

The pain still leapt and throbbed in her arm but by now she was barely even conscious of it for a thousand white-hot daggers were being thrust into her abdomen. Sweat streaked from armpit to waist to thigh. Sweat ran over her face, blending with her frightened tears.

She knew that she was losing the child – the son who would have been her posthumous gift to Gervase. In her heart she had somehow always known that it was a boy, but what did that matter now? Lucy's hatred had killed him.

Through it all Dr Hill was with her and also Mistress Hobbs, the enormous midwife who had attended Lucy's confinement last year. Alicia thought how gentle those big red hands were upon her body and weakly blinked back fresh tears.

'Rest easy, sweetheart.' Mistress Hobbs patted her cheek. 'It will all be over soon.'

Alicia attempted a grateful smile but another stiff wave of pain washed it from her face.

Suddenly she wanted her mother more desperately than she had ever wanted anything before. In her mind she saw the two of them sitting side by side on her bed at Greenthorpe. Dorothy's face was so wise and compassionate beside her daughter's stormy one. Her hands were like the touch of cool dock-leaves as they brushed the tears from Alicia's cheeks.

'Be still, Alicia.' The gentle voice lapped against her heart like candlelight. 'If you yield quietly, there is a chance that you'll find happiness.'

The pain rose again, hot and searing, smothering Dorothy's face, the sound of her voice. Relentless as a sea-tempest, it tossed and tore at her.

She was a little girl again, lost in the dense green woods surrounding Greenthorpe Manor. Sobbing with fright, her face scratched and tear-smudged, she stumbled through the clumps of overhanging trees, searching for the path which would lead her home. At last she cried out for her father, again and again, but he didn't come.

'Fool! Damned fool!' she whispered through sore, cracked lips, and turned her face into the pillow. For she *was* a fool to think that Richard would ever come to her rescue.

Nanty's face swam close above the bed, pale and frightened, the freckles glim-
mering like specks of nutmeg in the dripping light. The huge expressive hazel
eyes were fringed with tears.

'Nanty?' Her voice was little more than a dusty croak but Nanty seemed to
understand.

'I'm here, mistress. I won't leave you.'

The pain swept over her again, much worse this time; it was as if something
was wrenching itself from her guts. Dr Hill and Mistress Hobbs were talking to
her, urging her to relax, but she ignored them. Instead she clung to Nanty with
the last vestige of her strength and when a tear splashed into her neck she didn't
know if it was hers or Nanty's.

A rosy skein of daylight was curling through the clouds as Dr Hill emerged from
Alicia's chamber.

Shoulders slumped, his face latticed with fresh lines, he made his way downstairs. Although he had never veered from the regime which he prescribed for his
patients – plenty of sleep, daily exercise in the fresh air and a moderate diet
which included meat, fruit and vegetables – lately he found that these all-night
sessions left him feeling almost drunk with exhaustion. It was a reminder that he
was now in his sixties, though he liked to tell himself that he had the body of a
man of forty.

He paused on the bottom stair, looking about him in dismay. At dawn the hall
had a desolate air, cold as mist and filled with a creeping grey light. Trestles were
stacked against the walls as if waiting for a banquet that would never take place.
The great fireplace was banked with dead ashes, the rushes filthy and stinking of
greasy bones, dogs' urine – and worse.

As his eye alighted upon the figure crouched in the embrasure of the oriel, he
gave a little cough – no sense in startling the man out of his wits!

John Houghton was on his feet at once, his face sharp and tense like an
anxious greyhound's. Dr Hill noted the bloodshot eyes, the crumpled black
clothes, and knew that he hadn't slept. He also caught the smell of stale wine on
the other man's breath. Yet if Sir John had hoped to drown his worries in alco-
hol, he hadn't succeeded. It was clear that he was painfully sober.

'I'm sorry, Sir John.' The doctor carefully laid the box of medicine-phials and
instruments at his feet. 'She has miscarried of a son.'

The pale light fell across John's face, heightening every weary line. Then a
muscle began to twitch beside his mouth.

'How is she?'

'There was great loss of blood but I'm confident she will make a full recovery.
She's a hardy little thing.'

He paused, afraid that he might have sounded too familiar, but John didn't appear to notice so he went on: 'I've given her a poppy draught to help her sleep, and the midwife is still with her.'

He thought of the girl now lying in merciful oblivion upstairs, her face bleached as white as the pillow beneath it; thought of the tiny male child whom he'd last seen stretched out stiffly on a table like a rabbit waiting to be skinned. He had been perfectly formed but unable to withstand the violence and shock of last night's events, the full details of which were still somewhat hazy to Dr Hill. Yet he found his sympathy reaching out to the man standing before him, his face as bleak as a November landscape. Truly, John Houghton had suffered much. In a flash the doctor recalled the deaths of last summer. His skill had been like a rusty blade against the might of the sweat, and he had been unable to save either Agnes or Gervase. Also, there were rumours circulating the village that the younger daughter-in-law had grown weak in the head. In that moment Dr Hill had one of those bursts of clarity which often astounded his patients. Alicia had been attacked with a pair of scissors – a woman's weapon.

'Will you have some wine before you leave?' John suddenly remembered his obligations as host.

The doctor declined for he was impatient to be back at his own hearthside. His cheerful little wife would keep breakfast waiting till his return. With their six grown-up children all married and raising families of their own, he and Emily had grown very close and they cherished the few snatched hours which they were able to spend together. Meanwhile he felt duty-bound to offer some crumb of solace to John Houghton, who was alone in the world now.

'Mistress Alicia's arm will heal,' he said, picking up the box and moving towards the double doors. 'There will be a scar, of course, but it will fade in time.'

But the words were lost upon John. Left alone again, he sank down on a stool and gave himself up to despair. Burrowing his face in his hands, he willed the tears to come but to no avail. It was as if a great lead box had been dropped on to his heart.

'Father?'

Startled, he looked up to see Tom standing in front of him, his face white and scared. Gone was the purposeful strength that had sustained the whole household last night. His son was now a frightened little boy, slinking to his father's side for reassurance.

'Alicia has miscarried.' John's voice sounded flat and dull. 'It was a boy.'

Tom sucked in his breath, then slowly crumpled to his knees.

'Oh Christ!' he whispered, his eyes stricken. Then he spread his fingers over his face, just as his father had done minutes earlier.

Instinctively, John stretched out a hand to stroke the bronze curls.

'Don't cry, boy,' he said gruffly. 'I've no stomach for tears just now.'

Without a word, Tom laid a hand on his father's knee and for a while they stayed like that, as if each drew comfort from the other's closeness, while the morning light turned from grey to apricot and the jewel-colours in the oriel began to shimmer.

Tom was the first to speak. 'What shall I do about Lucy, sir?' His voice was barely above a whisper.

John sighed. The lad was feckless – he realized that now. He found himself wondering how much of last night's tragedy was due to Tom's selfishness, his utter disregard for the needs and emotions of others.

'What can I say? She is my cousin's child and I cannot abandon her. But she'll have to be watched – constantly.' He sighed again, shifting his weight on the stool. 'Alicia warned me about Lucy but I thought she was exaggerating. Poor Alicia!' A bitter note crept into his voice as he looked straight into his son's eyes. 'We have none of us treated that girl well.'

Tom bowed his head, unable to hold his father's steady accusing gaze.

The days and nights seemed to have blended into an eternal twilight.

Lying in her bed, encased in the secluded shell that she'd made for herself, Alicia was blind to the light that rose every morning, shimmered and then died in her chamber. To her tired mind, the world was tinted with grey and chilly, impersonal blue. She didn't want to see the sunlight ever again.

It was the first time she had been ill since she was a child. She wasn't really ill now, not any more. The wound on her arm had healed, leaving a jagged pink scar that resembled a little girl's first clumsy stitches. She had also recovered physically from the miscarriage, though it had left her feeling weak and drained. Depression had settled over her spirits like a shroud. It reminded her of the grey-ness that had encompassed her when Gervase died, except that it was worse – much worse. Then she had not felt so cold and empty, so lost. *Now I know how Lucy must have felt.*

As the thought struck her, she turned her head as if trying to escape from it. She didn't want to think of Lucy. She didn't want to think of the baby either, but found that she was unable to avoid it.

Not long after she had lost the child, she began to wake in the early hours, thinking she could hear him crying in another part of the house. Once she even climbed out of bed and made her way swiftly down the gallery, thinking that the sound of his cries would lead her to where he was but Nanty came after her and gently led her back to bed.

But worst of all were the nightmares, for they turned sleep into a maze of torture and madness.

She would dream that the baby was in bed with her. His little body had some-how got entangled in the covers. As she worked to free him, the covers wound themselves about her wrists. Once she dreamed that she saw his face, tiny and still like a frozen snowdrop, the way it had looked before Mistress Hobbs had bundled him into a sheet and whisked him from her sight. That night she woke screaming like some unearthly creature. Kneeling up in the bed, her eyes like dark holes in her white face, she felt the screams being torn from her throat and was powerless to stop them.

'Hush, mistress.' Nanty's arms were locked around her, drawing her back to safety. 'It's all right, you were just riding the night mare.'

She rocked Alicia tenderly in her arms till she grew quiet.

Sir John came to see her every day. Sometimes he brought her presents – scented gloves of soft Spanish leather, a string of sparkling blue beads, a coif encrusted with Roman pearls. Seeing the tired lines on his face, the sadness in his eyes, Alicia would try to rouse herself but it was no use. She was sunk too deep in hopelessness.

And then one day Tom came. It was mid-October now, the world outside crisp and tinged with russet hues. Through the window she could see the dark flights of migrating birds fleeing across the ice-blue sky.

He stood stiffly at the foot of the bed, watching her with wary green eyes. Alicia could see that he'd made this visit as reluctantly as he used to visit Lucy after she'd borne their son. The sight of him nearly made her smile – he didn't belong in a sickroom.

He was still jauntily handsome, even in sombre black, but now his good looks left her unmoved. A stony distance lay between them; it was as if they were looking at each other from opposite ends of a bridge which neither cared to cross.

'I never thanked you.' At last Alicia broke the silence.

'Thanked me?' Tom wrinkled his nose like an urchin.

'For helping me that night. You probably saved my life.'

To her surprise he turned and began pacing the room in long nervous strides. Back and forth he went, then all at once he swivelled round and came to stand beside the bed. His hands were twisting around each other like two restless carp.

'Alicia, I know I have no right to ask you this but – do you think you can find it in you to forgive Lucy?'

He saw the violet eyes darken until pupil and iris were indistinguishable; saw the thin figure stiffen beneath the mound of bedclothes, and was alarmed.

'I'll never forgive her!' Alicia spoke in a hard voice that he had never heard before. 'God knows, I wish her no harm but I won't forgive her; I can't.'

He hesitated for a moment, gazing at her with an unreadable expression before turning and walking very quickly from the room. After he had gone, Alicia found that her whole body was trembling. She pressed her fists hard against her eyelids, trying to force back the tears but soon they were dribbling helplessly down her face.

That night, instead of dreaming about her baby son, she dreamed about Greenthorpe.

The house was steeped in darkness, the rooms dismal and bare. Starlight faintly silvered the black windows as she wandered through the house, her feet skimming along the wooden floor as if she were floating on water. Eventually she saw a pale stripe of light shining beneath one of the doors. Her heart swelling with apprehension, she sped towards it.

Once inside the room she hesitated, feeling like a trespasser. Then she saw the girl sitting in a tall curved chair beside a burning brazier. She wore a thick, high-necked nightgown patterned with cornflowers, yet the bare feet peeping out from beneath the hem were mauve with cold. A sheet of bright brown hair fell forward across her face, hiding it from view, yet she seemed very young. Nonetheless there was an air of profound unhappiness about her as she sat there, chin cupped in her hand while the candlelight played among those shining brown tresses and flung her shadow against the wall.

A young man, breathtakingly handsome, stood beside the window. Alicia caught the coin-smooth profile, lit by a mass of bracken-red hair that tumbled to his shoulders. Unlike the girl he was in full day-dress that belonged to an earlier age. His long sensitive fingers were spread wide on the window ledge. Neither of them seemed to be aware of Alicia.

Suddenly the young man swung round and crossed the floor to sink on to one knee beside the girl. Gently he reached out a hand to curve the hair back from her cheek, tentative as if he feared a rebuff. As he did so the girl lifted her face and Alicia saw that she was indeed young – barely into adolescence.

It was a plain face, yet at the same time arresting; pale as a December morning, with clearly defined bones and the strong jawline of one who knows her own mind. At that moment it wore a look of such misery that Alicia felt a great jagged lump fill her throat.

'You still love him, don't you?' The girl's voice was harsh and strained, but there was a look of desperate pleading in her green eyes, like a child begging not to be slapped.

'Cicely, do you think I choose to do so?' Beneath the rough tone there was a thread of despair. Fists clenched, he turned his face from the light. 'God's blood, but I wouldn't see a dog suffer like this.'

'I know something about suffering too, Henry.' Cicely's voice slid up an octave. 'Lying beside you night after night, listening to you weeping. Oh yes, I hear you even though you hide your face in the pillow. You even cry out for him in your sleep. It's unnatural!'

Alicia took a step nearer. In that same moment Henry rose and turned about so that he was directly facing her. The breath froze in her body – his eyes seemed to be looking straight into hers. There was such anguish in their dark-grey depths that her fear instantly evaporated, leaving only pity. He had the haunted look of a man who despises himself but feels powerless to change. As he ran from the room Alicia realized that he hadn't seen her at all – that she was as invisible as air to this tragic young couple.

As the door banged behind her husband, Cicely slid to her knees on to the rushes. Arms folded tightly around her tall slim body, she lowered her head so that the length of brown hair fell forward again. She began to cry.

The image fled instantly but Alicia was still in her childhood home and it was still pitch-dark. She was drifting down the gallery that seemed strange and at the same time familiar.

A girl came tiptoeing out of one of the rooms, her small figure wrapped in a heavy travelling cloak. She paused in the doorway, one hand resting lightly on the handle. As she stood there, the light from within framed her like an aureole.

Drawing closer, Alicia felt her heart give a lurch, for she might have been looking at a mirror-image of herself. Large dark-fringed violet eyes dominated a pale, vivid oval face. A wisp of auburn hair had escaped from the old-fashioned butterfly headdress, glinting like an ember against her temple. She looked both scared and determined. As she turned to close the door softly behind her, Alicia noticed that she was carrying a small bundle under her arm. She squared her shoulders as if bracing herself for some unpleasant task, then made her way cautiously down the dark, twisting staircase. Intrigued, Alicia trailed silently behind her.

A dark shape stood at the foot of the stairs, holding a candle. The thin flame soared, illuminating the frightened young face above it. It was a face which Alicia dimly recognized.

'You have my horse ready?' The girl spoke in a harsh anxious whisper.

'Yes, Mistress Alice, but I wish you'd change your mind.'

The boy looked unhappy but Alice merely smiled and flicked her fingers play-fully against his chin.

'Don't be a goose, Alban! Anyway, no one will guess that you helped me. By the time my parents realize I'm gone, I shall be miles away.'

The young Alban stared at her dumbly, sorrow and fear and admiration all struggling in his face. As if to hide some sadness of her own, Alice gave a sudden petulant flap of her skirts.

'You know I can't stay here now – my life would be intolerable.'

Then, without warning, her expression softened, the lovely violet eyes turning misty, and when she spoke again her voice was pulsingly tender as a lute. 'I shall never forget your loyalty. You've been a true friend, Alban.'

'I'll always be your friend,' Alban choked.

He turned away as if he could no longer trust himself not to cry, and started off across the vast empty hall. After a moment, Alice shifted the bundle beneath her arm and hurried after him.

Standing alone in the narrow little passage, Alicia suddenly felt very cold. The chill seemed to be swirling up from the floor, winding itself in icy folds around her body.

Then, somehow, she was in her old room where it was snug and warm, with a bright fire crackling in the hearth. Lady Dorothy was sitting beside her on the bed, her brown taffeta skirts gleaming like a copper bell in the firelight. Her face was very solemn as she slid the rose-ring on to Alicia's finger.

'This ring was once worn by queens,' she was saying.

Alicia woke abruptly in her bed at Ryland Place, the dream still fresh upon her. The room was hung with mossy shadows – a sure sign that daybreak wasn't far away. She could her the clear clarion of birdsong outside the window. Still those disturbing dream-figures lingered – sad tormented Henry and Cicely, the girl-bride whom he could not love. Alice, starting out on her lonely journey in the middle of the night – who knew what terrors lay behind her sparkling, defiant face? And Alban, the servant who had been an old man for as long as Alicia could remember but who in the dream was a lad too young to hide his love for the wilful girl who needed his help.

Alicia knew that she wouldn't be able to sleep again. She sat up, swinging her feet to the floor. Nanty lay curled up on her pallet at the foot of the bed, her face rosy and smooth as a baby's in a nest of hazel-brown curls. She looked so peaceful, Alicia decided not to risk waking her. Nanty had suffered many a disturbed night because of her lately. She slid back under the blankets again.

She realized, of course, that the people in the dream were her ancestors, bound to her by blood – and by the pale stone house that they had loved as she did. Lying there in the watery half-light, she tried to recall what little she knew of her mother's people.

Her great-grandfather, Henry Marsh, had become a drunkard after a shameful love-affair, causing his wife Cicely such anguish that it had killed her heart. Their daughter Alice, pregnant by a man whom she'd obstinately refused to name, had fled to the protection of Elizabeth of York and later died giving birth to her love-child, Dorothy. They had belonged to Greenthorpe, and so did Alicia.

'I must go home,' she told herself, gazing up at the canopy overhead. 'I'll tell Sir John today and ask if I can borrow his carriage. I'll have to go soon, before the roads are too bad.'

No sooner had she made the decision than her mind felt calm and clear, all doubts swept away as if by a cold autumn wind.

Within minutes she fell asleep again, and this time her dreams were untroubled.

*

Afterwards she believed that her mother's letter was an omen, arriving as it did that same day.

It was her first day out of bed and she was sitting alone on the terrace. It was a bright blustery day with the wind blowing russet and yellow leaves across the land. She huddled snugly into her fur-trimmed cloak. It was the one which Kathryn had given her two Christmases ago, carelessly flung over her black gown that morning, before Nanty's scandalized gaze. Alicia had steeled herself against the girl's disapproval. Perhaps it was heartless of her, but she was tired of looking like a sick little mole.

The cloak glowed like a flame, echoing the October landscape. She smiled to herself, fingering a soft velvet fold. Then she set her mind to planning the future. She was still trying to decide how and when she would tell Sir John she was leaving Ryland Place when the messenger appeared on the terrace.

Without pausing to think, she snatched the letter out of his hand, then told him brusquely to go round to the kitchen for a glass of ale. Standing before her in his mud-caked riding boots, the man shot her a black look, but she was tearing excitedly at the seal and seemed to have forgotten that he was there. He muttered something under his breath, then turned and stomped away.

The letter opened with the usual enquiries about her health. Lady Dorothy hoped that she'd recovered from her tragic miscarriage. *Nobody can understand your heartache as I do, for I know what it is to lose a much longed-for child. Be assured that you have your mother's love and prayers at this unhappy time.*

There was no mention of the horrific injury she had suffered. Alicia smiled darkly to herself. So her parents had not been informed of Lucy's frenzied attack. Would Sir Richard have called for his horse and come galloping across the miles if he knew that his daughter had been slashed by a lunatic?

He came to find me, that day I was lost in the woods.

He had also punished her harshly, it was true, but now for the first time she was able to view his actions as the response of a parent who has suffered hours of tension and alarm.

She skimmed the next few lines, which were full of assurances that her pain would eventually pass; that faith in God and frequent prayer would help her best. She rattled the sheet of parchment somewhat tetchily. Her mother understood nothing, after all. For Alicia was convinced that the pain would be there, twisted inside her heart like a coil of wire, until she died. And she had never found solace in prayer – God had always turned his face from her.

It wasn't until she reached the final passage that she learned of Joanna's illness. For a moment it was as if the bright October sun had toppled out of the sky. The delicately calligraphed words writhed like black beetles before her eyes.

Her heart fluttering, she read those lines again but there was no mistake. Joanna was gravely ill.

The local doctor had examined her but was frankly baffled. There was no apparent cause for her collapse yet she had taken to her bed, complaining that she felt weak and tired. Only one thing was certain – she was dying.

It is as if she has grown weary of living. Poor Alban is inconsolable. They have been friends for more than forty years, ever since Joanna brought me home to Greenthorpe as a little baby. And now, Alicia, I must ask of you a great favour. Joanna has asked that she might see you again before she dies. I know that you have been ill and have suffered dreadfully, but if you are strong enough to make the journey I implore you to come home.

As Alicia came to the end of the letter, there were fat tears rolling down her cheeks. Crabbed old Joanna was dying. Joanna, who was as much a part of Greenthorpe as the stone-carved angels above the gatehouse. Joanna who had cared for her for the first ten years of her life and whose face was the earliest she could remember.

After a long while she wiped her face on her sleeve. Then she wondered why Joanna would want to see her again. There had been little love between them, and many battles, for the young Alicia had taken a pert glee in baiting the nurse, though she seldom succeeded in outwitting her. She could remember many a scolding, many a sharp cuff. But she also remembered the songs.

Joanna had never petted the Westbrooke girls when they were small but every evening – unless she was feeling particularly displeased with them – she would sit beside the nursery fire with Alicia in her lap and Kathryn curled on a cushion at her feet, and sing melancholy ballads in her strong, mooing contralto. On one occasion Sir Richard chanced to overhear the singing and had coldly asked his wife if the children were keeping a pet cow in the nursery. However, to the two little girls the songs were like kisses, drawing them into Joanna's private world.

Now she was dying.

As if through a cold swirling fog, Alicia recalled last night's dream. The terrace seemed to lurch, swimming drunkenly around her. In a flash she saw herself standing at the bottom of the lime-avenue approaching Greenthorpe Manor. The dream-figures were smiling and beckoning to her from the other end of the pale-green tunnel; Henry and Cicely, Alice – and dear old Alban who even at this moment was weeping beside the deathbed of his friend, Joanna.

She stood up, the letter spilling from her lap, and ran lightly across the terrace towards the house, the wind flinging her hair every which way. Inside the hall two maids had started to lay fresh rushes on the floor but were now quarrelling at the tops of their voices. Alicia gripped the nearest one by the shoulders and spun her round.

'Where is the messenger?' she demanded, her fingers digging into the plump flesh.

'Mistress?' The girl blinked, alarmed by the feverish glitter in those violet eyes.

'The messenger from Greenthorpe – has he left yet?'

'No, mistress, he's still guzzling ale in the kitchen.'

Alicia abruptly released the girl who pouted and rubbed her shoulder.

'Tell him to come to me within the hour. I want to give him a letter for Lady Westbrooke.'

She swerved round, caught up her skirts and headed towards the stairs.

She found Nanty kneeling beside the fire in the bedchamber, patiently brushing the tangles from Hero's coat.

'We're going home, Nanty!' she cried joyously as the girl sank back on her heels to stare at her in amazement. 'At last, we're going home to Greenthorpe.'

With that she jerked Nanty to her feet and flung her arms round her, laughing and crying, while Hero circled round them, barking dementedly.

CHAPTER FIFTEEN

1528

The courtyard was alive and ringing with early morning activity.

From her window, Alicia could see the stable grooms, weighted with harness, moving as slowly as caterpillars over the cobbles. Maids were emptying the chamber pots on to the dungheap in the corner with merry abandon. Two sturdy grooms laughed and exchanged cheerful insults as they heaved the great wooden travelling chests into the wagon. And all the while the horses pranced and snickered, violently jerking their heads.

Slowly, Alicia raised the pewter cup to her lips and tasted the warm sweet malmsey. An official-looking scroll lay in her lap; it contained the deeds to John Houghton's riverside house in Chelsea – the house she had been so certain he would give to Tom and Lucy as a wedding present.

'I know that just now you feel as if you want to hide yourself away at Greenthorpe,' he'd said sagely, as he handed her the document yesterday afternoon. 'But later you'll feel differently. You'll want to enjoy life and be a part of it again. When that time comes it will be a comfort to know that you have a home of your own; somewhere to entertain your friends or simply to enjoy the hours of solitude that we all need.'

Feeling somewhat dazed, scarcely able to absorb the meaning of his words, Alicia had somehow managed to stammer her thanks.

Sitting at her window on this, her last morning at Ryland Place, she realized what a blessing the house would be, even if she only used it occasionally. It was also a relief to know that she needn't worry about being a burden on her father. Sir John had settled a generous jointure upon her, in accordance with the marriage contract signed some four years ago. For the first time in her life she would be completely independent, no longer the property of her father or her husband. Unlike most women, she would be free to live her life exactly as she

234

chose. But for the present she needed the healing tranquillity of Greenthorpe.

She tilted back her head to drain the last drops from the cup, then stood up, the scroll curled in her hand.

Nanty came to lay a thick velvet cloak around her shoulders. Alicia swung round and saw her own excitement mirrored in the other girl's eyes. They smiled at each other, then Alicia tucked her arm through Nanty's and they walked to the door, Hero padding behind them.

Alicia paused in the doorway, turning her head for a last glimpse of the room which had been the scene of so much heartache. In a flash she saw herself on her wedding night, being undressed by the babbling women, then getting into bed beside her nervous, embarrassed husband. She remembered all the tears, the angry reproachful words, the tension and bitterness. She also remembered the rapture they had known in the big curtained bed. Last of all, she had an image of herself crouched like a terrified animal in the corner, cowering away from Lucy. Feeling slightly sick, she closed the door.

Downstairs in the hall the household was assembled in a double row reaching to the great middle doors. Alicia stopped at the bottom of the stairs, her face registering surprise, then lively suspicion. She had always believed that the servants disliked her, in spite of the respect they'd shown her since Lady Agnes's death. Yet here they were, gathered as if to see a dearly loved mistress on her way. Then she glimpsed the steward's sullen face – Sweet Jesus, must he always look as if he had a toothache! – and knew that they had received their orders from her father-in-law.

Sir John stood in the middle of the two rows, flanked on either side by Tom and Molly. Fortunately there was no sign of Lucy.

Tom came striding up to her, laid his hands on her shoulders and kissed her lightly on the cheek.

'May God protect you on your journey, dear sister,' he said softly.

There was a spark of the old audacity in his eyes, almost as if he wanted to assure her that he bore her no malice. Yet what did he have to forgive? It was childish, arrogant and wholly insensitive; it was typical of Tom, yet Alicia wasn't annoyed. Like him, she no longer harboured feelings of ill-will. In fact where Tom Houghton was concerned, she had no feelings.

Tom stepped back on his heel and Molly glided forward, a self-possessed little person now that she was to be married and no longer lived in the shadow of her ghastly mother's tyranny. Alicia embraced her warmly.

'I pray that God will watch over you always,' Molly said in the prim little voice that had barely changed since she was eleven years old.

'Thank you, sweetheart.' Alicia smiled at her. 'And I hope – I mean, pray – that you will be very happy with Master Jennings and have a dozen babies.'

'Oh no!' Molly's eyes widened and Alicia reflected that, in spite of her new self-confidence, the girl still had no sense of fun. 'Oliver's eye is sure to wander if I'm constantly breeding. Four children will be plenty.'

Before Alicia could think of a reply to that, she heard footsteps behind her, accompanied by a child's protesting squeals. Then Mother Luke appeared round the bend of the stairs, leading Jack with one hand and holding up her skirts in the other.

'I was afraid you might have gone,' she panted, descending into the hall. Jack, finding himself in the midst of so many giants, lapsed into silence. He thrust his thumb into his mouth and stared gravely about him.

Mother Luke started to curtsy but Alicia put her arms round her and kissed her shiny pink cheek. The nurse was probably the only one among the servants who genuinely cared for her.

'I pray that you find peace one day, mistress,' she said in her country burr that was as warm and comforting as the smell of freshly baked bread.

Alicia felt tears and laughter struggling inside her. It seemed that she was leaving Ryland Place with everybody's prayers. And yet, how much more affectionate those words sounded, coming from this homely, undemanding woman who could never see ill in anyone.

She bent down to kiss Jack but he wriggled away from her, burying his face in his nurse's skirts.

'He's shy with strangers,' Mother Luke explained kindly.

Alicia felt slightly hurt, though she knew she was being foolish. She guessed that, to small Jack, she had always been a stranger.

She searched for the merry face of Father Charles in the crowd before remembering that he had taken to his bed with a feverish cold. She felt a jab of disappointment, for she was very fond of the old priest.

'Are you ready, Alicia?'

Sir John caught her by the elbow and steered her through the avenue of bobbing servants, out to the courtyard where the escort of six mounted men was waiting. Thin sunlight pierced the pale furry clouds, glinting coldly on the harness. The horses stamped and chomped their bits, nostrils steaming in the frosty air. The last of Alicia's luggage had been piled into the wagon. All that remained was for her to say goodbye to Sir John; that was the hardest part of all.

They stood beside the carriage, the tired man and the now pitifully-thin girl whose fragile figure appeared swamped by her widow's weeds. Alicia felt a thick clot of tears rise in her throat. This was too much like that other parting a few years ago at Ashby Place, when she'd clung to Lady Bess, feeling as if the living heart were being torn out of her body.

Why must I lose everyone I love?

For she had come to love this kindly, dignified man, though once she had thought him a bumbling fool. She wondered if he had any inkling how much he meant to her.

'I shall miss you, Alicia.'

Her eyes blurred until his face was no more than a pale puff of mist in the sunshine.

'Your kindness has been a great comfort to me, sir,' she choked. 'Without it I couldn't have borne to live.'

John gave a mild shake of his head. The girl was exaggerating as usual, but it was a habit that no longer irritated him. He realized by now that she was more prone to flights of fancy and seesaw moods than his own more phleg-matic children. Lord, but his heart ached for her! Life was rarely kind to people of her type. He could only hope that one day she would find a strong man who would provide an anchor for that restless spirit. He would also need a rich heart – one which would yield the love that she needed more than most women.

'You will marry again.' He found himself speaking his thoughts aloud, unaware that he sounded like an amateur soothsayer at a country fair.

'Never!' Alicia's voice sounded like a twig snapping. 'I know now that marriage isn't for me.'

John gazed steadily at the rebellious young face, then he smiled.

'Alicia, you are young and pretty, and as fond of admiration as any other pretty girl. Do you really think you'll find happiness, hidden away from the world like some musty old scribe?'

Alicia's mouth was sulky but she didn't reply so he continued:

'When you first came to Ryland Place, I confess that I didn't much care for you but I admired the fire that I saw in you. My daughters were always so . . .'

He broke off at that point, uncertain how to explain those pale, spiritless little girls to this wilful creature whose flame still shimmered beneath the frozen shell which she had built around herself. Besides, what purpose was there in flaying himself with the old guilt? One daughter was dead, struck down like a leaf in her twelfth year, the other was soon to leave his house for ever. Neither cared now that he had failed to protect them from Agnes.

'I understand, sir.' Alicia placed a hand on his sleeve. 'Truly, I do.'

She was about to climb into the carriage when something made her hesitate and look back at the house for the last time. It stood silent and aloof as ever, the rose-tinged walls seeming to shelter a coldly indifferent heart. Then her sharp eyes caught a white blur at one of the upper windows. As she continued to stare, it became clear that it was a face. Of course – that must be the room where Lucy was confined.

She frowned, catching her lip between her teeth. It must be a miserable exis-tence, cooped up with her maid, visited only by Sir John and the gentle old priest. In that moment she felt an unexpected pang of pity for the girl, abandoned by the husband whom she'd loved so obsessively that it had robbed her of hope, pride and, in the end, her sanity. She raised her arm to give an uncertain little wave, wondering at the same time whether Lucy could see, or would even care.

Sir John helped her into the carriage, then turned to Nanty.

'Here, girl.' Smiling, he pressed a florin into her palm. 'Take good care of your mistress.'

Nanty blushed, then began to stutter with gratitude, but John silenced her with a flap of his hand.

'It's all right, child. Continue to serve her as faithfully and it will be sufficient thanks.'

Nanty beamed as if her face had been lit up by the sun.

John swept the curtain across on its wooden hoops, shutting the two girls inside the cavelike dimness. Stepping back, he signalled to Dick Reynold, the leader of the escort.

'Look after her!' He called in a rather shaky voice.

'Yes, Sir John.' Dick's large red face broke into a grin. Sir John knew him well, for he used to play rough-and-tumble games about the estate with Tom and had once bloodied that handsome nose in a boyish skirmish. Dick gave a shout; the carriage lurched, then rolled forward across the lumpy stones and out through the tall curved archway, the riders forming a diamond around it. The park sprawled before them, sparkling red and topaz under the creeping sun. Down the avenue the horses went in high dancing steps. Beneath their hoofs the brittle leaves crackled like a woman's skirts while they arched their necks and whinnied in the clear crisp air.

They rested that night at a village inn on the outskirts of Guildford, in Surrey.

Alicia, anxious to reach Greenthorpe in time to say goodbye to Joanna, would have travelled on through the night, but she knew she must consider the others. Now, as the carriage swayed through the narrow archway to the dark little courtyard within, she stole a look at Nanty, half-asleep on the cushions beside her and knew that she'd made the right decision.

As she stumbled out of the carriage, a groom came hurrying to seize the horses' bridles. Another stood by, holding a horn lantern. Alicia looked blearily at the stone building which surrounded the courtyard on three sides.

The landlord was standing in the doorway, wiping his hands on his leather apron and smiling rather obsequiously while the light from inside danced on his bald head. His wife, a trim little woman who unexpectedly reminded Alicia of Mother Luke, darted out from behind him and dropped a curtsy.

'I'll take you up to your chamber now, mistress,' she said kindly, after Alicia had explained that they needed food and lodging for the night. 'You look fit to drop where you stand, if you don't mind my saying so.'

Just inside the door she took up a candle, then led the way through the taproom, where several men sat bunched over the tables, drinking and dicing, raising their heads only to call for fresh jugs of ale. The air was cloudy with smoke from the wood fire, where a joint was slowly turning. Dogs roamed between the tables, looking hopeful. A fat little minstrel sat alone in the dusky blue shadows of the chimney corner, singing a bawdy song to the accompaniment of his lute.

Alicia and Nanty followed the landlady up a narrow flight of stone steps. At the top she turned into a dim little passage, pushed open a door and stepped aside to let them enter ahead of her.

Alicia looked about her, pleasantly surprised. The room was richly furnished and had an air of ripe luxury, like a sensual woman who knows that she is still beautiful even though she is no longer a young girl. Bright tapestries hung at the panelled walls. Several velvet-covered stools, a highly varnished cypress chest and a couple of tables were set at intervals about the room. There was even a red-tiled gaming-table. The plum-coloured velvet curtains had been drawn back from the bed, where the sheets were turned down invitingly.

A thin girl of about fourteen was getting a fire going in the hearth. She was rather small, with a curtain of dark-blonde hair framing her pretty, sullen face. She had sunk back on her heels as they entered, but regarded them without interest.

'My daughter.' The landlady nodded in her direction, then spoke impatiently to the girl. 'If you've done in here, Susannah, you can go and fetch some more bottles up from the cellar.'

Without a word Susannah scrambled to her feet. She curtsied meekly and turned to go but not before Alicia had seen the look of hatred she sent her mother from beneath downswept lids.

The landlady smiled apologetically as the door closed behind Susannah.

'She's a good girl, but sometimes needs reminding of her manners. Will you have supper in your chamber, mistress?'

'That would be wonderful.' Still wrapped in her travelling cloak, Alicia went to stand in front of the fire, stretching her hands gladly towards the blaze. She suddenly felt so weary that she nearly swayed forward. The prospect of food and a soft feather-bed grew more and more seductive. However, the landlady showed no inclination to return to her duties. One hand resting on the doorknob, she fixed her guest with a friendly, confidential smile.

'They say her Grace may be forced to go into a convent if Mistress Boleyn has her way', she remarked. 'That foreign cardinal – faugh, but I can't recall his outlandish name – he's put it to her, sweet as sixpence I daresay, that it'll be easier for everyone that way. Easier for the King and his goggle-eyed whore! But Queen Catherine is standing firm, poor lady, and rightly so. The very idea – a Queen of England to join a nunnery!'

'King Louis the Twelfth's first wife entered a convent so that he might marry his second, as all the world knows,' Alicia pointed out mildly.

The woman bristled; she had not known it, but didn't wish to appear unsophisticated before this self-possessed young woman. She pursed her lips with the air of one who has a vast fund of knowledge if only she could be persuaded to impart it, and continued smugly:

'Ah yes, but that's the French for you – yellow-livered dogs who'd run from a thunderstorm. In England we're made of stouter metal.' (Alicia tactfully refrained from reminding her that Catherine was Spanish.) 'It's one thing for a man to take a whore, though I'd pound my Matthew to a powder if he ever took such a notion into his head, but to marry her! Why, it makes a mockery of every decent Christian woman in the land!'

Alicia giggled, for the words sounded exactly like Agnes Houghton's. The woman flushed a dull red, thinking she was being mocked.

'I expect you'll be wanting your supper now,' she said coldly.

She bobbed the briefest of curtsies, picked up her candle and went stiffly from the room.

Weary after the long jouncing hours on the road, Alicia and Nanty went to bed soon after supper, while their escort sat below in the taproom drinking far into the night.

At dawn Alicia was woken by a sharp rap at the door. Nanty, already up and dressed in her blue linsey-woolsey gown, went to answer it and the landlady sailed in, carrying a tray. Her haughty expression told them she had not forgiven Alicia's rudeness.

Susannah followed at her heels with a basin of hot water, soap, and a clean towel flung over one arm. If anything she looked even more morose this morning and Alicia was disturbed to see that her lower lip was cut and swollen – no doubt the result of one of her mother's 'reminders'.

Alicia washed hurriedly, then Nanty helped her into her clothes.

'Aren't you going to eat anything, mistress?' Nanty eyed the breakfast tray longingly.

'I'm not hungry. You have it.'

Alicia, impatient to be back on the road, could scarcely bring herself to look at food. She poured herself a glass of ale and carried it over to the window where she stood, slowly sipping it. The pale light slanted across the courtyard, where the horses were being harnessed. There was a faint thread of lilac in the eastern sky, promising a bright day. A small boy was darting in and out between the horses' legs, crawling beneath their bellies as if they were a tunnel. He kept this up till one of the grooms cuffed him.

Alicia swallowed the last mouthful of cool golden ale. She was amused to see that dainty little Nanty had wolfed down the cold beef and bread and was now reaching for a mutton pasty.

'You'll have to eat that on the way,' she said sardonically. 'It's time we started out.'

Somewhat regretfully, Nanty bundled the pasty into a napkin.

The morning air was tinged with ice as they made their way across the court-yard. Alicia couldn't help noticing that some of the men looked rather pale. As Dick Reynold came to hand her into the carriage, she hastily averted her face from his bloodshot eyes and sour breath.

Within minutes they were out on the road again, heading north towards Greenthorpe.

They arrived in the depths of night, amid a November drizzle that covered everything with a gauzy mist.

The house was blanketed in darkness, just as it had been in Alicia's dream, except for the candles glowing like fireflies in several of the windows. Everything was silent, the only sound that of the horses' hoofs striking the cold wet stone beneath them. Alicia's heart seemed to dive into her stomach; the place had a deserted air that frightened her, and she found herself groping for Nanty's hand.

Then there was a flare of light as a groom burst out of the long dark hollow of the stables and came running towards them.

To her amazement, Sir Richard came out to meet her.

Shivering in the dank night air, she looked up at the tall shape outlined against the house like a sentinel. Her heart fluttering nervously, she went slowly up the steps. She remembered to curtsy, then received his cool kiss on her forehead. She couldn't tell if he was pleased to see her.

'You look half-chilled,' he said abruptly. 'Come into the parlour and get warm. Those men can have their supper in the kitchen when they've done.'

It was the first time he had ever shown concern for her comfort. Feeling a little bemused, Alicia followed him through the empty, echoing hall to the winter parlour.

A fire was crackling away merrily in the hearth yet Richard stooped to throw another log on the flames. As he straightened up and turned to face her again, she was shocked by the change in him. Silver flecks were sprinkled in the deep-gold waves of hair, there were harsh lines etched around his eyes. His face, once the rosy-cream colour of a healthy Englishman who spends most of his time in the fresh air, was red and puffy, with little purple pouches under the eyes. He had also put on weight. Yet traces of the aggressive beauty were still there, along with that air of wholly masculine power that had always frightened her.

They stood facing each other, as if each was taking the other's measure. Then Alicia remembered Joanna, the real reason she had come home.

Surprisingly, Richard seemed to guess her thoughts.

'Your mother is in the gatehouse, seeing to her maid.'

Her maid! Was that all Joanna meant to him – a nameless, faceless creature who sewed on buttons, emptied chamber pots, picked clothes up from the floor where their owner had casually dropped them? Alicia felt her whole body tense up with annoyance.

'The woman was a fool!' Again he seemed to sense her emotions, a gift she would never have ascribed to him. 'And your mother was a greater fool to listen to her mawkish nonsense. Her only excuse is that she was very young.'

'Father, I . . .'

Feeling frightened and confused, for the words made no sense to her, Alicia looked round the room as if for inspiration. Then she spotted the wine jug standing on the mantelshelf. For the first time it occurred to her that her father might be drunk.

Her mind began to reel with the strangeness of it all. Richard Westbrooke had always had a fondness for claret but she had never seen him clumsy in his cups.

'Only a fool drinks himself insensible,' he had declared on more than one occasion. 'A man should always have full control of his mind.'

A crafty smile curled around Richard's mouth.

'I'm forgetting myself. You know nothing of that unfortunate business.' His voice suddenly changed to the old whiplash tone of authority. 'Sit down, girl!'

Numbly obedient, Alicia lowered herself on to a stool while Richard refilled his glass then went to fetch another for her from the cupboard. Watching his movements through the curtain of her lashes – stiff and slow, exaggeratedly cautious – she realized that he wasn't quite drunk yet.

He brought her the glass, brimming with claret, then went to stand on the other side of the hearth, across from her. His big body seemed to dominate the room so that by contrast it looked dingy and cramped. The grey eyes staring unwinkingly at her were just as bright as she remembered – cold crystalline eyes with no hint of softness in them. She gazed into her glass, her fingers curled tightly about the stem. He hadn't bothered to make the usual polite enquiries about her journey, nor had he mentioned the misfortunes that had befallen her – the loss of her husband, her child. She knew then with chilling certainty what she had always suspected, even as a little girl. Richard loved nobody, pitied nobody. The only person who figured in Richard's life was

Richard. She wondered if he had ever cared for anyone – as a child, a youth, a man.

Her neck whipped round at the sound of the door opening, then Dorothy came in – an older Dorothy with grey frosting her temples and the band of golden-red which showed beneath her hood. Her figure in the violet-wool gown had the sharp thinness wrought by worry and too many sleepless nights. And yet, she was the same Dorothy. Alicia set her glass down on the hearthstones and ran to her.

'Alicia, sweetheart!' The soft green eyes glistened with tears, then Dorothy's arms went round her daughter.

Alicia wanted to cling to her mother's neck and weep until all the grief and tension had flooded out of her body. It was only Richard's withering presence that stopped her.

'How is Joanna?' she managed to ask. 'Will I be able to see her now?'

'Not tonight, child.' Dorothy sighed and for the first time Alicia noticed that her mother's eyes were swollen with crying. Was it possible that her old feud with Joanna had been swallowed up by the shadow of death?

She must have looked disappointed, for Dorothy went on:

'Joanna is very weak and needs to rest. I've given her a poppy draught which should help her sleep. You can see her tomorrow if she's feeling any stronger.'

'She'll be no stronger tomorrow, nor the day after that!' Richard's face jeered at them from the bright haze of the fireside. 'The old hag is dying. If you had any charity you'd let her go peacefully, like a dog grown too feeble to lift its leg.'

Alicia stared, appalled that even *he* could be so callous, but Dorothy remained composed.

'I know that she's dying,' she replied quietly. 'But I have a duty to care for the servants in old age, sickness and yes, in death itself.'

'There speaks a true daughter of the Plantagenets!' Richard scoffed.

He raised his arm and flung his glass against the wall with a resounding crash that made Alicia jump. The glass cracked into splinters, wine trickled down the panelled wall like a thin stream of blood. Then he turned and stamped out of the room, missing the satisfaction of seeing that his wife's face had turned white as paste at his words.

'What did he mean?' Alicia glanced curiously at her mother.

Dorothy smiled shakily. 'It's an old wound of mine that he likes to prod sometimes.'

'But what. . . ?'

'Go to bed, Alicia.' Suddenly Dorothy sounded very tired. 'You need to rest after your journey. Your old room is ready for you.'

Alicia curtsied and turned to go. As she reached the door a thought struck her.

'Have you sent for Kathryn?'

Dorothy shook her head. 'She knows Joanna is sick, but I didn't think it right to call her away from her duties. Besides, you are the one Joanna wanted to see.'

Tiptoeing up the dark stairs, her hands pressed flat against her skirts as if to prevent them from crackling, Alicia suddenly remembered her dream. By the time she reached the top, her knees were wobbling. Turning into the gallery, she half-expected to meet Alice – or, rather, Alice's ghost.

The gallery was black and bare, unrelieved by starshine. She saw the narrow chink of light beneath the door at the far end. By now her heart was screaming with near-hysterical terror. Would she find Cicely there, quarrelling with her husband, or weeping on her knees? She had a sudden picture of that clear-cut face, bleak and white against a fall of hazel-brown hair.

But of course there was only Nanty, airing nightclothes in front of the fire, her expression so innocently absorbed that Alicia nearly sobbed with relief.

The room was exactly as she remembered it. High on the mantelshelf was the little gilt clock that her uncle Nick had sent her one Christmas, and the silver rose-bowl which had once belonged to her great-great-grandparents, Thomas and Anne, the parents of tragic Henry. Last of all her eyes swung towards the bed where she had slept beside Kathryn for so many years, and then later alone. There was the same moss-green counterpane, the emerald velvet curtains – she remembered how she and Kathryn used to pretend they were sleeping in a tree-house.

Everything was the same, except that now there was no Joanna to tuck her between the sheets with dire threats of what would happen if she got up again.

Joanna had been installed in a secluded part of the gatehouse wing, seldom used any more except on those rare occasions when Kathryn and her husband came to stay. It was the room where Henry Marsh had lived as a virtual prisoner for so many years – sick, wretched, half-crazed with loneliness – and then died, still alone. But Henry was not in the thoughts of either Dorothy or Alicia as they tiptoed across the floor, cautious as if an infant were sleeping.

The room had an air of faded grandeur, crammed as it was with threadbare tapestries and scarred oak and rosewood furniture from an earlier, more romantic age when the Marsh family had enjoyed prosperity.

Alicia thought it a dismal place, solitary and dark with the dust lying thick as snow upon the forgotten treasures. Splendid it might be, but it was a singularly cheerless room for a dying woman.

The red-brocade curtains were drawn about the bed; Dorothy opened them a crack. The first thing she saw was Alban, hunched over the bed like a faithful old wolfhound while the tears ran silently down his face.

He stood up as the two women approached, edging round the bed so that they might have his stool.

He was old – older than Joanna, who was now in her sixty-second year. But as he smiled at Alicia through the haze of tears, she had a glimpse of the boy who had waited at the foot of the stairs, risking his livelihood to help a desperate, fleeing girl.

Sniffing unashamedly, he pushed back the floppy white mane of hair and shambled off to the far end of the room, leaving them alone with Joanna.

Alicia barely recognized her. A wispy braid of hair lay curled on the pillow like a white snake. Her face was a shrivelled mask, all the flesh fallen away from it. For some reason she remembered a half-starved bird that Isabel had found in the garden at Ryland Place one freezing winter day. By some miracle, and with Isabel's anxious vigilance and care, the bird had survived – would Joanna?

Slowly she grew aware that the hollow old eyes were peering at her through the gloom. She attempted a smile but her mouth felt stiff and numb.

'Mistress Alice?' Joanna tried to raise her head from the pillow but it lolled back like a puppet's. Then she closed her eyes as if the effort had tired her.

Alicia glanced questioningly at her mother, who shook her head very slightly, then bent forward to smooth the counterpane.

'No Joanna, it's Alicia. You remember, I promised to send for her.'

'Alice, Alice . . .'

They might have been forgiven for thinking that her wits were wandering when all at once her eyes flew open again and fastened themselves on the young face above the bed.

'Just like Mistress Alice – just like her. Aye, I recall now – I wanted to warn you.'

Alicia sat up very straight, gravely attentive as a schoolgirl on her best behaviour. Did Joanna have some portentous message for her, or was this merely the babbling of an old woman close to death?

Joanna must have guessed her thoughts for her face suddenly twisted and her mouth went down at one corner, the way it used to do when the child Alicia had been in mischief. Then she gave a dusty little chuckle.

'You were always wild – headstrong too, like her. Maybe that's why I was so hard on you – who knows?'

'It doesn't matter.' Alicia's voice wobbled on a sob, but Joanna didn't seem to hear.

'Be careful, child. Be careful or you'll come to a sad end, even as she did. She was kind to me.' The frail voice plodded on, pursuing a path she had half-forgotten. 'She was always kind – not like the others, they thought me a clumsy dolt, but not her. Flighty as she was, she had a good heart. But they didn't like her – Mother Peake and Lisbet and the others. They said that, for a harlot, she gave herself airs. Only I knew the truth.' For some reason her eyes suddenly shifted to Dorothy.

'Hush now, or you'll tire yourself.' Dorothy's voice sounded silky-smooth yet Alicia wondered why her hands were shaking. 'We'll leave you to rest now,' she added brightly.

'But I have to tell you – have to explain . . .'

'Rest easy, Joanna.' She laid a cool hand against the old woman's cheek. 'It can wait until later.'

Joanna was still muttering fretfully as they crept away from the bedside.

They found Alban standing beside the window, staring blindly across the barren park. It had started to rain, not gently as it had last night but in cold grey spikes that pummelled the windows and slashed through the naked trees. Alban's mouth began to quiver like a hurt child who is trying to be brave. Without a word Dorothy put her arms round him. After a while his big head dropped on to her shoulder.

'I wanted to marry her, you know,' he said at last.

'I know.' Dorothy kissed the grizzled old head. 'I know.'

'She's so thin, doesn't she eat?'

Mother and daughter were sitting in the winter parlour, each steeped in her own thoughts. The rain had stopped as abruptly as it had begun, leaving the countryside dull and crushed beneath the sodden brown leaves.

'She refuses most food now.' Dorothy glanced down at her hands which for once lay idle in her lap. 'Some wine, a little broth, but that's all. No wonder she's faded to a shadow.'

'But madam, can't you make her – order her to eat?'

From her place beside the fire, Dorothy smiled at her youngest daughter. There was a kind of tired pity in her eyes, as if not one but several generations lay between them.

'Alicia, no one can be ordered to eat. It's like ordering someone to sleep. Joanna is tired and weak and old. Her will to live has gone. That is something the young can never understand.'

Alicia's eyes fell before that steady green gaze. Lady Dorothy was more indulgent than most parents, but for a daughter to argue with her mother amounted almost to heresy.

She picked up a book which someone – probably Richard – had left lying face down on the window seat. She turned to the first page and tried to read but it was as if Joanna's grey, shrunken face was tattooed upon the paper. Suddenly she threw it down and looked almost accusingly at her mother.

'Something is troubling her, I can tell. Please, madam – let her talk to you.'

As Dorothy gazed back at the tense white face, her own was a mask of fear and anger and wild, driving pain. Her hands uncoiled in her lap, then flapped like a swan's wings swishing across water.

'In time,' she said, and her voice was frayed with tears.

Alicia stared at her with near despair. Had she forgotten that, for Joanna, there was so little time left?

'There's no time left, I have to talk to you.'

It was late, the windows smudged with black. At the far end of the room the fire snapped and bounded like a pugnacious dog, flinging a patchwork of light and shadow over the dark huddled shapes of the furniture. On a table close by the bed, a single candle flamed, swaying in the draught that came hissing under the door.

'I have to explain.' Joanna's eyes were both impatient and pleading and for some reason Dorothy remembered that night, so long ago, when the nurse had blurted out the confession that had smashed her life to fragments. But of what use to think of that now, when Joanna lay dying?

The new chaplain, a plump young man with a tired face, was standing in the shadow of the bed curtains. He had heard Joanna's confession, given absolution and could do no more for her, but he would stay till the end. The dying always wanted him to stay.

'There's nothing to explain.' Dorothy's face was strangely wooden. 'You lied to me – lied for years – and I believed you. What more is there to say?' Yet she caught the withered old hand in hers as if to soften the words.

'Please, hinny.' A note of urgency had slid into Joanna's voice. She shifted slightly, clutching the hand holding hers with all her fading strength.

At the old endearment, Dorothy's heart relented a little. She inched her stool closer, steeling herself to listen to whatever excuses Joanna was about to give for her despicable deceit.

'I've confessed everything to Father Philip.' Joanna's eyes slid to the priest who smiled and bent his head a fraction. Suddenly her face softened. 'Mistress Alicia has the ring. I recall the day her Grace sent it. It was your sixteenth birthday.' She smiled to herself, seeing again the bright young girl in her shabby gown, running upstairs to show her the jewel.

'Did you ever wonder why the Queen should send you such a ring, hinny?'

'She always sent me gifts on my birthday.' Dorothy spoke more sharply than she'd intended. 'She felt a duty towards me, because of her friendship with my mother.'

The nurse shook her head. 'Nay, it was more than that. It was because you were of her blood.'

Dorothy gasped, then her face turned an ugly dull red. However she remembered that Joanna was dying and strove to keep her tone gently reproving.

'Joanna, I thought you'd done with that nonsense. I'll hear no more of it now.'

Joanna glanced again at Father Philip. And again it was as if she had sent him some secret signal, for he turned and padded gently away, leaving the two women alone.

'You hated me because you thought I lied to you. I did lie, but only to save you – from him.'

'What are you saying?' Dorothy's fingers tightened on Joanna's wrist. Seeing her wince, she released her grip but her eyes were burning feverishly.

'I saw that he was cruel, the day he came back from London after leaving you here alone all those weeks, and you so newly a bride. I saw that he was hard – a stone that looks like a man. I feared for you then, hinny – feared that he might even kill you if he thought you better than him.'

'How better?' Dorothy gave a short laugh. 'A bastard!'

'A royal bastard.' For a moment the nurse looked almost fierce.

'So you said it was a lie, a pretty fancy of your own.' She paused, her expression one of sheer bewilderment. 'By all the saints, why?'

'It was better he thought you a fool than a threat to him. It was safer.'

As she heard those words, Dorothy felt as if all the breath had been punched from her body. She found that she was unable to drag her eyes away from the face on the pillow.

'You *are* King Richard's daughter. With my dying breath I swear it. Your mother told me before you were born. Oh, I know.' She gave a little chortle as Dorothy's eyes narrowed in suspicion. 'I was only a stupid serving-girl, but you see, she had no one else. The Queen – or my Lady Elizabeth as she was then – was a good creature, but maybe Mistress Alice was afraid to tell her lest it unsettle her. King Richard was her uncle, as you know. But she knew. Innocent as a suckling babe she may have been, but she was no fool.'

'They said my mother was as proud as Lucifer. She never once mentioned my father's name, so why . . .'

'Think of it, hinny,' Joanna pleaded. 'A young chit far away from home and soon to bear a by-blow. She couldn't bear the burden alone and her family would have none of her. I used to wait on her, you see. She knew I had no friends so was unlikely to gossip. It was one night – oh, a month or so before you were born. It was fearful hot, not a breath of air to be had, and she couldn't sleep. I think in her heart she was homesick – and lonely. Anyway, it was then that she told me.'

'That the King was her lover?'

'Nay, not her *lover* – she only lay with him the once.' Joanna didn't see the other woman flinch. 'She said he forgot her as soon as she put her clothes back on. But she didn't forget – he had her heart.'

Spent with talking, Joanna turned her face into the pillow and allowed her thoughts to drift.

The thoughts were tearing through Dorothy's brain, so fast that she was unable to grasp them and set them in a straight line. She felt chilled, dizzy, swimmy-headed, as if she were catching a cold. Joanna's confession had brought neither peace nor comfort. If anything, it had only raked up the ashes of her old anguish. She did not doubt that the woman had spoken the truth as she perceived it, but it resolved nothing. Alice might have been a naïve and emotional young girl in the throes of first love when she gave herself to King Richard, or a whore who sought her pleasure greedily among the ranks of his courtiers, never questioning or even caring that they would 'forget her as soon as she put her clothes back on'. Any one of those men might have been her father.

'Who else knows about this?' At last she'd found her voice.

'Only Alban. I didn't tell him, hinny, but somehow he found out.' She paused, running her tongue along her lower lip. 'You will look after Alban, hinny?'

Dorothy nodded, only half-listening. So Alban had been part of the web of trickery and lies. Strangely, she felt no resentment. Perhaps she was too tired, or it had all happened too long ago.

'Hinny.' Joanna's voice was little more than a whisper. 'Please say you'll forgive me.'

She hesitated for barely a heartbeat before leaning forward and tenderly kissing the old woman on the cheek.

'I forgive you,' she whispered, and the tears were thick in her throat. 'With all my heart I do.'

Joanna died just before daybreak, when the world is at its lowest ebb. She slipped quietly away, her hand curled inside Dorothy's.

'She is at peace now.'

Dorothy jumped as a hand landed lightly on her shoulder. She swung round to find Father Philip standing behind her. There was pity and concern in those eyes that were soft and grey as sealskin.

She bent her head and stared very hard at her gleaming gold wedding ring. If he was kind to her now she would weep like a child, and she wasn't ready to weep yet. Like praying, weeping was best done when you were alone.

'She never meant to hurt you, daughter.' The priest spoke very gently, as if Dorothy were suffering from a serious illness. 'It was wrong of her to lie, yet no wrong was intended. She did it out of her great love for you.'

'I know.' Dorothy swallowed, then gazed past him, at the windows that were already turning pale. 'But I wish she had said nothing, for now my mind is in such a whirl I don't know what to think – what to believe.'

Alban came to her as she sat alone in the winter parlour.

Her heart was as wintry as the world outside Greenthorpe's mullioned windows. It plunged still further at the sight of the old man. She was well aware that he was grieving even as she was – probably more so – but just now she lacked the strength to comfort him.

Yet Alban was not looking for comfort. In spite of his red-rimmed eyes and shock-bleached face, there was an air of dignity about him which plainly told her that he meant to mourn alone.

'I kept this, my Lady,' he was saying. 'Maybe I should have spoken out long ago but – well, Mistress Alice was dead and the whole house in a spin. It seemed best to say nothing.'

Then Dorothy noticed that he was holding a little wooden casket in his hands. She sat very still as he laid it carefully in her lap.

'It was your grandfather's,' he explained as she looked up at him questioningly. 'I tended him when he was sick.'

There was no trace of emotion in the old man's voice and his face was a blank mask.

'Thank you,' Dorothy murmured. She could think of nothing else to say. Then, as he started to move away she added impulsively, 'I'm sorry, Alban. I know how you loved her.'

Alban didn't answer, but merely smiled the way one might smile at an engaging little girl.

Dorothy's fingers were shaking as they opened the casket, though she didn't pause to wonder why. Inside was a bundle of faded old letters, loosely tied with a black velvet ribbon. She glanced through them but with little interest until at last she unfolded a sheet of parchment, cracked and yellow with age like the rest. As she read, it was as if her heart had come to a standstill.

My dear Father,

I am writing this because I think that, although you are very angry, you still have some love in your heart for me. I am in good health, but we are all of us here very anxious for his Grace the King as he makes ready for battle. May God protect him from his enemies!

My heart is filled with sadness because neither you nor my mother can find it in you to forgive what you think of as my sin. Yet I swear that I have committed no sin. It is the King's child that I am carrying in my belly. I feel no shame, for I gave myself to him in love, but I grieve for the distress I have caused you. His Grace doesn't know that I am to bear his child, nor will I trouble him when he has far weightier matters on his mind.

Her Highness the Lady Elizabeth is a truly kind mistress. She has spoken to no one of my plight, but I don't doubt that they already know of it in London, for such things are not easily kept secret, and I shall be branded a harlot. Yet it is not harlotry to lie with a man whom you love as I do him. Upon my faith, he meant no dishonour towards his Queen but she was ill and tired, and he much troubled in his mind. He took me in sorrow and despair but I regret none of it, even though it meant so little to him.

I expect to be delivered of the baby in October. I confess that I'm afraid, for death is always close at hand when a woman lies in, but the midwife says I am strong and shouldn't suffer too greatly. My little one, if it lives, will be your grandchild. I beg that you will give him or her your blessing, even though you cannot forgive me. I wrote to my mother last month but she hasn't answered me. I beg that you will be kinder.

Written at Sheriff Hutton this sixteenth day of August 1485

From your loving daughter

Alice.

Dorothy didn't realize she was crying until a tear splashed on to her wrist. All at once they were streaming unchecked down her face. She was crying for Joanna, who had loved her enough to lie to her, because she saw it as the only way to protect her, even though it must destroy their relationship. She was crying for the proud, wilful, high-spirited girl who had been her mother. Above all she was crying for herself; for the empty years, the lost friendship, for the person she might have been and the life she might have had.

The candles guttered and the winter light crept in, winding itself in pale streamers around the mellow old house. In spite of the fire now sinking low in the hearth but still giving out a faint sputter of heat, Dorothy felt so cold that her teeth were juddering and her hands were mottled with red and blue. She wondered if she would ever really feel warm again.

Some instinct made her look up to see Richard standing in the doorway. He seemed to fill the narrow space with his presence. At the sight of him her heart gave a fearful little quiver, until she realized that he was sober. Of course – it was too early in the day for him to be drunk.

As he started towards her, it struck her anew how much he'd changed from the blond handsome boy whom she'd married – the past few months of heavy drinking had seen to that. The once hard-muscled body was turning to fat, something Dorothy could never have envisaged. All his life he'd striven to prove himself a cut or two above his fellow men but now, in his middle years, he no longer cared.

'So she is dead.' He stood over her, his eyes scanning her face as though it were covered in hieroglyphics. 'Why are you crying?'

Dorothy didn't answer and when he spoke again there was a rough edge to his voice.

'Are you a fool, madam, or a hypocrite? We both know you didn't love her.'

She started at that, ready to protest that she and Joanna were reconciled at the end; that she understood, forgave and finally loved again the old woman who had cared for her since the day she was born. Then she realized, with something of a shock, that she was not compelled to explain her feelings to Richard. It was an intoxicating thought.

Meanwhile he had gone to pour himself some wine. He didn't ask her if she wanted any and she sat like a woman carved in ice, listening to the splash of claret against the glass.

'She did you a great wrong, filling your head with her fairy-tales.' Richard swallowed noisily. 'I still marvel that you were stupid enough to listen to the cackling of an old crone. A royal bastard!' He gave a short laugh, swirling the wine round the glass. 'Couldn't she think of a better story? Every milkmaid and serving-slut in the land probably imagines that she's the bastard daughter of some king or duke, but imagining doesn't make it so.'

There was a silence then while he studied her over the rim of his glass. He seemed to be waiting for something – some response from her.

Instead she looked back at him, her gaze steady. She saw a man, clever and indomitable – a man who had once been ambitious. As a youth he'd managed to gain a footing at court, but had stumbled on the sharp stones of his own arrogance. His plans had been thwarted by a curt tongue, a graceless manner, a stubborn refusal to 'toady to whoremongers and fools'. But he had never understood that. He still believed that he'd been deliberately snubbed because of the petty jealousy of his peers, and therein lay the tragedy of Richard Westbrooke.

It now occurred to Dorothy how frustrating it must have been for a man of her husband's energy and ability to have spent all these years kicking his heels on a small country estate when he might have sat in the council chamber, been a foreign emissary, reaped manors and revenues from a grateful king. For the first time since she'd met him she almost felt sorry for him.

Her fingers were curled around the edges of the faded old parchment. She had only to thrust it under his nose now and that sneering superiority would crumble like a piece of chalk.

Richard was still standing by the chimney breast, the empty glass in his hand. Beneath his watchful gaze, Dorothy rose and walked towards him, her silk skirts whistling over the rushes. She stopped in front of the hearth, hesitating for the briefest of moments before tearing the letter into pieces and flinging them into the fire.

The flames rose and curled around the yellow strips, sending out an acrid smell as they turned them first red, then black. Then she turned away and found herself standing face to face with the man who for nearly twenty-seven years had been her husband and her tormentor. Their eyes locked; she knew a sweeping instant of panic and regret for her rash action but it quickly died. She realized with a sudden flash of clarity that it no longer mattered whether her father was the last of the Plantagenet kings or an inarticulate farm boy. She was Dorothy, a daughter of this house that she loved so unreasoningly, and had nurtured since she was seventeen years old. She was Dorothy, wife of Richard, mother of Kathryn and Alicia.

She curtsied before him, graceful as a cat, skirts billowing out so that she appeared to be kneeling in a pool of shining russet. It was a gesture both mocking and submissive but Richard was too startled to be offended. He could only stare dumbly as she rose up again, a strange little smile on her lips.

His eyes were still following her as she went slowly from the room but she didn't look back to see the expression on his face.

EPILOGUE

1529

The two women stood at the edge of the lake on a cold bright afternoon in March. Neither spoke as they gazed out across the sage-green water which the wind had lashed with little frills of white.

The younger of the two leaned forward as a swan suddenly sped across the lake, great snowy wings furiously beating the water. She laughed, a high clear sound that seemed to quiver on the keen air, then tossed back her flapping black veil with an impatient jerk of her head.

The older woman smiled. It was good to hear her daughter laugh again. These past few months it had seemed as if a ghost were creeping about the place, silent and withdrawn. A sad ghost whose thin black shape was relieved only by the white hollow of her face. The girl still looked frail, still grieved for the cruel loss of her baby, but at last she was beginning to mend. That fragile body housed a resilient spirit – she must have inherited her strength from her great-grand-mother, Cicely.

And perhaps – a little – from me.

The thought struck her without warning and she mulled over it for a while. It was true that she had passed through a nightmare maze of rejection and violence and deceit, that she had been hurt by the three people who should have cher-ished her – Cicely, Richard and Joanna. But somehow she had survived; they hadn't completely destroyed her.

However it was not the strange and troubled past that concerned her now, but her daughter's future.

This was Alicia's last day at Greenthorpe. Tomorrow at first light she would leave for Greenwich Palace. She had as yet been offered no official post at court, where Anne Boleyn looked no nearer to becoming queen, although Catherine's position was decidedly shaky.

Even the most stony-hearted must pity her Grace, surrounded as she was by

254

spies and ill-wishers, denied the right to seek advice from those who had her interests at heart, like the Spanish ambassador. Bullied and harassed by her husband, who was in turn being chivvied by the increasingly fractious Anne, the Queen was standing firm by her convictions. She would not admit that she had been Prince Arthur's wife in the true sense, and wryly maintained that she would only enter a convent if Henry agreed to join a monastery. It was a nerve-wearing situation and Alicia was glad she wouldn't be taking up permanent lodgings at court.

Meanwhile the house at Chelsea was waiting for her. She wanted to hug herself every time she thought of it. And yet . . .

'I can't help feeling a little sad.' She spoke the thought aloud, looking about her at the vital greenness sprawling towards the skyline – the tall tangled reeds fringing the lake, and the graceful leaning willows. 'It's hard to leave Greenthorpe.'

Dorothy laid one arm across the girl's shoulders.

'There is always some sadness in every parting, Alicia, but it's soon forgotten. You are young and must make a life for yourself outside these gates. That is the natural order of things.'

Alicia dipped her head. They were almost the same words that Sir John had used, that last morning at Ryland Place.

'One day you will marry again,' Dorothy went on. 'You'll find true happiness with a man you respect and love, and you will bear children. Then all the hurts of the past will fade.'

The thought of George Boleyn streaked across Alicia's mind. He had written to her that winter, just when she had begun to think she would never hear from him again. It had been a disturbing letter, flippant and at the same time tender, as one might expect from George. It had also left her in little doubt that he was eager to see her again.

She frowned and stared at the onyx buckle on her shoe. Ever since Dorothy had confided her story during those dark days following Joanna's death, the two had grown very close and there were times when each seemed to sense the other's thoughts. Alicia didn't want anyone, least of all her mother, to know that George Boleyn was frequently on her mind these days. Dorothy would be appalled to learn that her daughter hankered after a married man, and would fear for her the whole time she was away.

Meanwhile she knew that Dorothy's advice was sound. Her life stretched before her like an unexplored country, waiting for her to claim it. For the first time for four years, her heart was high with elation and hope. As she stood outlined against the crisp spring landscape, her eyes took on a greedy expectant glitter so that she looked very much like that girl who had danced in the torch-light while the king's musicians thumped out a lively galliard.

In that moment she thought not of the hurt and sorrow she had known, but of those whose love had enriched her life and given it warmth; Dorothy, Kathryn, Sir Walter and Lady Bess, Sir John. And, of course, Gervase.

The air had grown stingingly cold while they stood there. The wind hurled itself all around them like a large exuberant puppy, nipping their cheeks, jerking their veils and heavy circular skirts.

'Come.' Dorothy spoke with the quiet decisiveness that was often in her voice nowadays. 'It's a pretty spot but it will always be here waiting for you. We must see that your luggage is packed and ready.'

As they picked their way across the grass, they could see the sunset glowing cold and pink above the tall chimneys of Greenthorpe Manor. Thin arrows of light glinted through the trees, now pronged with pale-green buds. In a few weeks they would be swollen with fresh-scented blossom but Alicia would not be here to see it.

'But I will come back,' she told herself.

They passed beneath the gatehouse arch, into the dark little courtyard where the fountain danced on the grey stones. Alicia paused, conscious that her mother had fallen a few steps behind. She sighed under her breath, tugging a stray curl as it blew against her cheek. Sometimes Dorothy looked so frail that it twisted her heart. There was a wry smile on her face now as she drew closer, almost as if she knew what Alicia was thinking. Then she laid her hand on her daughter's arm and the two women mounted the steps and entered the house side by side.